Nest of As

Book One c.
The Phoenix Trilogy
Story of Jane Seymour

By G. Lawrence

Copyright © Gemma Lawrence 2020
All Rights Reserved.
No part of this manuscript may be reproduced without
Gemma Lawrence's express consent

This book is dedicated to all the friends I found again,
during dark times,
And to lessons learned in lockdown.

"… and provide for those who grieve in Zion to bestow on them a crown of beauty instead of ashes…"
Isaiah 61

"I will sing of mercy and judgement:
Unto thee, O Lord, will I sing.
I will behave myself wisely, in a perfect way.
O when wilt thou come unto me?"
Psalm 101

"There is a species of bird in the land of India which is called the phoenix… When the priest has been signalled, he goes in to the altar and heaps it with brushwood. Then the bird enters Heliopolis laden with fragrance and mounts the altar, where he ignites the flame and burns himself up. The next day then the priest examines the altar and finds a worm in the ashes."
On the Phoenix, from Physiologus, a book of Nature Lore.

"I will show you fear in a handful of dust."
T.S. Eliot, The Waste Land

Prologue

Hampton Court Palace
London

October 19th 1537

A boy...

They all said it, did they not? After pain, after suffering, they all said I had succeeded, ascended. From obscurity to notoriety, shadow to light, ash to flame. The myth the King sought had been found in flesh. His perfect woman had brought forth his perfect boy. Someone whispered I was as the Virgin, who had brought forth the saviour of the world. My son was a more humble offering than hers, but he would save England, save the King, save us all.

They all said it, yet it feels now like a dream.

I struggle to remember, to hold on to thoughts. As light, as ghosts they are there, gone in a moment. My memories are birds in the sky, dark and vivid against blue light and then they are gone, as though never there. A call echoes in the clouds. Like memory, my thoughts hit me hard in the gut, the heart, yet images in my mind are vague. What a strange trap the mind is, a barn full of shadowed corners, an attic of holes and hay and barrels.

I cannot think. My mind is become a trap for memories, and for images of the present. They whirl like smoke in the wind, linking together, melding, breaking apart, cringing from one another as a worm does from vinegar, reaching out and fleeing back, confusing each other, confusing me. What is real? I see birds in the shadows. Have they fallen from those skies of blue, of memory? Some are fire feathered, some bear cruel beaks. Some are phoenixes, some falcons. Light bounces from black beak and black eyes. She had black eyes. Anne watches me.

Secrets, shadows, ghosts... The past is here. It moves, soft-stealing phantoms, in the present. It has not gone, it cannot. All that was left unsaid, all lies told as truths, they become as one in the end. They fall as shadow upon each other, layer upon soft layer. They fall, ashes in the fire, flakes rippling away, flying in the breeze of a warm summer's day.

What is real? I am in a bed. Sheets of fine linen are over me. They should be cool but they are not. They are hot and clammy at the same time, drenched in my sweat. They stick to me and hurt me; too cold, too hot. My skin is fire. My flesh aches. Bones are calling out from inside me, yearning to break out of skin, scuttle away, clicking as across the rushes on the floor they race. I see a skull grinning from the shadows. Why does it smile at me so? What amuses it? Amuses Death? There are flames in my belly, a sickly scent on the stifling air in this dark chamber. Where am I?

It is a chamber, gracious and rich. Tapestry hangs on the walls, rippling azure and shocking crimson glows, flickering in candlelight from guttering flames. Thread of gold catches the floating light, stealing it, holding it for a moment and then releasing, as a falconer does his bird. Cupboards stuffed full of shimmering plate of pewter, silver and gold stand, looming, casting shadow. I can smell plates of treats; sugared plums and figs, comfits of almond and caraway, put here for guests. What guests? Something in me knows there should be people come to honour me, honour my son.

There are many people, all dressed in fine clothes. Are they the guests? They do not look merry, but fraught. Pale skin, wide eyes; sweaty hands are wiped carelessly upon rich gowns of silk and satin, on tunics of finest wool. They hurry about, all trying not to look at me. But I am used to that, am I not? Being passed over, that was always my place. A fire roars, adding smoke to air, making it taxing to breathe. Why do I lie here and what is this pain I feel? I was brought to bed of a child. I am a mother. Is this but pain of childbed? I thought I was done, had given birth, but I still feel pain. But I cannot feel the lump of my child on my front, cannot feel the presence of another soul inside the cage of my flesh. I feel flat, empty. I do not seem to feel the heartbeat of my child inside me, and I mourn it. When he was inside me, it was the only time I ever felt not alone.

No… I have given birth. He has left me and entered the world. A son, a son for the King and he is safe, my little prince, my little saviour! Edward has made me safe. What if he had not been a son? Better it is not to think of such horrors. Wraiths of past fears cannot come for me now. That glint in the King's eye will not become a dagger as it did for Katherine, for Anne, for all those men, those friends he loved and friends he killed. That danger will not come for me. All is well. I bore a son. A living son. I succeeded where other women failed. I will not die for the King's displeasure.

How long is it since I birthed my child into the world? It seems long, long since I heard the cry of my child as women pulled him from my body. Long since I fell back on the bed, exhausted, triumphant.

But it was a boy… was it not? I have done my duty as others who came before me failed to. I have given the King a son. I am safe, as the others never were. Is it true? Or does the heat of my skin and the fire of my mind deceive me? Have I done as I was supposed to do, or does he turn his head from me? Have I failed him? Does he plot my death? Is he now talking to his men in careful rooms of hushed quiet, seeking the removal of yet another useless wife, another woman who could not deliver the son he desires above all things? Above love, above friendship, above morality, above faith?

Am I safe? What is real?

I know not. I try to ask people scurrying about me. They are shadows, shifting lights and dimness slipping about. Sometimes a face emerges from darkness; an eye looms, large, white, desperate before me, making me start. There are hands touching my head, lifting me, trying to make me drink bitter potions, cutting a vein in my arm. I stutter, mumble as I did when I was a child and was passed over, unimportant Jane, little mouse. No beauty, no wit, no fire in her soul to kindle love in a man. And that fire, I was told, was all that mattered. It would protect me, shelter me from the hostile world, complete me. I had nothing to light that flame in a man, that too I was told often.

Yet now, fire burns in me.

"My son…" I croak. I know not if they hear me, at first.

"My lady, Queen of this realm and of all hearts," says a kind voice, a rushed voice full of tears. It is one of my women. I know her voice but cannot recall her name. "Your son, Prince Edward, is safe and well and hale."

I hear others speaking, words of encouragement and hope, like a fall of water from cliffs of grey rock they fall, one on top of the other, another on top of that. Words crash in my ears, some bounce as droplets of water; those words alone I catch. I think the people are responding to the croaks that slip from my lips. My tongue does not fit my mouth. I think I speak, but I know my words are unclear and I cannot seem to cling to the words they say to me. Water rushes up, over my ears, but it does not cool me. My flames make it searing, uncomfortable… it will boil and I will cook like a leg of mutton. I am weak, so much weaker than I have ever felt and never did I feel strong. It is as though I myself am a new babe; helpless and fragile, skin screaming against the cold, sudden shock of the world. I cannot seem to ask what I need to. Have I pleased the King? Am I safe? Will I end my days on the block, or shivering beside a mean fire in a cold manor house surrounded by ice-cold fog? Will he turn his face from me? Will I die for his displeasure?

Will I die?

I shiver and I moan, but it sounds as though another woman makes such noises. I toss and turn in the bed, looking for the woman I hear groaning. She is lost and in pain. "Where is she?" I shriek. "Where is Katherine? What have you done with the Queen? My good mistress; she deserves this not!"

"Majesty, *you* are the Queen," says a voice.

I am Queen? I laugh. How can that be? Plain little Jane Seymour a Queen? Anne Boleyn was the Queen. She was born to rule all with those black eyes that saw the darkness in every soul and that crisp light wit that could brighten the saddest day. No... Katherine; she was Queen. Katherine of the sorrowful eyes and quiet dignity. Katherine the woman with more courage in her soul than a lioness, more power than a goddess of old. Katherine who knew what it was to suffer agony upon agony and never hurt others. Katherine, Anne. Those women. They were Queen. *They cannot both be at once*, something whispers in my mind, but as I open my eyes I see them, side by side before me. They are standing at the foot of this bed. Both wear crowns. They are Queens.

Or is this not real? I think I remember a man, the King, putting a ring on my finger. He clutched my hand after, hard, pressing the ring painfully into my flesh. I was his, I knew that then. When I twisted the ring later, there was a circle bruised into my pale finger.

Memory swirls, smoke and ashes playing in my mind. I remember a large chamber filled with blue incense, many of the court processing to watch my son be blessed, baptised. There is a face amongst the other faces, and it is a face I know. It makes my heart leap and fall at the same time, with joy and guilt and pain and devotion. It is my brother, Edward, smiling, his handsome face alight with pride and love. He took the babe from my arms. I remember people bowing, congratulating me. I was carried to a room at the side of the smoke-filled chamber to listen to a priest baptise my son. What is real? It all feels like a fantasy born of desperation.

I must be in the Tower. I must be waiting for death, waiting for a trial where men will lie, say I did things. They will slice my head from my neck so the King can be free to wed again, try again. I will become like the Queens, just another wife, another woman to throw away. A dirty cloth he has wiped his nose on, tossed into the fire. Another failure. I am waiting for death, for the scaffold, the axe. He granted her a sword but not me. The sword is to prevent suffering, and he loved her. I am waiting for death and I have gone mad as she almost did. The fire in my head, this confusion, it is lunacy and I am in it. I have fallen into madness. I have failed. He has sent me to my end.

"My son…"

"Prince Edward is hale and well, a bonny boy!" says a voice. There is a ring of false brightness in it, a light which bounds out and shatters against the wall. It is easier to hear lies than to see them. The voice has a harder time succeeding with falsehoods than the face does. I know this. Are they lying? Is my son dead?

If I am not mad, what is this fire?

My head aches. I yearn to follow the path of memories back to another place, a place where all is cool and quiet; a place of shadows, safety and no people. I remember a time more peaceful than now. Remember the place this began. I was a shadow in the darkness. The creature no one noticed, standing in the background, overlooked, underestimated. That was my place until he saw me.

Did he love me? Is that why the King wanted me above her, his wife, Anne, for whom he had moved the boundaries of all that was possible to possess? I know not. He was looking for a woman as unlike his wife as was possible to find, and found me. But was it love? I did not love him. I loved the place he brought me to; such a strange and different place from that in which I had stood before. To be bowed to, not ignored, revered rather than overlooked. I loved the throne, but I did not love him. How can a woman love that which she fears? But I had grown used to fearing. I knew what it was to fear long, long before I ever came to court. I learned to find power in submission, control in gentleness. I wore a mask. The King did not see it; he believed I loved him true. How could a man such as he *not* believe every woman in the world loved him? He is a creature of fantasy and flight. He believes he is the true knight of tales of old, but he is, in truth, the monster. How could I love such a creature?

I did not love him. I became what he wanted of me, in order to move from the shadows, and into the light.

And for her... for Katherine. I was Katherine's revenge made flesh, grief given form so I might avenge her. For all the power Anne Boleyn seemed to have it was a pale ghost who destroyed her in the eyes of the King. Katherine... do you look on me now and find peace? I brought your enemies down, my good, sweet mistress. I came to do your will. I had my own reasons, ambition too, I do not deny it, but it was you I served. Always I wanted to serve you, my Queen.

And Anne? She never realised how dangerous I could be; such a slight wisp, such a pale, little mouse. How could something so insignificant be so perilous? I took satisfaction in her fall, and yet I wronged her. Evil she did, yet much I know now was unconscious. I cannot claim the same, though I might protest to have done all I did for love.

I knew the trick. The King is not a man to be alone. He must be loved, adored, or all that he is crumbles before his eyes.

He fears to be alone. I thought it was clever to see something so simple.

But I remember. I remember the promise. I remember the truth. Anne, she did wrong indeed and yet I wronged her.

Am I in Hell? Is this why I burn? I thought to become Katherine's revenge, thought to come as a pale fury, make all well again. I did not see the evil I was within, a part of. A promise made, pact forged so long ago. For love what was sworn was upheld. Evil was done. Do I burn in Hell for the death of the Queen? For the innocent blood? Crimson on tapestry seems to wash, a flow of blood from the walls. I cry out, for it comes for me and in its waves I see faces; men who once the King loved, men who lived, and her, black eyes flashing from within the tide of blood. I turn my head. The wash hisses up my skin as a wave upon the shore.

"I have a son?" I croak feebly to shadowy shapes that huddle about me. A hand presses, warm and painful against my own. I shudder from the heat on my already scorching skin even as I cling to it. Weak and feeble, my fingers curl about the hot hand.

"You have a son, my lady," a tearful voice wavers as though far away, as though I hear it through water. "Do you not remember, the Prince Edward?"

"Edward." I speak the name as though I have never heard it, but somewhere in my memory there swims a vision of a crumpled tiny face, bright blue eyes staring up at me as he screams. "Edward is my son?" I ask, fearful again that these words and images are not real. That I have not won. That I have lost, as Katherine and Anne did by giving birth to a daughter, or to death.

"Prince Edward is your son, my lady," the voice assures me. "You have done your duty. The King is more proud and happy than any have ever seen him, and now you must get well, for he fears for you greatly and despairs in his love for you."

His love for me? Does the King love me? I know not if any have truly loved me. They have not known me. I hid too well.

The voice tells me my husband is at prayer, begging God to restore me to full health so we might celebrate the hale and hearty boy that is our son. The voice tells me my husband loves me, the country loves me, that I will get better.

I hear lies. They know I am dying.

My womb aches. There is a sour smell in the room which emanates from me, from between my legs. Something is rotten in me, perhaps it always was. My skin shakes and sweats. I am not long for this world.

"We must get cold herbs into the Queen," says a worried voice. The doctor. My husband paid for this man for he was supposed to know more than midwives. I hear him listing cold herbs, lettuce, which will aid me, bring down the fever. It will be too late. I think their coldness will be not enough. There is a fire in me. There always was, I think. Before it was ember, ashes, now it is lit. It wants to consume me. The heat in my blood is a mouth, it will eat me.

I feel a beak, pecking at me. The falcon of the shadows has come to me, biting me. It is her, her ghost, her falcon come to peck me bit by bit to death. People pull me up, make me drink. I taste ale and violet leaves, lettuce, and purslane. I was always good with herbs. I was taught well and often by my mother.

"My mother..." I whimper. I think it strange I wish so for her. She never was nice to me, but now I want her. I want to be a child and curl up in her arms, safe. This place is not safe. It is too hot and there are demons waiting for me, birds in the blankets that the others do not see. How do they not see the falcon pecking at my skin? I can feel it, can see it, beak cruel and black and pecking, pecking, pecking. The witch has come to torment me, but which witch? I laugh and they all rush to me, staring. They did not hear my jest and would not understand it. They know not the women I have faced in life, the battles fought. They see only Jane the Queen. Only the good wife, the quiet woman. *Little mouse...*

Not mouse. Not creature of fur was I in soul, but of feathers. Feathers of flame, born of a nest of ashes. And to ashes I shall return.

I lean my head back on sodden sheets. I shiver in painful cold as a wave of heat rushes over my flesh. The blood falling from the tapestry is hot. It joins the flames of my skin. The shades about me hurry to tend to me; they know they can do no good. Ghosts, ghosts, ghosts are about me, racing to me and gone again. They make me dizzy. Why do they race, so? Birds are in the blankets, hopping, pecking; scaly feet scratching, beaks digging into me. Raw is my flesh and my soul. I am so hot.

I remember other fires: a hearth of home burning in the great hall; bonfires alight for Midsummer, dark shapes prancing about the flames. I remember the mean fire in the Queen's chamber at the More. I remember there were fires to celebrate my son, lit on the night he was born. Fire, it has marked out my life.

"Throw me to the flames, that I might burn," I groan. I want it over, done. If I am to burn then let me. Lay me in the flames, stoke my flesh with wood, douse me in pitch and let it be done. Let me become ashes. Let me be by fire cleansed, my soul made pure. Let me start again.

But they will not. There is no relief. I cannot be by fire consumed. Shadows shift, flames dance. A bird is in the fire, wings outstretched. It falls, that gracious bird, into a nest of ashes.

I close my eyes and seek a cooler, quieter place. I, like the bird will fall, find somewhere safe to hold me. I will hide. I have been hiding for most of my life. Perhaps it will serve me now, at the end, as it did so well in life. Where to go when one has come to the end? There is nowhere to go but back. No future to make for, so one must flow into past.

The past was marked often by fear.

Chapter One

Twenty-Four years earlier

**Wulfhall
Wiltshire**

Autumn 1513

It is cool and dim and I am hidden. I see breath floating from my mouth; little puffs of white panic. I must stay quiet; someone is looking for me. He hunts. I do not want him to find me. I am afraid. I press my back to the wooden wall of the barn, willing the boards to open as arms, take me in, hide me. They do not. I hear his step. Against the wooden wall my heart thunders. I think he will hear it.

It is Thomas, my brother, *one* of my brothers; he is six. I am five, born the year after him. Thomas is the sibling I am closest to in age and farthest from in friendship. He is a monster.

He is seeking me, searching the outbuildings. He wants to taunt me and tease me. He finds a reason to do this each day. I am his amusement. He plays with me like a toy, stealing my doll, ripping woollen hair from her head. He likes to pinch me when we are in our lessons, so I earn a beating from our tutor for making noise when Thomas's sharp fingers twist my skin. Thomas likes to watch when I am beaten; it amuses him. He hurts anything smaller and weaker than him. Bugs and butterflies come to his hands, soft wing and scaly leg pulled to bits. He sets light to tapers and ties them to the tails of dogs, cats. And now he is looking for me, and for my doll. I am hiding. It is my only defence. I cannot fight. Thomas is older and stronger than me and a boy. Girls are not allowed to fight as boys do. It is wrong. I cannot run to my mother or father, for they will believe whatever lies Thomas tells them. They always do. Even if they did believe me it would not help. Boys are boys and girls are to accept what boys do. I should not complain, but have patience instead, be a lady of good manners. This is what they will tell me. But *please* and *thank you* and *no, please do not*, do nothing to hold my brother at bay. He likes to hear things squeak in pain or fear. Both please him deeply, combined they please him more. All I can do is hide, hope he does not find me.

Here, the dark shadows of the great barn are redolent with the smell of hay; a creeping scent of warm, wild summer, of possibility and clement nights. Golden strands are piled up to one side of me, fodder for beasts of our farms for the winter. It is a sweet smell, but it sours, mingled with the scent of my sweat and fear as I hear Thomas outside. He knows I am in here. I always run for the shadows. I am too predictable.

About the barn, hunter's feet pad, soft and careful in velvet slippers. Thomas should not be wearing expensive shoes out of doors, but he always does. Mother and Father never reprimand him as they do me; boys always get away with more than girls. Mother tells me girls are subject to falling into sin with greater ease than boys. We are crafted that way, weaker, more fragile than males, therefore we need to be corrected more, set and kept firm on the right path. Mother says God made us this way. I wonder why. Why would God have made His daughters more prone to sin? Why did He not make us strong, as strong as men? Why make one sex so weak, when that would cause such problems? Does God not love His children? Did He want man saddled with partners who always would be liabilities?

But it is not my place to question. I know this for when I do, I am beaten for it. When my mouth, a woman's mouth, opens to ask questions it is another sign I am sinful. Curiosity caused the fall of man; Eve wanted to eat an apple and gave it to her husband, Adam. The woman fell for the wiles of the slithering snake and innocence was lost. The curiosity of women, the searching in their souls, questions on their lips, these sins caused the fall of mankind from Grace. This is why we must be silent, accepting, patient, why we must submit to the will of men. They are stronger than us, better than us. They will keep us safe, from ourselves.

Girls should not ask questions, should not talk, not make noise, not want things for themselves, should not answer back. Sometimes it seems all I do is sinful, that all I am is sinful. I do not mean to be so wicked. Perhaps this is what Mother means when she says females are weak. We do not even know when we are falling into sin. It comes naturally as breathing.

Another step, closer this time. I press my back hard against the wall of the dark barn, try to make my breathing quieter. It wants to flout me, even now, when I need it to obey. My body is a traitor, it will see me caught. I clutch my doll tight. Katherine is her name. My mother named my doll, named her for the Queen of England; the only woman of whom my mother seems to approve. It is fitting such a lovely doll, with auburn wool hair dyed by our maids, who wears a glorious gown which I made myself from scraps of dark velvet, should bear the name of the most gracious, godly woman of this world. She must be so, Queen Katherine, for my mother would approve so wholeheartedly of no one who was not perfect. Queen Katherine is the perfect woman, the perfect Queen. That is who I must emulate. I must aspire to become perfect.

If you are not perfect, you cannot be loved. I have been told this.

I love my doll. I talk to Katherine at night, whispering into her ear of cloth, brain of grain, telling her my secrets, my hopes, wishes. Katherine is the only one I trust, aside from Edward, my oldest brother. He is my protector, the only one who seems to love me, but he is not here. Edward is kind and sweet; he looks for me when others fail to notice me, seeks me out when no other would. He is my friend, and I love him. Thomas is another matter. I *must* love him since he is my brother, but secretly, sinfully, I know I would not love him if I did not have to.

If truth could be told, I would speak. I would tell him I hate him.

His steps have slowed. I can almost see that cruel grin twisting up his handsome face like the curve of the crescent moon. Thomas knows where I am. He is playing with me. Bile rises in my throat. *He will not get her this time,* I think, fingers digging deep into Katherine. I will run if he finds me, run with Katherine, make for the forest where I will hide for the rest of my days. I know what plants are safe to eat. I will feed us; make traps for hares and take my bow that I might hunt deer. I am not good with my bow, but I will learn. As I grow I will learn. Katherine is perfect, so she can tell me what I do wrong. She will instruct me, teach me, as the Queen teaches her women. I will find soft fruits of the briar for us to feast upon and collect Alexander leaves, wild onions, apples, and pennyroyal to infuse and drink. I will make a house of branches, willow woven whilst still living, so we can hide. We will watch from behind soft, downy leaves as men rush past, not seeing us, and we will laugh, Katherine and I! No one will miss me, none will find me, and Katherine will be safe.

I pull Katherine close. The beating of my heart sounds, echoing against her soft gown. Sweat, slick on my palms, seeps into her linen and velvet body. *I will keep you safe,* I promise silently.

His steps have rounded the barn. I hear him at the entrance. The wide doors of the barn are open; like a mouth the barn gapes, surprised, perhaps afraid. Men on our father's lands are moving hay to fields to feed sheep and oxen. Winter is on the wind. I smell it when I wake in the cold mornings: a sharp scent of rain lashing land, water mingled with shards of snow. There are tiny running streams which spill from fields and onto roads, in the morning they shimmer blue-silver with frost. By day, red-brown water flows, melted and cool, down the edges of tracks through the fields and into the roads; ice gathers on my wash bowl in the morning light, becoming a mirror I turn my eyes from, shatter with my hand before I can catch a glimpse of my face. Scent of iron is on the air, snow coming not far behind.

Animals are fast gathering what they can to last through winter. Squirrels in red tunics bury nuts in deep, dark earth and scamper off to find more, bounding over the frost-cloaked land on their merry paws. Birds are flying from our shores to see other lands of which I will only ever dream. Soon will come the time of slaughter, beasts brought in to the outbuilding where Death lives, waiting. There will be cries as their hooves slip on the blood of those killed before them, more as it runs past their eyes, bright and sticky over cobbles, over the mud of the yard. Their eyes will roll as they catch the scent of death and fear on the wind. They will struggle against hands that guide them. Men who lead them will whisper false comfort into soft velvet ears.

Mother does not like to watch the beasts led to slaughter, does not like to hear their calls, but I watch. I know it is only another part of the many pains of this life. They die so we may live and feast upon flesh through winter. I watch each year, standing beside Thomas as beasts are killed one by one. I watch as a knife is stuck deep into their necks. They buck and squeal, blood runs from them, fighting death. Harvest is the only time Thomas does not seek to tease me. When I stand at his side, watching calmly as pigs and sheep are butchered, he seems to possess a quiet respect for me. He watches because he likes the look in their eyes as they die and relishes the sight of sticky blood, flowing red, mingling with rain on the floor of the yard. In time it all flows away, into soil, into land. On such days, Thomas tells me that one day he will be a celebrated soldier, a knight in the King's armies, and therefore must never be squeamish, as women often are, about blood. He watches the yearly procession of death to prepare himself for his future. I do not know why I watch. Perhaps it is just because it is the only time he does not torment me.

Breath catches sharp in my throat. He steps into the barn. I hear his feet tread as though he is stalking, hay and straw crackling lightly under his toes as he sneaks to the murky corners where I often hide. I can see his back. He is two heads taller than me, limbs long and gangly but still he is strong enough to always best me. I am small, even for my age. And I do not have a demon in my soul, pushing me on, urging me to inflict pain. There are times I think Thomas is possessed. When I see that detached look in his eyes as he hurts something, I see a demon, a cat, something dark hidden deep rising to the surface.

"Where are you, little mouse?" he calls in a sing-song voice, tone mocking, taunting. There is a darkness at its edge, something cruel. I hate the name mouse. Many people call me it. "Come out, come out, wherever you are. I won't do your dolly any harm, Jane. I just want to admire the new gown you made for her…"

Tears bound into my eyes. I know he lies, and he has given away what he wants to do to Katherine. Her dress! I have just made it, and I love it. He knows. Thomas always knows where to poke so it will hurt. Thomas watches. He is clever in cruelty. I do not smile often but when I do it shows not on my lips but in my eyes. He knows I love the new gown I have made for Katherine, that I am proud of my work. I turn the doll over in my hands, glance at Thomas. He is still on the other side of the barn. I start to undo the pins and ribbon which hold the gown in place. *I can hide the dress*, I think, *I must hide the dress.*

A hand suddenly leaps over my shoulder, snatches Katherine. He tears the doll from my shaking fingers. The gown falls, Katherine falls. She lands in the hay. I cry out, a fearful, heavy noise of sorrow and anger as Thomas crows, grabbing Katherine roughly and dancing off across the barn. Before he notices, I seize the dress from the floor and stuff it into the deep folds of my own gown.

I walk out from the shadows. "Give her back to me," I say, voice shaking as I stare at him with tearful eyes. My heart is pounding, but I gather all the courage I have.

Thomas prances with my doll, moving as though she is his partner at a dance at court before the King. His hands are covering, smothering her tiny ones, and he bends and bows to Katherine as though he respects her. "She wants to dance, little sister," he jests, spinning her in his hands. I hear a rip. He is pulling her apart as he dances.

"Stop it!" I shout. I hate that she is naked, without her fine gown. It makes it worse. "You will hurt her!"

"Hurt her? Me?" His voice is incredulous, but there is a wicked edge to it. Thomas's dark blue eyes sparkle in the dull light of the barn. He looks like the Devil, like pictures of the Prince of Darkness in prayer books Mother shows us. "I would never hurt such a fine lady. Although…" he trails off, pulling Katherine close to his eyes, "… I do not think she is as well-dressed as she normally is."

My heart falters as he looks at me. "Where is her new dress?" he asks.

"I did not like it, so I burnt it," I lie with solid conviction. He laughs.

"Liar!" Thomas accuses, and quicker than a heartbeat he is on me. Hands snatch and grab at my dress; his arms reach about my shoulders. I struggle, but he pushes me to the floor and sits on my back. He is bigger than me. My ribs creak painfully as he bounces once on my back to teach me to submit. My hands are under my body, pressed painfully against the ground. I feel every blade of straw and every cobble. My knuckles scream in agony, bone grinding on stone. I call out and he stuffs straw in my mouth. Laughing, he makes me eat it.

"Lie still, little mouse," he says as tears come from my eyes and fall into the dirty hay. The strands of thick straw in my mouth taste foul, as though animals have soiled them. My cheeks are red with anger, but there is nothing I can do. Thomas rifles through my dress and finds the gown. I hear it ripping as he pulls it apart. Every careful stitch I made, every loving tuck, he destroys. "Dear, dear," he says, "you *have* been careless with your doll, sister... what will Mother say?"

I let out a noise, half scream and half whimper. My spirit does not know what I am, coward or fighter. My tears fall into straw. I spit out the foul-tasting grasses as he climbs off me. I turn over to see the dress ripped into four pieces. All my work, work done over many weeks to make the perfect court gown, all ruined. I grasp bits of material, hugging them to my chest as I sob.

"I think her hair needs a little work too, sister," Thomas taunts. I look up with swollen and red eyes to see him rip Katherine's woollen hair from her head. For a moment he holds my doll in one hand and her hair in another, as though she is a traitor and he has beheaded her, and then with a flourish, he throws both in the air. Katherine lands face down in a dirty puddle. I scramble to her with a scream. Thomas laughs heartily and runs off.

I gather the bits of her dress, hair, her soiled body. The bits I put in the folds of my gown, hoping somehow I can mend them before Mother sees and punishes me for not taking better care of my toys. She will not believe Thomas did this.

I take Katherine to the trough in the yard and plunge her into cold water. Fragments of ice float still on the top of the water, even though it is already afternoon. I try not to look into them, try not to see the ugly, red-stained face. I focus on Katherine. I soak her to remove the stain from her perfect face, then head for the kitchens. Marge and Kat will help me dry her, to mend her if we can. They are our kitchen maids. I am not supposed to spend time with them, but I do. They are the only ones who are kind to me in this house, my home, Wulfhall.

I do not succeed in mending the dress. Mother notices. She beats me for not having more care for my things. Bent over a chair in her chambers, the light of the fire glowing on Mother's willow whip, I look up and see Thomas hiding in the doorway. Mother does not see him, but I do. There is a malicious smile playing about his lips as he watches the whip fall on my skin over and over again.

Chapter Two

Wulfhall
Wiltshire

Spring- Summer 1514

"You will never a beauty be, Jane."

I remember that sentence said to me more than any other. Through childhood it echoed, said by many people, voices bouncing from the walls of my memory as glass shattering against a hard surface.

Why did they repeat it so? Did they think I had not noticed, had forgotten? People love to say what is obvious. They love to speak aloud observations that enter their minds, hoping that others will suppose them wise and not understanding a thousand minds have thought and tongues have said the same thing before. It is as when a man is tall and people look at him and say, "You are tall!" as if he will look down his legs and notice his height for the first time. No one had any need to remind me I was not a beauty. I had eyes. My father could afford a mirror.

It was an important lesson for a young girl to learn, however, which mayhap is why it was repeated at me so. From the moment I was born, or so it seemed, I knew the truth. Beauty was what a woman *should* possess. Beautiful, woman *should* be. If she was not, something had gone wrong. She had failed. She was defective, unnatural. Without beauty, one was barely a woman. Beautiful women were rewarded for doing as they should, for being correct. Ugly women were punished for not looking as they should.

Devoid of physical perfection, a woman had few things she might try. One was to try to be good. That was the only thing that could recommend her as highly as beauty. Another virtue was to be quiet. The striking may speak, indeed may speak nonsense and have all people hanging on each word as sparrows to a bough in windy autumn. What is ugly may not speak. The ugly are to be silent, and good. Good must you be if beautiful you are not. If you are ugly *and* nefarious of character you will be swift found out. The Devil wears horns and has a pointed tail so men may spot him at a distance. It is the same if you are foul of face; there is no hiding the evil within.

As I grew, of course, I understood it was not as simple as beauty was akin to goodness and ugliness betrayed badness. What is beautiful may hide a wealth of evil, but people are fools all. They want to believe in the beautiful, to believe in perfection. They look upon what is pleasing and think it wondrous. They forget, because they want to, how pretty are poisonous flowers of the forests, how bright are berries that kill, how a sweet face may hide a sinister heart of wickedness. They forget the Devil comes in many forms, possesses a wealth of tricks. They do not want to see truth. They want to believe in beauty.

I say *they*, but I too was taken in by beauty once. Unlike others, I learned my lesson and never did I make it again. All other times if I was deceived, it was for love I became a fool. That I cannot regret. For love I would gladly be deceived, for what else is there to believe in if one cannot believe in love?

With speed, for fool I was not, I learned to hide as a child. I was not pretty so I should be quiet, try to make people think I was good. I knew I was not good, many of my thoughts were not pure, but I hid them. I did not know then that no people are good, or only very few. I was told often I was wicked, and wicked was what I thought I was. Repetition breeds certainty. We believe what we are most often told. And we believe in the words of those we are told to trust. I was ugly because I was so often told I was. For a long time, I never thought to question what I was told by those who supposedly loved me.

Devoid of beauty, I hid behind walls crafted of silence and goodness. There was a rebel within me I had to repress, for I wanted to be neither silent nor good. Words, naughty and rebellious, were always trying to leap from my mouth and there was much that was not virtuous inside me. But that, no one could know. And all that *was* worthy about me was not me or mine in truth, as my mother often reminded me.

"Your royal *and* noble blood flows from *my* line, Jane," Mother would inform me. Usually twice, but sometimes thrice I was blessed with such important information in the span of a day as we sat and sewed in her chambers by the light of the fire. "Never forget; you are a descendant of King Edward III, through me."

"I forget not, my lady mother," I assured her, drawing a thread of yellow silk through the sheet I embroidered, wondering how I was ever to forget such a thing. She said it as often as she said her prayers.

"Your father's side may not be *as* noble in origin," she went on, speaking mainly to herself, often the way in our conversations, "but he is a man of nobility in *spirit*. The King will note this soon enough. Your father will be elevated to where he, and our whole family, belong truly."

"Yes, lady mother," I agreed in a humble tone. To say anything else was to incur her wrath. So easily was her temper unleashed when it came to me. I was her daughter yet nothing I could do was good enough. I was not graceful enough, not beautiful enough. I was dull of wit and slight of charm. My mother made this plain as the looks upon my face. I had let her down.

I know not if she loved me as a baby. Perhaps when we are babies it is easier to think we will all be beauties, since infants are generally adorable whether pretty or not. I had been born in 1508, the year before the old King, Henry VII victor of

Bosworth died, and his son Henry VIII came to the throne as a fresh young prince of promise. As I saw my first summer, my pale eyes starting to take note of the world, the new King was busy rescuing and then marrying his Queen, Katherine, Princess of Spain. She had been languishing alone, lost and cast off in the country after her first husband, Prince Arthur, died. Our new King, Arthur's younger brother, swept in, saving young, lovely Katherine from a life lived in darkness, and brought her to sit at his side, as his Queen.

I was left in the nursery at Wulfhall as my mother and father went to London to watch the coronation of the new King and Queen. When I grew up, Mother told me of the glory of the occasion, of the processions through London, the King's men, newly created Knights of the Bath, dressed in flowing blue robes, riding at the head of the winding, glittering snake of courtiers. She spoke of hangings of tapestry and painted cloth that had been hung out to decorate London, cloth flapping from every window, balcony, every house and merchant's shop of London along the route from Palace to Abbey where they were crowned. The King's horse had been draped in ermine and cloth of gold and the four barons of the Cinque Ports had held a golden canopy over him. In crimson and ermine, cloth of gold and glittering with more gems than a man could count, the fresh young prince had gone to Westminster Abbey and there been crowned our King.

People told me later that Henry VIII was not supposed to have become King. His brother Prince Arthur had been the eldest, and intended successor. "The old King loved Arthur more than Henry," Kat of the kitchens whispered to me when I was old enough to hear her tales. "But God loved our Harry, and knew he was right for the throne."

I felt for King Henry, for not being as loved as his brother. We had something in common, I felt. I was the first daughter born to my parents after a string of sons. My mother told me that whilst sons, many of them, were good for a family and she had clearly completed her sacred duty as a woman by providing so many, it was a relief to finally have a daughter, one she might pass knowledge of herbs, remedies and embroidery to. She hoped, after having done her ultimate duty so diligently in birthing many sons for my father, God would permit her to bear a beauty, a girl who would charm all she met. But then there was me.

Not beautiful enough, not clever enough, not graceful enough. Not enough. Had I been perfect no doubt my life would have been different. But I was not, and I was not allowed to go unpunished for failing to be the daughter my mother wanted.

She had a never-ending stream of pride for her sons, my brothers. My eldest brother John had been dead four years by 1514. I did not remember him. Taken to his grave in the local church I had been, stood over the brass with his name on it I had. Maids of the kitchens said that metal plate was kept bright by my mother's tears, for John had been her first child, and he had died not of fever as so many children did, but in an accident. He fell into a river, his clothes pulled him under and he drowned. When we all went to see my eldest brother in his tomb, I made a show of sorrow, but I did not grieve. I never knew John. It is hard to sorrow for something unknown.

The eldest of my brothers living was Edward. My oldest brother was sandy of hair and grey-blue of eye like me, and had recently been named a page in the household of Princess Mary Tudor, sister to our King. Edward was to go to France that year, for the Princess had done as all good princesses should and married a King to become Queen.

My brother Henry was next in line, but he had no time for me; too grown up to spend time with Thomas and me. When he was old enough, Henry was to be sent to the house of Richard Foxe, Bishop of Winchester, to train for a role in the Church. Father had taken Henry to court along with Edward, so they could be seen and serve in honorary positions open to children at state functions, but it was plain to see Mother and

Father thought Edward had more promise than Henry. Henry was more like my father, a solid, plain kind of man.

Thomas was the youngest son and I shared some lessons with him. Supposedly we played too, but his play often took the form of my punishment. There was also a distant cousin of my mother's line living in the house, Edmund, and his wife Mary. Edmund was a poor relation, of an obscure branch of my mother's family. I believe he may have been a second or third cousin, but cousin we all called him. Edmund and Mary lived in our house, but Edmund was often seeing to Father's business on the Seymour estates, and he too had little time for me.

If you were pretty, everyone would have time for you, I often told myself.

Quickly I learnt that no one wished to look at me and I followed suit. I avoided mirrors and surfaces that might reflect my face, which was my mother's first and most lasting disappointment. My hair was fair, like hers, and my eyes grey-blue. Thus far the head and face I wore would seem to be in keeping with commonly-held ideals of beauty, yet thus far was as far as it went. My face was not arranged as pleasingly as my mother would have liked. Women were supposed to attract good husbands, who would keep them safe in life, see their children elevated. I was not beautiful therefore my chances of a high marriage were damaged. My family were not poor, certainly, but not flowing in wealth either. Mother would never admit it, but we were the lower of the high; poor nobility. Without a large dowry to recommend me, I had only my looks to rely on and they were lacking.

My cheeks were round, eyes small, lips slight. I had a habit of tucking in my chin to reduce the space I took up in the world so people would not notice me, stare at my ugliness. This affectation made my chin appear smaller and gave an onlooker the impression I had grown another chin, of fat, under the first. My nose was not large, but it seemed so against my diminutive features. Its prominence gave me a heron-like appearance, as my mother often noted, tone dark with disapproval as though I was in control of the way my features had been arranged. My small lips, too, conspired against me. Pale and thin, they gave my face an expression of constant censure, as though I were judging what I saw and found it wanting. My skin was pale, which was often considered a mark of beauty, but I was so *very* pale. If I turned my arms over, a keen eye could trace blue veins towards my heart, and no one wants to see the blood of a woman.

No, I was no beauty, not like my mother. She had hoped to have a daughter who grew up to become as a mirror to her. I did not reflect well. My mother had been a young ornament of the English court, of whom all spoke of with reverence for her comeliness and natural grace. Mother still served the Queen on state occasions. Margery Wentworth, as she had been before she married and became Lady Seymour, had been written about by poets. Other maids of court had sighed with breath of bitter jealousy as she sauntered past. In the house of her aunt, where she had served as a maid of honour as a young girl, the court poet John Skelton had seen, and fallen for, each of her many charms. He wrote verses, and her beauty was proclaimed far and wide, lauded into eternity. That was what beauty brought a woman; rewards of love and eternal life. What is ugly passes un-noted, swift forgotten.

My mother was fond of reciting one of the poems written for her, an ode entitled, *"To Mistress Margery Wentworth"* which I soon knew by heart, even as a child.

> *With margerain gentle.*
> *The flower of goodlihead,*
> *Embroidered the mantle,*
> *Is of your maidenhead.*
> *Plainly I cannot glose;*
> *Ye be, as I devine,*
> *The pretty primrose,*
> *The goodly columbine.*

With margerain gentle,
The flower of goodlihead,
Embroidered the mantle,
Is of your maidenhead.
Benign, courteous, and meek,
With words well devised;
In you, who list to seek,
Be virtues well comprised.
With margerain gentle.
The flower of goodlihead,
Embroidered the mantle,
Is of your maidenhead.

Women of court had set the poem to music. It was sung by common people through our lands. Often on a spring morning, if seeping or sweeping rain were not our companion, I would rise from my bed and hear a kitchen maid singing it as she plucked sorrel leaves for green sauce or herbs for the pottage that night. And the song was more than a laud for my mother, but also for the Seymour house.

It was a sign of immense honour that a celebrated, noble beauty like my mother had been given in marriage to a man of slighter birth and blood such as my father. My father was descended from the St Maurs family, who had sailed to England with King William the Conqueror, but faded into obscurity after that. Although my Seymour grandfather had managed to get a post at court, and one for his son, it was really through the military endeavours of my father, John Seymour, that our family started to truly rise once more. And rising was what mattered. "What good is bread without yeast?" my mother would ask no one in particular as she considered the position my father should hold in England, and did not. Position at court, favours from the King and Queen, these were the things that mattered, we were told. Men gained such honours with their brains, women with beauty. Blood helped of course. To be born into the right family was a gift from God, and nobles ruled commoners as the King ruled them. That was the way of things, the hierarchy handed down from above, where the saints watched over us and God watched over them.

My mother knew what it was to be of good and noble blood. My mother came from the line of Sir Henry Percy, *Hotspur*, and was indeed a descendant of Edward III, but we had other connections too. My maternal grandmother Anne Say had married twice. Through the children of her first marriage I and my siblings were related to the Howards, lords of Norfolk and Surrey. Distant though the connection might be, I was a cousin of sorts to the newly reinstated Duke of Norfolk, and his son the Earl of Surrey. Mother was pleased to inform us of this often, although I came to understand fairly early in life that almost all the nobility were related to one another in some way. It was also true that almost all the nobility were distantly related to royalty. My mother's grand claim, therefore, was all but meaningless.

But this, I could not say aloud. To question my mother was to be beaten, and good girls did not question; they accepted. And I had let Mother and my family down enough. I had to be good, if I was unwilling to be beautiful.

Chapter Three

Wulfhall
Wiltshire

Late Summer- Autumn 1514

It was only when Mother ran her hands over my hips, large even when I was a child, that she seemed to find anything to approve of. "Breeding!" she would crow, slapping her hands on my sides as though I were a fat cow. "Good wide hips. Even if you have no other charms, daughter, men will mark this about you."

"Yes, my lady mother," I would say, and flee her chambers feeling as though I was about to be herded to market. But if she thought my hips a virtue one day, on another she could find nothing to please her.

"Jane has but small charms to recommend herself to a husband," Mother mourned to my father one wet morning in late summer, within my hearing.

We were in the great hall, where often we went when it was pouring with rain outside. The days of summer had been long and hot, sultry and lazy that year, but in the lateness of summer muggy skies broke, sending thick, fat droplets of rain upon us. The skies were warm and grey and blue. Thunder rolled, often and ominous, in the low-hanging heavens. The grass, parched and crisp, spare and yellow after so long without rain paying a visit, turned lush green seemingly overnight. Ivy bobbed in trees along the edge of the woodland, bouncing as large drops hit and shattered. Cattle and sheep were hiding along blackthorn hedgerows, trying to stay dry.

I cringed as I heard Mother. When one is pale as a ghost, a flush is hard to hide. I hung my head, my head bowing low to the floor, chin tucking in. Shame flooded into my blood, hot and bitter as bile. I stared at the rushes on the floor. It often felt as though I saw nothing but floor, so much were my eyes downcast.

"Jane has her own charms," my father said, putting his hand to my shoulder and squeezing even as he walked away to talk to his steward on matters of the estate. Tears of gratitude raced to my pale eyes, but I always wondered what charms I had that he saw. He noted none aloud.

Although often away from home at court or on local business, and although he seemed absent even when present, my father did at times try to calm the continual criticism of my mother. He failed. My mother was a force all her own within our house, ever-conscious of the droplet of royal blood she had graciously bestowed upon my father's line, ever-aware of the *vastly* more noble connections she could claim. Her father had been an important man in Suffolk and Yorkshire where he held estates, and my mother was a fine prize for my father. My mother and her father had thought him a rising star, but John Seymour had not flown as high in the skies as they had wanted. Other stars blazed brighter. Yet for all that she reminded him of, for all the many steps down she had apparently taken by marrying him, they were not an unhappy couple.

My father was, like any man, apt to stray from the bed of his wife, particularly when she was with child. The prodigious amount of children born to my parents, something which became a jest between my father and the King for a time, allowed him many chances to exert his natural right to seek comfort in the arms, or more often between the legs, of other women, usually our maids or daughters of his tenants who caught his eye. But he was not open in his affairs as many men are. Father was careful, and as long as he was careful in his dalliances I do not think Mother paid much heed to his absence from her chamber at night… not until later in my story. She ignored his infidelities. It was the way many women, including our Queen, coped with straying husbands; pretend something shameful exists not, and it does not. It was the way I felt, at times; ignored so I would not cast shame on my family. In truth, it was the only thing wives could do to retain dignity. If they complained they could be beaten, or punished in other ways. What choice did they have but to submit, yet try to make it look as though they were rising above the insult of a husband choosing another woman? Ignoring a man's infidelities was, for wives, like tripping on a step, recovering and walking on, head up high. Everyone knew they had stumbled, yet they tried to pretend they had not.

Father was more at home with the company of other men, however much he loved women, but he admired the beauty of his wife. Just as she ignored his lack of fidelity, he tried to ignore her waspish nature. They had both, in different ways, apparently agreed to ignore the ill and uphold the good in their marriage. It seemed to work. They rarely argued. My mother usually had her way, whilst on the surface Father remained lord and master of the family. Mother oversaw the household and the raising of the children and my father got on with business of his estates, occasional appearances at court, and whoring. Peace prevailed, through fantasy.

The year of my birth had been the same year in which my father had been promoted by the old King Henry VII, and made Sheriff of Wiltshire. He had served his King at the Battle of Blackheath in 1497 when a rebel army rose from the wilds of Cornwall to test the, then, new King Henry VII, and later in France in 1513, when the old King's son went to war my father had led a band of one hundred men. Father had fought, although I was later told no one really fought, as the enemy ran away so fast, at the Battle of the Spurs, but John Seymour did not rise high in royal estimations. At Blackheath he had been knighted in the field by the King himself, and he served well in sieges at Tournay and Terounne, but his ambitions, if high in war, were lower than my mother would have liked during peace.

In war my father knew his place, at court he had but small place. The old King had honoured him, our new King knew him, and he was called to court from time to time for he was a knight of the body to King Henry VIII, but my father was no prancing, dancing gallant. He was not talented in arts of jousting, or in the subterfuge required for the dark politics of court life. To succeed at court in these modern times meant men must excel at many things. They had to be poets and warriors, jousters and dancers, lovers and men of hard and unflinching cruelty.

The truth was, as later I heard whispered in the kitchens, that my father was a solid man, but not one of vast prospects. The King honoured him with positions, but they were granted more because of Father's local importance than thoughts of his future greatness. The King needed men loyal to him in all shires of England, so appointed men like my father who were useful in battle, to keep the peace and to deal with rebellion if it broke out. Like a spider with legs on the many silver strands of its web a king had to be, and my father was one of the outer strands. Many of his positions were nominal. When there was war, he would be called, when there was a court event or foreign lord come to call on the King, Father was present at court to boost numbers, make the King look even grander for his many attendants, but boon companion of the King Father was not. He was older than the new King by a good decade, and Henry VIII was a man of many passions, and liked his friends to help him indulge them all. My father fitted one block of life but was not able to assume many shapes. He was not a creature born to adaptation, but to specialisation.

My father was a soldier. He had small patience for witty conversation that appeared to be about one subject but was in truth about another, had no interest in fawning over women he did not like for the sake of advancement, or flattering men with lies. He was not a man made for court therefore, where it was a good thing if a person had many masks up their embroidered, velvet sleeves, ready to bring out and slip on at a moment's notice. Think not he was devoid of charm; when he liked a maid the full force of his eyes and handsome face would fall on her and he would smile as though she was the only pleasure in the world, but he was not talented at pretence. The King said he liked that about my father, admired his plain ways and honest character... but perhaps the King lied, for he did not promote him high. John Seymour was ever in the thick of war and at the edge of court. Sheriff of Wiltshire was a good appointment, granted to him for his service to his young, war-like King.

But Father, if not one of the most important men of England, was not unimportant. He had importance locally, and in a more limited fashion at court. In times of war he was needed by his King, and was present at ceremonies. The King, so he said, liked to talk of war and battles and appreciated his views.

"The King can make any man feel like his best friend," he told me once. "High or low, Harry will sling an arm about your shoulder and walk with you, jesting and laughing as though you are brothers." There was a note of admiration in his voice. It was always there when people spoke of our King. People had admired and respected Henry VII, but they loved Henry VIII. It was something I understood quickly. Our King, so beautiful, so wise, could do no wrong.

My father was not as rich as he might have been, but certainly we were not poor. He had a house at Wulfhall, in Wiltshire where we spent most of our time, and another at Elvetham in Hampshire where we spent less. Wulfhall was a manor house, with more than a thousand acres, much of which was farmed by tenants. There were acres of garden to walk in and orchards which gave fruit. There were deep plots of good, rich soil for vegetables, and long expanses of glittering fishponds. We had more than a hundred acres to grow food for the house, but much was also left to become pasture for cattle and sheep. There was no finer house in the neighbourhood. Wulfhall was made of timber for the most part, and arranged in blocks surrounding a central courtyard. There was a long gallery with leaded windows installed at high expense, which my mother claimed credit for, as long galleries and leaded windows were the height of fashion. There was also an older great hall, the like of which were falling out of fashion. There was a chapel in the grounds although we used the local church at Great Bedwyn a great deal, and Father kept a chaplain, which was a mark of wealth. The innards of the house were lined with panels of wood, painted in white and other bright colours so the house was not too dark by day. There were good bedrooms, and for a while I had my own for I was the only girl. I often had a maid to sleep in my bed or on a pallet bed on the floor, as girls were not to sleep alone. It invited too many questions later in life about their morals.

I was much in the company of my nearest brother, Thomas, but Edward was my hero. With golden hair and eyes the same colour as mine he was an older, impossibly elegant figure to me. Edward wore clothes suited to a young man at court, even though he was only a lad then. He was kind to me, unlike my mother and Thomas, and would always bring gifts on the rare occasions he came home. Edward had given me Katherine, my doll, purchased from a travelling merchant. Father took Edward to court every time he was there, and left him in the houses of kin who were more regular attendants at court than Father was. He was trying to grant Edward the best start in life and it had worked. That year Edward would become a child of honour, a page of lesser station, in the household of Princess Mary Tudor, sister of the King. It was a high honour, although a position of small significance in practice. In some ways my brother was to be an ornament for the chamber of the Princess. Father had managed to gain this appointment with help from the Bryans, our kinsmen, who were much at court. Lady Bryan was a favourite companion of the Queen's.

Princess Mary was to wed the old French King, Louis XII. He was grey and toothless, broken and crooked and she, poor thing, was eighteen and lovely. The loveliest woman of the world, some claimed, with red-fair hair like dragon fire, skin clear and pale as fresh milk and her blood as royal as her brother, the King's.

"It is said the French King is a leper," my mother whispered. We all crossed ourselves. Even I knew a leper was a cursed man, skin rotting and body too, falling into the grave whilst still walking about the world.

Louis XII was fifty-two, an old man by the standards of our time, and he had lived a quiet life of near retirement with previous wives. His court, although beautiful and rich, was said to be nothing to the splendour and sophistication of Mechelen where the Archduchess Margaret lived, or to England where King Henry had created much in the way of wonder. "Courts tend to reflect the personality of their ruler," Mother told us. Louis's court was good, and dreary. The greatness of the French Court seemed to have faded in the twilight years of his reign.

The common people of France adored Louis, partly because of his frugality. To his people, Louis was *"Le Père de France"*. He imposed few taxes and did not waste the money he did take. His nobles hated this, thinking that a king should make much show of magnificence, not only to his own people, but to the world. It was the way rulers imposed on other rulers how superior they, and their countries, were, after all. A king should be easy to find in a crowd; he should be the richest, most noticeable of men. Louis, it was rumoured, was more like one of the servants than a true son of France. He went to bed early, rose before dawn, was careful with his money, staid in appearance. He was not fond of dancing or hunting and preferred books to the companionship of his nobles. He was, in short, an old man, retiring from the world.

But this was all to change when Mary Tudor arrived. The old man was suddenly invested with a bride who loved everything he did not. Unhappy though she was to be placed in a match with an aged man, Mary Tudor was fond of many pleasures that her new position could bestow. She wanted endless rounds of dances, feasts, hunting and masques. It was obvious from the start that the court was about to change. And my brother was part of that change, that court, that wondrous marriage. My brother was in France, serving a Queen.

I missed Edward as the night misses the sun. He had been at school before that time, often at court with our father too, which is how he had come to be noticed and promoted, but he had come home from time to time. When he went to France I thought I might not see him again. I imagined what he was doing; serving wine to the Queen of France and the King, opening the door for cardinals and bishops, dukes and lords. When he was older, I thought, a young beauty of France would fall helplessly in love with him and refuse to wed another man. Fearing for her health, her noble father would allow the marriage. My brother would become a duke later in life, promoted by his Queen. He would be the greatest knight of the French Court, and then he would come home, and be the same in England.

Then, a few weeks after the wedding, I thought my dreams might turn to ash when I heard that King Louis had sent Mary's attendants home. "It is cruel!" my mother said.

"It is quite normal," my father contradicted calmly. "No King wants his wife surrounded by attendants from her homeland. It introduces too many spies into his court, and keeps the Queen from being close to her new people."

My mother pursed her lips. They became as thin as mine. She would not disagree, even though I could hear her doing so in her mind. But much to the relief of my parents, and my dreams, a few people stayed with Mary in France. She had her pages, and Edward was one of them. It was likely he was thought too young to be a threat to anyone. The Queen of France also retained a few women, two of which who happened to be relations of ours.

"How Thomas Boleyn arranged that, I know not," Father mentioned to Mother.

"The girls are related to the Howards," Mother said. I watched as motes pranced in a beam of sunlight near her gable hood, as though they were dancing with her.

"Howards went home, Boleyns stayed," he said, shaking his head. "That man has a tongue that could talk the Devil into virtue and angels into sin."

"John!" Mother reproved, crossing herself.

"I just mean, when he starts talking it seems all men lose their own thoughts and take on his," said Father. "It is a rare talent."

The two girls who had stayed on were named Mary and Anne Boleyn, and they were my cousins, albeit distantly. "Mary served in the Princess's household in England and is the elder," my mother told me. "Anne has come from the household of the Regent Margaret of Austria, and is the younger. She is so young that normally she would not be considered for such a post, but her father, Thomas Boleyn, has talked her way into a court position as she has a talent for languages after serving for a year in the Court of the Regent Margaret. She is there to aid the Princess with French."

"Does the Princess not speak French?" I asked, a desperate note of hope in my voice. I spoke it so badly. It would make me feel less foolish if a Princess of England and Queen of France also had not mastered it.

"Of course she does!" my mother said, *tsking*. "But it is good to have an expert with her, in case there is something she does not understand. Consider, daughter, that a Queen must talk to ambassadors and men of other lands, and if there is even a slight misunderstanding much might go awry between two countries. Being Queen is a high responsibility. She must not waver or slip."

Be perfect, I thought. *A Queen must be perfect.*

So Edward stayed on, and I missed him, especially since I was left with Thomas. My brother was a poor substitute for the brother I had lost to France. He was a brutal boy, cruel to me, vicious to his pets. He was a liar and a teller of tales, some true, many not. Usually the tales he told were falsehoods made up for his own amusement, but he also could not be trusted with secrets. Thomas was much annoyed that he could not leave home as Edward had, for he was sure that he would make a better page to the Princess, or to the King. Thomas was a braggart, a boaster, and a liar. He amused himself by telling tales to our mother that were not true, but were always believed, to get me into trouble.

He enjoyed my hate. It made him feel powerful.

The times I was happiest were when I was in the saddle of one of our horses, riding out over my father's estates. I would feel the wind searching through my riding bonnet and under the mask I wore to protect my pale skin from sunlight. On a horse I knew what it was to feel free and whole, be devoid of care and concern. Servants were sent to ride out with us, but Thomas would often urge me to ride on, lose them in the paths of the deep, thick forest of Savernake. I learned not to do as he bid, in time. When I was young and fool enough to obey his reckless notions, thinking that to do so might make him a friend, he would double back to tell tales that *I* had urged our flight from our servants. More than once, because I was a fool for hope as I was for Thomas, this earned me a beating from our mother.

Once, I followed his call and we rode deep into the forest. We galloped down wide paths, plunging ever deeper into the heart of the woods. The chalky ground was firm beneath the hooves of our horses, and the sound of their clipping echoed through the trees. When I realised Thomas was no more behind me, I pulled my horse up, afraid for a moment to be alone in the heart of the woods. But as I looked about, I could not feel fear. I had not room enough for it in my body, my blood, my bones. Wonder consumed me.

Shadowed glens where woodcutters had felled trees for the use of the King in building ships to sail over wide seas were dappled with bright, fragmented sunlight. Trees were green but also gold and brown. They flickered, leaves dancing. Long grass swayed and bowed in the lightest breeze. Autumn air, chilled, fresh and sweet flowed over me.

I loved autumn; a season where the purple-black fruit of blackthorn was abundant in spiky hedges which kept our livestock away from fields of crops or from wandering into the forest to become lost, or stolen. Old men would ask permission to cut from the blackthorn soon to make walking sticks which lasted, so it was said, the rest of a man's life and were hardy and true. Some said this power came from witches, for witches lived in blackthorn, the thorns holding them safe. If so, perhaps witches favoured old men, or wanted to aid them, for it was true blackthorn made the best sticks for legs that had gone past their prime.

As we had left the house that day I had smelt pork and salt; slaughtered hogs being preserved for winter, cooked flesh soaked in brine so strong that eggs would float in it. The salt had been brought to the house in barrels, having come all the way from the Bay of Bourgeneuf or Northern Spain. It was a dark, sea-sourced salt and made the hands of our maids raw as they rubbed it into flesh. There had been too, a scent of apples and honey and pears. Fruit gathered from our orchards was being cooked down into preserves; jellies and jams and marmalades, some thick enough to be sliced and eaten on crumbling biscuits accompanied by sweet hippocras at Christmas. Peas and beans were being dried, more apples cleaned and set into dark barrels where they would winter. We would take them out to eat, each month their skin more like leather and insides spongy, and tart. I had caught a scent of barley being brewed for ale, too. The kitchens had been busy that day. They always were, but autumn was the busiest season. There was much to store and preserve for winter, much to prepare.

But such things were of house and home. I was in the wilds.

Spindles of light cascaded like delicate, searching fingers through the leaves, motes of dust were flecks of gold chasing one another in streaming sunlight. The green of ferns, the sharp, verdant spikes of leaves on bushes flew into my eyes. In the distance I could hear the singing of men about their work, the slight rustle of bushes speaking of small creatures that lived within. Even with the falling shadows and indistinct patches of shade where danger might lurk it was beautiful. Perhaps the light was made only prettier by the dark. Green fell to deeper green, then to black. And what beyond black? Tiny darts of glimmering gold; the sun reaching through with her thin fingers, caressing deepest shadow.

A breeze blew, trees tossing, wind rushing, the sunlight bursting through clouds and then leaves as an unexpected guest. Wind flowed down paths of the forest, tousling trees, blustering this way and that, leaves waving as though a procession passed.

I felt at home in that shadowed place. I lifted my nose to the air and caught the scent of flowers, gazed up at the rooftop of trees waving in the wind above. I stretched out my neck, so often stiff, accustomed to bowing, and I felt as though there, hidden from the prying eyes of the world and the taunting of my brother I could be as I was supposed to be; a free soul, unbidden, at liberty and beholden to none.

It did not last, of course. A moment in a life is not all there is in a life, and does not grant freedom, but life is made of moments and the ones we cling to when times are hard can become lasting, can become the essence of a soul if we so choose.

When the harried servants found me I was already bringing my pony to trot back to them. They took me to my mother's chamber in Wulfhall and I was beaten until the backs of my thighs bled. When my mother left me, I went to the kitchens where Kat and Marge took me aside from the main throng of servants and slathered goose grease and arnica on my wounds. I hid in a corner near the fire, and they fed me secret treats of honey tarts. They were kind to me. The head cook of the kitchens, Mother Cooper, was too distracted to notice me hidden away as she shouted and barked commands to her other maids. There were six in the kitchen, but Kat and Marge were the ones I came to when I was in trouble. Kat and Marge led me to a side chamber of the kitchen, where Mother Cooper would not see me.

"Master Thomas was the one to get you in trouble again, wasn't he, Mistress Jane?" Kat asked, kneading dough with her rough hands. Against the dark oaken table, the dough swelled and folded under her power, seeping into deep, black scratches cut by so many knives slicing so many foods through the ages our line had lived at Wulfhall. I watched her pound the dough, pushing and kneading with strong arms. An apron tied over her serviceable and warm gown and kirtle of wool protected both, which was good as she had only one gown. It was a mark of a well-off servant to have a gown at all, for many women of England just had kirtles. Kat had wages enough to wear a gown over the kirtle. It was not taken for granted. Kat might have a second kirtle, to wear underneath, but her gown had to be protected. It was warmer in autumn to wear both. Our servants wore good wool, from our own lands. Father sold it to them at a fair price, if they could card and spin it, send it to be woven or do it themselves. Mother had asked him do so. If they were well-dressed, our family looked only the better for it.

I nodded, but I did not answer. Staring down at the slate floor, washed and scoured that morning, I bit into my tart, feeling the sweetness of honey and the slippery egg and flour which held it together slide over my tongue. My rear and thighs were stinging from my mother's willow whip, but a sweet honey tart was good compensation.

"That boy…" Kat sighed, pounding the dough into submission then turning it to force more air into its flesh.

"He's a rare charmer, though," chuckled Marge from where she was chopping herbs to put into a blackened pot of steaming pottage hanging over the fire. "He'll be one to watch with women, just like…" She stopped herself and glanced at Kat who had a warning expression on her face. Kat shook her head curtly, and Marge faltered. "Just like… many other men…" Marge finished, her tongue clumsy upon the words.

I pretended to note nothing as I felt their eyes fall on me. I knew that was not what Marge had meant. She had meant my father. I knew from scraps I heard in the kitchens what my father was known for; a roving eye and a willing hand. Many women of the household allowed him to do as he wished. He was their master, after all. Should they displease him, they could find themselves seeking employment elsewhere. It happened in plenty of houses, and when girls got with child often they were turned out for whoring. That did not happen in our house. If I had bastard brothers or sisters I knew not of them, but my father, for all his faults, was not a man to abandon children.

Many women of the house were actually fond of him, admiring of his exploits in battle, his easy charm. Some, I knew just as well, did not want the attentions he offered. But they did not have a choice. What the master wanted, the master got. That was the way of things. But I said nothing of all this, for I did not want to make Kat and Marge uncomfortable for saying something potentially reckless, and I could not speak ill of my father. It would have been as speaking ill of God. When people we love do wrong, we say nothing of it in public. That was something I learned young. Family secrets were just that; secrets only for the family.

Kat shook her head at Marge and glanced at me. "It's so easy to forget you are here, even when a body is talking to you, Mistress Jane," she noted. "You are so slight and quiet. Just remember we keep your secrets and you keep ours. Your mother would not like you coming down here, would she? Not a fitting place for the young daughter of the house to be?"

I shook my head. "I do not say anything I hear," I assured them. Kat did not need to threaten, however kindly. I would not have said anything.

Both looked relieved. Another maid came in to ask where the chafing dish was, for she needed to seethe spinach so it was soft enough to spread on toast with egg and ginger, a dish my mother was fond of. Marge pointed to the dish with her nose as she gathered the chopped herbs in two hands and brought them to the fire. She opened her palms, scattering them on the top of the steaming, savoury broth, and patted her hands until all flecks of pungent delicious green had tumbled into the stew. With a long-handled spoon of wood she stirred it. Green rosemary and sage, marjoram and lettuce disappeared under bubbles of brown pottage, soft chunks of pale turnip and white carrot floated up to take their place.

I breathed in the scent. Meat juices from gamey pheasant and mallard swam in the air, mingled with herbs. I could smell honey and mustard leaves too. My family could not afford much in the way of spices, or the heated black pepper which I loved and only seemed to taste at Christmas or when we had company from court, but our proximity to the forest and our good gardens meant we had much in the way of fresh herbs, vegetables and wild plants to flavour our food and grace our table.

The game of the forest, and the fish of our ponds and lakes too, were favourites of mine. I loved tasty, tiny songbirds our men caught in nets and the rich, soft flesh of hung game birds, pheasants, pigeons, duck, goose, and on rare occasions, quails. We did not often find them wild, but sometimes they were brought for special occasions to the house. We did not eat a great deal of sugar, most of what was bought for the house was used to preserve fruits and vegetables, but we had honey in plentiful amounts from the many working hives on the land. Mustard and honey roasted mallards, boiled larks with wild endive and home-made verjuice, baked duck with rich yellow butter, fresh or salted from our own herds, old hens done with laying soft and tender in tart-sweet gooseberry stew… these were dishes I adored. They tasted of home. My mother despaired of our inability to purchase many things that she missed from life at court, such as rich spices and barrels of fish from the coast, sugar loaf and saffron, but I thought we had more than enough, and the skill of her kitchen maids was great and good.

"You are a good secret-keeper, Jane," said Marge with approval. "And we will honour your secrets as you do ours."

I nodded and nestled my back into the warm hearth, trying to keep my thighs from the hard surface below. I watched ash and ember collapse on top of each other, grey softness falling, slipping upon the blackened floor of the fire.

Of course I would keep their secrets. These two women were the only ones, aside from Edward, I truly loved.

Chapter Four

Wulfhall
Wiltshire

Spring- Early Summer 1517

"No, no, *no!*"

I sighed, trying to conceal my frustration, roused sour and chafing only more as Thomas accepted the challenge I had failed, and executed the Latin phrase from the Holy Bible perfectly. Of course he did. My brother's tongue was born to twist and slither like a snake, and he did everything perfectly, in front of others. The malice in him he kept just for me.

In truth, Thomas's Latin was not that good, as I was later informed by Edward, who was learning it from experts and was therefore proficient. But Thomas's Latin did not need to be that accomplished. Rudimentary though his skills were, largely because learning any language, but especially Latin, requires dedication and discipline, Thomas only had to be better than me to impress our tutor. If there is always someone behind you in the race, you look better by comparison. That was something that in later life would restrict my brother's abilities. I never knew it then, nor did he, but Thomas's habit of only attempting to surpass others, and usually those he already knew he could beat, led to him never becoming the best of himself. I thought what he did harmed me, but it wounded him far more. Sadly, I never knew that as a child. I might have pitied rather than feared him.

Despondently I gazed from the window, looking beyond the oiled parchment covering the open hole. In the better rooms, like the long gallery, there was glass but in our rooms cheaper materials sufficed. I tried not to sigh, whilst wishing I was anywhere but there, but home. Although in truth I knew nowhere else, and all my days were much the same. That did not mean there was no beauty or wonder in my life, but there was not, either, much variation. Tedium breeds restlessness. Thomas felt it too, but he was allowed to express his feelings of a need to roam, to exercise by riding or practising with his sword. I had to swallow my frustration at the routine of our lives.

We had risen at dawn that day, as usual, waking with the bells pealing for Prime. It was sensible to be awake when there was light upon the world, as candles were expensive. We rose always just before light crested upon the long horizon of Wiltshire, roaming gently over fields that were wide and elongated, the land spread out and flat, for the main part, so the skies seemed vast, never-ending. On summer days the skies would be a pale blue, like the robes of the Virgin, and they were spread over us as an immeasurable hood, so wide, so tall, limitless.

I climbed from bed to the scent of curling smoke flitting through cobalt blue light. Mother and Father had wax candles in their rooms, but they were the best and cost much coin, so we children had rush-lights made of tallow which smelt a little. The servants had worse ones which smoked and stunk, or they simply worked by what little light the skies had to offer, which in spring or winter was not a great deal.

To the sound of birds trilling outside my small window, which was covered by a wooden shutter, making the room gloomy, I would wash with the help of my maid, and dress with her aid also. When it was cold there were clean smocks of linen, then thick garments of wool to put under my kirtle; the under-gown. A gown, usually of fine wool but sometimes of velvet if it were a special occasion, went on top, the front open to reveal the kirtle and with separate sleeves hooked together underneath. I had many kirtles and pairs of sleeves but only four gowns. Using many sleeves and a few kirtles, a girl could make it appear she had a varied and large wardrobe by swapping them about. It was a trick Mother had taught me. "Used often at court," she had said, nodding sagely. Anything of court was right and proper, even lies, as this fakery with gowns was.

I wore my hair loose as a child, as was expected of a maiden. Girls who were unwed wore their hair unbound and flowing down their backs, older or married women usually plaited their hair and kept it under a sheer veil of white or black, with a hood or headdress on their heads. Most popular was the English Gable hood, which was bulky but made the face under it look slim and the neck too. The Queen favoured it, so many women of England followed suit. I wore one infrequently, usually only for grand occasions. The rest of the time my hair, pale and fair, was allowed to show. Sadly it was not golden, as the hair of the most admired girls was. It was paler, more like moon than sunlight, more silver than gold, but it was not glossy and it did not shine.

To chapel and Mass we of the house trooped as maids went to our rooms to take down window shutters and put up cloth or waxed paper, to make beds and empty chamber pots. In church we would take to our knees upon the swept earthen floor, strewn with straw and rushes, praying to God to save us and that we might save ourselves from sin. Some elders who came to Mass had stools they brought with them to sit upon, since their knees were too old and swollen to last long on the hard floor, but the rest of us knelt or stood in the empty belly of the cool church. Then back to the house we went, where a small plate of bread and honey would be sent to our rooms, each of us children, and then to the schoolroom we went. I did not like the schoolroom.

Most information we had to be taught was learnt by memory. Books we had, but they were expensive, as was paper and parchment. So memory was how we learned; our tutor reciting, we copying him. Thomas and I shared a hornbook, although he used it more. It was a wooden board with a handle. On the front a sheet of vellum went which contained the day's lesson, such as the alphabet, a prayer, or numbers.

This was covered by a sheer layer of horn, which protected it. We could then read it, committing it to memory by repetition. Hornbooks were common in noble, royal and even merchant houses but often were made of more expensive materials if the owner was wealthy. Ours was made of wood and horn, as all used to be, although many belonging to wealthier children were silver or pewter, and ours allowed the vellum to be taken out so another lesson could be inserted. In this way we could each learn many lessons, committing them to memory.

With a tutor and resources to hand, we were more fortunate than most children of England, so perhaps my education should have seemed easy. It is hard, however, to concentrate when the other pupil in the schoolroom draws his finger across his throat when the teacher's back is turned, flicks spit at your ear, pokes you in the side or whispers you are a failure in all you do. It can be taxing to pay attention when your brother is pinching you, twisting skin under the arms or on your back. Attempting not to cry out kept my mind from paying attention too. I spent more time worrying about what Thomas would do to me that day than ever I spent learning anything.

Our tutor never saw what Thomas did and I never told. Telling, apparently, was a worse sin than any of his crimes. In silence was my brother's power as my tormentor made most powerful, and it was a power maintained by me. Fool that I was, I thought silence might make him my ally, might keep me safe. Nothing was safe from Thomas when he had a mind to tug wings until they snapped off in his hands. When my brother looked at me, he saw a fly or a mouse, something to toy with. Sometimes I thought he had been born to the wrong body. Surely he was a cat. His malice had an almost innocent quality, for although he enjoyed it he seemed unable to understand why others would not. I should *want* him to torment me, for it would make him happy, that was how Thomas's diseased little mind worked. The world was made for him. Anything he wanted should be his, any pleasure was his right.

I wished I had a sister to be my companion, but I was still the only girl of the family at that time. At times I thought of the Princess Mary, daughter of the King, named for the King's sister, wishing she and I could be friends, although she had only been born in 1516. It had been a cold and bitter night in February when we were brought the news that the King had a daughter, and even more miraculous, that she was living. Church bells had rung all the next day up and down the country, the sound of the bells crisp upon the snow that fell upon England. Many people, however, looked a touch hesitant about celebrating.

"Let us pray the Princess will live and sons will follow," my mother said when we were to go to our prayers one night not long after the Princess was born, and suddenly I understood, reading the pale worry on her face as if it were a lesson in my hornbook. She did not think this princess, like other children our Queen had borne, would live. A little prince born in 1511 had lived for but two months and had been followed later by brothers. Three years before the Princess entered the world the Queen had borne a stillborn son and the year following another who was dead. England had been offered many princes, yet all had been called from the world. Father had served at the funeral of the first prince as a pallbearer, a high mark of honour considering his rank. Perhaps in a time of such raw sorrow, the King only wanted honest and plain men about him.

Princess Mary, however, was still alive as I sat in that schoolroom making my tutor sad, and she was the joy of her mother's life. She was also the hope of the country. "It shows the Queen is not barren," said my father. "And sons will come soon."

Daughters, it appeared, were good enough for no one, not even when the daughter was a princess. Certainly I was not good enough for my parents in the schoolroom, or any room. That March, another Princess Mary, the elder who once had been Queen of France but had returned and was now Duchess of Suffolk, had borne a boy. She named him Henry.

The marriage of the Princess Mary and King Louis of France had been exceedingly short. On New Year's Day of 1515 the King had died and after the period of mourning, and watching to see if she was with child, which she was not, Mary had come home along with her attendants. *"The only soul of England who remained was Mistress Anne Boleyn, and that was because the new Queen Claude asked for her to enter her household,"* my brother, Edward, wrote to us.

Most of Mary's attendants had to be sent away from her household quickly when she returned to England, and for good reason, since she could not afford them. It had all been a bit of a scandal. The Princess, finding herself a widow, feared that her brother would make her marry a stranger again. And she saw a way out.

Long had the Princess harboured love for Charles Brandon, Duke of Suffolk, whom she had known as a child. When he came to France to escort her home, she talked him quickly into marrying her. Brandon did.

Despite being a Duke and boon companion to the King, Brandon was a lowly match for a woman of Mary's blood. Brandon's father had been the standard bearer of Henry VII at Bosworth, and he and Brandon's grandfather had fought in the Civil War between Lancaster and York which had ripped our country asunder before I was born. At Bosworth was the last fight between those ancient houses decided, as Henry VII, young and inexperienced in warfare had come with his army of French, Welsh and mercenaries to face Richard III. Henry VII had been, some said, outnumbered two to one that fateful day, for Richard, a tried and tested warrior and general had more than eight thousand men. Yet God smiled on the Tudors, and Henry VII won, his foe falling in battle, and the crown, it was said, tumbling from Richard's head into a hawthorn bush.

The red dragon of Tudor and the white boar of England met, fought, and the dragon won.

Upon the death of the standard bearer, the son, Charles, had been taken on as a ward by the old King, Henry VII. Raised near court by his grandfather, then placed in the household of Prince Henry at the age of about thirteen, Charles Brandon and Henry Tudor became friends, and Brandon also spent time with Henry's sisters, Margaret and Mary. Mary, five years younger than her brother Henry and always the beauty of the family, grew up at Eltham Palace with Henry and Margaret. Their elder brother Arthur had his own household by then. Promised in marriage many times was pretty Mary, from the age of two, yet no matter what princes and kings she was offered to by her parents, one man had stolen her heart in childhood, and would keep it all her life; Charles Brandon. And with the death of Louis of France, Mary got her way.

"They say she danced the poor man into an early grave," my mother whispered, speaking of the King of France.

In the kitchens, rumour was the Princess had been too exciting for the old King in the bedchamber, and that had hastened his end. I heard men japing about the "little death" but I knew not what they meant. Surely death was always a large event?

When the King found out about the marriage between his sister and best friend he was enraged. It had been done and consummated without his permission, which could be seen as a direct challenge to his authority as King and as a brother. The King was head of the country and his family, therefore in both respects his sister Mary was his property. It was up to the King who she married. Brandon was saved from the rage of the King and a swift, short trip to the block by Cardinal Wolsey, the King's chief advisor, who arranged a public apology and set vast sums the Duke was to pay to the King to compensate for the dowry the King had paid out to France in order to make his sister Queen. Years of paying fines would leave the premier couple of England without much coin, but mere months lessened the anger of the King. He had a romantic side, so I was told, and would sometimes talk of how important it was for love to live in the world. Seeing that he had been well compensated for allowing love to flourish, the King could say he forgave the Brandons because they loved each other. It made a romantic tale of it. I wondered if the King would have been so forgiving without being so very well paid. But for all this, love had prevailed and now the Dowager of France had a child, a boy.

"She has an eye on the succession," whispered my mother, who went on to explain that if the Queen did not bear a son, the son of the Duchess of Suffolk might succeed to the throne. Although this Henry's father was noble only by title rather than blood, his mother was of the Tudor line. It might be enough to recommend him for the throne, if the King and Queen had no male heir. The Queen had, that very year, made a pilgrimage to Walsingham to ask God for a son. It seemed she too was concerned about her ability to provide a male heir for England. Listening to my mother talk about the designs the Duchess of Suffolk might have on the throne, which clearly belonged to the offspring of saintly Queen Katherine, I wondered how my mother thought the Duchess had affected the sex of her child. I knew there were things a woman might do, such as lying on one side in bed, to make the conception of a son more likely, but for the most part I had thought the choice was up to God. "This boy born to Charles Brandon and Mary may not carry the Tudor name, but he has enough Tudor blood to become King, one day," Mother went on. "It is not right."

"What of Princess Mary who is daughter of the King, my lady mother?" I had asked.

"Girls and women do not rule countries," I was told.

Perhaps it was because our brains were too soft. Our tutor certainly thought mine were.

Our father kept a chaplain, Master Thomas Thatcher, who taught my brother and me, but our tutor's main preoccupation was Thomas. Boys were offered more education than girls; their minds were stronger, more capable. The female mind was weak, insipid, incapable of holding on to wisdom and likely to do ill with what it could manage to retain. I was supposed to learn my paternoster in Latin by heart, sign my name and read well enough to have an understanding of missives and household accounts, but my education was rudimentary. My mother taught me French, but only enough that I could get by in a simple conversation. I never excelled at it and she ran out of patience swiftly when teaching me. My lack of ability in that sophisticated language was a terrible failure in my mother's eyes, for she said I would never become a lady of the court; a damnation most grievous from one who had, apparently, been one of its brightest ornaments. French was considered the height of refinement at court.

But my mother was less cankerous when it came to my embroidery and needlework. I was good with my needle and it was a suitable occupation for a woman. No person should be idle, for that was when the Devil would use your distraction to work his wicked wiles. Women were especially vulnerable because of our feeble souls and fragile minds, so should be always occupied. Some read as well as sewed, but many men did not think women should read at all for they might be carried away by the ideas in books and not be capable of judging if those ideas were ill or good. A creature so easily corruptible should be kept away from corrupting influences. Sewing was safer, and it was practical. It was less selfish too, as a woman usually was making garments for others, her husband, children or father. Reading, unless done aloud to others, was insular, selfish. Women were to offer themselves up, to think of others first and always, to be charitable and self-sacrificing. Sewing and embroidery upheld those virtues, reading did not.

From an early age I was taught to sew, to mend shirts and make clothes so I could one day make them for my husband

and children. I was taught to embroider, so the clothes I made would be exquisite and my husband could take pride in wearing them. I was taught to make altar cloths, so the Church would be granted gifts from my husband's house and would honour him. I was also taught how to wash clothes, not so I could actually perform that menial task, but so I could oversee servants when they did. I was taught to remove stains using piss, to use bread to clean heavy, thickly embroidered tunics that my husband might wear to court or to special occasions. With bread, stains could be teased from bright cloth and rich, heavy thread without damaging the precious, costly fabric. My mother took me to her still room, where she made medicines for the family. We could afford a doctor when we had need, "And you should always take the advice of cunning women, or men, if they are good of character and use magic only for good," my mother told me. But a good wife could make medicines, soaps and potions herself, so could tend to her family and not waste her husband's money, spending coin on remedies from doctors that could have been created by her own hands. Mixing remedies and medicines was another worthy pursuit women might undertake, for it was done for others, for the most part. At times I thought a wife was a servant, just like any in our house. There seemed small difference, except that a man's wife was not paid for her work.

Sewing, aside from riding my horse, was my greatest pleasure. I was not dull of wits when it came to plants and herbs but my mother made me nervous, always watching, waiting, sometimes breathlessly, it felt, for me to make a mistake. And when I did, *thwack*! She plunged on me like a triumphant hawk. She did not strike me always, but always there was a blow, by words if not by hand. Feeling the anticipation of making a mistake made me make them. Under the scrutiny of her eyes I became clumsier, stupider. It was as if I failed because she expected it of me. Perhaps I made her happy, in that way. It can make people feel merry to be right.

I was good at herbs, but never seemed to shine in front of my mother, but sewing was easy for me, and I made beautiful things even as a child. I was careful and took my time; patience and perseverance are good qualities for crafting something fine. It was a quiet pastime, and in this realm of hush and thread and cloth Mother did not seem to think I would make a mistake, so I did not. It was a refuge, in truth; concentrating on sewing allowed me to drown out my mother's relentless chatter. My father was happy enough with my achievements. He did not hold that women should be too educated.

"It spoils them," he said to my mother when she spoke with caustic bitterness of my lessons. "Women should not be too educated. What man wants a wife who lectures him on the Bible, or law? The role of women is to bear children, to make the home a pleasant, restful place, keep kitchens and accounts in order when needs be, and maintain peace in the family. Too much learning can make women wish to spend all their time in a book, and none with the family!"

An expression of weariness crossed my mother's brow, followed swift by irritation. I knew, even then, what my father said was false. Women were, in fact, expected to know and do a vast deal in the household and for it. Accounts, figures, the education of children, overseeing servants and the running of the house, brewing potions, medicines, making soap, clothes and hangings for chambers… and that was just the basic skills that were expected. Higher women also studied the Bible and royal ones ruled as regents, as well as doing all that lower women did, or overseeing such things at least. The truth was women were supposed to do much, but not talk about it. We were to know much, and admit nothing. Certainly we were not to speak of our work, education or minds with *pride*, for pride was a sin. Men liked to think women knew not much, did not much, and this pretence was maintained because women did not speak of their achievements. This was useful for the world, as it explained why men had all the power; they were better suited to it, minds capable of bearing the heavy burden, and they did all that was important, whilst women relied upon them. But women knew, and did, as much as men. Our work was hidden, our skills just as varied, if not more, but men were allowed to speak of what they did. Women were not.

Aside from Mother, of course. Superior breeding made her more outspoken than most women might dare to be. It was something I was to learn later. If a woman happened to outrank a man, before marriage at least, she was offered more in the way of freedom to talk of her worthiness within marriage. Sex determined position, but position determined the ranking of the sexes, too.

"*I* was educated well, John," my mother reproved, ruffling her shoulders like an old hen in the yard. "Yet I am a good wife, am I not?" She pursed her lips, offended. At such times she looked like me. Seeing that thin-lipped expression, my father paused. He was no fool; he knew when his wife required a compliment, even if peace between them came at the cost of insulting his daughter.

My father put his hand on my mother's shoulder. "Jane is not the same as you, my love," he said carefully. "She is no beauty, no lady of court as you were. There are limitations upon her which would never have applied to you. Jane is destined for a quieter life. She never will rise high, but that is as well. Not all can have a distinguished destiny."

"That is true, perhaps," Mother said, mollified.

"Think of what husband our daughter will have, my love, and give Jane the skills she will need to please *him*," Father went on. "To manage a house, know what to order for dinner, how to check supplies. Her husband can read letters to her, and as for French, what need will she have of it? She will bear many children; that will be her main prize for her husband. And we may have other daughters in time more suited to a life at court and a grand husband. You can give those daughters all the education they will need to please in noble households or court if we send them to serve. Do not seek to make Jane something she is not. We all have our place in the world, ordained by God, and if He has seen fit to make our first daughter nothing other than a good wife, we must be satisfied, as He is."

My mother agreed. They set me to learning simple numbers and accounts, so I could run a household, but my book-learning and languages were reduced. When I did try to read, even in English, it was always a frustration, for I was not taught enough for it to become fluid. Books were no pleasure to me. They became a place I was dragged to, where I would suffer shame, be shown up as a creature of small understanding, thought stupid for lack of education. I looked at books and saw humiliation waiting, taunting me. The only book I loved was the Bible, and that was because God was in those pages, so I was told. Noble and royal women and men, even children in some households, were learning to read the Bible and study it themselves, without need for priests to interpret the meaning God intended. Mother did not hold with such an idea and neither did Father.

"It is all part of the New Learning," said Mother. "Just another word for heresy."

Heresy was a terrible thing. People who did not believe in God or questioned the ways of His Church were heretics. They were evil, sent by the Devil, so Mother and priests said. When I heard that Katherine of Spain was in favour of studying the Bible, however, it made me wonder, for Mother was so much Katherine's advocate that it seemed the Queen could do no wrong. But Katherine *was* Queen, and a woman of far superior education to me. There were things she understood that I never would, and much she indeed needed to understand since she aided the King, had acted as his regent and would oversee the education of their children. It was fitting that such a person knew much. I did not need to know a great deal because I was destined for lowness. So, just as I set aside matters I did not understand from lessons of the priests, believing it was not my place to question, I set aside the notion that Katherine the Queen could do anything wrong.

I learned my prayers and paternoster by heart. I learned the words for capon, beef, and other meats, grains, drink or fish that might be bought by a household. I was taught to add and subtract short rows of simple numbers, was shown what weights and measurements of foods were so I might know if a servant was stealing or if I were being cheated by a merchant. I learned little else, and for ever after in my life I struggled with reading; a task others seemed to find such ease in doing, and pleasure in. Books simply had no place in my life, and none of my family thought I would have a destiny beyond being a wife to a country knight, so would have small use for them. My sons would be taught by a tutor, my daughters by me, and I had just enough education for a woman. I needed no more.

But it upset me. Without a position with Mary of Suffolk, since she had to watch her spending with so much money heading into her brother's pocket, and without a new position at court available, Edward had been put into education again. My brother had come home and had been placed with kin so he might attend Oxford University. That house of learning would teach him much. He might not take a degree, but it was traditional for a young man of a noble family to have some education in a high establishment. Edward spent time in London with our kinsmen the Bryans. At their table he learnt to carve meat and fish, and in their parks and grounds was learning to hunt. When at Oxford he was learning much, building on his youthful Latin, his hunting and sportsmanship skills, studying arithmetic, astronomy and rhetoric, and he would learn more French, for he had hardly had a long time to learn when posted in France.

Edward was also attending court. He had ridden in the lists, against other young men, and it was said the King had been impressed. The Duke of Suffolk, too, thought my brother had promise. Edward wrote often, telling us at Wulfhall of his accomplishments. When I heard I was to be taught less, I felt ashamed. Edward could do so much, I so little.

"He is young, another position will come, perhaps in the household of the Prince of Wales, in time," said my father. As he spoke of the Prince of Wales, of the heir we did not yet have, a shadow passed over his face.

"There will be one soon," Mother said stoutly. "The Queen is the most blessed of women. God will send her a son when the time is right."

Chapter Five

Wulfhall
Wiltshire

Early Summer 1517

"What do you want with book learning, in any case, Mistress Jane?" Kat asked when I came to the kitchens wearing a downcast face, and told them of my new lessons. "There's an awful lot of knowledge which lives outside the pages of books."

I nodded but I did not agree. I could not and would not explain it, but misery had fallen upon me. It seemed my fate had been decided, and I had nothing to do with it. My life would be simple, low, tedious. Girls only a little older than me, like my cousins Mary and Anne Boleyn, were serving royalty. They were learning languages and dancing in fair and gracious courts about the world. I was only learning to read a little English and add small columns of numbers. They would be married to high and noble men. I would have a husband worthy of my own meagre talents and beauty.

You are not only ugly, but dull of wits, said a voice inside my mind. It sounded like my mother. *You will end a spinster, and not even that for you cannot work for money!* To be unmarried was, I believed, the worst curse a woman could endure. Spinsters at least earned their own money. I could do no such thing. The fate that was open to me was to wed, but I had little to recommend me. My husband would be old and uglier than me, if such a thing were possible. It was as though I could see my future laid out before me, unchangeable and hideous, and I was helpless to alter it.

"I don't hold with books in any case," muttered Mother Cooper in a dark tone. "How does a soul know if the person who wrote those words down is of a good soul or bad? There's many who came to trouble, through *reading*. Words can corrupt a soul, if the author is possessed of a bad spirit."

"The Bible is a book, though, Mother Cooper," protested Marge, who, as the younger daughter of a town merchant had been taught in a nunnery when she was small, so knew how to read simple things. "You can't fault *that* book, surely?"

"The Bible is another matter, Marge, as well you know, for God told men what to write in that book. And in that case we have priests and bishops to read it for us, to tell us the lessons it contains in their sermons. *Thems* the ones who have to read; men of God, not the likes of us. They can tell us what we need to know, speak the words Jesus wrote down for us, to lead us and bless our lives. That is the way of things. It was *other* books I spoke of. Books can be dangerous, especially when none knows for sure who wrote them."

Mother Cooper nodded her large head, her magnificent bosom wobbling like one of her quince jellies. "Don't you sorrow for losing naught, Mistress Jane," she continued. "For naught have you lost. Priests will tell you what you need to know, and your husband can tell you what they don't. Anything else, you can remember, if you have a need to." She tapped a floury finger against the side of her head. "I remember every recipe I was ever taught," she said. "And none have ever left me, for I used them all over and over. That's the way the Lord intended us to keep what we needed in our head, and He is the one who guides your parents now. Trust in the Lord. He'll do you right. He has a plan for all of us, no matter how small or how poor."

"I do trust in Him," I said softly.

I did, of course. I knew that even if my parents were largely indifferent to me, Edward absent and Thomas spiteful, the Lord God loved me. I was told this every time we went to church, which usually was three times each week, and in return I assured God that I knew He loved me when I prayed each morning, before each meal, and every night. It was God who made everything, and whilst that made me harbour some confusion about why He had made Thomas and cast my brother of so cruel a mould, I also knew God made the forest. He had made my pony, the horses of my father's stables. God had crafted bluebells, trees and exquisite, watery-eyed does who wandered through our parks in the blue-grey dusk, their coats shimmering in shades of gold and fawn and russet. The Almighty had created glittering frost which made autumn mornings stunning enough to steal my breath, and brought balmy winds flowing over us in summer, which lifted loose hair from my neck and made my soul sigh with pleasure. The Lord of Heaven made flowers bloom and smell so sweet. He made crops rich and waters fresh. God had created all I loved in this world, and I loved God. Not because I was told to by priests, but because He had made so many good and wondrous things. Anyone who crafted such beauty deserved all the love I could offer. It was the least I could do.

I wept for God at times. I thought God must be lonely, and He had done such good for us. When I thought of God sacrificing His only son to cleanse the sin of mankind it made me sad. Our chaplain told me I should not weep, for Jesus had gone willingly to his fate and now rested in the arms of his father. I should follow the example of the Lord of light and surrender my own desires and wishes in favour of those of others. At times I thought it odd that I was expected to do so, when Thomas and Henry's wants were often pandered to. We all were Christians, were we not? Should we not all follow the example of Jesus?

I tried to do as our chaplain said, follow Christ, emulate him and honour his sacrifice, but I found it hard for much did I pity that poor man as he hung upon the cross. I pitied too that his Father would have had to witness that suffering. Although I had not followed his teachings, the chaplain praised my piety when I told him this, and suggested a career in the Church as a bride of Christ. I think my mother considered sending me to become a nun many times during the years I was a child. It was where one put daughters who were not beautiful, had few prospects, or when a family had too many to find dowries for, but for some reason Mother did not pursue it. I always wondered why; it would have been a goodly way for her to rid herself of me. Perhaps it was simply that for a long time I was her only daughter.

And so, I continued with my education, moulded and made to be a wife and not a lady of court. There were times I resented it. Resented being thought of as having so few prospects by my own family, but what could I do? Daughters were supposed to obey and serve. My mother and father had chosen my destiny, I would accept it. That was the way of things. But I felt sad when Mother told me of court, of the dancing and feasting, of the games of love, things I never would see.

"The games of courtly love keep the court of the King gracious and refined," Mother told me. When in a good mood she would tell me tales. That day we had heard Father had been granted the keepership of Bristol Castle, an honour bestowed by the King himself. Edward had been named constable of the castle along with Father, and although it was an honorary appointment in truth, as their main duty was to ensure the castle was serviceable, it was a good appointment for my brother. All this had pleased my mother enough to be generous with her stories that day.

Courtly love was, I was told, an ideal. The games revolved about women who were high of station and beauty. They were the objects of poetry and music, the muses young gallants sighed over and sang to. Young knights rode for them in tournaments, wearing their ribbons on their armour to show where their hearts lay. Young men were allowed to perform for the women of court. Their poems, songs and feats of arms celebrated the talents of the young men and placed ladies at the centre of this intellectual adoration. And it was *intellectual* adoration.

"The women never give in to the pleas of poets or the fearsome strength of warriors," Mother said. "Noble women smile, receive attentions publicly with pleasure, but always express disbelief in the honesty of the protestations of their admirers, causing the game to continue to higher levels and greater feats."

That was the point, apparently; a continual round of romantic, intellectual sparring. The poetry and songs were superb, but the game was power. If women surrendered to advances or protestations of devotion, the men would tire of them quickly. And our Queen, good Katherine, would not suffer her women to debase themselves in such a way. If a woman was found dallying physically with a man, the pair would find themselves married, not always to each other, and usually banished from court. Quickly I came to understand the *value* of virtue. Virginity was a woman's greatest asset, greater perhaps than beauty.

As long as women withheld their bodies from men who worshipped them, they kept the power; if knights succeeded in seducing women, they won. Courtly love maintained the romantic atmosphere of the palace and gave young men a way to advance through intellect and skill or warlike talent and sportsmanship. Young men could rise high with generous patronesses. High-born men who were already established as lords and knights, or even princes of neighbouring lands, paid court to women who were not their wives in order to demonstrate their sophistication. The object of the game was actually rarely true seduction. It happened of course, but most who played understood the real goal was to advance within court by display of natural talents, or by being the object of desire. The women were to be eminently desirable and utterly unobtainable, the men to be sighing, dying lovers of a love they could not obtain. They might wither in joyful sorrow for their ladies, as the women might reign in cruel kindness. That was the game. It worked as well for women as for men, as long as the women remained unobtainable. Young ladies, singled out as objects of devotion, became more desirable as matches in marriage, and men could become renowned for their talents and prowess. For those looking to wed it was therefore a showcase for their talents.

And it was one I was never to know. I was not destined for court.

Thomas was a different matter. My parents wanted him to move in court circles, as Edward was to. Henry, like me, learnt enough so that if there was a place my parents could afford, he might go, but I think they believed him not talented enough as they did not put a great deal of effort into his education. My parents were not the richest of nobles, so they had to invest in the children they thought most promising. And we were investments; those who rose high might one day help those who were lower, so it was in all our interests for the best of us to be endowed with more benefits. Henry was too straightforward for court, and my parents knew his plainness of character and speech would not go far in society. It had not for my father. But in Thomas was a slippery intelligence. His mind was made for court.

Thomas learnt French, Latin, reading, arithmetic, and studied rhetoric and map reading. He was not an apt or a willing student. More often than not Thomas was to be found staring from a window rather than putting his nose into a book. He dreamed of the life he would have, but was not willing to do work that might earn him such a life.

Thomas was much better when it came to learning to fence and ride, to hunt and do archery. He was talented at running at the rings and everyone said he would make a champion jouster one day. Jousting was not his only ambition, however. Even at the age of nine he was planning what he would do when he was grown. He wanted to be away from Wulfhall, he told me, away and with the King, being a soldier, invading France.

"The French hold lands that are ours," he boldly announced to me one day when he had decided to take a break from tormenting me. "It is our duty, as Englishmen, as knights, to win stolen lands back from them."

His tutor must have mentioned this, I thought. Often Thomas would hear another say something and repeat it to me as though it were his own thought. Stealing came naturally to him. It was much easier than working for something, remembering it. Deserving it.

"I will go to the King on bended knee and assure him that I will take back the lands that are his by right," Thomas went on, setting his hands on his hips, standing as though he meant to crow. *You are more ass than cockerel,* whispered something sinful in my mind.

"And when I have won them for him, the King will reward me with lands of my own in France. Then I will never have to come back here again!"

I nodded, making an admiring face, even though I thought him ridiculous. I doubted our King would think much of such a small, ineffably annoying boy. Our father was a huge man, much bigger than Thomas, and he had fought in wars in France. If the King had not rewarded our father overmuch, I doubted he would reward a weedy, foolish little lad like my brother. *Still,* said that fiendish voice, *when men march to war they walk with Death…*

Such a wicked thought I tried to cast away, knowing it was the Devil whispering in my ear.

Thomas strode off to boast to women in the kitchens, and I stared from the window. I was in our great hall that day, as it was raining outside. A fire burned in the large hearth, my father's emblem of the peacock above it, its wings erect, neck azure. It was a symbol of pride. As flames danced, light licked the peacock and for a moment it looked like another bird, one not of pride and pleasure, but of resurrection and self-sacrifice. For a moment a phoenix stood above me, then it was gone, gold fire replaced by boastful blue. Ashes slipped in the fire, the flames burning not as bright as before. More fuel was required. I shivered as a damp wind rushed through the hall and down the chimney. Scented smoke wafted into my face, up my nose, the smell rich and welcome.

Not far away was the source of the pleasant scent; one of many fuming pots kept in our house. They were small pots with an upper and lower shelf. The lower held hot coals or glowing twigs and the upper incense, dried herbs or scented wood. Charcoal, wood or glowing coals burned, leading whatever was on the upper shelf to smoulder, releasing scent. Fuming pots kept the house cloaked in perfume. They were kept on surfaces not likely to catch fire, for over time they grew hot. Hot was something I wished I felt that day. I shivered, moving closer to the flames. The spring and early summer had been wet. They had also been dangerous.

Though it happened far from us, there had been much unrest in London. Preachers had gone into the streets, stirring people up against an influx of foreigners they said were coming into England. "That Doctor Bell does no good," Father had said in March, upon his return from a trip to court. "He tells people to defend Englishmen and their rights, and all he says is nonsense, but it is firing people up."

"Foreigners take jobs and houses, income and food from Englishmen and women, though, lord husband," my mother said.

"More often they *bring* employment and wealth," he said. "There will be trouble because of this, mark my words."

There was. A poor harvest had made food expensive and people miserable and disgruntled. They blamed men who had come to their country from other lands. Men of Italy and Spain were thieves and had been taking grain, it was said. Foreign merchants charged high amounts for food and drove all prices up. Men of France and other lands brought sickness into England. As food prices went up and the weather was poor, I seemed to almost hear dangerous discontent muttering all the way from London. There were reports soon after of Englishmen setting upon foreigners, French, Spanish, Italians and Jews, in the streets, breaking their houses and looting their shops. The mayor tried to impose a curfew, and that sparked a riot. We heard a week after it happened. Two thousand men had risen up, gathering in Cheapside and had marched into the city to St Paul's, where many men of other countries lived in the St Martin le Grand area. Houses were attacked, doors broken, possessions destroyed, and homes looted. Merchants and their families were assaulted. Many Englishmen were arrested and the King had to send in his own guards to quell the rioting in the streets.

"Thirteen troublemakers were condemned to die," my father said, reading a report aloud to us. "But the Queen along with her sister Queens, Mary of France and Margaret of Scotland…" Margaret Tudor had arrived in England some time before, fleeing her cruel second husband who she had married when Queen Katherine's troops had killed her first husband, King James of Scots, at Flodden Field. "… went down on their knees before the King and begged him for mercy. All but one of the rioters were released because of the intervention of the Queens, and the King thanked them for reminding him that God's work was mercy and justice combined."

"Never had England a finer Queen!" crowed my mother.

"I hope England's people understand and remember that men of this country were saved by a woman of another," said my father.

"What mean you?"

"Katherine is of Spain, my love, or had you forgotten?"

"Queen Katherine is now as much an Englishwoman as I!" she said. "And she hails from the house of Lancaster, from John of Gaunt, does she not?"

"That is true," said my father, knowing when to surrender.

Although a few troublemakers had been pardoned in public, more were arrested afterwards. I was told not long after that so many had been arrested that the gaols of London overflowed as rivers in flood. Fortunately for the rioters, the King was merciful, and, presiding over a mass sentencing, pardoned them all. The Queen and her sister Mary, both swelling with child, had been overjoyed. It was said that with the Queen pregnant, the King could deny her nothing. That summer the Duchess had given birth to a daughter, named Frances. She stayed at her house in the country as the plague known as the sweat was upon London. The Queen was not to be so lucky in her child. Before summer was gone she would lose her babe.

But that was of the future, I try to leap ahead from the day in the great hall, rain lashing the timber roof, my brother prancing about, performing for titbits of adoration and praise.

My mother's maids were sitting by the glowing fire on large floor cushions, giggling about the handsome, proud boy that Thomas was. They favoured him, as did my mother. In their eyes he could do no wrong. I always was puzzled when they mentioned his looks, for I could see little in Thomas that was attractive. Dark-haired like our father, but with deep blue eyes like my mother's, I suppose Thomas was handsome but he never seemed so to me. All I saw was the cruelty in his spirit, the callous arrogance in his soul. No manner of fresh skin, high cheekbones, or pleasing arrangement of features could mask the nasty little beast within.

I smiled, thinking of Edward. To my eyes he was the handsomest man of the world. My eldest brother was sandy-haired and pale of eye and skin, much like me, yet he wore his looks with more ease. His mouth was quiet and free of boasts, but full of wit and intelligence. His temper was clement but there was fire in him. Like me he kept it carefully contained, but Edward was allowed to release it from time to time as I was not. He was not a flighty cock like Thomas. I saw Edward as some kind of pale raven; something that might seem everyday, and yet was one of a kind. Perhaps I thought more of him because I saw his soul with ease. We looked so alike, it seemed at times that we had been crafted of the same materials, perhaps even the same stretch of soul.

*

Later that year Edward came home for a few days. My brother was seventeen and was to be married.

When I heard his horse I ran down the stairs from the attic rooms where I had been sewing, and flew to his side. Edward, fresh off his horse, the scent of the road and his mount upon him, grasped me, laughing, and swept me up into his arms. I giggled, putting my hand over my mouth to cover the noise. Mother said ladies of good breeding were not to titter like apes in public, so I tried to hide laughter on the rare occasions it escaped me.

Edward pulled my hands from my lips with teasing fingers and a kind smile. I turned my head from side to side to stop him seeing my smile, but he followed my movements and eventually won, claiming my eyes. I turned a beaming smile on him, feeling my heart surge as I looked into his glorious pale eyes. He laughed merrily.

"That is what I came home to see!" he announced and planted a kiss on my lips. "The beautiful smile of my sweet sister. A man will ride far to witness such a sight, Jane."

I giggled. "I thought you came home to be married," I murmured. "Father and Mother have been preparing the barn.

They will be most disappointed you only came to see me smile."

Edward chortled and put his hand encased in its riding glove against my cheek. I smelt orange and bergamot, and just the slightest hint of shit. It was used liberally in the process of softening leather and leather always retained a hint of the smell. "Where do you find that humour of yours?" he asked, pinching my cheek with gentle affection. He looked about and whispered in my ear, "Not from our mother, I'll wager."

I laughed aloud. I could not help it. He looked so mischievous and so merry, and it was nice to hear someone criticise our mother for a change.

"Come, sister," he said, taking my arm and leading me to the door. "When I have washed and changed my smock, I wish to know all that has happened since I was away. Omit nothing, for I am a curious fellow!"

"I sent water to your rooms already and there are fresh clothes Mother sent up," I told him. We had known he would want to change his underclothes. The linen smock all people, low or high, wore next to their skin was the first layer to encounter sweat as it flowed from the body, and therefore it soiled fast. If men engaged in sports or hunting, they changed it several times in the day, as long as they were rich enough, of course. Heavier outer clothes, bulky with gorgeous cloth, thread or jewels sewn into the material, were harder to wash and did not collect ill scents of the body so easily, but underclothes did and were changed and washed frequently. Mother had laid out a good linen smock for Edward already, and I had spoken to Kat in the kitchens, ensuring that water was on the fire in his rooms, ready for him to wash, and that there were rose petals, dried last summer, to scent the water. I wanted Edward to have the best.

"I am a well looked after man," he said, beaming. "When I am changed, I will meet you in the long gallery and you will tell me all."

"There is not much to tell, brother," I said. "Not a great deal happens here."

"But *you* are here, Jane," he said. "And therefore *here* is the most interesting place in the world."

I led Edward inside, feeling awfully grown up on the arm of this handsome brother of mine. My heart glowed brighter with his every word, my head lifted higher. In my eyes, he was the sweetest soul who ever lived.

Chapter Six

Wulfhall
Wiltshire

Summer 1517

Edward was marrying a lady called Catherine Fillol, daughter and co-heir of Sir William Fillol, a knight who held lands in Dorset and Essex. They had been promised to each other for a year or so, and had gone through a kind of ceremony already, but had been thought too young to live together. It was dangerous for young men to bed wives too early. Young men of fourteen or fifteen could exhaust themselves by entering the marriage bed as husbands. The same was not thought dangerous for women. Women were intended to breed; their curse from God as well as their blessing. Girls as young as twelve could share a bed with their husbands. The old King, Henry VII's mother, Margaret Beaufort, had been just thirteen when she gave birth to the old King. She never had a second child.

"It is foolish," my mother had told me, under her breath as it was not sensible for a woman to be heard condemning common law. "Bearing children too young is perilous for the girl and her babe."

"Sometimes women of a young age are not wide enough in the hips," she went on to explain, although I had not asked a question. "The babe gets stuck, both mother and child die. Sometimes, even if the child comes out successfully, it can damage the mother so she never bears another child. One heir is not advantageous for a house. Better to wait, better for the mother, her child and the line of her husband."

Men, it seemed, were not keen on waiting, but in Edward and Catherine's case my mother had had her way. She had insisted to my father that we were not to exhaust Edward, her precious eldest boy and a man so promising, and we were not to put Catherine, his bride, at risk either. Mother wanted plenty of grandchildren to grace the Seymour line. Catherine and Edward had been promised, vows exchanged, but consummation had been delayed and Catherine had remained in her father's house until the year she came to Wulfhall. There was to be another wedding ceremony, in public with many witnesses, and after the couple were to share a bed. With Edward busy with his studies, and hoping to win a permanent place at court, my brother and his wife would be separate a great deal but together enough, Mother hoped, for Catherine to have children.

"He can visit, get her with child, then go back to his studies," she said.

I smiled and nodded, yet it sounded to me as though Catherine was not so much a wife, but more a prize cow for breeding. What would her life be? A series of pregnancies, babe after babe in her belly as she sat at home sewing with us, whilst Edward went off to enter a glittering career at court, or learned wondrous things at university? If I had had the nerve, I would have said the life of a woman sounded awfully dull. Mother, at least, had experienced a little excitement, had lived at court a while as a maid before retiring into marriage and the country. Catherine would have nothing so interesting to experience or memories to comfort herself with in the long, monotonous nights at the fireside in the great hall. Not for her would there be endless tales, all variations on the same tales, of court that she could tell her maids and attendants. *Neither will you,* said the voice in my head. *Court and courtly love are for women of beauty, not ugliness!*

I winced. My inner voice of condemnation had a fearsome whip, it lashed a stinging wound in my soul.

Courtly love was something I knew to be beyond my reach for I was neither rich nor beautiful, but even though my exclusion from such wonders made me sad, I loved to hear stories of poetry and love, of the King and his men dressing up as beggars to fool the Queen and her ladies. The King's gallants would come to Katherine's door, my mother said, faces covered with masks and bodies draped in rags, and they would spin woeful yarns that they were wandering poor men who wished to dance before her for her pleasure. Once inside, they would cast off those rags and reveal the King and his knights! Mother laughed with hearty affection when she told that story, and although I had heard it many times before it never failed to make my heart glow with warmth.

It sounded such innocent, foolish amusement, dressing up, playing the fool. I marvelled at the tales and thought Queen Katherine fortunate. She had a husband who loved her so dear that he would seek to surprise and amuse her in so many ways. He jousted for her, it was said, and he danced for her. He sent men to ask after her health each day if he was too busy to go to her himself. That, I told myself, was love. That true care and attention to the needs of the other. So few had that. My parents certainly did not. Theirs was an arrangement of mutual contentment, but I did not think it love.

But my brother and his wife will know love, I thought as I came down the stairs to the hall a few days before the wedding. I smoothed my russet gown, not my best, for there was work to be done that day. The house was in a roar of preparation, cooking, cleaning and making ready accommodation for guests. There was a sea of tents being erected in the pastures, our cattle and sheep herded to other fields. All attics of the barns were prepared, hay moulded into beds for servants. Standing in the great hall I watched maids run hither and thither with baskets of eggs and vegetables, some with cloths and polish of beeswax in hand, and I watched my mother, strong and proud and bold, a force of nature in her truest element, ordering everyone about. At times, were I not so afraid of her, I might have admired her. She was so unlike me, so as I would like to be.

It was not many weeks after the May Day celebrations. We had watched in the great hall as the Lady May had stood in the centre of a group of dancers all dressed in green, with garlands of flowers about their necks, reciting poetry welcoming in the summer as they pranced about her. Hawthorn, its flowers known as *the May*, had been scattered all around, flying through the air as soft, warm snow, handfuls gathered up by our maids to strew in their rooms, under beds, in their clothes to bring them good fortune and fine husbands. At court, as June came tramping in bold and scorching, Father told us there had been jousts most fearsome. Lady May, presumably a different one unless the same woman had roamed all the way to London, had presided, calling on her fair knights to defend the rights of chivalry that held sway over sweet England and her good King, Henry.

"Some young knights became foolishly overexcited," Father had told us on the night he returned from court. "I thought we might have another accident, like the last time, but they managed to scrape through." He looked vaguely disapproving. Father was not talented at the joust and therefore looked down on it. He thought it frippery, and he was a soldier who had fought in true wars so perhaps I should simply have accepted his opinion, but my mind was wicked; I suspected his disapproval had more to do with his own lack of talent. I knew, even then, how people come to dislike that which they are not good at, or what they lack. The poor hate money, for they have it not, as I resented beauty, for it was something I lacked.

"The Queen graciously oversaw the tournament," Father had said. "She manages to keep the young men in good order by merely demonstrating her grace and godliness."

"Of course," my mother said, voice throbbing with respect. I could hear her heart in every word. "When I think of all those years poor Katherine spent in Durham House, cast off by the old King and by her own father, pawning her jewels and clothes to pay her servants and buy bread…!" My mother clasped a hand to her chest as though in physical pain. "It was a disgrace to treat a woman of such Christian goodness and gracious bearing in such an infamous way! And then our good King Henry married her and brought her from the darkness to light." Mother sighed, a breath of pure pleasure and contentment. All women should be saved by a man. It was the end of every story, much as marriage was. Sometimes I wondered what happened after a woman had been saved and married. The stories never told us. Perhaps it was because marriage was where a woman surrendered all of her self to others, to her husband, her children. As maids requiring rescue, women had a little self. As wives, they surrendered what little they once had possessed.

"Yet adversity taught the Queen many lessons," our father said, twiddling his signet ring of gold upon his finger. It held his initials and a carving of a peacock, his emblem. When he sent messages he pressed it into wax or resin on the page, so all knew it truly was from him. "Perhaps the Queen is now so good, because she was treated so ill."

"Of course you are right, lord husband," said my mother, in a tone that indicated she was about to disagree whilst making it sound as if she was agreeing. "Yet I think Queen Katherine a *naturally* good woman. The way she was treated may well have *enhanced* her natural graces, but I think she was strong of character before, and her ill fortune simply brought out her fine and noble characteristics. Yet still, even if suffering did make her good, I think it a crime she was so cast down, and by her own family!"

Thinking of this, I was distracted when my mother called my name across the great hall. When finally I noted my mother waving, her cheeks red, I understood she had called me at least once, and I was therefore scolded for not paying attention to my elders. I was quickly set to tasks; some of commanding servants, as though I had become my mother's second-in-command, and some of doing jobs myself. All that day I trotted about the house, for walking was too slow if I was to get everything Mother wanted done, and I thought of the Queen, of how she had been cast down and had risen high. How her family had abandoned her, but she had made a new family in England, with the King. I could not imagine doing to my brother Edward the ills that had been done to Katherine of Spain. Even Thomas I would have trouble treating so ill.

I was to learn soon enough that family means little to some.

*

Catherine arrived at Wulfhall a few days after Edward. They were to be wed in the church of Great Bedwyn and after Catherine was to live with us at Wulfhall. Edward would visit Catherine often, so they could work on breeding heirs. The country would be a healthier place for children in any case. It was well known that the ill scents which roamed in London and other cities carried spirits of sickness who could invade the body through the mouth, nose, eyes or pores, and make a person ill. "That is why each year in summer the King and Queen leave London on progress," said Mother. "They go to their country seats, and see favoured courtiers, staying away from the miasmas that cause illness."

I was jealous of Catherine from the moment I heard she was to be the wife of my beloved brother. It was a strange jealousy, for I hardly wanted to be the wife of my brother myself, but I adored Edward, and he was the only one who loved me back. Much as I wanted him to be happy, have love, I did not wish to share him with anyone. Catherine's arrival would alter that. My brother had always had others claiming him, my parents in particular for they thought he would be a star of court when he was grown, but whilst he respected them I knew he often found them as trying as I did. We were not to say anything of course. Children were bound by law of God and man to respect their elders, and we were fed and kept in clothes by their coin. They had brought us up, paid for our education and our food, had made sure we did not fall to death as so many children did. We were in their debt and that, as much as natural obedience and the hierarchy of society, kept our mouths closed when we were tempted by the Devil to say something in retaliation for cruel words, or indifferent ways. Bound to obedience we were, and in many ways we were their servants as we were their children. The bond Edward and I had was different. He owed nothing to me, but treated me with respect and love. In some ways the love for him I possessed was a kind of debt, for I felt indebted for his loving me, but I also knew he would not hold me to account. The gratitude I felt for his love was not something he required.

On the day Catherine arrived, I was watching from one of the attic windows. Up high I was, thinking that if I could see her from far away I might in some way prepare myself to lose my brother, to share his love. It was the thought of a foolish child. For one, I knew not that I would lose him, and even if that were so the preparation a few more minutes might offer could never compensate for a loss of love. There is nothing more haunting or terrible in life, than losing love.

But, being a child and knowing nothing, I was watching.

There was no glass in the windows of our attic. Shutters were pulled across when it was wet, or in the winter, keeping stores like barrels of honey, apples and salt fish in gentle, dry coolness. But on summer days, like the day Catherine arrived, they were pulled back. Cloth covered the open spaces, but I had pulled many of the sheets back. No one would mind on a warm, bright and dry day as that day was. There was no danger in allowing in fresh air and good light.

I liked our attics. They were a good place to hide from Thomas as for some reason he never thought to go up to look for me, but they also afforded a fair view of the countryside. I could see the shady edges of Savernake Forest from the windows. Far off though it was, the sight of the first dark leaves of that wood, the bruise of purple and black on the horizon, always gave me a shiver of pleasure, a teasing, gentle finger running down my spine. I felt anticipation when I gazed upon the forest, for I knew the delights it held. Anticipation, the thought of something good on the way, was often, I thought, more like true happiness than when an event actually occurred. It is always easier to make something better in the mind than it can ever be in real life.

There would be otters playing in rivers that flowed along the base of the forest, young pups gambolling in streams, fighting and yowling, wrapping their serpentine tails about each other as they rolled into the flow of the river, wrestling. Grass, some green and some topped by fluffy purple and white seed heads would wave gently in the slight breeze in glades where spindles of light tripped through tree leaves above, like thin, skeletal fingers. Motes would be chasing each other, gliding in a gentle dance to the earthen floor, weaving about butterflies in brown and black tunics, soft as down. As dusk fell, russet foxes would trip out of bushes and bracken, sniffing the night breeze, their paws light as air on the grass, wandering about deer who gathered in their herds, taking a seat in the shade after a sweltering, sunny day. There, in the flickering blue light of bracken would be shambling badgers, long, striped noses close to the earth, snuffling, round eyes bright in the gloom as they hunted wriggling pink worms or slinking slimy slugs. There were not many boars left wild in England, for the King had killed them all, but in the deepest parts of the forest there might still be some, round black eyes bright with rage and madness if they heard a human step. Some said there were wolves still in Savernake, though it had been an age since any had been seen loping through the darkness, amber eyes keen for prey.

In the wide skies above the house there were rooks and crows in flight. They were trying to see off birds of prey; kites and buzzards who hovered in the heavens, watching for mice in the grass, or for nests with eggs or young remaining inside, the second clutch of the year for most birds. Brave black darts were the rooks and crows, the jackdaws and ravens of the world, for up against much larger foes they flew, trying to see them off, trying to defend their children. I had great admiration for those who risked so much for others. Not sure I had such audacious courage inside me, I admired it in others. Even birds. Perhaps birds more so than humans. It seemed to me humans had many weapons of word and war to hand. Birds had little but beak and claw.

Casting my eyes away from the blue skies and wispy clouds, and along the road, I could see the houses of my father's stewards just outside the boundary walls of our house, plumes of blue wood smoke rising from their small chimneys. They were larger houses than those of the poor in the village nearby. They were modest dwellings, usually comprised of two storeys, made of wattle and daub. The poorer folk of the village would keep their livestock in a room at the base of the house, which kept the upstairs, where they slept, warm. Many in the village had houses of several rooms, however, and there was a good well, good work and good prospects for people in Wiltshire. My father was a fine lord, they all said. He made sure they were taken care of in hard times and in good times they made sure the estate flourished and we prospered. It was the bargain struck between servant and master, tenant and lord; mutual care for each other.

My father's stewards' houses were larger. Each probably had a hall for guests and dining. It would not be as large as ours, and their children like all children would share rooms, but they were comfortable. Each had a plot of land at the back to grow food, and many kept hives, geese and a goat or a cow. Several had hogs, or owned them together with a neighbour, sharing the care and feed, which offered good eating when one was slaughtered in winter. As I looked at those houses, I used to try to imagine what the wives of those men were cooking for dinner, what they were doing; baking bread or brewing ale, tending to wailing babes or chewing meat to put into the mouths of infant children, making the flesh easier to eat. In the distance, I could see the village, many houses clustered together as if sheltering from the sun, its packed, muddy streets thick with pigs being herded to water or woodland, or with the market set up there every Friday to sell many wondrous things. Too far away to see was Marlinges Boroe, a town where there was a mound of earth called Merlin's Barrow. People said it was where Merlin, soothsayer of King Arthur himself, had been laid to rest. The magician slumbered, waiting for the day his master the King rose once more, and on that day Merlin too would rise. If England called, he would come.

It was a little world I looked out on, but I knew that not when I was a child. I stared over farmland, smelling hay and dung in summer, the freshness of creeping, silver mist in autumn, sparkling snow scented like iron in winter, or wild blustery wind in spring, and I thought it perfume made by God. The skies seemed huge about Wulfhall, the heavens above wide, never-ending. On days when the skies were light blue, clouds loomed as vast, benevolent mountains guarding the roof of God's realm. Rooks and crows glided, cawing in warm air, wings ruffling with the breeze. In spring swallows looped and curved in the heavens, tiny dark arrows making the skies joyous.

The attic smelt good. Pots of pickled beans and vegetables were stacked along the walls as well as baskets of other foods that would last without being sealed in a pot or barrel. Onions with their crisp skins and subtle smell, when uncut, were tied in huge belts and suspended from rafters. Turnips, earth still clinging to their roots, for it kept them fresher, lay piled, pink, purple and white balls. Bundles of leather-skinned carrots were tied together, black-purple, white or yellow skins scrubbed fresh and clean by our maids. There were small barrels of pickled beans and large ones of salted meat. Chests of salted fish, salted butter and hard cheese lined up as soldiers along other walls, kept cool and away from each other. This was not our main storeroom, there were others, larger ones about the estate, but it was one the kitchen servants could reach with ease. The attic was a good, dry place to keep food in winter and the wind rushing through open windows kept it cool in summer, so produce did not spoil. There was a scent of spices, nutmeg, cloves, orange peel and cinnamon as well as sharp-sweet vinegar. It rushed to embrace the smell of dust and dry wood, the faintest hint of mouse droppings, and all scents of farmland for miles about which roamed into the house, carried on the arms of the wind. It was a glorious place; heavenly-scented, warm and cool at the same time, and it was dark. I always felt safer in shadow.

There was also company; a cat who lived up in the attics, and feasted well on mice that came to pilfer. The cat had no name, but I called him Alfred, after the King who had rid England of invading Danes. I thought this a fitting name for the cat, since he spent most of his life fighting and eating invading mice. Alfred the King had lived in Wiltshire, fought battles here, I had been told.

I liked Alfred's eyes, sometimes green and gentle, sometimes evil yellow. When yellow, full of wickedness and contempt, he was bound to scratch, a pearl-white claw leaping from the folds of his soft paw. When green, he was a kitten born anew. And he was a wise cat. When storms were on their way the pupils of his eyes would swell so they seemed to take up all space there was, and he would race, fur on end and tail twitching, around and around, up and down the walls. This was how he warned others that a tempest was about to break. Something of the wild madness of a storm raced ahead, invaded his blood, and sent him out to warn others. When Mother Cooper saw Alfred leaping about, unhinged, fur on end, she ordered shutters to go up and washing to be brought in.

Alfred was not as busy in daytime as he was at night, and when I came to the attics he would climb into my lap for a sleep. He liked the warmth. The cold, indeed, was something he did not stand for. Alfred would fall asleep purring soundly as I stroked him. I was the only one of the household he would come to. My brother tried often, but Alfred was no fool. He knew Thomas only wanted to pull his hair, or tie a rag to his tail and light it to make him scream and yowl. Alfred was far too clever to be caught by Thomas. Alfred would wait at the kitchen door for scraps, but if anyone tried to pet him he would scratch. He never did that to me.

My secret was hardly a secret. I waited for Alfred to come to me. I sat still and if he wanted to come and sleep on my lap, I let him. Cats infinitely prefer people who do not fuss them. They are much more likely to seek out the one who does not wish to pet them at all, and sit on them, than they are to come to one who calls them. It is because cats like to pretend they are self-sufficient and need no one. It is not so, of course, all creatures want comfort, but cats will always go out of their way to make it look as though they are bestowing a favour on the one they sit on.

Alfred liked me because he knew I would not seek him out, but always would accept him when he came. He had dignity, and did not want to be used as a toy, a passing amusement or something to fill the time. Alfred had pride in himself. It was something I admired, having so little myself.

We had an understanding and it suited us both, for I liked him on my lap. Something about his purr calmed me. I stroked only his head, for Alfred was particular and did not like people touching his belly or back. I had found that out quickly, found myself staring down in horror at a bleeding finger, one glittering, white claw deep in it, a yellow eye glaring balefully at me. But I did not scream in pain as his black-tipped tail swished menacingly back and forth. I merely lowered my hand, allowed him to remove the claw and from that day onwards stroked only his head. And he allowed me to. That was our understanding. I did not mind that the friendship was on his terms. I was accustomed to that being the way of things in all relationships I had. I was not the one to set pace, or define borders in a realm made between two people. I followed, agreed, submitted. Aside from Edward, that was how it was with all people I knew.

On the morning Edward's bride arrived, I was at one of the open windows. The summer breeze was piling in, ruffling Alfred's fur in a manner that seemed to please him. He was asleep, legs twitching on my lap, but every now and then would open an eye, green that day which meant he was merry, and he would yawn and stretch in kitten-like contentment. It was a strange look on a cat so war-beaten and scarred from battling rats and mice, but even the rangiest cat can look like an innocent kitten when he yawns, or when asleep.

I sat by the window watching for Catherine. She was due at any time, as a messenger had ridden ahead saying they were close by. Edward, my father, and Edmund had missed the message as they had ridden out before dawn to take a tour of the estate. My mother was busy ordering Mother Cooper about in the kitchens, and commanding maids to ensure that Wulfhall looked its best, so no one had noticed when I slipped away. I was already in my best gown of crimson velvet, a gable hood of the same colour on my head. There was nothing more I could do other than get in Mother's way, so I went to the attic.

I was in my usual seat, on a flat-topped chest near the window. Alfred had emerged from the shadows, stretching his back, pushing sharp claws into the wooden planks of the floor. He had yawned and arched, a sight which made him appear demonic and endearing at the same time, and padded to me, looking at me once before he leapt into my lap as though he wished to re-establish our agreement that I was to only stroke his head. I allowed him to paw my legs, turn three times as he always did, and sit down before I put my hand to his soft head and stroked him. Under my fingertips I could feel scabs and healing wounds, inflicted by mice or rats he had fought the night before, and from fleas which roamed his fur. He liked me to scratch around these scabs a little. I never minded for it made him purr all the more when I did. I ran my fingers through his soft fur, scratched his itchy war-wounds. His purr and the soft breeze ruffling through the attics were the only noises.

The only noise, that was, until I heard shouts. I glanced to the distant road and saw a party on horseback approaching; men and one woman, possibly with a maid behind her. This was the woman who was to marry my brother, the woman who might steal his affections from me. I grumbled to Alfred under my breath, mumbling and resentful, telling him that I did not want her to come. I wanted to remain, as Edward often called me, his favourite maid. I did not want another to take my place in his heart. It was the only place I had, besides the attic, or a corner of the shadowy barn. The only place I knew to be mine, I knew to be safe.

I think I was afraid of her, fearful of losing the little love I had.

The riders were getting closer, plumes of dust, yellow and grey, rising into the air behind them, whirling in sultry air and catching sunlight so it glittered as gold. I could not tarry much longer. I would have to go. Mother would soon be looking for me, and would be displeased if I was absent. I was supposed to be at her side as she greeted this young woman, welcomed her into our home. But I wanted to see Catherine before I left this sheltered alcove. I wanted to see what she looked like. For some reason, it was most important.

The party clattered into the courtyard, hooves as thunder on the cobbles and earth. Lads of the stables rushed forwards to take reins so the riders could climb down off their mounts. I saw Catherine immediately, even surrounded as she was by two other maids and guards, probably employed by her father to escort her to Wulfhall. I gasped, breath catching in my throat. Until that moment, I had never known what beauty truly was.

Catherine was young, seventeen or eighteen perhaps. No one had mentioned her date of birth to me. All I had heard was she was a little older than my brother. To my eyes, eyes of a child, she did not look young, but grown up, and she was the most sophisticated creature I had set eyes upon.

Her hair was concealed under a covering of dark silk, and on her head was a hood in the style the French wore. Princess Mary had brought the style back, I had been told, from France and it had become popular at court. It was more daring than the hood I wore. The French hood sat farther back on the head than the gable, and showed just a touch of hair. And the hair I saw that day on the head of my brother's bride was *golden*. I had often heard people speak of my hair, or my mother's as golden, but upon seeing Catherine's hair I knew it was not so. My hair was straw; it was dun and hers purest gold. Her hair caught the sunlight in the skies and twinkled at me.

She slid from her saddle, holding her arms out to a servant who aided her, and let out a small laugh as her feet hit the cobbles in the yard. She smiled at her helper, and giggled again as a light flush raced swift along his cheekbones. There was not an eye anywhere but on her. From the first moment she commanded all who stood in that courtyard. She was a blazing light, all were dazzled.

Catherine smoothed her gown of crimson, clearly new, and shook an over-cape of deepest black, lined with fur. It was a warm day, so the only use for it was to keep her gown clean. She glanced up and around at her new home, clear eyes, blue as forget-me-nots, roaming, taking everything in. I gaped at this magnificent creature. She was entirely out of place. Catherine was glamorous, lithe, beautiful, with a full bosom but a thin waist. Her fingers had rings of gold and silver on them which caught the sun and flashed light up, over me. I blinked and moved my head. Her eyes darted up. Shadowing her eyes with a hand to see better, she looked in my exact direction. Eyes of a hawk, that woman had.

I gasped, and swiftly drew back, causing Alfred to drop from my lap in an ungainly fashion. There was a short snarl of protest as he hit the floor and bounced on his paws. With one disgusted glance over his shoulder to demonstrate I had displeased him, Alfred walked away, tail twitching. As I darted out of sight I heard that throaty giggle and I knew she had seen me. I felt shamed by her laugh, by the pretty eyes that had caught me and by her beauty. The glimpse of her face, young, fresh, with clear skin like milk, showed me a vision I had only ever thought belonged to old stories kitchen maids told in long winter afternoons as they worked; tales of Guinevere, and King Arthur, of Isolde and fairy maidens. Such beauty was not for this world, and yet, I had seen it. I had seen her.

I thought Catherine Fillol the most perfect creature I had ever set eyes upon. And the first thing I had done, naturally, was to shame myself in front of her. *You always do,* said the voice inside my head.

I heard a shout; my mother calling for me with growing impatience. She was trying not to surrender to an impulse to scream. She must be growing desperate for Catherine was there, in the courtyard and the family was not assembled!

I brushed my skirts, trying to rid them of cat hair, tell-tale and white, and climbed down the attic ladder. Down long staircases I scampered, reaching my mother and earning a clip about the ear as I rushed, pink-cheeked and out of breath, to her side.

"Where have you been?" she scolded, but did not wait for an answer. "Edward's new wife is here. Your place is at my side, child, not running off, wherever you were!" She *tsked* at black and white hairs still clinging to my skirts and bashed them with her heavy hand, slapping my legs in the process. She turned me about and *tsked* even more at the dust on my back. I had to grit my teeth as she hit that dust, making it fly off in little clouds. Thomas grinned at me from the other side of the hallway. Perfectly presented in a stunning doublet of black with silver-gilt buttons, a white shirt, and black jerkin, he was the picture of nobility. Black hose and breeches and a black cap with a large russet feather sticking out from it completed the costume. And my brother, of course, did not have flushed cheeks and was not covered in cat hair. *You always shame yourself,* the voice said.

My mother swung me about and pursed her lips, eyes critical. "You'll have to do," she sighed, "we can leave the poor girl waiting no longer in that hot courtyard." Mother screwed up her lips and narrowed her eyes. "But think not, Jane, that you have escaped without punishment. I will remember this, and when the time comes, when we are not due to greet your brother's wife into this house for the first time, I shall make sure you are punished for this insolence!"

Unsure as I was as to how I could have been insolent when I had said nothing, I kept quiet and hung my head. *Absent is not the same as insolent,* I thought.

Edmund's wife, Mary, looked at me as though disgraced to be seen with me. Henry was shaking his head and I could feel Thomas's glee at my scolding positively burning into my skin. Mother whirled me around and pushed me to walk just behind my brothers. I trotted, feeling my cheeks flame, into the courtyard.

And there she was. Catherine. Gazing about, a merry smile on her lips and critical evaluation in her eyes. Was Wulfhall as grand as the house from which she had come? I wondered. Was my father richer than hers? Was our house better? Our lands? I saw calculation in her blue eyes, and I believed she was looking down on what she saw. Perhaps her father's house was much grander than ours. Perhaps she was sorry about her fate.

But when she saw us approaching she smiled widely, any hint of displeasure peeling itself from her face, floating away on the breeze. She spread her arms gracefully and dropped her knees, performing a delightful curtsey which was low, poised and elegant. She kept her head bowed as my mother approached, only lifting those bewitching eyes when my mother asked her to. From the first moment Mother was entirely won over by this enchanting creature. Catherine was far and away more beautiful than Edmund's wife Mary, a thick-hipped creature with a sour expression and eyes the colour of mud, and she was superior to me in every respect. Catherine was all a noble beauty should be, all the court of the King would yearn for. In the face of Edward's wife my mother finally glimpsed the daughter she had wished, nay deserved, to have been granted.

Catherine was charming. She kissed my mother's hand, complimented her on her beauty, her dress, home and her lands all in one breath, and even made a light jest about the roads, which my mother laughed at. I blinked. It was a revelation that my mother was capable of laughter.

After a brief introduction for Henry, Mother turned to Thomas. "This is my youngest son, Thomas," said Mother, extending a hand which almost hit me in the nose as she brought Thomas forwards to meet his new sister. Thomas bowed in a flamboyant manner and kissed Catherine's hand, causing her to let out a bright tinkle of laughter and respond with a playful curtsey. I could see Thomas found her attractive, for he had already started to fawn about her.

They had almost forgotten me when my mother's glance lighted upon me. "And this is my daughter, Jane," she said in an offhand way, as though I was one of the horses.

"Jane," Catherine breathed, as though mine was the most exciting name she had heard. She came towards me, much surprising my mother, and curtseyed, then took my hand. Hers was warm, smooth. I could smell roses, sweet and soft, on her skin. "I am so pleased to meet you. I think it a fine thing I have a younger sister. I only had an elder before. It will be pleasant for me to be the older sister for once. I do hope we will be good friends."

My feet stumbled, surprised, and I curtseyed awkwardly. "I hope that too, Mistress Fillol," I mumbled, not trusting myself to look into that striking face.

Catherine took hold of my chin and lifted my eyes to hers. My cheeks flooded with colour. Her touch made my heart race. Perhaps Thomas and Mother were not the only ones already in love with her. "Call me *sister*, Jane," she insisted, "and I shall call you the same."

"Yes… sister," I stuttered, both glad and sorrowful when she released my chin and patted my cheek by way of ending our introduction. I could smell her perfume on my skin. Something in me never wanted it washed away.

"And where is my dear Edward and his noble father?" asked Catherine of my mother. "I have so looked forward to seeing them, my lady."

"They are riding the estates," said my mother, a throbbing apology in her voice. She really was captivated by Catherine. She would never have shown such respect otherwise. "They rode out before your messenger arrived, my dear, but they will be back by evening."

"And tomorrow, my lady, I shall be married!" Catherine said with a laugh. "It feels as though it were yesterday I was a young maid, like sweet Jane here, watching as my older sister went off to become a bride and a wife, and now here I am!" She smiled at Mother. "But it must feel the same for you, my lady," she said with respect. "It cannot be long since you were married, indeed, your marriage must have occurred when you were very young, for I can hardly believe children so grown as Thomas and Jane, here, are yours!" She put her hand on Mother's arm. "I heard the men of my father's household speak in awe of the beauty of Lady Margery Wentworth before I knew of my engagement to your son, but I never imagined such stories were true. And now I find they are. You are enchanting to behold, my lady."

"Well, well," said my mother, flushing, but looking boundlessly pleased all the same. "How now... I am a matron now; a mother, a wife with a brood of many."

"I can only hope to be as fortunate as you, my lady," Catherine went on. "To grant a large family to my husband, and yet manage to retain the figure and face of a young maid? You must tell me your secrets."

"Call me lady mother, or just Mother, if it pleases you," my mother said, her words rushed as affection, so lately seeded but already grown hale and thick in her soul, flowed out of her mouth.

"Mother," said Catherine. She touched her eye as though blinking back a tear.

Mother linked her arm into that of Catherine, and walked with her to the house. I stood staring in abject amazement, and I was not the only one. Mary was gaping at my mother and Catherine as though she could not believe it. Thomas, however, was staring after the young beauty with narrowed eyes. There was something in the way he looked at her I liked not. I shivered, but knew not why. In that moment, all I wanted was to protect Catherine. I think I had fallen for her too.

Chapter Seven

Wulfhall
Wiltshire

Summer 1517

Edward, Edmund and Father arrived back that afternoon. By that time Catherine had washed, changed her linen smock and was so at home in our mother's chambers it seemed she had been there all her life. My new sister gushed over my mother's embroidery, and was careful to praise mine as well. She had already gathered our mother into her confidence and it had been reciprocated, as Catherine was being told things about my mother's time at court of which I had never heard. The only one my new sister seemed to have made an enemy of was Mary, who was glowering from the back of the room. Mary had always known herself to be the wife of a poor relative, but she had enjoyed Mother's companionship and confidence, especially since I was a disappointment. Catherine's arrival had just altered her position in the house, knocking her down a level.

By the time Father and Edward arrived, it seemed Catherine had been crowned the little Queen of our house. Mother was hers entirely, Thomas obviously wanted to offer himself as a bridegroom despite being only ten, and the servants were already talking of Mistress Fillol as though she was the only being in the world. And me? I could not stop staring. Catherine was a bright comet descended on our household of shadows. I thought her remarkable, witty, amiable and magnificent. Something about her shimmered, like the white paint on our walls when the morning sunlight hit it. I felt as though I had become a lap dog, ever-content to follow her about, sit at her feet. In the few hours that had passed since she had walked into the house, Catherine Fillol had made more of an impression than I had in the nine years I had lived there.

I was jealous of her no more. I did not mind if Edward loved her, for I loved her. I was proud my brother was gaining such a prize as his bride. I thought of the beautiful children they would have, the life they would lead at court, for *of course* this creature would *have* to go to court. She was too glorious to be left at dull Wulfhall for the rest of her days. No, Catherine would go to court, and charm the King and Queen just as Edward would, and our royal masters would see what wonderful creations these two were and elevate them to become their personal servants, and friends. Catherine was made to be a Duchess. This, I was sure, was the destiny for Catherine and my beloved Edward.

When Edward arrived, he was clearly nervous. I understood that he and Catherine had only met a few times. She had been brought to court with relatives and they had met for an hour or so perhaps twice, so although they were to wed and be bonded for life on the morrow, that day they were relative strangers. Knowing each other would come later, of course. That was the way of things. Couples had a lifetime to spend getting to know one another after they were joined.

My eldest brother was obviously enchanted with her manners and beauty, as all of us were. Edward bowed to Catherine, enquired after her journey and the state of the roads, and introduced Cousin Edmund and then the servants. She received each new person she met with pleasure, kissing them on the cheek, and doing the same to our father. Father, who was obviously more acquainted with Catherine and her family, since he had arranged the match, asked after her father, mother and elder sister. Catherine answered all that was put to her with a ready grace and happy smile.

The next morn, they were married in the church on our lands. The ceremony took place first in the doorway, a tradition starting to fade out of fashion for the nobility, but Mother liked it and it was still honoured in many places, so it was done. Vows and rings were exchanged in the doorway, then into the belly of the church we were taken, to watch the rest of the ceremony performed at the altar.

Once inside the church, the priest spoke in a harsh, grating voice on the reasons for marriage; to procure children and to stay far from sin. I wondered what sin he spoke of, for in love I saw no sin. But he knew these matters better than I, in my ignorance, ever would, so I bowed my head and prayed to God that my brother would find great happiness with his wife.

We came back home, and as Catherine entered her house as a married woman, we threw handfuls of wheat over her and Edward, blessing them with fertility. She presented a wreath of flowers to Edward, as we unmarried women gave them to all men of the house. All of these little ceremonies were intended to bring children to the marriage. I was proud of the garlands. Although no one thought to ask, I had made all of them.

That afternoon, all noble and merchant families from the area came to our house. Wulfhall was suffused with scents of fatty, roasting meat, of herbs curling on flames of the fire, bleeding flavour into meat and grain and ale. There too was the scent of rich pottage bubbling thickly over the fire in the kitchen, mutton falling from white bone, beef bobbing alongside cabbage and lettuce. The great barn had been cleared of all stores and hay, and huge tables were brought out in pieces, legs set out, tops unfolded and arranged to make several long tables. Our family were to sit at the table at the top of the barn, arranged so it was horizontal to other, longer ones. My place was to be at the very edge of the high table, on the end, in accordance with my rank. Eldest and only daughter I was, yes, but a girl sat lower than boys, even had I not been younger than them all. But I did not mind that I was not as close to my brother as I would have liked. I knew I would have a good view of him when I glanced along the table. Merely to see him flushed with wine and happiness was enough for me. I was warmed by the joy I had already seen on his face and hoped I would glimpse more come the evening.

As servants set up trestle tables, long boards on frames, and swept the floor one last time, I stood outside the barn. I was in my best gown of crimson velvet, adapted from one of Mother's court gowns. I felt grown up, a part of something although I had taken no part in the ceremony. Perhaps it was the gown, or anticipation of the feast and dance to come. Mayhap my young heart was struck by the moon, already in the skies though it was not yet night. Perhaps it was the happy buzz of conversation, a sound humming all over the lands of Wulfhall, like a thousand merry bees gathering food from willing flowers, but a hush fell in my soul, as if dusk had fallen not only in the skies of the world, but in my heart, bringing peace. I stood a moment to try to catch the feeling that fell upon me. I wanted to name it, possess it, make it mine. I knew it not then, but I have come to think the best feelings, the best moments, of life, are the ones we cannot name, the wildness we fail to possess; something that comes to us, lifting our hearts and inspiring our souls, but for what purpose or reason we never understand. The moments and feelings that matter most, are those we are least able to explain.

In my nose was the scent of the approaching night. I stood in the doorway of the barn. Great eaves stretched up, cresting behind me into the barn's belly, light wood then darker reaching as rib bones towards one another. Outside in the cobalt skies bats were flying, black arrows whizzing through warm air, swooping gracefully as they caught flies and bugs. White moths hovered, winging towards blazing torches that lit the outside of the barn, and more on poles, lining the path, leading a procession of gaily dressed guests, who had come to the church that day, towards the barn and to their tables for the feast. I could see them walking towards us, many of them with linked arms. The air echoed with laughter and the sound of teasing voices. There was the scent of spices and ale, wine and burning scented logs on the air. About the land bonfires had been lit to celebrate the marriage, purify the air, wash clean the old, and to usher in a new time. Common people would dance about them that night, awash with ale my father had sent that they, too, might celebrate the wedding of his eldest son.

I breathed in and closed my eyes. *Usher in a new time,* I thought. That was how it felt; a new time, the start of something. I felt expectation, anticipation settle on me even though the day and the night and event were not mine. Something was to happen, and happen soon, and it felt like something good. Rare are times like that in life, where we feel something coming and, whether we are right or not, stop and allow the feeling to flow into us, suffuse our souls and hearts. But that night was one such night for me. Edward's wedding was the start of something, not only in his life, but mine. The feeling within me was as the sound of thunder on hills of the horizon, as the feeling when the skies crackle in summer before a storm. It was the intake of breath the world seems to make before rain starts to fall after a long time of dryness. It was the hush of dusk and dawn, when even birdsong cannot shatter the stillness of the world. It was a moment of change. Somewhere, a fairy was crossing a boundary between her world and ours, tripping out of a mound of earth covered in daisies. Not far away a spectral hound had broken loose and was leaping a ditch into the world of man. Change was coming. Borders had broken. That was how it felt; magical and strange.

We feasted in the barn under the glowing amber and yellow light of hundreds of torches, blazing in metal sconces on the walls. Shadows leapt, long, strange and spindly, like the wraiths of fairies, on the roof, along the walls as people moved. There was a loud hum of conversation, shattered now and then by happy laughter. The scent of warmed wine with spices and fresh ale infused with summer herbs filled the air, along with smoke from the fire and incense from braziers. Mother was all that was beautiful in her gown of red with azure sleeves, and Father was handsome as the Devil in a black and red tunic, and a tight jerkin of black leather. His sword, the mark of a gentleman, was at his side, clinking as he laughed and it banged against tables and stools. I was even proud of my brothers; pale and dark were Edward and Thomas, with Henry as ever between them, just as in the order of their births. Edmund and Mary looked handsome that night too, and Mary was happy, which suited her. It gave her a lightness she seemed to lack at other times. I think she found the position of being a dependant of a dependent kinsman of our family trying. She was an elevated servant, but not one of the family, and at the same time she was family and not a servant. Edmund could at least claim blood with the house. She could not. Hers was a place between places, utterly reliant not only on her husband, but on those her husband relied on; my mother and father. It cannot have made her feel secure, and she never had a chance to express her own thoughts or feelings, for she had to placate Mother.

Mary had borne no children and knew the servants spoke of her badly for that. If there was a fault of fertility, it was always the fault of the female, not the male. Perhaps she feared that Mother, a greatly fertile woman, thought badly of her for it too. But if such unhappy thoughts haunted her, my cousin's wife did not say anything. Mary did not talk a great deal, since Mother did enough for all of us, but in truth Mary bore a lot with a quiet grace, perhaps more than Edmund did.

"To table!" my father called. "And may you feast well this night in honour of my good son and his beautiful bride!"

To table indeed, tables soon groaning with the weight of food placed upon them. Pottage of fresh trout with herbs, and bubbling stews of blackbird, woodcock and lark were brought to us in huge serving bowls. Diners dipped pewter spoons into shared messes, ladling portions onto trenchers of sliced thick bread if they were people of the estates, onto platters of pewter if they were noble guests.

Bowls of perfumed water, pretty with flakes of orange peel and marjoram floating in them, were brought out before and between courses so we could wash our hands, particularly the fingers used for eating. Our guests wiped their spoons with bread before dipping into another bowl, and laughed, talking and jesting as servants moved between them, placing more food on tables or refilling shared goblets of fine Malmsey wine or fragrant ale. Then came more dishes: hens boiled with green and white leeks bobbed in a pale green broth, and bone marrow served on slices of toasted bread tickled the nose with its rich scent. There were artichokes, roasted in slices on the open fire until black and sweet, and quince pies covered with golden pastry. We cried out to see roasted pheasant, partridge, glistening mutton with onions and sausages of pork and apple. Whiting, crayfish, shrimps, smoked eels, oysters brought in huge barrels from the coast and roasted turbot came next, making the tables creak in protest. Fruit tarts, honey tarts, decorated eggs marbled with bright saffron and sweet, pale cheese pies wobbled as they were set down. Bowls of fresh green peas, thin-sliced boiled cabbage glistening with oil and verjuice, many-coloured carrots shining under melted thick butter, slices of peppery turnip and expensive olives made the tables gleam. Roasted geese, fat and golden, sat beside owl, bittern, gull, crane, heron and duck, all hunted and caught on our lands. And then, to thunderous applause, a whole roasted peacock was brought in, served dressed in his own iridescent feathers, his beak gilded with gold leaf. I gaped until my mother told me to close my mouth, for it made me look like a salted herring.

The feast finished with grand jellies made into heraldic devices of the family, more peacocks for my father and Wentworth leopards for my mother, and thick slices of quince and peach marmalade were served on tiny wafer biscuits. We drank sweet hippocras and I felt my young head swim with heady alcohol. Afterwards, the tables were cleared and musicians struck up a lively tune. My brother led his new wife to the centre of the barn and together they performed a dance popular at court that season.

I watched as their hands met above their heads, as they came together, feet moving elegantly and quiet over the earthen floor and the rush mats atop it. I watched Edward's eyes sparkle as they rested on Catherine's laughing face. He looked so happy that night, joined to a woman of such grace and loveliness. Each time their hands met in the air, each time they clapped, I felt my heart rush faster, surging as the waves of the sea, powered by a love for them so strong it was painful.

I only partnered one man, an ancient friend of my father's who moved so slow and creaking that I had to force myself to think about every step I made so I did not lose him in the dance. If he fell I feared every brittle bone of his aged body would shatter. But I cared not that I was not asked to dance more. I stood at the side of the hall, watching with wide, happy eyes.

When the time came to take the couple to their beds, Mother, Mary and I went with Catherine. We helped her to undress and washed her, perfuming her skin, which was clear of marks or scars all over her blessed body, with rose and lavender water. There was much said during that short time that I did not understand. Catherine did not seem afraid, as Mary and Mother evidently expected her to be. She changed into her shift and got into the bed prepared for her and her new husband. Mother spoke, warning her softly.

"Sometimes, men can be rougher on the first night than they are at other times," she consoled her new daughter. "But make no noise, try to relax, and it will pass easier for you." She handed Catherine a pot of salve, made of oil and angelica. "It will aid his passage, and hurt you less if you apply this."

I was lost. I had some knowledge of what passed between a man and a woman in bed. We lived on farm land, and I had seen pigs or rams mount mates. I had heard their squeals. Was *that* what my brother was going to do to his wife? I hardly wished to think on it. What a horrible idea! And yet, from the way my mother spoke of the encounter, it seemed there was pleasure that might come from this ungainly experience.

"You may not feel it the first few times," Mother warned, "but the joy of the marriage bed will come in time. It is important it does, for when a woman enjoys her husband she is more likely to conceive a child."

Catherine nodded, cheeks flushed with wine, with excitement and fear. Downstairs, we heard the raucous sound of Edward being carried through the doors by his friends, laughing and shouting as they heaved him up the stairs. It sounded as though they might have dropped him several times, if all the crashing and banging was anything to go by. I hoped they would not hurt him. Mother's lips thinned as the noises got closer, as we could hear some of the jests. They were crude. She pressed a hand to Catherine's arm, her expression sympathetic. "I watered his wine during the feast," she whispered to Catherine. "So I hope he is not as deep in his cups as my own lord was when first he came to my bed."

Catherine giggled nervously as the door flew open, bashing from its hinges, and Edward was carried into the room on the shoulders of his friends. They were singing a ribald song full of dirty words which made me blush. As they poured into the chamber I saw there were more men behind the ones who carried Edward, all singing, japing, some making lewd motions with their hips. They roared to a stop and almost threw my brother onto the floor. He flew along on feet that could not seem to stop, but managed to stagger to a standstill just before the curtained bed. There was another anxious giggle from Catherine as she saw her new husband before her in just his nightshirt, legs bare, eyes as unsteady as his feet. Edward grinned at her. He looked a little foolish and I looked away. I did not like it. I felt shamed for him.

"We will leave them to bed, then," said my mother sternly, fixing her eyes on my father to command him to take control of the men.

"To bed," Father agreed, leering at his wife with bloodshot eyes. He laughed when she turned a disapproving look upon him and he lifted a goblet of Romney wine, spilling a fair slosh as he thrust it into the air. "To my son, and his beautiful wife!" he cried, words slurring over his tongue. "May you find much joy in one another this night and all to come!"

There was a huge roar of laughter, and more jests. Many men were speaking of *ploughing*. I did not know why farm work would come to mind at such a time. Catherine was bright red, and my mother firmly ushered my father to lead the other men from the room, and to ensure they did not listen at the door. *She* stood at the door for a moment, glaring at any who seemed likely to linger. Mother indicated I was to stay with her, guard the door for Edward and Catherine a moment, so I stayed. Mother sighed as she watched my father link arms with two other men, slopping wine all over his shoes, heading back out to the barn to continue drinking.

"Let us hope your brother is not as far gone in his cups as your father is," she muttered, almost to herself, "or that poor girl will have a hard night of it."

She looked at me as though she had just realised I was there. "The wedding night can be a testing time for a woman, Jane," she said, her tone gentle. "The man is often too eager, and can be rough with a maid."

"Yes, my lady mother," I said, although I did not know of what she spoke.

"Do you understand what happens between a man and a woman in marriage?" she asked.

"I think so, my lady mother," I replied. "I have seen how lambs and piglets are made."

My mother laughed. "Then perhaps you *do* understand what the wedding night can be like!" she said, amused. When I looked baffled, she laughed harder.

She gazed down at me and breathed in, letting it out through her nose. "Well, I will tell you tonight, then. It is apt, since this is the first bedding ceremony you have been to." She led me to my own room, next to Catherine's, and there explained what occurred between a man and a woman. Mother undressed me, which she never did at any other time. She put me in my night shift as she explained, and I was so surprised by her gentle tone and caring manner that I had the courage to wonder aloud why on earth a woman would wish to be married, and have such things done to her.

My mother smiled. Perhaps it was the revelations she had offered, or the large amounts of wine she had drunk, but she seemed like a friend that night. "It is not *all* bad, Jane," she said as she pulled the sheets up about me. "There is even pleasure to be found if the man has skill, and is patient. And, of course, the main aim is to have children, bear heirs for the family, bring consolation to one's life in that way. There is no other way to get a child in the belly of a woman, so, even if we women do not find pleasure we must endure, for that is the task God gave us, and us alone. Men cannot bear children, but we can, and we are blessed."

"The Virgin Mary did not lie with a husband to gain a child," I disagreed. "Perhaps it is better that way, rather than… this way."

"The Virgin was singled out of all women and blessed by God Himself, Jane," whispered my mother, "we cannot expect to be as fortunate, nor as loved by God. He loved her above all women. He chose her to bear his son, for she was the purest of all of us. She was the perfect woman. The rest of us can only hope to emulate her." Mother rose and nodded to me, making for the door. "Sleep well," she said as she closed the door.

That night, I lay thinking long into the hours of darkness. The sound of revellers in the barn kept me awake, as did noises coming from the chamber next door. I got up, late in the night, and gazed out through a crack in my shutters at men still dancing in the barn with women. There were others, too, sitting around a bonfire, telling old tales as some half-dozed and others drank. Around one corner of the barn I could see a man bent over, folded in half as he vomited long and hard onto the muddy floor. There was a friend beside him, rubbing his back.

But from next door I could hear sounds which troubled me more; the noise of the bed rocking against the wall, the muffled sound of a man groaning, and the soft whimpers of a woman clearly in pain. Whatever the pleasures that my mother had spoken of were, Catherine was not enjoying them.

Chapter Eight

Wulfhall
Wiltshire

Summer 1517

The next morning, Catherine's bride sheet was stripped from the bed she and Edward had shared and pinned up in the great hall for all to see.

As we came down late to share a light meal it was there, waiting for us. I gazed up in horror, for on the fluttering white linen were brown-red smears, streaks of blood. The sheet seemed to speak to me, echoing all the unhappiness I had heard in Catherine's whimpers from the night before. Like a ghost it floated over Catherine and Edward, who sat at the head of the table. My mother had explained that a maid lost her virginity with blood, but the amount on that sheet, the wide spread and splatter, spoke to me of pain. Catherine's pain was pinned upon the wall, and her pain had become a mark of pride for my brother. It made me uncomfortable. I knew not why but it felt wrong, so unlike Edward.

Under the fluttering cloth, Catherine looked pale and wan, but she offered me a smile as I took my place at the end of their table. My brother seemed to be suffering, and was drinking deep from a cup of hot, spiced ale, calling for it to be replenished often. My mother was sitting primly by the side of my father. Father ate nothing, and when the obligatory time had been spent at the table he went outside to stick his head in a trough of water in the yard. For the rest of the morning he was to be found at the side of the fire still burning in the yard, a flagon of ale his only companion. Evidently, when one drank too much at night, more drink was needed the next morn. He did not even seem to note maids of the kitchens scouring pans and knives with sharp river sand, or the plant known as horsetails which we used on pewter plates, nearby. He just stared into the flames and drank.

Edward went hunting with Edmund, Henry and Thomas later that morning, and I went to seek Catherine. She was sitting by the fire in the great hall, a piece of embroidery in her lap. Her feet were tapping restlessly on rushes, meadowsweet and wormwood strewn on the floor, there to keep fleas at bay. Her eyes seemed lost in the flames. She was alone, but for her maid at her side.

"Was it very awful, sister?" I whispered fearfully as I took to a stool beside her. She turned to me and laughed a little.

"I will not lie, sister," she said. "It was hardly what I would call pleasurable, but my lord husband was deep in his cups. We did as was required for the marriage to be legal. I have hopes that as we are together more it will get easier." The edges of her lips lifted as she read the dismay on my face. To think ill of Edward was as natural to me as thinking ill of God. I did not want to imagine him being rough or careless with such a wonderful creature as Catherine. Seeing my concern, and confusion, she pressed a hand to mine, and I felt her fingers, long and cold, as they wrapped themselves about my own. "Worry not for me, dear sister," she whispered. "And tell your mother naught of what I just said. No mother likes to think that her son is not... gentle with his wife. It is our secret."

I blinked, amazed anyone would want me to be their secret-keeper. "Do you promise?" she asked, her eyes catching sight of Mother, bustling towards us from the other side of the hall.

Quickly I nodded, breathless with excitement, and of being so trusted. It distracted me for a moment from the bafflement of thinking of Edward as not perfect. Catherine rewarded me with a bright smile. It was as if an angel had cast radiance upon me.

Mother was almost upon us, one of her maids trotting at her side, carrying a basket of many-coloured thread and another with a small pile of linen shirts for mending. "My daughters," she said, manoeuvring her rear into one of the wooden stools opposite Catherine, "I trust you are both well?"

"Heartily well, my lady mother," said Catherine, taking up her needlework and regarding it critically before pushing her needle into the fabric.

"And was last night… acceptable, my dear?" Mother asked Catherine.

Catherine glanced up and gave her a pretty smile. Her cheeks coloured pink and glowed with the amber light of the fire. "Your son was gentle and kind, my lady," she lied in a bold tone. "Rest assured I am happy in my union. Edward will be a fine husband, much like his own father."

Mother was visibly relieved, and took up one of the shirts from the basket, threading white through the eye of her sharp needle. "I explained much to Jane, on matters of the marriage bed last night," she said to Catherine in a low, amused voice carrying a conspiratorial tone. "And my innocent daughter said to me that it seemed the manner in which the Virgin got her child was a better fate for women!" Mother laughed. "But she will come to know, as you and I do, there are many compensations for a woman when she has lost the flower of her maidenhead."

Mother chuckled as she pulled her thread through the shirt. She nodded to me and I took another shirt, mending the button hole. I hated mending button holes, and it seemed that Father and every one of my brothers seemed to rip this part of their shirts and breeches the most. Button holes were fiddly affairs, requiring the sewer to loop neat stitches around and around, to protect the rest of the shirt from ripping. *Men should wear pins, as we do,* I thought. Buttons were rare on women's clothing. Most gowns were laced or held together with pins.

And we do not tear our clothes as often as they do, I thought. Perhaps it was because we had to fix them, and knew what toil that took. Men never saw all the work that went into mending clothes, not truly, so did not appreciate it. They wanted something, it was theirs, wanted something fixed and it was. Perhaps if they had to mend the clothes they wore, they would not rip them so much, might not take them for granted.

I kept my face straight, but my eyes blazed at the offending button hole. Whatever men did, women always seemed to be there, mending after them, fixing what they broke. I mended shirts Thomas had torn, as Catherine lied about my brother and his abilities in the bedchamber. I narrowed my eyes and held my thin lips together. In the poor light provided by the fire, the intricate work demanded by this most tedious of tasks made my angry eyes water.

"I hope that one day my dear sister Jane finds herself a husband as good as mine, or yours, my lady," Catherine went on.

I was amazed, not so much by her lies, but the easy manner, the fluid grace with which she told them. Catherine, when she had first come to the house, had seemed such an open woman, a creature of natural refinement and virtue. That was part of her charm. I suddenly realised she was capable of telling falsehoods with as much ease as another spoke of the weather. It made me wonder whether my new sister had meant any of the compliments she had handed out so liberally to my mother, Edward, or to me, but I consoled myself that she was only lying now in order to spare Mother's feelings, and perhaps save Edward from embarrassment as well.

She is not truly a liar, I thought, as I pulled thread rapidly through the button hole, trying to get it done as fast as possible so I might work on something else. *She is being kind.* Catherine was trying to make Mother happy and preserve

Edward's reputation, so there could be no sin in a lie told for such a purpose.

As I finished the button hole on one shirt, Mother handed me another with more button holes that needed fixing.

*

My brothers came back that night as dusk was falling, a grand stag bearing thirty points on his antlers as their prize. Father declared the head would hang in Edward's room, a reminder of the day. He put his arm around his eldest son, his face shining with pride. I remember that moment well. Some moments of life become etched in memory, pictures drawn with a diamond on glass.

Many more nights that week I heard the bed rocking, squeaking against the wooden panelling of my walls. Sometimes I heard a cry of pleasure from him, and sometimes a squeal of unhappiness from her. It seemed that no matter what Catherine said to my mother, my brother Edward was not a skilled man in the bedchamber. I was unhappy with this knowledge, for it marred the ideal I had of him as a perfect young gallant. I hoped that for his sake he would get better as time went on, and he was young after all. But they barely had time for that.

A letter came from our kinsman Francis Bryan. There was a temporary position vacant in the King's household. Edward was invited to fill it, and if all went well, he might end up with a permanent position at court. There was no mention of Catherine. It was not expected that a junior man of the King's household would bring his wife to London and to court. Edward would be in a dormitory with other lesser servants, so there was no place for her. Catherine would stay with us, Edward would go.

We said goodbye to him a day later. There was no time to lose. He embraced me as we stood gathered to see him off, and promised that if he found anything he thought I would like as a present he would send it to me.

"I would you would simply bring yourself, brother," I said in a voice thick with tears. "You are always the greatest present of all."

"Sweet Jane," Edward said, stroking his hand in its leather glove over my cheek. "I promise you, my favoured maid, that I will return whenever I can." Under the glove's perfume, I caught a scent of shit again.

He parted from us in the courtyard, promised to return as soon as he could, and then, he was away. I watched his horse trot, Father's servants riding beside him, until he was too far away to see. I was the only one to do so. Catherine went inside as soon as Edward's horse reached the first gate, and went to help Mother with her household accounts.

The days which followed Edward's departure were wearisome. Life returned to normal. There were no visitors, no more dances late into the night, no more men vomiting in the shadows or torches blazing red and golden against the dark cowl of night. There was little music, little dancing. Wulfhall became as it had been. I had never noted just how dull it was before.

I helped Mother with the sewing, for many garments had ripped on the night of the wedding whilst people danced. I brewed a wash for my father's best hound, who had mange and needed to be treated with dogberry. But even tasks I had once loved I did now with an ill grace of heart. There was nothing to excite me. The sense of wonder and expectation I had felt left me. I felt Wulfhall had grown smaller, as though the excitement of the days just passed had made it seem bigger, and now that this was over it had shrunk. Catherine, too, seemed less animated when Edward was gone. She often stared into the fire, lost in thought, needlework forgotten in her lap.

Mother thought Catherine was pining for Edward, and I allowed myself to believe this was the case, but there was something nagging at my mind, something which told me that Catherine was not as my mother thought. It was as though Catherine had become lost in herself, as though there was a choice or a path she was thinking of. In time, I came to know her secret, and it was a secret which was to come close to destroying our family.

Chapter Nine

Wulfhall
Wiltshire

Autumn 1517

It came, as all the worst things do, when I did not expect it. Demons of chance and ill-fortune know how to catch a soul off-guard. They watch. They are patient. They know when to strike.

Perhaps a month after the wedding of Edward and Catherine, on a morn when high winds rocked the house and rattled the roof, my mother announced she was three months gone with child. She had felt the quickening of the babe, its first movements. Now she was sure it was alive she was happy to tell those about her. It was often the way that mothers did not tell others about their condition until the quickening. The risk of losing the child was greater in the first months.

Although it had been long since I had entered the world, it seemed God had decided my family were to have more children. Mother had lost a child she carried a year back; that sibling of mine had lived in her belly for but two months before slipping out, straight into the arms of Death. Mother had sorrowed, but taken comfort in the words of her chaplain who had baptised the dead babe so it would not to limbo go, who said that sometimes children are called away before they have known life to become as angels at the side of God. Although I had not been present, Mary told me the chaplain had spoken words of blessing and baptism over lumps of blood and gore which fell from Mother's womb on that day. He said that it would aid the spirit of this child who never was alive to find its way to God. I do not remember my mother crying, but when I think of it she must have. Hard she could be, devoid of heart she was not. But it was not usual to demonstrate grief publicly when a child was lost. Grief was private, and to question the will of God was not fitting. If He had not wanted this child to live, there was a reason, little as we could understand it. And now there was another waiting to be born. My parents had suffered in losing one child, but been blessed with another. The trials God sent often were baffling, and hard, but clearly my parents had passed and pleased the Almighty.

Mother and Father were not, I think, *trying* to have more children. I believe it was just the opposite. They had three living sons and a daughter. That was enough to ensure the future of the house. There were certain herbs a woman could drink or eat to bring on her monthly courses, prevent pregnancy if required. Although the Church did not approve, it was often necessary, my mother said, for a woman to protect herself. Having children too close together, bearing too many babes or breeding when past one's prime were dangers to women.

"God does not mind if we are sensible, Jane," she assured me. "After all, He made herbs and flowers, and placed them in the earth for our use. The Lord of Heaven understands we women need, from time to time, to use them to enable us to live, so we might remain with our families, husbands and children, for as long as we can. The birthing chamber is a place of peril. A woman can die from the effort it takes to bring a child into the world, or after of fever of childbed. God does not mind, as long as we do our duty and breed, if we sometimes spread the gap between our children, or cease to breed when we have passed the time of our greatest strength."

When Mother spoke of death in childbed, she never said "I". She spoke of women in general, or of "we". I think it was how she lessened fears growing in her mind.

"Yes, my lady mother," I agreed. Although I always agreed with Mother, I also thought she was right. God loved us. He would not mind if we took steps to protect ourselves. "Would it not also work to ask a husband not to lie with his wife, if she was put in danger from having more children?" I asked.

Mother's lips grew thin. "It is the duty of every woman to submit when her husband requires it, daughter," was all she would say on the matter. I came to the conclusion that asking a husband not to lie with his wife was not likely to be successful. And she was correct it was the duty of a woman to submit. It was in the marriage vows, a special clause in that contract only for women, to be "*bonny*", which meant compliant, in bed.

On the day she told us she was with child, Mother also told us she was praying for a daughter like Catherine, apparently forgetting she had a daughter of her own already. I bowed my head and bit my lip. This daughter growing in Mother's belly was to be all that I was not, as far as I could tell. My mother wanted to teach this daughter to learn the ways of court, to speak French and possibly Latin. She would be a revered beauty; an object of courtly love. As Mother spoke, heading deeper and deeper into her fantasy of the perfect daughter, Catherine glanced at me with sympathy, but she could not lift her voice for me. Just as Catherine had her own mother, now she had another, one she had to please in order to survive in our house. I understood. Rare was the time anyone, even Father or Edward, tried to speak for me against the torrent that came from Mother. There was simply no point. Actually, it only seemed to make her worse. At times I wondered if Mother needed me to be so different to her, so disappointing. It was as though my ugliness and ineptitude made her more beautiful, more intelligent. As though I had to be small and pale, not only of skin but character, to make her shine brighter and bolder. I said such iniquitous thoughts to no one, but they grew in my mind.

Mother sent me out to collect haw berries that afternoon. They were thick on the hedges, hanging long and scarlet like open wounds. I brought back many, for they were good for Mother's remedies, but I had little thanks. Catherine was with Mother, and although my new sister had not been aiding the house or doing anything other than gossiping with Mother, Mother was better pleased with her than with me. I should have been used to it, but it stung.

But it seemed Catherine was not only set on pleasing our mother. I, who was not noticed much, noticed much others failed to see. Perhaps the eyes of others were busy elsewhere, and mine, being occupied only with the floor and the rushes, had more time to see. Mayhap I saw what they did not want to see. Perhaps I, who had run so often from Thomas, noted danger better when that old ill demon came stalking.

Our father had been more often at Wulfhall since the wedding. He said there was much on the estate which needed his attention, but the business of riding out to see tenant farmers, or observing cattle and crops was more often left to Henry and Edmund even when Father was at home. It seemed other things much more closely associated with the house required my father's attention.

It started with glances. My father looked for Catherine when he entered a room, and she did the same for him. They were often to be found in conversation, and it seemed whenever Edward was away from the house she sought out our father, praising him on his finely kept stables or the bountiful produce of his lands. Catherine always had a reason to find him, speak to him. My mother approved of all Catherine did, and mentioned many times that I could do no better than to ape all she did, but there was something about the manner that Catherine and my father had between them which gnawed at parts of my mind, biting suspicion into my flesh. Of what, I knew not, until one day in autumn.

It was one of the first days of autumn. I had gone upstairs to find a section of needlework I had left in my chamber. The day was misty, and a cold dampness had settled all about us. Leaves on the trees were rapidly turning from green to shades of amber and gold. Stopping to glance from one of the hallway windows, covered with oiled parchment to keep out the damp, yet open for light, I saw a fox scrabble up a short, bent tree; just a flash of red and he was gone. The tree was bent low to the ground, like an old man whose bones are failing, so he did not climb high, but into a nook he scrabbled, curling up, becoming small. Men came running after him and ran straight past the tree. It made me smile. Clever fox. They do not climb trees with grace, nor naturally, but apparently this one had learnt a trick to perform when pursued. Amongst leaves of fire and copper he would not be found. He must have raided a coop, or taken a young lamb perhaps. Foxes rarely did such things, but they would try if opportunity arose and their hunger was great enough. Shaking my head at bold Master Raynard, I walked on. The dim hallway, not lit by candles and oil lamps as it was by night, was shadowed, shades leaping as I wandered past painted panels decorated with the pomegranate of Queen Katherine and her portcullis, and the Tudor rose and lion of the King. They were always with us, our royal masters, little reminders each and every day.

I welcomed autumn. It was a cold but gentle season with much to surprise a soul; many tiny beauties. I loved the glistening spider webs in the low grass of the fields, the glittering sunlight in the daytime, wild winds at night; trees ablaze with colour and fruit to tempt the tongue and apples raining from branches as water from the skies. Red lights entered the heavens at night, roasting the skyline with brilliant shades of fire-like hue. Since the day was chilly and air sodden, my mother had ordered a good fire in the great hall, and brought us together to sew by it.

"On your way, Jane," she had said, turning her head my way as she barked orders at the servants, "bring Catherine down to join us. The fire will be warmer here than the one in her chambers."

"Yes, my lady mother," I said dutifully, and went upstairs, thinking that Catherine would probably rather sit at the hearth in her chambers. As a married woman, Catherine should have had the option, occasionally, to stay in her own chambers. As a daughter of the Seymour house, however, she did not. Mother was our Queen.

I found the needlework on my bed where I had left it, and, it in my hands, I went to seek Catherine. I came along the shadowed hallway at a normal pace, but at the edge of her door I stopped. I do not know what made me stop, but something did. It was as though a hand reached out and put itself to my breast, warning me. I heard whispered voices, a conversation that was pressing, heated. The tones of the voices made my cheeks ignite with colour although I knew not why. I could not hear what was said, but I wanted to. My curiosity was so intense it burned; black pepper on my tongue. I glanced up and down the corridor and saw nothing. I could hear steps sounding below, but not on this floor. I slid sideways to the hinge of the door, peeked through the tiny gap, and into Catherine's room.

I saw two figures, standing close together. They were whispering; words strange, insistent, earnest. It was Catherine, and my father. They were turned a little from me. Of Catherine I could not see a great deal but I could see my father's face. He looked strained, shocked, angry and oddly, pleased.

Catherine stepped forwards and put her hand to his face. "I cannot stop thinking of you, John," she whispered, her low voice throbbing with heat. "You are all I think of, every night, all day, in my dreams you are there. You haunt me."

"You are married to my son," he murmured, but he did not remove her hand from his cheek. He was staring at her as though his eyes were fixed to her face. "You know nothing can be between us, Catherine. You are my own daughter in the eyes of God!"

Still he did not remove her hand. He did not move away. I could see his eyes. There was a desperation in them I had never seen so plain, so obvious on a man's face.

"An accident of marriage, not one of blood, John," she said. "I am not your daughter in the eyes of God… how could I be?" Her fingers rose up, into his hair. I could only see her back, her body moving closer and closer to my father. His eyes closed, as though her touch was all the pleasure the world would ever hold for him. "If God knows all things, He knows for whom my heart sings. I knew, did you not know? From the first time I saw you in my father's hall I knew I had to be with *you*. I was meant for you and you for me."

"You are my son's wife." My father's voice was a croak.

"I agreed to marry Edward only because it would bring me to your house, John. I married *him* to bring me to *you*. You are the light of my heart, my true love. What else could I do? I could not allow my father to marry me to another man, be sent away, never to see you again! We are together now. Do not say you do not love me, for I see how you want me in your eyes." She stepped closer, bolder now. Breath caught in my throat. My heart was pounding so loud in my ears I thought they would hear it. But they could hear and see nothing but each other.

His hand caught hers, stopping her as she shifted towards him. His eyes opened, bright, hostile, and he stared fiercely at her. "This can be nothing, Catherine!" he said, his voice rising. "Nothing!"

He did not let go of her hand.

"Yet you do not deny you want me, my lord," she purred, head tilting, her tone teasing.

My father swallowed hard and dropped her hand. He ran his own through his hair and shook his head. "I do not want you," he said, his voice utterly unconvincing.

"You are a poor liar, my love," she said, "and it is as well for I love an honest man. I will wait. Know I wait for you to come to me, as I know you want to and as I want you to. Whenever you are ready, John, I will be too. Whenever and wherever you choose, I will be willing."

By God! Even I could feel the power in her words! It was as though heat rushed into that chamber, the haze of the sun stuck in air as light hits a cobbled courtyard. He was staring at her, naked lust in his eyes. I suddenly knew what the priests spoke of when they talked of the power of temptation. This was it! I had thought they talked of an urge akin to that when I wanted a honey cake, but this was something different. This was more powerful than anything I had seen. *Catherine is a witch,* I thought. She could not a normal woman be, with powers such as these, with the willingness to say things such as this to my father.

If I heard more I would faint or cry out, I knew it. I drew back from the door, shaking, nauseous, and slipped along the corridor. When I reach a bend, I put my back to the wall and stood there a moment, my heart pounding in my ears. What had I just heard? Catherine married my brother so she could come to Wulfhall because she loved my *father*? Was it possible, or was I running mad, my mind infested by the winds of autumn?

I heard the door of Catherine's chamber bang, footsteps retreated in the opposite direction. From the sound of the tread, the weight, it was my father. Catherine never moved with anything less than fluid, liquid grace. I waited a moment, then skittered to Catherine's door.

I knocked. There was a short laugh. "Enter," her voice called, faintly mocking. *She thinks you are Father, back already to beg for her bed,* I thought. A wave of nausea hit, threatening to knock me over.

I walked in as she turned, a great smile of triumph on her lips. Her blue eyes were bright as skies in winter before snow. If before she had looked beautiful, in that moment Catherine was too dazzling to behold. There was something terrible about her, dangerous, powerful. When she saw it was me she stopped, her smile falling. She managed to restore it, but it did not shine in her eyes. *Because it is not you she loves,* said a voice. *She loves your father.* Rage kindled in my soul.

"Jane," she said in a warm tone. "What an unexpected pleasure. What brings you to my rooms, sister?"

"Mother asks if you would like to join us at the fire in the great hall," I answered, wondering if she would note the heavy flush on my cheeks, the disgust and shock in my eyes. I dropped them to the floor. They were safer there.

"I would be honoured," she said gaily. "Let me gather my things and I will be with you directly."

I nodded and made for the door. As I walked slowly downstairs and back to the hall, my mind was in a riot of confusion. All I had thought of Catherine wavered and distorted within my mind, my soul. It was as though I had, all this time, been seeing one person and that person had shifted aside, revealing another behind them. As though a mask had been peeled from her face, revealing a demon underneath.

All admiration I had possessed for her, my fantasy of her and Edward as the perfect couple, my dreams of their children, their future at court, their love true and everlasting… all that was false. I thought my heart might break and my mind might shatter, a glass bead thrown to the ground.

But something in me could not believe it. I was unaccustomed to the art of placing trust in myself, after all. I so often was wrong. *I must be wrong about this,* I told myself. Catherine was too perfect to be so sinful, so wanton, so different a person from all she seemed. *I must have been mistaken.* I tried to banish what I had heard from my mind. Perhaps I had misheard. *That must be it.* I had misconstrued what I had seen and heard. I was constantly being told how ignorant I was, how foolish. Perhaps she was still the exquisite angel I had believed her to be; the one who was going to bring such happiness to my brother, and to me, to this household.

I was quiet as I sewed at my mother's side that day. She noted nothing. I was often quiet. I allowed her idle conversation with Catherine and Mary to flow over me as though I was not there. I was trying to convince myself that the dream I had had was still real; that Catherine was still my ideal, my golden, wondrous lady; that she must love my brother, as I did.

But I had a feeling, even as I tried to crush it. It was the same feeling I often had when I woke and a dream, so clear when I was within it, slipped from my mind. A dream that whilst I dreamt had seemed impossible to forget, became forgot, as my eyes opened and the sunlight of the day rained upon my face, banishing images of the night.

Chapter Ten

Wulfhall
Wiltshire

Autumn 1517

It was not long after my ears had been set afire and mind ablaze, that I was once more in the attics. I had come to seek out Alfred, the company of a friend, after another beating from my mother. Thomas had told her that I had stolen his best quill, and broken it. It was a way to explain the crime, as he had done it himself and did not want to be held responsible. Mother, as usual, believed him and took out her frustration on my rear with her willow whip.

Even with her belly swelling, my mother had possessed enough spirit to give my backside a rare beating that day. When she was done, she let me flee. Instead of the kitchens, that day I chose to go to the attics. I know not why. Many times since I wish I had done otherwise.

I was not in my usual seat by the window, but crouched at the back of the attic, behind chests of preserved potted marmalades, petting Alfred. I had not wanted to sit at the window and see the world that day; I wanted to hide from it. My inflamed buttocks did not wish to sit on anything either, so I was crouching, hidden away, when there came the sound of steps on the ladder.

I slid backwards into the dim corner, thinking it was Thomas come to attack me or a servant of Mother's sent to bring me back for another scolding. Alfred noted my stroking had ceased and dropped from my lap, wandering off to find a warm place to sleep away the afternoon. As the steps came higher up, I thought I recognised them as my brother's and I feared it was indeed Thomas, seeking to compound the nastiness of the day by smacking me on the fresh wounds my mother had inflicted. But as a head rose into the attic, I saw a hood covering golden hair. Catherine. No other in the world had hair like hers. Thinking she might have come to seek me out to comfort me, I almost emerged from my hiding place, but as she gained the top of the ladder, she looked back and down. There was something agitated, excited, and rushed about her. I kept still. Another figure was climbing up rapidly behind her.

Father.

As he reached the top, he stood for a moment staring at her. Her eyes gazed boldly back. There was a challenge in them. He rushed towards her with a sound as though he was in pain. Pushing her up against one of the beams of the attic, he pushed his body against hers, forcing his lips to her mouth, running eager hands over the curves of her breasts. He pulled at her gown with rough and violent hands until her large, pert breasts came from their velvet coverings. He buried his head in them, groaning, moaning her name.

Catherine's face was a mask of triumph. She laced her hands through his hair, grabbed it viciously, making him wince, and pulled him to her, tipping her head back and laughing softly as he began to push up her skirts. She did not stop him, but hopped backwards, so her rear was on one of the chests. He fumbled at the strings of his breeches, pushed her gown up, so it bunched and gathered at her hips. My sister opened her legs eagerly, pulling him to her with little high sounds of impatience. He dropped his breeches so they were about his ankles, and thrust into her. Catherine let out a short noise of surprise and pain, but wrapped her legs about his hips and scrambled ever-closer to him.

My father was letting out sounds as though he was in agony, muffled and strange from against her neck. Catherine breathed out in quick, high sighs. She clung to him, whispering his name and words of love.

I stared in abject, mute horror as I watched my father driving into her like a rampant boar. He got faster and faster. His hands grasped hold of her hair, pulling at it as she had done to him, but Catherine merely smiled and tipped her head. He rutted into her with such force that the chest under them shook, banging against the floor.

Catherine fell backwards, her hands on his shoulders, letting out eerie, high noises of pleasure which only seemed to encourage him. I could see my father's buttocks, shining white in the dappled light from the closed shutters, battling against her with such speed that I thought he must be hurting her, but she seemed not to mind. And then, as he seemed to reach the height of his speed and force, he pulled backwards in an ungainly manner, stumbled. He spilled his seed onto the chest under them and into the gathered bunches of her skirts.

I seemed to have stopped breathing, but I knew I had not, for I could smell them. Their sweat, Catherine's rose perfume, the seed of my father. It was on the air of the attic. I was breathing in their lust. I thought I might be sick.

For a long time, they lay half over the chest. He on top of her, panting, and she with her beautiful gown creased about her hips, stroking her hands through his hair. "I have wanted you so long, my love," she whispered, kissing his face. "I wish you had spilled your seed within me." He lifted a weary head and abruptly stepped back from her, swiftly wiping himself and pulling up his breeches.

"It was a moment of weakness," he muttered. "It will never happen again."

"It will happen again, and again, and again, John," she said, still lying there, breasts exposed and soft curls of fair hair between her legs in plain view. "It will happen because I know how you want me, and I want you too… it will happen because you will know I will always be ready, whenever you want me. It will happen because you will not be able to help yourself."

"It will not happen again," he said. I too could hear the doubt in his voice. I despised him for it.

Catherine laughed her low, throaty laugh. "Deceive yourself if you wish, my love," she said. "But you will think of me. My bed is cold and empty, John, and you will come to it. We were meant for each other, you and I. When you stop denying it, the happier we all will be."

"You are my son's wife," he said, tying the last strings of his breeches and running his hands through his hair.

"I am *yours*, and ever will be," she murmured, stretching her arms back over her head and gazing at him, long sooty eyelashes resting on her pale cheeks. She was so very beautiful. "And I promise you, John, none shall ever know of our love. This is the perfect arrangement, is it not? For you can take me whenever you wish, and if there is a child then all will believe it is your son's."

"I will spill no seed within you," he said, his voice harsh. "I will not make my son a cuckold."

"Edward will never know." She ran a fair hand over her breasts. "Come, John, what harm do we do? If none ever know, there is no sin for any to see. I have my love, you have yours. Edward will have the wife he wants and children to please him. None will ever know they are not truly his."

"You are a witch!" my father gasped, although I noted he was staring at those delicate fingers which wended a path over her breasts. "You have enticed me into sin."

"I hardly had to *try*, John, did I?" She giggled. "You wanted me, and now you will want me all the more. You have but sipped from the cup of pleasure. Be honest, my love. Does not the danger and secret excite you? It does me." She sat up, running her hands up his chest and staring into his eyes. I saw him shiver as she dropped her hands to his breeches, and started to slowly unlace them, eyes darting to his face as she spoke. "Come, my love, come to me once more…"

He pulled back from her and walked to the ladder. "It will not happen again, Catherine," he said, his back to her.

She lay back on the chest and I heard her soft laugh. "It will happen, many times and in many places, my love," she said. There was certainty and triumph in her voice. She knew she had won. And from the way his back stiffened, wincing with pain or humiliation, or both, my father knew it too.

Father's back remained taut a moment, then he clambered over the ladder top. I heard his footsteps retreating along the hall. Catherine sighed and stood up, rearranging her gown and smoothing her skirts. Before she left, she gazed about the barn. For a moment I thought I would be seen, but I was not. She put a hand to her mouth, feeling the impression of my father's lips on hers, and she smiled. She had never looked as wondrous as she did then, nor as wicked. She smoothed her hair, rearranged her hood, and carefully climbed from the attic.

I stood in the shadows. The strange scent of sweat and seed polluted the air. I had been struck dumb and numb. I could feel nothing; not even the wheals on my rear from my mother's whip. It took me a long time to climb from the attics that day, and when I did I felt as though I had come to the steps of the ladder as another person. One who has seen what they should not; one who understands things they never should have. It was true. I had been right. I had not mistaken what I had seen or heard. I was right.

Catherine and my father; my father and Catherine. She said that she loved him. She was betraying my brother, and my father was betraying my mother. My father was bedding his own daughter! Not flesh and blood was Catherine, but his daughter in the eyes of God she was because she was married to his son! Although I knew my father was far from faithful to his wife, this was different. This was a sin beyond any I could imagine. I was dazed with the knowledge I possessed. Sick with it. And I was lost.

I felt my mind come undone, a frayed rope tied to a boat and a post, threads unwinding, unclasping, one at a time falling away.

Should I tell someone? *But who will believe you?* I asked myself. My mother would not, I knew that. Edward? Even if he did believe me, could I hurt him so much? Could I tell him that his wife was lying with his own father, under his nose? That she was going to have our father's children, our half-brothers, sisters, and pass them off as Edward's children? I knew not. For now, I kept the secret. I knew not what else to do but keep it.

In my heart and belly it sat, a little worm. From time to time I would almost forget it was there, and then it would shift, a rotten core within me. Something that could shatter all I knew. Within me was the secret of our family's destruction. Within me was a darkness I had never known existed.

Chapter Eleven

Wulfhall
Wiltshire

Winter- Spring 1518

That year, in the depths of the winter snow, my mother took to her bed and brought forth a hale, hearty and screaming girl. The noise of my new sister shocked me, for snow had made the world fall silent, so it seemed. All I had seemed to hear for the time before her calls entered the world was stillness; a hushed hiss of snow falling at night, the soft thump of a pillow of snow falling from a branch, the quiet *pat, pat* as a robin hopped along, seeking a shallow place to hunt creatures hiding under the vast, open whiteness. Snow had piled about the outbuildings, up one side of the barn in particular after one driving night storm. Men had tied lengths of rope from stables to barns, and then to their houses, otherwise at night, blackness broken only by whirling white, a man might stray from the path and die in the cold.

For many days we had lingered in my mother's chamber, Mary, Catherine, me and my mother's maids, waiting for the pains to start and the child to be born. Only female relatives were allowed to be present when a woman gave birth, and Mother wanted me to be aware of how a child was born. I was considered old enough. I was ten.

For weeks we waited and it was dull as dirty dry sticks. Supposedly there was much to see and do, as hangings had been sent for from other houses of kinsmen nearby, to decorate the rooms, and Mother had the best candles, as pregnancy and childbirth made the eyes of women weak. Cabinets filled with the best plate of the house were heaved up to her rooms before the lying-in time came, so the babe would be surrounded by our wealth when they entered the world, making them aware of their place in society. Symbols of power would greet the next sibling I possessed. There was, too, a Bible in the room and other books, but all must be worthy books, nothing flighty or romantic, in case it affected the mind of the new babe. But for all that there was that was supposed to entertain or divert us, it was not enough.

The shutters were up all night and most of the day, making the rooms dark and no windows were opened, so it became stuffy despite the cold air outside. Not a window was opened because not only was it winter and we had no wish to fill the chamber with snow and icy wind, but it would bring spirits of sickness upon Mother and her child, and women were more vulnerable to wandering demons in pregnancy or childbed. They might come for the child, or kill Mother. They might try to steal the soul of mother and babe.

Time passed. We played cards and dice, Mother read to us from the Bible and Mary recited passages too. Catherine sang. We sewed by the fireside, hearing, rather than seeing, snow wash down the windows like water. We went to bed early as the light faded and rose late, when it returned. Oftentimes, as was the way in winter, there were two sleeps in the night, one early and one later. We would sleep, wake in the cold, black night and talk a while, then enter a second slumber. Some people got up at such times, sat by the fire, ate a plate of food or did work. Mary told me that some couples used the time to embrace. Supposedly it was the best time for the conception of children. Thinking of my father and Catherine, I flushed and looked away. Mother and Mary laughed at my innocence.

Days became as one. Although I was accustomed to spending time indoors, indeed, occupied with the self same tasks I did during that winter, I came to feel tired of it. Before I had even opened my eyes I felt weary, as though I had not slept, which was strange for in some ways it felt as though we were sleeping all day, as if we had fallen into dreams unending which all were the same. As days began to blur, all lifeless, all the same, I felt faded and weighted down, stuck in some otherworld, an underworld-like limbo where nothing was good or bad and nothing ever changed. There was no sorrow and no joy, no laughter and no tears. The monotony of our existence became exhausting. It was supposed to be restful but it did not feel that way for me. My heart wanted a chance to leap, in fright if not for pleasure, but nothing was there that could do such a thing. Nothing was there at all.

At night when I lay in bed with Catherine and Mary, for we all had to share beds inside those chambers and were not to leave and sleep in our own rooms, I heard the wind keening, screaming at times, about the walls of Wulfhall. It did not scare me, but felt like it was calling to me. I wanted to followed the lunacy in its wild call, to rise from the bed and run to it, leap into its feral arms, but I could not. Where would I go but out into a storm of snow that would kill me? Yet the wildness and recklessness of that voice in the wind of the storm kept calling. If I asked a priest, I knew he would tell me it was the Devil trying to tempt me from my dutiful place at my mother's side, pull me from the warmth and safety of the house of my father. Yet I was so restless all I wanted was to run into that tempest of white and wailing wind, even if it cost me my life.

I could not wait for my mother's childbed to begin. And when it did, all I wanted was for it to stop.

It was horrific. Nothing could have prepared me for the deep, guttural screams my mother made, for the thick, gamey smell of blood and membrane which spilled from her, or for the blinding terror in her eyes as the pains grew worse. The midwife who came from the nearby town for the birth said my mother was lucky; it had been just ten hours from first signs of pain to the birth of the child.

"A fortunate woman brings her children out fast," she gloated from between my mother's legs as she watched the head of the child cresting from my mother's body. "Pant, pant, my lady, do not push whilst the head is coming, or you will tear yourself and harm the babe."

My mother, her shaking hands slipping in her own sweat on the sides of the groaning chair, a special chair with a hole in the seat so the child could be received through it, gave a wail of frustration and agony as she did as she was bidden. This old crone crouched under her had been at each one of her labours since my dead brother John had been born. My mother trusted her with her life, which was what childbirth was all about for women… life… either to lose theirs, the child's, or win both. No one could ever be sure how a birth would turn out, and the more children a woman had, the more chances for her to die during it, or after. Mother had confessed and made her wishes for her private goods known to my father before she entered the chamber. The priest had blessed her before her pains grew bad so if she died she would die with the last rites upon her soul. The midwife would bless the child if it was thought to be in trouble, baptise it so it would achieve Heaven. The thought of death was present even as Mother struggled to bring life from her body.

"Now, my lady," cackled the old woman, revealing a black, empty mouth, devoid of teeth. "Push!"

My mother let out a groan like a ewe in labour, and threw her remaining power at the push. The child seemed to slip from her, plopping into the hands of the midwife and almost immediately letting out a huge, crackling, healthy cry. The midwife measured the cord binding baby to mother, and cut it. Happy though I was to see the child, and my mother safe through this, I almost vomited. The smell was like game hung to rot a while, to make it rich, succulent.

"Good lungs," said the midwife, rubbing the child with a linen cloth and taking her to be bathed in oil and good Rhenish wine. "A fine and pretty daughter, my lady," she announced to my mother, who had fallen, exhausted, leaning over one arm of her groaning chair as Catherine bathed her forehead with a cloth soaked in vinegar and water. There was a muffled cry from my newest sister as the midwife wiped the baby's gums and tongue with honey and wine, to encourage her belly to lust for food.

"A daughter." My mother sounded as triumphant as she was tired. She had wanted a girl. Sagging in the chair, she allowed herself to be washed and cleansed. There were more pains, not as bad as the ones that brought my sister to the world. I watched with fresh revulsion and fascination as the slippery mess of the baby's cowl fell from my mother. The midwife stuck an exploratory finger into my mother to check it had all come out. "Best to make sure," she said, looking at me and clouding my face with breath so foul I thought I might faint. "If it's not all out, it can cause fever and death for a poor mother."

But she was satisfied. The midwife did not think there was an urgent need to baptise the child here and now, for the little baby seemed healthy and not about to die, but she did it anyway, just in case. She burned the baby's bloody cowl in the roaring fire. "To keep the Devil from chasing the soul of the babe." She nodded to me. "'Tis important such things are done for the protection of the babe until she is baptised in church. Until a priest has blessed the child the Devil may still try to come for her, and we must protect her from him, and from limbo."

I shivered at grim words, spoken so blithely. But I supposed she dealt with such things as the Devil and eternal exclusion from the realm of the Almighty every day, and clearly she knew her profession well. I wondered what it was like to bring babes into the world, and often, to see them and their mothers die on the same day; to know what prayers and magics to use to protect the child from the Devil. A midwife had the power to perform baptism if she thought the child was likely to die, and it was a power granted by the Church. *Such a power, given to such crude and basic peasant women,* I thought. To have the power of a *priest*, to bless and save the soul of a child! There were few times in this world a woman could be so important, could make as much impact, as this woman and others like her.

I brought Mother her caudle, a drink made for women who had just given birth, rich with spices that would aid her recovery and brewed in hot wine, to revive her. My new sister was cleaned with oil and wine and swaddled; wrapped in clean linen cloth bands from head to toes. She would be unswaddled and cleaned each day, but as all babes would spend most of the time bound in cloth. It was necessary or her limbs would not grow straight. Some mothers altered their baby's natural appearance by swaddling, binding one part tight or another loose to change the shape of the body, the bones, but my mother did not hold with it. She refused to allow my sister to be bound tight about the chest, a trick some women used which might grant my new sister a fatter appearance by creating the impression of a thicker neck. She thought Elisabeth, as her name was, beautiful as she was.

"God made her this way, so this is how she stays," she told the midwife.

"I think it healthier in any case, my lady," the crone agreed. "Some think crushing a babe's chest healthy, for I have heard it can prove beneficial against consumption, but I have ever thought the opposite." The midwife explained that sometimes patients did things she did not think wise and much as she might try to offer other alternatives, they would do as they wanted. "People do as people want," she said. "It is up to them, for all were granted free will, and only a parent is master of their child."

The wet nurse arrived to try my sister's appetite that same hour. It was best, it was said, for the babe to start feeding immediately. My sister was a hearty eater. The wet nurse, selected for her clear skin and fair hair, had been on a good, plain diet of white bread, meat, almonds and hazelnuts and fine wine for weeks before the day she was to start feeding my sister. She was not to eat onions or garlic, vinegar or spices, as they would make her milk poor. Medicines for the baby, if required, would be eaten or drunk by her, and enter Elisabeth's belly through her milk. It was thought the best way. When my sister grew in years, the wet nurse would chew meat for her. It was a good position in the household, and one that came with gifts, for it was traditional to bestow many upon a wet nurse. It made their character sweet and clement, therefore their milk too.

Mother looked sad as her child was fed by another woman, but it was ever the way of things. Women of noble blood did not feed their own children; that was something only peasants did, and feeding a child inhibited a woman's ability to conceive. No man wanted his wife unable to bear more sons.

We bound Mother's leaking breasts, weeping at the sound of her child crying or feeding, in cabbage leaves and linen. Changed and washed each day these pads were, until her milk dried safely. "Bind not too tight," said the midwife as I aided her. "Too tight and the milk is trapped, and makes the mother sick."

Mother was confined to her bed for three days, the room kept dark for the sake of her eyes, damaged by childbirth. After three days she was allowed to sit up in bed and upon her *upsitting* we celebrated with a meal in her chamber, where we all drank to my sister and to my mother's health. After that, she was allowed up and about but only in her chamber. She had to wait forty days to be churched and was not allowed around the house during that time, but she was allowed visitors.

My sister, Elisabeth, pleased my mother more than I ever could. Elisabeth was a charming baby who hardly seemed to cry or fuss, and was simply sweet and gentle through her childhood. My mother praised her, showed her to all who visited, and always, I think, loved her more than me, her most disappointing daughter. My sister seemed, from the first, to have inherited the lion's share of my mother's beauty, and my mother often mourned that Elisabeth had not been born before me, so that she could be the first daughter to offer as a marriage prize. Oddly, I did not mind. Having witnessed the horrors my poor mother had endured, and endured with prodigious courage I might add, I was glad she had emerged with a reward so great. I was accustomed to her criticism, though I liked it no more than I had in the past, but I was glad my new sister was not to share my fate. Any fool could see Elisabeth was a beauty, and was good by nature. I did not resent my sister. I loved her.

As my mother, confined in her chambers, crowed over her new daughter, Catherine grew in prominence in the house. With Mother absent, Catherine found new power. She requested changes to her chambers. The ones she held presently, she claimed, were too small for her and Edward. She kept her bedroom, but Father granted her more chambers, had them cleaned out and painted so they were dazzling. She seemed also to be the recipient of more money than Mary or I were from our father, and Catherine bought herself fine bolts of cloth to make new gowns, hoods and sleeves. Mary grumbled about this to me, but she could say nothing against our father. He was the head of the house, and it was up to him which dependant or daughter he favoured more. But I knew the reason Catherine got all she asked was because she was secretly my father's mistress. That encounter I had witnessed in the attics had not been the end of their affair, no matter what he had protested at the time. Before we had entered the lying-in chamber and after we emerged, I heard Catherine's door creak and the bed in her room rock in the small hours of the night when Edward was not at home. I knew my father was bedding his daughter again and again. His wife, my own mother, was recovering from the ordeal of childbed and this time, rather than seek the comfort of a maid's body he slaked his lust on the wife of his son.

They were careful, covert, but I saw the glances which passed between them. I heard the sighs and groans in the night. I knew he visited her almost every night, and I was sure there were many other encounters in dark corners of the house.

I was not the only one hiding in the shadows anymore.

*

Edward came back to visit just after Mother walked to the chapel with her lighted candle and was blessed at the pew by the priest. Her churching complete, Mother was allowed back to roam freely about the house and land. Mother returned from her blessing and greeted her son, removing the veil that she had been required to wear during her churching to kiss him. She was overjoyed to have Edward home. Catherine looked pleased and said she was, but I caught a sour whiff of disgust coming from her when she glanced at my brother. She was not merry he was home, just as she was not that my mother had rejoined the household. Both of them stopped her doing what she wanted to do. Both of them reduced her power in the house, as my father's mistress.

When my brother went to her bed I did not hear her call out as she did when my father visited; a muffled cry of deep pleasure called into the sheets of her soft bed. When Edward was with her there was the rocking of the bed, the groans he made, but she was silent. I imagined her, lying there, with my handsome brother doing the things that my father did, and I imagined her face. She did not love Edward. She loved my father. She welcomed my father to her bed. Edward she merely endured.

Edward did not seem to notice anything was amiss. He would come home for a few days, take meals with us, tell us court news, bed his wife, and leave for court once more, never knowing that all this time his wife was playing him for a fool.

I watched her power growing in the household. I came to hate her for it. She had my father bound to her in sin. She had charmed my mother so she thought Catherine the perfect daughter, and all others seemed to recognise the new power in the house, and bowed to her as well. I was the only one who knew her secret. In time, I decided I must say something, or see my soul fly apart with the pressure of knowing things born of sin, darkness, and deceit.

Chapter Twelve

Wulfhall
Wiltshire

Early Summer 1518

I went to Catherine's chamber one afternoon. My mother was busy with her babe, with her new wet nurse, and with Mary, who, finally, after so many years of marriage to Cousin Edmund was at last carrying his child. Such happiness had fallen on Mary that she had become almost pretty. Joy was shining from her every pore.

I was happy for her, and as I noticed my mother's distraction that morn, happier still. I was going to use this time. I would confront Catherine. I was determined to tell Catherine that I knew about her and my father, and to tell her to stop, or else I would tell my mother.

As all best and wildest plans made by children, this one was of fantasy formed. I had seen it all already in my mind. Catherine would hang her head in shame, would say she knew what she had done was wrong. The affair would cease that day and none would ever know it had happened. My father's soul would be saved from sin of incest, my brother would never know the shame of his cuckolding, or of raising children that were not his. And I would never have to tell anyone else that I knew. I would never have to tell my mother, my brother, anyone. The secret would be kept. The people I loved would be saved the truth and live in happiness, for ever more.

If only such dreams as dreamed by children could be.

Yet for all my fantasy about how this would turn out, I was nervous as I stood at her door. Palms sweating, brow damp with perspiration, I looked at my hands and saw them shake. I had almost lost my nerve entirely when she opened the door and stared at me in surprise. Catherine was dressed for riding; a tight tunic over her gown and a cap on her head. Her black mask, there to shelter her pale skin from the sun, was in her hands as well as her gloves. The sun mask, devoid of features with but holes for the eyes and mouth also had a cord with a dark pebble attached. This was to go in her mouth, to hold it in place. Some had ribbon that went about the head, but most were like hers. The pebble rocked against her gloves as she opened the door. For some reason I was, for a moment, mesmerized by it.

I knew she was to go out with my father that day and take a tour of the estates, but I also knew they were going to find another place, more quiet than the house, to rut. Perhaps in the forest where none would hear her cries of joy at his touch, or in one of the hunting lodges which he maintained on his lands. She stared at me as she opened the door and smiled. "Sister," she cooed. I hated the way she spoke. Once her voice had sounded like music. It seemed so false now. "What are you doing, hiding there?"

"I came to speak to you, sister," I said and nodded to the chamber behind her. "I think we should speak in there, in private."

"How very mysterious." She laughed, opening the door wider and turning to walk back into the room. "But I cannot stay long, Jane. Your father awaits me. We are to view lands to the east of his estates, for he thinks that perhaps, when there is money enough, a hall could be built there with chambers for Edward and me." She widened her smile. "For the time may soon come when we will have a child of our own, and we will need a larger place. You can come and see us there, would you like that?" She chuckled. "Mayhap you can come live with us, escape your mother."

Intended though it was as a bond between us, I knew her reasons for wanting to escape my mother were very different to mine. Cruel though my mother could be, thoughtless at times, she was nothing as wicked as the woman before me. It had not occurred to me until that time that there were different kinds of sin. The kind my mother favoured was not conscious. Ones Catherine revelled in were.

I shut the door and looked at her. She was so striking in her black riding coat. The cap on her head held a long white feather, which drooped becomingly over one side of her face. They were more gifts from my father, I had no doubt. Payment for whoring.

"You are the mistress of my father," I said, words falling from my lips in a rush. I blinked, surprising myself. I had not meant to say it so bluntly.

Catherine laughed, shaking her head. "What is this, Jane?" she asked as though thoroughly amused, "is it a jape you and Thomas have thought up to tease me?" She looked about. "Is he hidden nearby?"

"It is no jest, nor jape," I said, my voice faltering, falling to a whisper. "I saw you in the attic. I was hiding from Thomas and I saw you, and my father. I saw what you did."

Her smile froze. Her eyes became hard, blue ice, as she narrowed them. "I know not what you mean," she lied. "I have never been to the attics, why would I? It must have been a kitchen maid you saw your father with. You should not say anything, Jane. It would upset your mother. Men are apt to stray from their wives when they are carrying children. I am sure it was nothing to worry on."

"It was you," I insisted. "And I have heard him come to you many a time since. Do you think the walls between our rooms are so thick that I could not hear you? Hear you call his name and tell him that you love him? And hear him... when he groans." I shivered with revulsion. "It is disgusting. You are his daughter in the eyes of the law and in the eyes of God!"

"And what do you intend to do with the information you have, little sister?"

Catherine smiled no more. Her tone sounded light, yet something bristled inside me, telling me it was dangerous. Her eyes were no more sky, blue and sweet, but burning coal, fixed on mine. She seemed to have ceased to blink. Catherine had become very still. I did not trust her stillness. I took a step back. It felt like the moment before Alfred jumped on a mouse, before a snake strikes.

"You will end this affair with my father," I commanded, trying to keep my voice firm. "You will stop playing my brother for a cuckold, and be his true wife, as you promised when you married him, otherwise…"

"Otherwise, what?" She was dreadfully calm. I had expected tears, protestations, threats, but she was still and quiet, watching me.

"Otherwise, I will tell my mother, and she will put you from this house!" I said boldly. "Edward will leave you, and you will be known throughout the land as a whore, a jade! They will shave your head and parade you through the streets. You will be whipped in the centre of the town and…"

Quick as a hawk, she was on me. I barely had time to cry out in shock before she leapt, talons out so they dug into my arm. She pressed one hand over my mouth, and with the other took hold of my ear, pulling me down towards the floor. I felt a ripping, stretching pain and called out. I was silenced. Her fingers pressed into my mouth.

"You will say *nothing*," she snarled through gritted teeth. Her eyes flashed with fury, her nostrils flared, white-tipped, as she pushed her face close to mine. "*Nothing*! Do you hear me, little *sister*? If you breathe one word of this to another soul, I will go to your father and tell him I found you bent over a hay stack with stable boys lining up to take turns between your thighs! I will tell your mother, too. Which of us do you think they will believe? The little liar, constantly beaten and corrected for her many, many sins, or the perfect daughter, married to their perfect son?"

"My father will know I speak the truth," I said, words squeaking from me as she pulled painfully on my earlobe again as though she meant to rip it from my head.

"Your father will agree to label you the whore, Jane, not me," she boasted, and let out a mirthless laugh. "He is head of this house, not you, and not your miserable sow of a mother. He will keep my secret and sacrifice you. He will keep the mistress whom he loves, and his reputation too. Do you think he will allow you to spoil him in the eyes of his sons, his wife, his servants? Do you think he cares for you at all? Many a time, in my bed, he has spoken of his disappointment in you, his ugly little Jane, and now, they have another daughter. What need have they of you? An ill-favoured, dim-witted little fool who sneaks about in shadows taking note of matters which do not concern her? Do you really think they will believe you, over me, when I am everything and you nothing?"

She sneered into my face. Searing tears sprang to my eyes. Catherine spoke truth, and I knew it. I knew it, for only truth can hurt the soul. Lies cannot. They have not that power. All she said cut to the quick of my spirit so all she said was truth. Nothing had ever hurt me as much as the truths she lashed me with. Catherine was cleverer than me. She was beautiful. If she indeed had such control over my father as she believed she did, there was nothing I could do to stop her. It would be *me* cast out, not her. Me who was branded or had my head shaved, who would be stripped to the waist and marched through the streets so all could witness my shame and see my sin. And my father would allow it. He would allow me to be treated ill to save Catherine, to save his reputation. I would be sacrificed. I would be cast down to keep them high.

"You are a witch," I hissed, tears burning my eyes. In all my feeble life I never felt so helpless, so useless. "You are a witch."

"Say you will say nothing, Jane, *nothing*!" Spittle dropped from her lips, falling onto my face. It ran slow and sullen down my cheek. "Or I will go to your father this instant and tell tales of his daughter which will turn him green. Before this week is out, I will have you whipped from this house and sold to a nunnery, or to the lowest bidder he can find."

"I have never known a man," I protested. "I am only ten years old!"

"Many a whore started her career earlier," Catherine hissed. "And you are not listening, little mouse. It does not matter what the truth is. It matters only what I choose to say. If I tell your father you are a threat, he will remove you. Now, swear to me you will say nothing."

"I swear..." I gasped as she pulled my ear again. "I swear!"

"Swear on the lives of your family... on the life of your precious brother, Edward!" she demanded and then stopped. She let go of my ear and got off me. Catherine walked to the other side of the room and picked up a book from the table. I got up and staggered away from her, clutching my throbbing ear.

"Swear on this," she said, and thrust the book towards me. It was Catherine's copy of the New Testament. I felt my face run pale. If I did such a thing, I was bound to keep my promise, for to swear on God's Holy book and then go back on it was to ensure my soul was damned. To swear an oath on the Bible was to make God your witness and if you went back on your word it made God a liar. I would be cursed. I would go to Hell, if I did not keep my word.

She took a step towards me. "Swear it," she hissed. "Or I go to your father now."

I put a shaking hand on the book, sick, and dizzy. Catherine no longer looked beautiful. She was wild, fierce, and ugly. Her nostrils flared with rage. Her cheeks were crimson, her eyes burned. She looked like the Devil. I wondered how she did not burst into flame, holding a Holy text in her hands.

"I swear," I choked.

"What do you swear?" she pressed.

"I will tell none that you are the *whore* of my father," I said bitterly, looking up at her with fire in my own eyes. My jaw wobbled, tears fell, but I kept my eyes on her. "I will tell none that you betray vows you swore before God to honour my brother. I will tell none that you use Edward, my brother and a good and honourable man, as a cuckold. I will tell none that you are a filthy, stinking jade who takes her own father to her bed. I will tell none you are a liar, a trickster and that you will place a cuckoo in my brother's nest. I will tell none that I hate you more than any other being of this world, for all that you do, for all that you are."

She did not flinch once. When I finished, I took my trembling hand from her book. "Then we have an understanding, do we not, sister?" she said.

She turned from me, and flounced from the door. I sat down on the bed, shaking. I felt I might vomit. Never had I felt so sick and lost in my life. And I had sworn to protect her secret, for fear of what she might do to me. I had sworn on the Bible! It could not be undone. I had no way to save Edward from humiliation, from this evil between my father and his daughter. I had no way to show anyone the Devil in a dress hidden under the rafters of our own house. I was trapped, and she would be allowed to continue to corrupt my father and to bring sin to our house.

I left the room that day utterly defeated. I knew Catherine was right. If she told my father he would move to destroy me first. Even if they did not defame me in public for being a whore, I would be packed off to a nunnery, or sent to another house. If I did marry, I would marry so far beneath my already spare expectations that I would never know what society was. Only a man of evil would accept me. I would end my days in terror and tyranny. I was a fool to have gone to Catherine. I had revealed myself and my intentions, trusting that she would agree to end this and be a good wife to my brother. But there was nothing of goodness in her. She was evil, and worse, she was evil hiding behind a pretty face and a bewitching manner. She was the cleverest of devils, for unlike ones in the books my mother showed me Catherine did not wear horns, or have an ugly face. She was hidden in plain view. No one would believe she was as depraved as she was, because she was so very beautiful.

That night I dreamed I was walking down stairs. The stairs were made of glass. They shattered as my foot fell upon them and I tumbled. Space and darkness, barren and wide, was all that was beneath me. I fell. I fell forever, and did not stop.

Chapter Thirteen

Wulfhall
Wiltshire

Autumn 1518- Summer 1519

That autumn as mist swirled about Wulfhall, we were plunged into mourning. The Queen had been with child again, and again had lost her baby.

"A daughter," my mother said, sorrow dripping from her voice, as she read aloud a missive from Edward at court. "She was stillborn." Mother was six months gone with a child herself, and this news affected her greatly.

Mother insisted that the entire household wear black armbands to honour the Queen and show respect for her pain. "At least she still has the Princess Mary," said Catherine. Mother nodded, wiping tears from her eyes. Never did I see her more upset than when on behalf of Katherine the Queen.

"It is just…" she said one day out of nowhere as winter flew upon us, "… the Queen is so good, Jane. So very good and so godly. There never will be a heart more pure than hers. It seems so unfair that God should deny her a son. It seems not right, in some ways."

She stopped and crossed herself. Speaking against the will of God was something only heretics would do. "God must have a plan," she said. Her eyes went back to her sewing, yet not a stitch more did she sew that day.

But I sewed. It was my solace then, as it had been before and would again. With every stitch I bound the darkness in me, the fear, the hatred. I pinned down my feelings, impaled them; prisoners upon that cloth. My hatred could not escape, fear could not harm me, whilst I lashed it to cloth. Sometimes I thought I sewed my sanity to me as well, tied that down so it could not escape. So young was I, and so haunted.

That was to be the last time our good Queen was made sad by death emerging from her womb, although at the time we knew it not. Queen Katherine never grew thick with child or giddy with promise again. That stillborn daughter was the last her womb would try to bear, the last child she would lose; the last hope. I did wonder, as time went on and it seemed less and less likely the Queen would bear another child, if it was a relief. Although Katherine could not have known for sure, as we did not, that that was her last pregnancy, I had to wonder if coming to the end of her time to try to bear children would bring respite. To know hope only to have it dashed so cruelly to the ground time after time must have been a tortuous existence. At least when hope was gone, there was no lifting of the spirits only for a corresponding fall to come, no great, blinding light that faded to obscure darkness.

All the Queen's efforts went into her daughter. Katherine believed Mary would marry and be the Queen of England, perhaps Queen regnant, although such a thing had not been done before. It was said the Princess would have a son, and that son would rule, as King Henry II had when his mother the Empress Matilda had handed her claim down to him. What people did not dare mention was that before that time there had been civil war raging in England for decades as Matilda fought Stephen, another claimant, for the throne. But that ill-boding thought was in people's minds when they spoke of Mary Tudor and her claim. I could see a silver glint of sword and armour in the eyes of people when they thought about the lack of a male heir. I could see they thought war would come.

*

Christmas came and went as always it did. We gathered in the great hall to tell stories on Christmas Eve where, after an entire Advent of fasting and prayer, eating fish rather than flesh and taking no meat, milk, eggs or other treats on the Eve of Christmas itself, our hungry minds were played by hungry bellies. It was easy to believe anything. Ghosts could walk and monsters breathe upon our necks on the Eve of Christmas. All was possible. The borders between worlds might open, as they did at Midsummer and Allhallowtide, but unlike those times, we were safe at Christmas. That was why we could dare to tell stories, risk saying aloud the names of spirits which at others times might come to haunt us. Christmas Eve was safe because demons and spirits were rendered powerless that night. The light of the Lord of Heaven, Jesus Christ, was already entering the world on the Eve of Christmas. He held us all safe.

As we heard tales by the fireside that Christmas Eve, there was a roar from outside. In through the doors burst performers, mummers and singers. Father must have paid for them to come, or they would have called elsewhere. One did not go about invading the house of a gentleman after all; it was likely to lead to death by the hand of one of his men mistaking performer for pilferer. Father pretended to know nothing of it, however, laughing and welcoming them in, cheeks flushed bright with wine, as if he had not seen them before. Mother smiled, her face gentle, pretty, at his antics. No doubt he reminded her of the King in his old romantic days with Katherine. Mother was upon her good seat near the fire, one hand on her swelling belly, watching her husband cavort and laugh with the performers. But when they came to do their pieces, tableaux acted out with one player reading stories from the Bible, and later as the singers sang old carols, Father was not looking at my mother and smiling at her. Another lady had his eye.

At the stroke of midnight it was said all the cattle all over the world would kneel, letting out a long groan as they did so, to honour the coming of our Lord Jesus. I often wondered if anyone checked. It was unlikely. Men of my father's lands gave extra fodder to livestock on Christmas Eve, partly to honour the event, and partly so they did not have to feed them so early on Christmas Day when they wanted to be celebrating, or nursing swollen and painful heads. It was hard to know, therefore, if the tale of the cattle taking a knee was true, for no one was ever there to witness it.

Not long after the performances that night Mother retired to her room, and just after Christmas went to her lying-in chamber. She should have gone earlier, but had tarried, wanting to join in the Christmas celebrations. I did not blame her. As I remembered from Elisabeth's birth, those chambers were a dull and frightful place. I would avoid them for all time, if I could. *One day it will be you who enters, not knowing if you and your child will live or die,* my mind told me. I tried to pretend I heard the voice not, but the hammering of my heart showed up my pretence.

The New Year brought me a new sister, Dorothy, who was born much as Elisabeth had been, a child of snow. I attended to Mother again, and found it not as appalling as the first time, perhaps because I was prepared for the horrors that would come, and knew what I was supposed to do. One of the worst things, guaranteed to disturb the mind, is to be in a situation frightful and not know what you are doing. There is a sense of such helplessness, which stokes the fear burning in your belly, your heart. Knowing what to do granted purpose, tasks to be completed one by one, and that kept my mind from racing away on the wild feet of terror, making me imagine the worst that might come. It was long, two days passed since the first pain came, but eventually I had a sister. We emerged from the chambers of my mother just as men were making new bee skeps for the year to come, binding straw or willow to form hives, and arguing about which was best, for some said straw only was to be used and some favoured willow.

"Men never can agree about anything," Mother said when she was released of her chamber, and was watching a new wet nurse feed her baby. "And quick as a slip if they are told to do something they do the opposite. It is why there must be a King to keep them in line, you understand, Jane? Allow men to do as they will, and it all ends like that." She pointed to the end of the hall where two of father's men looked set to draw daggers, arguing over willow and straw.

Mother smiled at me and walked along, past them. That stopped the fight dead in its tracks. It seemed to me perhaps the country needed not a King. If England had my mother there would be not a fight ever known.

Dorothy was not the only child born that year, there was one far more important who came to the world. As summer broke upon England there was word from court. The King had a son. But not a legitimate son, a bastard.

"Bessie Blount," my mother hissed. "That fair-haired strumpet!"

I doubted my mother had really known the lady well, and from what I heard Bessie had been the mistress of but one man, and that man was the King, so it was unlikely she had had a lot of say in the relationship. She was unmarried at the time of conception, but married off to a nobleman not long after, yet the King, who was not one to make much of his affairs since adultery was hardly a virtue, acknowledged the boy. He was named Henry for his father and if any was in doubt where he came from, the surname of FitzRoy was granted to him; a title given only to royal bastards.

It was said the Queen was sad, but sent congratulations to her husband upon hearing of the boy. "Truly, Queen Katherine is a saint," said Kat to Marge in the kitchens one day. "Most women wouldn't want to say a thing to their husbands again after such a humiliation."

"And the Queen desires a son so," mourned Marge. "It shows boundless nobility of character to do as she did."

"A saint," said Mother Cooper, nodding over her steaming pot of mutton pottage.

Midsummer came but a few days later, and it seemed fitting, for Midsummer was a time of boundaries and change, confusion and alteration as the summer starts the path to autumn and harvest, and winter. May Day Eve was when the fairies came to call in truth, but Midsummer was when people tried to find the future. It seemed the King was too, since he had acknowledged a bastard son. There was talk that this bastard boy might be made legitimate, and he might become our King one day. There was other talk that the King might gain a dispensation and wed his daughter Mary to his bastard Henry. Such a thing sounded shocking to me, as they were half-blood to one another, but I was told royalty often were closely related.

Nothing came of those rumours, but of ones about the succession there were many more in the years to come. Yet as Midsummer dawned there was small talk of much apart from pleasure.

There were bonfires, lit near our fields of crops, so the smoke could purify them. Processions and parades went on about the land, and young women peeled apples from the stores left from the year before, throwing the peel upon the ground, and hoped it would form the initial of the man they loved.

The churches were garlanded in greenery, and our doors with birch and fennel. There was a scent of green and grace upon every doorway, fresh and clean. Events went on for days. Processions marched through villages and towns, and Father allowed one on his lands, with his tenants invited to Wulfhall after, for a feast in the barn. Statues were taken from the church and held aloft, with people praying as they passed, and cheering too. There were drummers and men playing the horn, players acting out famous scenes of the Bible, as they did at Christmas. Each year a giant, looking somewhat moth-eaten that year as he had been made a long time ago, walked out with ten men working his arms and legs, waving his great hands to make all the children squeal in delighted fright and run away. They came back, of course, to poke him and run away again.

Men drank in plentiful amounts and women could often be found singing. At night I stood by the door in the great hall and I smelt bonfires burning on the skyline. I watched shadowed shapes bound and dance about them, legs leaping high, men bounding through the centre of the flames, testing their courage. Tiny specks they were from so far away, but I loved to see them. Something in my heart wanted to go, to dance, to lift the hem of my skirts and whoop with glee as all who danced there did. To be free.

And then I would have to turn back and go to the empty fire in the great hall, where there was greenery and flowers rather than flames.

Hard work was coming with the harvest, and then with autumn and winter too and spring where little grew could be a time of hunger and danger as our winter stores were tested sore. There was strain to fall, so celebrate before that strain people did. Midsummer marked the descent to winter, the turn of the year, but there was time yet to celebrate, to rejoice, to honour the land that provided for us, and the God who kept us safe.

It was a good thing our people did celebrate, for that year was worse than any imagined, but not because the work was harder than usual, or the harvest not as good. The bonfires were supposed to cleanse the air, drive out spirits of malice and sickness. Ash was taken from those fires and scattered about, a charm against illness and ill fortune. But perhaps the dancers danced not well, do not leap high enough, perhaps the ash was not potent, not infused with all that had gone before, so could not protect against what was coming.

That year the bonfires did their task not well.

That was the year sickness came.

Chapter Fourteen

Wulfhall
Wiltshire

Summer 1519

That summer, in 1519, the plague known as the sweat came to Wiltshire. Usually, when such plagues crept or swept upon England we were far enough into the country that we only heard reports, but this time Death came calling, He came to our house.

It started with a creeping feeling, hints and rumours that trickled as a leak in the roof, reports of the sweat in cities, then towns, and then in villages. People came to our gate to sell produce and pins, told us there were people dead not only in towns where people lived close-packed, but that they had seen bodies along the road. It was spreading, and fast. We heard that the King had left London with the Queen and their daughter, heading into the countryside with a small band of guards to stay safe. My father ordered that all of his tenants were to stay upon their lands, not go to market or to see friends and family, but it seemed this command came too late. Soon there were reports of the sweat in Marlinges Boroe, and then in villages close to Wulfhall. We knew we were in danger.

Other orders went out. Food was brought into the house, and stores were checked and double checked, people were to stay away as much as possible, there were to be no more wandering merchants coming to the gate to sell produce and pins. All tenants and stewards were not to meet with strangers, all coin was to be exchanged in bowls of vinegar. We, Father's family, and most especially all us women, were to stay inside. There was to be no hunting, no riding unless there was a dire need. Father and my brothers, along with Cousin Edmund, would go out when required to keep the lands and estate in peace, arrange supplies for those in need. That was to be the only travel permitted. That summer was scorching, and it was unpleasant inside, but as reports came of more deaths, and as we started to hear of people we knew who had become sick or died, I started to fear the outside world. I felt filthy when I had been in the courtyard, as though wandering on the wind the sweat had come, stained my hands, crept up my nose. I felt I had breathed death in, tasted it. I did not go outside any more than I had to. It felt dangerous, dirty... and predatory.

Mother started to look pinched. She spent much time in the nursery, washing the walls with vinegar and burning sage in the fire, or holding Dorothy or Elisabeth. Sometimes I would find her staring from the window at nothing. When she looked at me it was as though I was not there. As though she was staring straight through me. Worry was consuming her. She feared for Edward and other kin who had fled London, and for the Queen and King who had gone to a country seat to protect themselves. She feared for her family and for the village. Terror was filling her, a soft-stealing consumption; soon there might not be space for her soul.

One night, as we were eating in the great hall, my father was speaking to Edmund and Henry about the progress of the plague. My mother, who had been telling Catherine and me of some fawns she had spotted in the shade of the woodland, stopped talking. I wished she had not. More than a month ago I had seen an antlered stag, a trail of duller females behind him, wandering the open pastures at the back of Wulfhall. They had crossed the skyline as dusk fell, and the stag had turned, his red-brown coat lit up as fire against the setting sun, the females black shadows at his back, heather at his feet. *These fawns must be his*, I had thought as Mother told us of them. Children of such a mighty King of beasts as he, I would have liked to see. It would have been a nicer thought, too, than the ones that came as Mother stopped talking and as we heard the conversation of the men floating up from the other end of the table.

"It is something to be feared, in truth," Father said, taking up a spoonful of flayed eels in butter. He took several wobbling spoonfuls, then wiped his pewter spoon thoughtfully with bread. A shimmer of silver and grease caught the candlelight. "They say there are hardly any signs a person is struck with the sickness before they fall to death. Well at dawn, dead by dusk, some say, with delirium and visions coming in between."

"Old Thomas and his wife are dead of it," mentioned Edmund, taking three baked oysters to open and dip in oil infused with lemon balm. These were the last of the stores we had from the sea. Much trade had stopped as people feared to travel. "And their children are sick too, after tending to them."

"I am sorry to hear that," said my father with grief in his tone. "Thomas was my page in the Battle of Blackheath. He served me well."

"The plague seems to have spread to Bristol and to Bath," my mother said, lacing her fingers together and leaving the smoked fish pottage on her pewter plate uneaten. It was a Wednesday, and on Fridays, Wednesdays, all festivals and Saints' Days, we ate no flesh, but fish was allowed. "We have to pray, lord husband, that the Good Lord watches over us. I have asked for relics of the church to be brought out to bless the house with, that they might protect us from this dreadful disease."

"Good," muttered my father, his eyes lost as he gazed along the table. I saw his glance graze Catherine, who sat opposite my mother. She looked up at him and there was a small twinkle in her eyes. She looked back at her plate. He would visit her this night, I was sure of it. *Even now,* I thought, *even with Mother speaking about relics to bless the house and praying to God, they are thinking of coupling!* It amazed me. Sin brought sickness upon people, upon a country. We should be trying to be as good as we could in an effort to win the approval of God.

The meal went on with little talk of anything besides the plague. That night, as I knelt beside my bed I prayed for old Thomas and his wife, even though I had not known them. "God bless them and keep them," I whispered, feeling my toes go numb. I had lingered long on my knees. There was a certain pleasure in the pain that long hours of prayer might bring. I often felt I had small control over anything, but I could force my own body to do things, such as pray. That was a form of control, of mastery. "God send angels to watch over them, and bring them peace. Holy Father, watch over my family, over Edward who is not here. Lord of Heaven, watch over us…"

I faltered. I heard a noise in the corridor outside. Catherine's door opened quietly and closed. My father was inside once again. I heard muffled voices talking for but a moment, and then the sound of the bed. I glanced down at the maid who slept on my floor, Bess. She was young and they worked her hard in the kitchens. When she slept on my floor often she was asleep long before me and heard nothing. Other maids who slept in my room had heard things, I was sure. I was not alone in knowing my father's secret anymore, but not one servant of this house would say a thing. He was their master. Tell his secret to someone and they would lose their home, their job, and perhaps their families would suffer too. They were bound to secrecy due to fear, perhaps I was the same.

Unable to pray, unable to make my voice heard to God as I heard my father start to bed his daughter, I got up. My legs wobbled, blood flooding into parts of them that had been cut off. I ignored the rush of pain, the tiny darts hitting skin and blood. In some ways I welcomed the discomfort. I *should* suffer, for I was part of this sin. Keeping silent allowed it to continue. My oath had trapped me, silenced my mouth and imprisoned my soul.

I got into bed and pulled the covers about my head, trying to drown out the vile noise. How could my father do this? Bed a woman who I was sure was a witch for all her magic at capturing and controlling him! How could he rut in sin with her, so often, and for so long? I wanted the Lord God to raise His hand and smite them.

But the Lord of Heaven is subtle, as I was to learn.

*

The next day, my father had not appeared when Henry and Edmund were ready to leave. They were to ride out to talk to tenants and stewards, ensure everyone was keeping far from the village and other settlements, and find out who needed aid. They were, as Father had instructed in a stern tone the night before, not to get off their horses, or enter houses or stand close to the people they talked to. They were all to ride with coverings over their mouths and noses. They were not to accept food or drink from anyone, and if their horses needed anything they were to water them in streams or rivers, not troughs at people's houses.

"We'll not be long, Jane," Henry said. He looked around, wondering where our father was. It was not like him to be late. "I will go seek him," he said to Cousin Edmund. "You wait here."

I was at the doorway, enjoying a rare moment of Mother's absence. She was in the nursery discussing Dorothy's milk and Elisabeth's progress with the wet nurses. There were two now, one for each of my tiny sisters. Whilst it was usual to breast feed an infant for two years, at certain points other foods could enter the diet, such as sops of bread, honey or sugar, and a little chicken or gruel. Elisabeth was a hale babe, and it was thought she might try some of these foods soon. The new wet nurse, a woman blessed with huge breasts, clear skin and a clement disposition, had served in another noble household, that of the Dormers, nearby and was filling Mother in on what our noble neighbours had done with their offspring. Mother was determined that she would do as they had, only better, with her newest child, Dorothy and her most precious daughter, Elisabeth.

Elisabeth was Mother's favourite. She was a beauty already. It is easy to see in some children. Many babes, no matter what their mothers think or strangers say, are fearsome ugly. Elisabeth was not. She had fine hair, a little darker than that of Edward or me but lighter than Thomas's, and her eyes were a pretty blue, like summer skies. Her features had been arranged with care by the Almighty. It was easy to tell she was going to be the beauty of the family, and what was odd was I did not mind. Mother's remarks about *finally* having a child who possessed beauty rolled off me. Perhaps I was too busy worrying about Catherine and my father, or it was because I loved my little sister that could not resent her. I knew not, but either way Mother's remarks stung but did not affect my feelings for Elisabeth. She was an innocent, and I believed her perfect, as all who looked upon her did.

I sighed and stepped into the courtyard. The morning had felt strained. Talk the night before of death and plague had hardly been settling to mind or spirit, and even after the noises next door had ceased, I had passed the night in dreams of darkness and demons. I saw Old Thomas and his wife chased by spirits with tails and horns. I saw birds; falcons pecking exposed eyes and feathers of flame that came to chase the other birds away. I had risen that morning feeling at once as though I had not slept at all and that I had slept too deeply. It was as though I had not slept in truth, but had wandered from my bed into some other realm and there had spent the night. Gritty-eyed, muscles and bones sore as if I had been beaten, I had stumbled through washing and dressing, then chapel and prayers. The house was already hot, the air suffocating. It was one of those still, breathless days of summer where air hangs stagnant and oppressive, where it feels a dragon might open its mouth in the skies at any moment and unleash a storm of lightning and thunder. I went outside to find a breath of wind, and found none. I was about to go back in when my cousin caught my eye.

Edmund did not look well. He was pale, a sheen of sweat over his forehead.

"Cousin…" I said hesitantly, "are you well?"

Edmund looked over at me, his eyes glazed. Edmund stared at me as though he knew me not. He swayed like a ripe stem of barley in summer wind. And then, he fell. His legs crumpled like old parchment, his head lolled backwards, his spine seemed as soft as pottage as he slipped to the floor. With a cry, I held out my small arms and tried to catch him, but I was a child and he was a man, twenty-two, fully grown, so much bigger than me. My knees bent, screaming in protest as his weight came down on me. I fell to the ground, bashing my kneecaps with a sickening shock of pain on the cobbles of the yard.

"Edmund!" I exclaimed, trying to lower him to the ground. His head slumped into a puddle of dirty water awash with strands of straw. His eyes rolled back in his head and he curled up about his own body and shivered violently. A moan of pure misery came from his lips.

"Help me!" I screamed to the empty yard. Unusually, there was no one there, but at my shout many servants came rushing from the kitchens and the outbuildings. "Help me!" I shouted again in a high and eerie tone, fraught with desperation.

They carried my cousin inside the house, up to his room, shared with Mary. I marched behind them, shouting orders for water to be boiled and herbs to be collected from the kitchens. Never had I sounded so authoritative. Rounding a corner, I crashed straight into my mother, running from the other direction. As we separated, she looked at me, and then along the corridor. She saw Edmund being carried by our servants and a look of pallid dismay dawned on her face. She put a hand to her heart, and leaned against the wall, weakened by terror.

"Edmund…" she whispered. "What happened?" she asked, turning wide, wild eyes on me.

"I know not," I said, words stumbling from my lips. "He fell in the courtyard just now. He started to shiver, he looked pale, and he fell on me. Mother, is it…?"

"Do not speak the name of the sickness!" she cried, crossing herself violently. "To do so may bring it to this house, even more than it is now!"

"What do you mean?"

She dragged her eyes from her kinsman, the ward she had been given to care for by a relative. "Jane, your father, and Mary and Catherine, all of them! They are all sick and now Edmund too! I found your father in his room, on the floor. Mary and Catherine did not rise from their beds." She crossed herself again and I did the same, muttering a prayer to God to save us. "It has come!" my mother exclaimed. I could see the whites of her eyes. "Why would God punish this house? We are good, God-fearing people. We give to the Church, go to Mass, say our prayers… Why would God punish us?"

I could think of one reason God would want to punish my father's house. But I said nothing.

My mother pressed a hand to mine. "Your brothers, Henry and Thomas?" she asked.

"They were well when last I saw them," I said.

"Then they must be sent from here to the house of a neighbour," she said, nodding as she tried to remember, through dismay and fear, all she knew about tending the sick. "They will take Elisabeth and Dorothy with them," she continued, almost to herself. "We cannot risk them, Jane. Your sisters are too young to withstand this sickness." She stared at me. "But you must stay with me and tend the sick. Go, tell the others they are to leave. Henry will be in charge of them. Tell him to take them to a hunting lodge and there isolate them. And tell him to send a servant for the doctor, and another for the cunning woman of the village. We need help!"

I turned and ran, not caring ladies were not supposed to run. I found Henry pacing about the fire in the great hall, and told him what Mother had said. He listened, nodded and hurried away to find Thomas, shouting for my mother's maids to gather my infant sisters and their things, and be ready to leave within the hour. Everyone was running. The house was awash with footsteps. Yet despite all the noise of feet upon the ground, there seemed to be but little sound of voices. A deathly hush had fallen. Footsteps, just footsteps, echoing beats like a heart bounded through the quiet halls.

I ran too, back to Mother. My thoughts raced as my feet bounced along dim corridors, as I brushed past servants and maids racing along in many and various directions with their own orders. My father, my cousin and his wife, and Catherine, all sick with the sweat! God had been watching. He was punishing my father and Catherine for their sins. His wrath had fallen not only on my father and his whore, but on others, my cousin and his pregnant wife as well! It was like the plague of the first born in the Bible. I always shivered when the priest read it out to us in church.

The hours that followed were a blur. Mother and I moved from one bed to another, pressing sodden cloths soaked in cold water and vinegar to the pale, shaking skin of our patients. They flinched from the cold, but we could not wash them with warm water, for to do so would open the pores of their skin, and invite more sickness to enter their bodies. We washed the walls of chambers in vinegar to drive off the sweat. We changed soiled covers grown sodden with sweat and sticky with piss and shit. Waste came from our kin in streams of hot, black, ill-smelling foulness. I gagged as I bundled soiled sheets up and took them to be burned in a great fire built in the courtyard for that purpose.

When I came back in I heard them. Voices cried out, mumbled words and groans of pain. Each one of the sick sounded mad. Each one screamed, demons chasing them in their fever.

Mother boiled herbs; feverfew, dandelion, honeysuckle flowers, clover, fresh oak leaves, and she put dried leaves of holly into water over the fire. She gave me bowls of it to spoon into the mouths of our patients. She ordered bags of onions to be tied to the doors of the house and in each of the rooms. They were to be changed every few days, then burned in the fire. "The onions take up the sickness," she assured me, her voice weak with weariness and fear. "They will draw sickness from them."

The cunning woman of the village, or rather one of her granddaughters, arrived that same day. She cast an eye over my mother's efforts, nodded with approval, and went to work. She set about concocting salves, potions, and poultices to rub on, feed to or place on our patients' skins. "My grandmother has succumbed to the sickness herself, my lady," she explained when Mother asked why the cunning woman had not come herself. "But I am her eldest granddaughter, and she has taught me well."

"Should you not wish to be with your grandmother?" my mother asked, although she clearly did not want the young woman to leave.

The young woman shook her head. She looked calm and competent, her bonnet clean and her simple grey woollen dress neat and tidy. Her hands were those of a woman who worked hard for a living, but they were scrupulously clean. "My younger sisters are caring for her, my lady, and others in the village who are sick," she said, firm resolve in her tone. "You need me. My grandmother was well enough to insist I came to you, for you have done much for our village and its people. My grandmother knows you are a good house, of good and noble people, my lady, and she would not rest until I was sent to you. I assure you, I know all she does, for she has taught me well."

Deftly she bound a cloth about her face. That seemed to seal the argument, for my mother closed her mouth. The young cunning woman handed cloths to us and walked to the bed, where she put a cool hand to the forehead of my father, whose room we were in at the time. "The fire rages," she muttered. "We must break it."

Her name was Mistress Edith Grey. She came from a long line of cunning women; souls of wisdom taught to guide women through birth and tend to the sick, the injured and the dying. Edith knew the common name of every herb in the gardens and in the wild, and all their uses. She had learned when best to gather and pluck plants so the spirits in them were strongest. She had trained at the side of her grandmother, something she told me as we set to work, and her grandmother was the most knowledgeable woman in four counties, at least.

Edith seemed to not possess the fear that Mother and I were filled with as we scampered room to room to tend our family. Perhaps it was because Edith was accustomed to sickness, or because these people were not souls she loved personally, but her cool detachment was a balm to my spirits and Mother's. Edith looked over each patient swiftly and thoroughly, approved of all my mother had done thus far, then set to work. She took samples of their piss where she could, requesting anything we had in the house made of glass, a most expensive material, to examine the colour in. She held piss to the light, tasted each sample; a drop on her finger put to the tip of her pink tongue. Her large sack was unpacked; bundles of dried herbs were used to purify rooms and she sent maids to the kitchens with lists of more to be gathered. Everyone obeyed her without a word. There was no arrogance in her commands, but her authority was unquestioned, absolute.

She was most concerned for Mary and Edmund, and told us that they were far weaker than even we had thought. Despite this dire pronouncement, my mother was, I think, greatly relieved to have Mistress Grey in the house. Mother followed Edith about as I had never seen her do with another person, hanging on her words, obeying her every command without question. By the time the doctor arrived some hours later, a fat, red-faced man with a bulbous nose, Edith was in complete command of our house. Even Catherine, for all her wiles, had not the power this young woman possessed.

This is the superior power of goodness, my mind told me as I went to fetch clean water and sage to burn in the chamber of my father, to cast out the demons in the air. *Catherine had power indeed, but as a soul of goodness comes to the house, you see goodness is greater, more powerful, than evil.*

"You are doing all I would have recommended, Mistress Grey," the doctor said, looking about as he mopped his brow. He knew Edith's grandmother as it transpired, and unlike some doctors who objected to their trade being shared with women, this one did not mind. In truth, I think he was happy to have someone to tend to poor folk, as they could not afford his fees. Some doctors went into their profession out of a desire to aid people and some entered for money. This man was one of the former. In truth it looked as though neither he nor his horse had stopped all day or night.

His voice came muffled from under his cloth, sodden with vinegar, as he pulled it back over his face. "If, my Lady Seymour, you are happy with your woman here…" he nodded to Edith, "… then I will leave you pills I know to be effective, and continue on. I am afraid this part of the country has been much affected by this sickness, and the Dormers, your neighbours, have also called for me. I understand the entire household has fallen to the illness."

Mother paid for the pills and let him go on his way. I think she believed in Edith more in any case.

The days went on. Edith insisted that Mother and I eat, even though we had little stomach. She sent us to sleep in shifts, and she worked at the side of my mother's remaining maids when we went to lie down. Edith did not seem to tire. Her eyes were red-rimmed but always bright, alert. When I slept, when I could sleep, I fell into black holes of darkness. I often did not sleep for long. There were horrors waiting for me I would not allow myself to see in the daylight.

"It is good they are alive still," she told me after two days and nights had passed. "I am told that some are well at breakfast and dead by supper with this plague, but those who survive past that first test are more likely to become well again."

I almost burst into tears when Edith said that. The thought I might emerge with all my family intact was almost more than I had hoped for. I knew Mother felt the same, and I knew she was, too, worried for Dorothy, Elisabeth, Henry and Thomas, wherever they had gone. We had had no note, for sending someone back into a house of sickness would be foolish. And Edward, we both wondered about him. Had he made it from London and court soon enough? Was he alive?

Not knowing is more terrible than knowing. They say ignorance is bliss, but not always is it so. When ignorant about whether your family is alive or dead, ignorance is a curse. It plays with the mind, making you imagine the worst.

Another day passed. I grew dizzy from the cloth of linen fastened about my face infused with Edith's personal recipe of wormwood, lemon balm and vinegar. The servants, too, had cloths bound about their faces. Our house seemed to have become a silent show of mummers. Had I not been so scared, it might have been amusing. But after a time, eyes became all I could see when I opened my eyes or closed them. I began to read all emotion from the eyes before me. I began to think I would never see a mouth or nose again.

The scent of vinegar hung in the air and stung the eyes. Herbs were roasted on fires in all rooms to purify the air. Edith instructed Mother's women to light huge bundles of dried green-silver sage from our stores, and use its smoke to drive out the demons lingering in the air. Maids wandered the house, bundles of smouldering sage in their hands, wafting it into every corner where sinister spirits might linger. A pall of blue smoke hung in the air. When one walked along a corridor it shifted and wafted, danced; ghosts prancing on the breeze. There was dust on all things, embers of the perfumed sage sailed, bright amber flame in the air and then that flame was gone, grey ash remained, more phantoms whirling, motes chasing sunbeams which fought to enter the dark, shuttered house. I found myself staring at the dust, the smoke, the rooms once familiar that now were strange, full of terror and worry. Spirits seemed to shift and weave; the past haunting us, as we were trapped, stuck in a limbo of unsettled time and fate. I would find my tired mind watching, lost and wandering as I stared at smoke and ash, and then I would be wrenched back to the present by noise that shattered the stillness, made my heart race with fright.

My family cried out in their troubled fevers. Moaning and mumbling was the background noise, as the hum of insects in a field in summer, and then screams, screams shattering thought and stillness, a clap of thunder on a scorching, close afternoon.

The loud and muffled sounds of the sick echoed through the house. They became as one. It seemed to follow me, even in my sleep, where I dreamed no dreams in my exhaustion, the noise of their whimpering and moaning came after me. It was the sound of suffering, the sound of people I loved hanging on a cliff top of life and death. It was the sound of people I loved dying.

Every now and then as I rushed about in the daytime, I would bend over, a cry coming from my mouth. I did not weep, but sometimes the terror within me surfaced and broke loose, screaming from my mouth, bending my back and crushing my gut, my ribs, my heart. I sounded like my mother when she gave birth, and perhaps there was a truth in that idea. I passed fright and terror unimagined from my body. It rose up my gullet and leapt from my throat, a hard, harsh guttural call of pain and fear and grief. The noise washed from me, at times I almost fell to my knees, but I did not. I let out the sound, my hands on my knees, shaking.

And then I was up, and on again. On, on, on, trying to save my family from death.

Chapter Fifteen

Wulfhall
Wiltshire

Summer 1519

One day, I could not have told you which, during the time of sickness upon our house, I was sitting beside Mary, my head nodding against my chest. I was so tired.

The bones of my breast kept waking me, my thin chin hitting them and bouncing up, eyes for a moment startled awake, then falling to irresistible slumber again. I was exhausted. I could not have told you how many days or nights had passed since my family had fallen into sickness. I could not have told you what age I was, for I felt old, broken. My head lolled and my eyes closed. The cloth I was holding, soaked in wormwood and vinegar, fell to the floor. I felt it slip from my fingertips, but I could resist no more. Slumber had me, firm in his warm arms. There was blackness, lack of thought, more seductive than a thousand poets singing of courtly love. I think I slept, or passed from consciousness. When I awoke, hours or minutes later, I glanced dully at Mary. I stared a moment and blinked, and with a dreadful fear in my heart, I moved to her side.

She was lying upon the bed, soaked in her own sweat. Her face was grey. Her hand was on her stomach, where a slight bump was starting to show. Mary's hand was protecting her child. My eyes were drawn to her face. Her eyes were open, as was her mouth. Mary stared with unseeing eyes at the curtains above. Her mouth gaped as though she had seen something dreadful. She was not moving. Those staring eyes saw nothing. When I touched her arm, I could feel warmth leaving her body.

I let out a cry of despair, and fumbled, desperate to rouse her. Her body shook under my hands, limbs flopped uselessly. Mary was dead. Her brown eyes stared up in mute horror; as though she could not believe what had happened to her and her child. For a moment I stood there, looking down, my mind refusing to believe what I was seeing. My feet made the choice. Before I knew what I was doing I scrambled from the room, a strangled scream bursting raw and broken from my throat. My mother and Edith heard and came running to me. Flying into my mother's arms, I collapsed. Tears burst from me, not the quiet weeping so often I employed but vast, wracking sobs. I could not breathe. There was not air enough in the world for me. Mother enfolded me in her arms and together we fell to our knees. Meadowsweet posies crushed under us, emitting a sweet smell. I would always remember that moment, that scent. Never again did I smell meadowsweet without thinking of Mary's eyes, dull and brown and staring. Edith walked into the room with a steady, grim face, and emerged wearing the same expression. "I am so sorry, my lady," she said, pressing a hand into my mother's shoulder. "Mother and child are taken by the hand of God. There is nothing more we can do."

"The child..." My mother's voice was strained with pain. "Can the child be saved if it is cut from her?"

Edith shook her head. "The child is not yet grown enough to live if that were attempted, my lady," she said. "And I think it too late. Mary has been dead an hour or more, the child with her. I will cut into her belly, bless the child within the body of its mother. We must pray that God accepts my blessing, and welcomes the child's spirit into His Kingdom."

Mary, along with Father, Catherine and Edmund had received the last rites from our chaplain when they fell ill, just in case. Their souls were safe if the worst happened, but the child... In a birthing chamber it was usual to try to bless an arm, the head, if a child was stuck in its mother's body during childbirth, but Mary had died already. Even if Edith blessed the dead babe now, found a part of it in Mary's dead body to baptise, it might be too late.

It *was* too late. I knew it. I had felt the coolness of Mary's skin. The child was lost to limbo.

Edith went back into the room, but I knew what she had said to Mother were words of false comfort. The child was to linger for eternity in limbo, the place all lost souls go. I gasped and shuddered with pain. That such an innocent soul, the soul of a babe not even born, should fall into a cursed realm beyond the light of God without having had a chance to ever be redeemed, it was too much to bear. It was not purgatory, not Hell; the child would not burn, would not pay for its sins, but never would it see Heaven. *And the fault the child is lost is yours,* that voice in my head accused. *Had you not been sleeping as Mary died, the child could have been cut from her and baptised before death. You have condemned a child to limbo!*

No! my own voice screamed in the dark recesses of my heart. It could not be true!

My mother clung to me. I knew the same things were in her mind. Her kinsman's child was gone, not only dead, but lost to the blessings of God and His everlasting light. When Mother released me, her eyes were flat with anguish. Edmund and his family were her responsibility. She had raised Edmund almost as a son, and Mary had been with her every day. Mother felt responsible for Mary's death, and the dreadful fate of her child.

"I will go, see to Catherine," I whispered, leaving my mother and Edith to start the cleansing of Mary's body, so it could be buried in the family vault of the local church. It would be a swift, spare funeral; another indignity, another disgrace for poor Mary. With most of our family still either sick, or in other houses for their safety, there was no one to attend. Poor Mary; such a faded and spiritless woman, who had finally ascended to her greatest triumph by growing large with child, only to now have her child stolen from her by death, and for barely a soul to weep at her grave. Unappreciated by all of us save Edmund, in life, she would go un-honoured too to the grave. But Mary would live in the light of Christ with God. She had been a good woman. But her child… Mary would never see her child, not even in Heaven. They would always be separate. Mary would never hold her babe, never. In all eternity, mother and child would be strangers, lost to one another.

It cannot be my fault, it cannot be my fault, said my mind.

But it is, said the voice. *Who else is to blame?*

I walked to Catherine's room. I am not sure what was in my mind, but it felt like a worm was crawling through my brain, one of malice and unrest. There was something dark in me born of the dark secret I held, or that held me, I no longer was sure which. In my soul a wyrm, some twisted dragon of hatred, writhed. It set flames in me, fuelled my steps, sent me reeling towards the darkness that had been set into the heart of my family.

I knew the power of rage, of remorse, of vengeance and of hatred then. I knew the fire the Devil commands. It burned in me, no steady flame, but one of destruction, obliteration.

I wanted to look on the face of the one who had done this to our family. I wanted, needed, oh how I needed, someone to blame, someone other than me. Catherine and my father. They had brought the wrath of God upon us. Mary and her babe had paid for their sin. This, this hell we were thrust into, was God's punishment. God had killed this child to punish Father for his sin.

Perhaps I was being punished too.

My hand shook as I lifted the latch to Catherine's room. Quietly I closed the door behind me. I was so still. I felt like she had appeared on the day she had attacked me; so still, so motionless, a predator; round eyes watching, always watching for a movement. So still was I in form, in body, yet inside I was a tempest of rage. Something of fire was being born inside my soul, a dark fire, an eye and heart of purest wrath. I stood by the side of her bed and looked down on Catherine's sleeping face. Even pallid and grey, she still possessed the beauty which had bewitched my father, which had brought such grievous horror upon my family. She seemed to feel the burning fury of my eyes, for hers opened and stared up. Her eyelids flickered. She looked helpless. It made me hate her more. If she had shown her power plain, I could have struck then. Her helplessness made me stop.

"Water…" she croaked, dry lips fumbling, cracking, flakes of brittle skin falling to the bed linen like vile snow. "Water, sister… please."

"Mary is dead," I said my voice blunt, emotionless. "As is her babe. You have killed them."

Catherine's eyes opened wide at my words. She tried to push herself up in bed and failed, falling back down. I hated her helplessness no more. I liked it. I smiled to witness her weakness. I felt powerful in anger, spiteful. Filled with wrath, I was capable of anything. I had never felt like that, never felt powerful. Finally I understood why my mother took such pleasure in whipping me. I understood the bitter power rage bestows. I could do anything.

"You lay with my father, brought sin on our house," I whispered. "The hand of God has come to punish you and my father for your sin. Your whoring has killed Mary and her child. It is for your sin that she and her babe have died."

Catherine gazed at me. She was already falling from consciousness. I took up a cloth, dripping with water and herbs from the bowl beside her bed, and I held it over her. "I could kill you, Catherine," I whispered into her ear. "I should kill you now, for Mary, for her child, for my father…"

Her eyes flickered open. There was fear in them, yet she could not move. The cloth in my hand was wet. I knew that a person could suffocate another with a cloth. Just hold it over the mouth and nose and it was done. I had heard of a man who had done it to his wife, killed her so he could wed another. He had been caught in act of murder by their son and sent to the gallows, but no one would find me. Just a while, just a little time for it to be done and no one would know. Catherine was sick. Mary had died already. They would think the witch had died of the sweat. I could do it. I could rid our family of this evil. With her would die the secret. No one would have to know about my father and her, Edward would not be hurt, no one would know I had known. And she would be gone. Justice would be served.

My hand shook. My heart thumped loud and painful in my chest. I dropped the cloth and I turned from her. If I looked into that face any longer I would do it.

"To do such would be to make me as you are," I said, my voice shaking with the effort it took to stop. "I will not become that which I hate. I will not a killer be." I breathed in, heavy and hard. The air hurt my throat. I was shaking all over. Part of me wanted to grab the cloth and do it. *Do it!* With each breath I took I pinned the rage inside me down. Like as when I sewed to hold back my darkness and fear was that moment, each breath a stitch, pinning murderous intent down, deeper down, into my soul.

"Lie there, think of the good woman you have murdered, and the innocent babe you have sent to eternal limbo. Think on your sins, Catherine. Think on what you have done." Shaking, I walked from the room. Mother was outside. I jumped to see her. My heart burst into furious life. I thought Mother would hear it, guilt pounding in my veins.

"How is Catherine?" she asked weakly.

I nodded. "She is well enough for now," I said. "How is Edmund?"

Mother shook her head, and I knew it was bad. I walked to her and took her arm. We went to the bedside of my cousin and watched him gasp and struggle for breath. He died later that afternoon. Edith could do nothing. We could do nothing. Perhaps it was better this way, dying on the same day as his wife and child, Edmund never had to bear the sorrow of losing them, not as we did. He never knew they were gone, the child's soul lost. We had to endure that pain, but he did not. A slim blessing, but when all dreadfulness the world may contain has fallen upon you, any blessing is welcome.

Mother collapsed when Edmund died. She had to be carried to her bed by her women, and was soon in a fever which raged through the night. Edith and I were in control as Mother tossed and screamed in her bed. We worked on, heaving ourselves out of sorrow and fatigue like old dogs who struggle, bones and joints cracking and popping, from the fireside to heed their master's whistle. I did not go to Catherine's room again. I did not trust myself. I sent others to her, but I sent them more often to my mother and father. I did not care if Catherine died. I wanted her to. I believed it would rid the house of her evil once and for all, but I would not lift my hand to kill her. It was not my place to decide who lived and who died. That was God's power and His alone.

When I thought of how close I had come to killing Catherine, everything in me started to shake. I had always wondered how people fell into sin, and now I knew. It was so easy. Surrender to the hatred within, and it is easy. My only consolation was that I had stopped myself. Yet in spare moments between tending to Mother and Father I found myself wrapped in fear of another nature. Fear of what was in me, what I had seen, witnessed, the presence of evil I had felt rising in my hands and heart, the power that told me I could kill a person, that I was capable. Stopped myself I had, but never had I known that I had that within me. Wicked thoughts I had had, but to kill a sister, even one as evil as Catherine, was to become Cain to Abel. There was sin waiting to be born in me, darkness longing for a chance to claim me. I feared my wickedness would bring more horror upon the house. But God, it seemed, was done with vengeance. He had taken, and now, He gave back.

My mother, father, and Catherine recovered. Their fevers broke one after the other in the days that followed Edmund and Mary's burial in the family tomb. None of the family could attend the funeral, and the priest was overworked, burying vast numbers of villagers and farmers in mass graves where bodies were piled one on top of the other. For the sake of the living, the dead were granted little dignity.

When Thomas, Elisabeth, Dorothy and Henry came back, Thomas was surprised I was still alive. "I thought you would have died," he said in a careless manner, "you are so slight and weak, I thought you would have succumbed."

I stared at him with stark eyes. He seemed to care little that our cousin and Mary were dead. "You speak nothing but malice, Thomas Seymour," I said, making him blink, then stare at me. "I will hear you no more."

I walked away, him gaping at me. It was the first time I ever felt I had power over him. Perhaps it was strange such power could come from loss, from grief. Perhaps not. Priests say God has many ways of working His will, that mere mortals often do not see His hand upon our lives. God had taught me that I was strong even as I seemed weak; that I was capable when everything about me fell apart. He had shown me I could overcome hatred, not take revenge. It was a hard, bitter way to learn such lessons, but from that day onwards when

Thomas teased me, I offered him no reaction. I stood and stared calmly when he taunted me, gave up my toys without protest when he wanted to rip them apart. I calmly denied the lies he told about me, and accepted beatings if I was not believed with an impassive face. I had been hurt by sorrow more than he could ever hurt me, and I had faced a darkness greater than him, one inside my own soul. I had fought demons, and I had won. What power could Thomas Seymour, little fool that he was, have over me when I had faced that and lived?

For a time, Thomas continued as he always had, but after a while he slowed his cruel attentions and then stopped altogether. I had taken the amusement out of it for him. The year after the sickness came, Thomas was sent away to the household of our cousin, Sir Francis Bryan, so he could learn to serve in a rich house, make his way to court. After that, I hardly had to see or endure his company again, until we were grown.

Edith stayed with my mother for some time, feeding her syrup of St John's Wort, and blessed thistle mixed with mint to soothe her sorrows. Mother was the last to rise from her bed. When she did, Father came to her, and they wept together. Catherine stayed in her rooms. I thought, for a while, the witch might have felt remorse, that my words might have made an impression. But when Catherine was well and laughing once more about the house I heard her door open and close quietly in the night. The rocking of her bed started once more.

I knew that the sweat had been brought to our house to punish my father and Catherine. But they, in their passion, seemed to neither to know or care what they brought upon us. I hated both of them. They were evil; a rotten stinking apple hidden at the base of our basket, polluting and souring all about them. And nothing could I do. No shame that I could bring upon Catherine seemed able to make them stop. Not even death could stop them, not grief, not pain, not the lost soul of an innocent child.

I could not understand why she felt no shame, for I did. Guilt and shame, sorrow and loss. At night, sometimes I would wake suddenly, slippery with sweat. In my dreams I heard Mary's baby, a wail of sorrow and loss upon the wind.

Chapter Sixteen

Wulfhall
Wiltshire

Winter- Autumn 1520

As the year turned my father left in its first few days, bound for court, for like almost every man of any title he had been chosen to attend to the King at what was later to be known as the *Field of the Cloth of Gold*.

"Where is my lord father to go?" I asked.

It was a summit meeting of Kings, I was told. Father was to attend to represent Wiltshire, rather than as a personal attendant of the King, but the honour was still great. The King needed many of his men there. This was to be an occasion none would ever forget.

The King of France was to forge bonds of eternal and everlasting peace with our King, and their children were to wed to secure it. Young Princess Mary, daughter of the King, would wed the Dauphin, heir to the throne of France. This was a grand occasion, all said, yet many who spoke looked concerned. If the daughter of our King married the heir to France, what would happen when our King died? We were not to talk of the King dying, for it was treason to imagine his death, but the possibility was in many a mind. If the Princess became Queen of France, her husband the King, would that husband, too, become King of England? Would England become a part of France? It seemed possible. All property a woman owned became her husband's when they wed, and although England was a greater piece of land than that most brides could lay claim to possessing, it remained property. Were we English to cease to be, becoming French instead?

At the same time, most people agreed that eternal and everlasting peace was beneficial, and surely what God wanted for His children. That a sweet came with a sour, like the sauce we poured on roasted rabbit, seemed unavoidable. Uncertainty also made people wary.

But if his people were wary, the King was not. Into this festival of peace and, as it transpired, boasting on a royal scale, he entered with all enthusiasm. That March as a cold wind bit the walls of Wulfhall, six thousand men sailed from England to Calais, but not to war as men of England so often did against France. They went to that English city across the water to start work on the English camp. The Kings and their courts were to meet in the Val D'or just outside Calais itself, on neutral territory. The English were to stay in a camp about the town of Guisnes, the French at Ardres.

"Five thousand people are to accompany the King," my mother told me.

She said only the best were to go, herself and my father included. I pondered this. How many people were there in England? Were all five thousand going with the King *all* the best of people? Or did my mother just mean her and my father? Father was to take eleven servants and his chaplain, which demonstrated his wealth since only a prosperous man could afford so many, but I was told the King was to take thousands of servants and nobles. My father's prosperity was no lie, but other men were wealthier than he.

As it turned out, the Queen had a full contingent of attendants and did not require my mother. Mother served only on state occasions at court, so it was not surprising she was not amongst the first chosen, but she was sour about it for a long time. "It must be the King limiting numbers," she told me and Catherine one day, "for the Queen would have wanted me at her side without doubt."

We nodded. I could see Catherine laughing at my mother. Inside the eyes of the witch was a cackle.

Father, already at court for the King needed all his men to help prepare, sent word back often. At times I saw Mother glare at a missive just arrived from London, as though it were my father's fault she had not been selected and he had.

"In truth, Mistress Seymour, the King may have pitied your father," Kat of the kitchens told me as she washed pots outside. "I was told, by a peddler who was here selling nails and thread, that the cost of taking wives and servants, as well as dressing richly, as the King requires so England is not shamed before France, is bankrupting some of even the richest of nobles. Perhaps the King thought to save a few of his men some expense."

"And our master has his debts to think of," mentioned Marge as she put another armful of pots to be scoured beside Kat. Clearly this was a thought unbidden that should not have been spoken, as a warning shot fired from Kat's eyes in Marge's direction, pinning her mouth shut.

Seeing this, I said nothing more, but I wondered. I had known of no debts. I had always thought my father hale of coin, even though I knew little of the household accounts. But if the King was trying to save my father some money by excluding his wife, and if Mother had gone she would most certainly have needed fine gowns and hoods and capes, all new, perhaps we were not as wealthy as I had thought.

I went to go inside. As I walked past the barrel of steaming water, I caught sight of something. A reflection. I froze. And then it was gone.

"Are you well, Mistress Seymour?" Marge asked, looking up with flushed cheeks from her work. "You look like you saw a ghost."

I swallowed hard. "I am well. I just thought of something I was to do and had forgotten."

I hurried indoors. I had lied. Marge had the truth of it. For a moment, I had thought I saw Edmund standing behind me, scowling. A ghost whose eyes accused, told me that by my silence I was in league with the one who had killed him, who had killed his family.

*

A week later and Father wrote there was concern, for the Princess Mary, Duchess of Suffolk, who had to go to the summit meeting since she was the Dowager Queen of France, had been ill with a pain in her side at the start of the year and still was ill. Her ladies, Father wrote, were in a state of near apoplexy, for if Mary did not go they would not either. To miss out on what was likely to be the greatest event of all time would be a hard and unusual punishment. Fortunate it was for them that the Duchess went to London to help with preparations, and found that toil improved her health.

Just before the English party set out for France, there was word that the Emperor was to visit England. "I thought our King was making peace with France?" I asked.

I was told it was a good thing we were at peace with all countries. And the Emperor Charles V, King of Spain and Holy Roman Emperor, was the nephew of Queen Katherine, so it was even better that we should be friends with Spain. Edward, we heard, was to go with Father and attend to the King as he met his nephew the Emperor.

"*I shall go,*" Catherine said, almost to herself one day as she stood at a window in the long gallery, watching rain pelt the glass windows.

Father came home to report much, gather clothes and his men, and then left again. Edward was to go with him to meet the Emperor and then to go to France, but for all her boasts, Catherine was left behind.

"As Edward's wife, I should have gone," she said to Mother one day.

"I thought the same, my dear," Mother said, sighing into her embroidery. "But I have heard the truth from one of my friends at court. As you know, our royal masters are to go from meeting the Emperor straight on to France. The Queen, in her wisdom, knew she could not take more attendants than the Queen of France. In truth, it is the miserly nature of the King of France that led to our being left behind. If Queen Claude had been allowed more attendants, the Queen could have taken us all, but Katherine, kind and humble as her heart is, did not want to upstage the Queen of France, her sister upon a royal throne, so took only as many as Claude."

If Queen Katherine was concerned about not upstaging her French counterpart, our King was not. When Father and Edward returned, we heard much. There had been a short meeting with the Emperor in England, which apparently the King of France was unaware of, and then to France they had gone, and into a realm of wonder.

We were told of tents of gold and silver cloth the French had erected, so their side of the field blazed as if covered in dragon scales of precious metals. But we English had magic all our own.

"A *castle*?" I asked, leaning in closer to listen to Edward as he told the tale. "But our workmen only went to Calais in March, how could they have built a castle in such small a time?"

"Ah…" he said, touching his nose to show he had a secret.

"Torture us not, lord husband," Catherine said, pouting. She looked enchanting, innocent as the child she had killed.

"How could I deny you anything?" he asked, eyes glowing with affection as he gazed at her. I had to look away. Into fire I stared. If I imagined myself in those flames, I could almost feel myself purified by the fire, the heat, cleansed, my soul no more dark and soiled by all I knew.

"It was not a true castle," Edward went on. "King Harry commanded it to be built and told his men how. It was a castle built out of wood and cloth, the outside painted so it looked like stone. He called it the *Palace of Illusion*, and it was huge; four wings where all the royal family slept and ate and entertained, as well as a central courtyard. There were real glass windows! There was too a gatehouse, which had England's lions standing proud and bold on the top, painted to look like stone. Some statues were made to look like marble by using feathers, trailed through black ink and then laced light and free over white paint. Cupid and Bacchus gazed down from its walls, along with heads of ancient and noble Emperors of Rome. Outside there was an enormous fountain, and our Good Harry shipped forty thousand gallons of wine to France, so the fountain would flow always, never run dry." Edward laughed. "There were many nights and days men gathered there, drinking, trying to run it dry and none did succeed."

"What a sight it must have been!" I exclaimed.

From the bitter look on Catherine's face, she thought the same.

"The Queen, King and Princess all had rooms inside, as did the Duke and Duchess of Suffolk and Cardinal Wolsey," Edward continued. "The Dowager of France was the most beautiful of the three Queens, but Claude of France is a godly woman, like Katherine, and they were praised by all. In the Dowager's rooms, there were the monograms *M* and *L,* done in gold leaf."

"For her husband?" I asked.

"Her husband is Charles Brandon, little mouse," said Catherine. "*Louis* of France is the husband the Princess would remember, for he was a king, not a mere Duke."

"More importantly Louis is the husband the *French* remember," said Edward. "That is why it was done."

Catherine scowled and looked away. Edward became worried. He did not like upsetting her. The more detached from him she seemed, the more he loved her. My brother pressed a hand to her arm and she eventually bestowed a smile upon him, her little slave. I swallowed a lump that tasted of hatred which rose in my throat.

"Did the Duke not mind?" I asked, trying to draw Edward from the witch.

He smiled at me. "He did not. He knows his wife outranks him and has always thought himself lucky to gain her hand and keep his head at the same time. Mary was the one the French all wanted to see, as she was greatly loved during her time as Queen of France, and loved she was at this event. Everywhere she went, the men of France cheered her and women spoke only well of her beauty and her dresses. The King of France called her his beloved sister, and danced with her before his people."

"Did her husband not dance with her?" I asked.

"He did, but Brandon injured his hand early on in the competitions, so spent most of the time helping Wolsey to see all ran smooth."

"Cardinal Wolsey made the event run smooth?" I asked. It seemed a strange occasion for a man of God to organise.

"Wolsey makes *all* run smooth," said my brother. "He is the oil and grease in every cog of England."

I must have looked confused, for my brother went on. "Did you not know? Wolsey is the King's right hand, some say the left too. He runs England."

"Is that what a Chancellor does?" I asked.

"If the King desires it," said Edward. "What the King desires is what is. That is the way of things in England."

After our King left the King of France, he met again with the King of Spain, the Emperor. It was said this too was a magnificent occasion, but the King of France was not happy about it. Not long after we heard we were to be friends with Spain, not France. France, so lately a friend, might soon again become an enemy, we were told.

I found myself confused that promises of peace and friendship were so easily made and broken, but when I looked into the secret at the heart of my own family, I understood. People so rarely told the truth. More willing was the human heart to work deceit and trickery for the benefit of one, than to employ truth and friendship with honesty, for the good of many.

Chapter Seventeen

Wulfhall
Wiltshire

Winter- Summer 1521

The year after the Field of the Cloth of Gold, and just before the Duke of Buckingham, England's premier nobleman and once friend of the King, was arrested for being a witch, Catherine swelled large and giddy with a child in her belly.

It was not long after Candlemas that she announced her condition. Edward must have got her with child before Christmas, Mother said, for in the January of that year, 1521, he had been employed by Cardinal Wolsey and taken to the court of the Emperor of the Holy Roman Empire at Worms, on the Rhine. There was an assembly to be held there which was to denounce the heretic priest, Martin Luther, who had nailed a list of complaints about the Church to a door in the Holy Roman Empire and had, I was told, been spreading malicious dissent ever since. I had always been taught that to question the Church was to question God Himself, so Luther was a name synonymous with demonic evil to me. That my good brother was to go on a mission to aid the Church against her foes seemed wonderful. My brother was to become a knight of God, a soldier of the Church.

Edward had only been gone a month, but it seemed we may not see him for some time. He had sent word that in the spring he was to be admitted to the court of the Emperor and stay a while. The King and Wolsey had recommended him personally, he said. He was to be the eyes and ears of the Cardinal, report on all that went on. The Emperor had approved the position and had shown a brotherly warmth towards Edward. I was so proud of him I thought my heart would explode. Yet if my brother was all that was good, his wife surely was all that was ill.

I had watched her on the 2nd of February as we processed to the altar, we women, bearing candles representing the blessed light that the Virgin brought to the world in the form of Jesus Christ. To see Catherine that day, fair hair covered with a veil, her face shining lovely and innocent, you would have thought she could become a saint herself. Beauty is the best mask. It conceals all that is putrid underneath.

We had emerged from the church that morn into mist. Low and creeping it had come scuttling from the valleys and falling from clouds as we had honoured the Virgin. By the time we emerged it was thick, soupy, slithering across the paths leading back to Wulfhall. Ravens had called to us from the trees as we walked home. It sounded as though they called my name, as if they knew my secrets and were mocking me. Mother had insisted we walk that day, a pilgrimage of feet in honour of the Virgin, there and back to church. I did not mind, despite the mist and chilled air. The moss and the grass had been bright, gleaming gold with tiny touches of sun that glinted from blade and soft, downy lichen. Trees far away were dark purple and black, bruises and wounds against bleak winter skies. At one point, wood pigeons burst from the hedge in front of us. I jumped as though I had seen a ghost.

And then a week later, Catherine told Mother, and Mother told us.

I watched the witch pretending to be my sister and a good wife to my brother. Whose child was it? I doubted the fair-haired whore even knew. Edward visited with regularity, took care to bed her often when he came. And there were her nightly attentions from my father.

With a man so often in her bed, I wondered that it had taken so long for her to fall pregnant. Perhaps she had been taking something, some remedy or herb, to stop her becoming pregnant with my father's child, but when I thought of what I had heard in the attic, it had sounded as if Catherine relished the idea of bearing his children. Perhaps she took her herbs when Edward came to her instead.

So there will be a child, said my mind as I listened to Mother gush about Catherine's baby. *A child born of sin and evil, in the place of Mary's good baby, who died for it.* I know not how I congratulated Catherine. I thought I might vomit on her leather shoes.

I went out to walk about the fishponds much that month, a chorus of frogs in my ears, the wind trying to tear my hood from my head. Toads were on the move, roaming to a place unknown, oblivious to my presence as they hopped and fell across the paths, scrambling on ungainly legs into the hedge and beyond. Jackdaws croaked at me from the trees. Tenants of my father were out yanking blackthorn and hawthorn shoots from the land, the ploughmen were busy with oxen, ripping the dark, frosty earth asunder. The oxen dropped dung as they went, and men trod it in, knowing shit is good for soil. I wondered if the same was true of our house, that what was fetid and rotten could make it better. Catherine's whoring had made a baby, the baby would be known as Edward's son or daughter. A fertile future formed, from a past of waste. I hoped something good could come of it, hoped more than I could say. And I could say nothing, now, could I? Even if I were not risking my eternal soul and my present reputation by telling someone the truth of our house, there was a child that would be hurt now. Born of evil it might be, but I could not believe it was anything but innocent.

If people knew the secret, and this child in Catherine's belly was Father's, it would be cast off. Edward would be wounded, his reputation scarred. At times I thought it was better if all continued as it was, if the secret remained secret, so no one, Edward, this child, my mother, would be hurt. I stopped often on slippery paths covered in thin ice that month and stared into the world. In some ways, despite all the industry and roaming beasts, the world looked frozen, still, as though nothing would change. Perhaps it would be better if that was the truth.

Her child quickened in the spring, at the same time the Duke of Buckingham went to trial and was found guilty. Many were unsettled by the Duke's fate, for he was of ancient blood, some said blood more noble than our royal line of the Tudors, and perhaps that was why he had been arrested rather than witchcraft. People said Buckingham had called on men to predict the death of the King, which was treason, and had kept a knife up his sleeve that he meant one day to plunge into the King's heart. Carrying a knife was no crime, all people, even women did, for they were required for eating and were useful tools for other tasks. Men carried swords, if wealthy or noble. Carrying one with the intention of using it on the King was obviously treason, but I wondered how anyone knew the Duke had intended this? People said he had confessed. Other people, their voices lower, more careful, said he confessed because the King's men tortured him. Those who spoke in the lowest tones of all said the King wanted the Duke gone because he feared him, feared the power he had, the money in his coffers, his royal blood, the influence and soldiers in his possession and the love the people had for him.

But if England was unsettled about the Duke, Catherine was overjoyed about her child. My mother took great care of her, refusing to allow her to eat salad plants as well as fish or milk which were thought too phlegmatic for the babe, and feeding her jellies of quince to bring health to the child, along with raspberry tea to ease her eventual childbirth. Mother even sought out and gave her an amulet with powdered unicorn horn within it, to protect both her and the child. She also found an eagle stone and brought the rattling rock to Catherine in triumph. It had a hollow in the middle, in which something was trapped. It was a form of magic, of course, the stone with stone inside representing a mother and her babe. "It will relieve pangs of childbed," Mother told Catherine, "and prevent the child from leaving you before the time is ripe."

"They are mentioned by Pliny," Edward wrote. *"And Saint Isidore wrote of them too. They are believed to be most effective. You, my beloved wife, should keep it with you always, bound to your arm."*

Catherine, set upon by Mother, did just that, but she did not like it. The eagle stone might have been magical, but it was not pretty.

As maids of our house took tablecloths and bed linen out for the spring wash and soaked them in oaken tubs of steaming water, wood ash and soda, the Duke went to the block and lost his head for trying to kill the King. That same day Mother told us she had secured Edith Grey to aid with the birth of Catherine's child. Edith visited the house much after that time to discuss the process and advise us in the lead up to it. She was now the cunning woman of the village, for her own aged grandmother had died of the sweat along with so many others. On her first visit Edith felt Catherine's stomach, and said she was carrying low, which meant a boy, news which only increased my mother's joy.

Mother's full attention was upon Catherine, which made it much more difficult for Catherine to dally with my father. I went out of my way to aid my mother, insisting that Catherine was with us day and night, much to Catherine's annoyance. It pleased me to see her lovely face twist with sourness when my mother could not see. I often smirked at Catherine at such times, relishing her irritation. Oh, my wicked little heart and the comforts it took! When rendered powerless we often become petty creatures.

Busy with Catherine, Mother often sent me to tend to other tasks, such as overseeing maids as they shook, beat and inspected furs, kept in a chest when not being worn. I would have to make up a cleaning wash for furs that required attention, made of wine, lye, fuller's earth and verjuice. I restored colour with sponges soaked in verjuice and sprinkled fur made hard by damp with wine and flour. When that mixture had sat a while on the furs, I instructed the maids to rub out the paste, restoring the fur to stunning softness. Catherine liked it when I was handed such jobs, for she knew I did not like them. As I relished her misery she returned the favour. She suggested many a task to Mother that she knew I hated, knowing Mother would simply send me off to do them.

Catherine should not have continued to lie with my father in any case, for the safety of her child. But such concerns of morality and mortality seemed to little trouble the two of them. After all, if they cared not for the sin they were wallowing in, the death brought upon our house and on innocents for their misdeeds, what did they care for adding more sin to it? Once a body is dirty more dirt hardly matters. And they had no shame, no shame at all about the lies they spun as silken thread about the house. Father was as pleased, perhaps more so, as Mother at the news of Catherine's pregnancy. I knew he was thinking the child was his. He seemed to have managed to vanquish his disgust at the idea of cuckolding his son, and now was *proud* he might have laid a seed in the belly of his whore. It disgusted me to see him touch her stomach, put his ear to her belly to see if he could hear the child. I had problems stopping myself from physically retching to see the sloppy smile on his face.

And yet if they knew, Mother and Edward, if they knew it would be worse, I thought, trying to convince myself it was good if the lies of Catherine and my father concealed the truth.

Edward came home later that year to wait for the birth. Catherine was within my mother's rooms by then for her lying-in, and only female kin were allowed in to see her. As buzzards flew in the skies, and more birds than one could count sang with the dawn, Edward spent much time with Father and Henry. In the day they were drinking, hunting or hawking out in the marshlands. I thought about telling him, as I often did when he was at home, and then I could not. Not only was I trapped in Mother's rooms, where we waited for

Catherine to bring forth her seed of sin, but the thought of stealing that bright, proud expression from his pale eyes was more than I could bear. Even if I had not sworn on the Holy Bible to the imperilment of my soul, I am not sure I could have told him. My good brother never looked more handsome than when he heard he was to be a father. At times I cried at night, telling the darkness I could say nothing, that I could not hurt him like that, and I cried, too, for the guilt of not telling him. I felt weak, a coward. I hated myself for it.

Catherine went into labour one night in late summer. It was a sultry, stifling season which had made her last months uncomfortable, much to my satisfaction. But there my satisfaction ended. Her labour was short. The witch passed through it with more ease than my mother had. And the child was a boy. Catherine got all she wanted, just because she wanted it. Was beauty always rewarded for being beautiful, even if it was ugly inside? Childbirth was God's punishment upon women for our part in the fall of man. If this was the case, why had Catherine, who had done such ill, escaped so lightly? Why did not God make her hurt? Why did He grant her a son?

"Tell me, Lord of Heaven, Lord of Hosts," I mumbled in the house's chapel in the dusk of a summer's night not long after the birth of my nephew, or brother, which he was I knew not. "Please explain this, for I do not understand. How is it she can work such ill, commit sins so numerous I cannot count them, and be rewarded?"

There was no answer from God. I stared up into the eyes of the Virgin, painted on the walls. Her face was impassive, calm. *Wait*, she seemed to say.

Mother told us we were not to say that Catherine had had an easy time of the birth. It made her sound uncouth, for noble and royal women were supposed to have a harder time in childbed, whereas common women gave birth with ease. We had to tell tales to those who asked after "the fair daughter of the house", lie to say she had suffered much, but *sweetly* and with remarkable *strength* and *courage*. I almost choked on words of praise. Catherine, when she was accepting visitors in her rooms, kept her face pale with almond paste and milk, so she looked wan, as though she had suffered much.

If only it was so.

Catherine asked that the child be named John, for my father. Edward, poor, happy soul that he was, agreed, not knowing he was being made a fool of again. Mother was so pleased she burst into tears, and threw her arms about her daughter-in-law. I thought of how Catherine's heart must be laughing to pile humiliation upon humiliation upon my mother and my beloved brother, and them not only not know it, but rejoice in it. I wondered what my mother would have said if she had known that the squalling pink-faced child in Catherine's arms was quite possibly the bastard son of her own husband.

"It is not the babe's fault," I said in my prayers, trying to convince myself. "It is not the fault of the child that he was born to such sinful parents."

In merry ignorance, the household threw itself with gay lunacy into celebration and revels. The bastard was baptised, and forty days later Catherine was cleansed and purified of the stain of childbed by being churched. Until she was churched she was not allowed out of her rooms, or out of the house, nor was she to go near cooking food, baking bread, or crops, for she might spoil them. I thought that might be a good rule to follow in any case. The woman was clearly a curse. All she touched became rotten.

Before her blessing and welcoming back to the Church, Catherine was a target for evil spirits, and demons who might try to claim her soul in her unclean state. It was several weeks before she was ready to undertake the ceremony and much of that time she spent in bed. For my own part, I thought Catherine a demon in any case. I did not think it mattered if another came to her. She was already stuffed full of vice. Like as much, there would not be room for another demon inside her skin, and any who came calling would leave swiftly for there being not a seat left in her soul for them. The irony of her being cleansed made me shake my head at times, always when I could not be seen, although I was not careful enough obviously, as Mother started dosing me with warm oil in the ears, thinking there was something amiss with my hearing.

Nothing was, but my soul was troubled, always in a state of riot and misery. For much of my youth I had grown up with this secret pressing upon me, had known the fine reputation of my family was a lie. My family thought we were close, loved each other. What love was there here when my father and Catherine did as they did, when my mother was deceived and Edward was twice taken for a fool, by Catherine and by me, for I said I loved him but had not the strength, courage or will to tell him the truth? Truly, who was more immoral? Catherine who worked secret sin, or me, who knew of evil and allowed it to be?

I feared for my soul, to be cast out, to be not believed. I feared to bring pain upon those I loved. At times, it felt I had been silent on the matter so long that I had no words to tell of it. As though my tongue was in the hands of the witch, not mine anymore, but her servant, slave, bound to her will.

We attended her churching ceremony. She knelt, veiled, near the door, at a special pew made for women for this purpose. The witch carried a lighted taper in her hands, and made an offering of the chrisom of her child to the Church. Leading her inside, the priest blessed Catherine in the narthex, opposite the altar and sprinkled her with holy water, his hands moving to create the form of the cross in the air over her. He recited Psalm 24 over her head in Latin. "Who shall ascend into the hill of the Lord?" the priest asked. "Or who shall stand in his holy place? He that hath clean hands, and a pure heart; who hath not lifted up his soul unto vanity, nor sworn deceitfully…"

As I listened, I said Psalm 25 in my head. *O my God, I trust in Thee: let me not be ashamed, let not mine enemies triumph over me...*

Blessing done, he led her on as he intoned, in English, "Enter thou into the temple of God, adore the son of the Blessed Virgin Mary who has given thee fruitfulness of offspring."

For a moment I wondered if she would glance back, look at my father, the true seed of her fruit. *The meek will He guide in judgement,* said my mind. *And the meek He will teach His way. All the paths of the Lord are mercy and truth unto such as keep His covenants, and His testimonies...*

The priest took Catherine to the altar where she was blessed again and once more sprinkled with holy water, and dismissed her with the words, "the peace and blessing of God Almighty, the Father, the Son, and the Holy Ghost, descend upon thee, and remain forever, Amen."

For Thy name's sake, O Lord, pardon mine iniquity, for it is great...

Catherine looked pure that day. She returned to the house to celebrate with us all for the hale, hearty boy she had borne for the line of the Seymours. A month had passed since the birth of her son, and he was a handsome babe. For a while I was present at the feast, listening to Edward roar with laughter and tell tales of the Emperor and his court, of the King of Spain's good sense and long chin, but soon I could bear it no more. I pleaded a headache early in the night and left. I could not bear to watch Edward kiss and pet Catherine so affectionately, all the time not aware of the twisted horns of the cuckold sprouting from his head.

Late that night, when Edward had been carried to his bed insensible with drink, I heard whispers outside. I crept to the shuttered window and looked through the crack. Catherine was leading my father through the yard to the barn. I glanced down at Bess on the floor. Deep asleep, as always, curled up in her covers like a mouse. All others in the house were asleep, but I crept from my bedroom and went down the stairs, passing through the kitchens to the outside.

Turn Thee unto me, and have mercy upon me, for I am desolate and afflicted…

My bare feet tapped lightly upon the rushes in the kitchen. Carefully I opened the door, stepping out into blue and white shadows under the light of a half moon. Sultry air of a summer night washed over me, a breath of jasmine poured upon my face. I stole through the courtyard and about the side of the barn. My breath was short, as though I ran far, but I did not. There, I saw Catherine bent over, hands pressed against the wooden slats of the barn, my father standing behind her. One of his hands was on her head, the other grasped her naked hip as he rode her like a boar rides a sow in the woodlands.

"You are mine," he gasped as he thrust into her with vicious force, thighs slapping loud and true against her buttocks. "Mine and mine alone, Catherine."

I shivered to hear her wild, short cry of pleasure, her moans that she was his, that she loved him. "You are mine," Father said again.

Oh keep my soul and deliver me, let me not be ashamed, for I put my trust in Thee…

"Mine."

She is your son's, I thought. My heart was become dead inside me. He had surrendered. My father loved her. Whatever spells the witch had worked, they had succeeded. On the night our household, our family, had gathered to celebrate the birth of Edward's 'son', his own father had stolen Edward's wife away to lay claim to her again. I wondered if Edward had bedded her that day at all. I thought not. He was asleep in his bed, unconscious. I wondered if Catherine had ensured his drunkenness so she and her lover could rut against the barn, under the stars, like the animals they were.

Light from my father's signet ring flashed, catching radiance from the stars or moon, and swept over my face. I drew back, feeling exposed. Around the corner of the barn I closed my eyes and leaned against the wooden boards for a moment. Through the wooden panels, all connected, I could feel their hateful union, just as I could when her bed banged against my wall. Always I was connected to this, to them, to their sin. Never was I free of it, of them.

I thought I might lie down there, right then, and die. Little as I had liked what I had seen the first time, this was worse. My father was a weak, sinful man and Catherine was a witch who had him in her thrall. I hated them both, hated the mockery they made of all they touched. And I felt old. Children should not hate their parents, it was a sin, I knew, but what of love could grow in my heart for my father when he did such things? I felt most alone at that moment, and lost beyond measure.

I slipped away, making for my rooms. In the eyes of my family and the Church, Catherine was now a pure woman who could return to the bed of her husband. I felt sure this encounter, this night, was to set in the mind of my father, and in the mind of his mistress, that his whore was his alone. He was the first to take her, the first to spill seed in her after the birth of her first child. My father had stolen once more from my brother, my poor insensible Edward, sleeping the thick sleep of a drunken man who knows nothing. Churched Catherine had been. Pure she was not. Neither of them were.

Redeem Israel, O God, out of all his troubles…

Chapter Eighteen

Wulfhall
Wiltshire

Summer 1521

Whilst Edward was at home, revelling in his son although not in the work that came with the babe, he announced his intention to go on a long hunting trip to the plains of Somerset. Catherine was still too weak to go, so she claimed. I believed she relished the idea of bedding her lover whilst her husband was away. But Edward invited me and Henry. With Mother's permission, I went.

It had been pleasant enough to escape the chambers we had waited in for the birth of Catherine's bastard. A day or two spent in sunlight, a mask upon my face provided by my mother as all women of court wore, protected my pale skin from the reddening sun, and I all but forgot the stuffy indoors that had held us captive so long. I had gone out into the air to sit on meads now resplendent with wild flowers and thick, bouncy grass in the orchards. Looking across at the meadowland my eyes had lit up with a fire of flowers; yellow, violet, red, and brown that became purple at a distance, mingled together so all colours seemed one; a blended joy of blooms, light and sweet scent. Into the meadow I had walked, bees buzzing busily about my ankles, jackdaws playing in the skies, brown-coated butterflies dancing about one another at the height of my head, dipping and chasing each other in the warm skies. It had been almost possible to forget, on such walks, that there were ugly things in the world. *You are one of them,* said the voice.

Not as ugly as that which appears to be beautiful, I retorted. The voice fell silent. It was not often I won.

A trip away from Wulfhall, hunting, staying overnight in lodges on Father's estates and on land of his neighbours was even more welcome than a mere hour or so in the meadow, or walking along by the glittering fishponds. We rode out one morning before dawn, just as birds were starting to call from nests in the trees, just as the creeping light of the sun started to show, hesitant, glittering, over the forest in the distance. As we emerged from the house I saw a brown stoat snake across the grass, vanishing quick as a breath into the hedge. On the other side of the garden I saw the black-tipped ears of a young hare fade into shadow. In the blue light of that morn I could almost tell I you I saw Death gather his cloak about glaring white bones and stalk away. The young hare escaped death; the stoat would be hungry a little while.

Already maids were up. The fires had been swept, I gathered, for Bess came out and emptied ashes into a bucket, ready that they might be taken into the garden by one of Father's men, mingled with soil. Ashes seem as though they are dead, yet in them is life. Mixed with earth, they grant richness to plants. There is resurrection where it seems only dull death, the end of things, is present. Flakes of ash, like grey snow, drifted into the dark, yet lightening, skies. I watched, spellbound for a moment, as they floated away, out of sight, vanishing as the red light of the morning sun touched them.

"A good palfrey I chose for you, sister," Edward said, interrupting my silent revelry. He was walking ahead of the man leading my horse. It was a good horse indeed. I knew my horseflesh by then, and I was a fine and true rider. All things I took pleasure in I was good at.

"Beautiful," I said.

She was. She was pale of coat and gentle of disposition, my brother had chosen well. Palfreys were considered the best mounts for women, paler ones the best of those. Through the courtyard and out of the gates we rode, passing the orchards to one side where peach trees, my mother's pride, stood, their small fruit waiting for plenty of sun to ripen soft flesh in shades of downy pink and ductile yellow. Flanking them were quinces and pears. In spring the orchard was a blaze of blossom, white as snow, but now all there was to be seen was green and green in the orchard, flowers given way to fruit as yet unripe.

We clopped past the long and wide fishponds called *stews*, for that was what the fish were used for, where water was igniting as sparks upon kindling in the first light of day. Nodding wild irises, flags, stood yellow and green and tall along the edges of the water, whistling rushes at their sides, as fellow knights lined up for battle. Sedge fluttered, stroked by the wind. Not far away, the hedges were full of apothecary's rose, escaped from our gardens perhaps, and growing intertwined with sharp, dark thorns of briar and blackthorn. Blackthorn was the plant from which the crown of thorns had been made, it was said. With roses poking through, it was stained by beautiful blood.

"The rose of Lancaster," said Edward, spotting it.

In our gardens were herbs, with flowers and vegetables amongst them, as was the way. Lilies and peonies stood with marjoram and mallow, marigolds to decorate pottages were flanked by shallots and sorrel. Lettuce for stew and salad stood about roses whose petals would be sprinkled into puddings of custard and sweet milk. Currant and raspberry bushes were overshadowed by vines which twisted up, over arbours where we would sit at times to read or think.

Along the edges of the woodland, patches of trees dotted through fields and pastures, honeysuckle bobbed, pretty scents wafting from yellow and pink flowers. On sunny banks were late dog violets, and musk roses climbed in the trees of the hedgerows. White butterflies, silky wings dotted black, fluttered about alighting on flowers and grass with their spindly legs. We stopped to pluck sorrel, almost past its best, from the wayside, chewing the tangy herb as we rode, its tart leaves flooding our mouths with water. The trees were lush and green, their leaves filling the skies to compete with the clouds for space in the heavens. Buttercups dazzled the eyes as the sun reflected from their glossy petals. Meadows glowed as the haze of the morning sun hit them, flowers and grasses moving gently, waving to us as we rode along. Swallows were already swooping, hunting flying bugs in the air over the meadow. We passed a boy on his way to the woodland, herding pigs. Jostling and snorting, shoulder-barging and impatient the hogs wandered past, ready to root. The smell of their sweat and skin encrusted with flaking grey-brown mud rose pungent and heady on the air.

We took servants; two men to help with the hunting, and a maid to aid me with dressing and to cook for us when we stopped at hunting lodges on the way. Henry's hounds ran alongside, huge, long tongues flopping from their pink mouths. Henry chose the best dogs. He had a talent for it, often seeming more comfortable with animals than people. We were a merry band that morning, riding out with the warmth of the summer's day already wafting towards us on the fresh morning breeze. Squirrels in russet tunics skittered up trees and stared accusingly at us, as birds warbled to greet the sun. We rode not far the first day, and stopped at one of Father's lodges where we ate a simple meal and slept deep and well. The next day we rose early and whilst it was cool we rode harder than we had the day before. As the skies became striped, gold and pink touching hands with indigo and silver as though they were to wed, we slowed. Shrews darted, long-nosed and hasty, over the path, racing for home, and hedgehogs trundled to bed in the bracken, spikes glinting under the emerging sun. We sang songs from court, and Edward told us gossip from its halls.

"Queen Katherine cannot give the King a son," he informed us. "Her courses have ended, and all at court know now there is no hope that she can give our good Henry an heir."

"How do you know this?" I breathed, thinking my brother must be clever indeed to have discovered such information.

Edward shrugged. "Some women of Katherine's chambers are as loose with their tongues as they are with their virtue, sister," he jested. "They share the private secrets of their mistress with ease, and many are prepared to pay them a coin or two in return for information."

"Why would anyone but the King care?" I asked. Henry and Edward snorted in unison at my ignorance.

"The question of the succession is a matter of concern for *all* people of England, sister," replied Edward, pulling his reins as we crested the top of a small hill and stared out over the open plains of Somerset. "Without a male heir to succeed to the throne, we are left with only the infant Princess Mary to claim the crown. A woman cannot rule England. It has never been done before, and for good reason! Women are often weaker of mind, and they certainly cannot lead men into battle, cannot command. God made them for a life leading in the home, caring for babes, and bringing them to life within them. The Almighty divided our duties; men to lead in public, women in private; men to make war and craft politics, women to make peace and bring about charity. Some say Mary's future husband will become our King, but there are many, including me, who fear such a thing."

"Why so?" In truth I knew why, but I also knew that my brother liked to tell me things. If I appeared ignorant, he became wise, and that made him happy.

Edward glanced at me and smiled. He looked so handsome on his horse. With his riding doublet and cap of green velvet, a jerkin of dark leather, with the white of his linen shirt showing, and a large pearl set at his throat, he was the model of a courtly gallant.

"What if she marries the King of another land, sister?" he asked. "Think on that. A King of another land might envelop England as part of his territories. We could become no longer a strong nation, independent as we stand now, but a mere extension of another kingdom. Perhaps a King of another nation would seek to make us like his own people, impose laws which we did not hold with, or steal taxes from us to fund wars in which we have no part to play. We could become slaves to a foreign master, subservient to his people who he would always place above us. No," he sighed, eyes wandering about. "We need a prince. England must be ruled by an English King. And our Harry knows that as well as any man of his court."

"You speak of the King as though you are his friend, brother," I said with admiration.

Edward flashed me a grin. "I am a server in His Majesty's chambers, his companion on the hunt, and I have had the privilege of riding against His Majesty in the joust," he replied blithely. "The King is friendly towards me, warm even, but it would be an exaggeration to call me his friend. Yet I hope, in time, to rise in his estimations and trust. He is a fine man, sister, and a good King. We are a fortunate race. Not many people of the world are granted the grace of possessing a King who is both warrior and poet, defender of the faith and student of the tomes of history."

"It must be wonderful to know the King so well," I breathed. "I can hardly even imagine court, having only known Wulfhall. But to be as you are, brother... that is something I should dearly love."

"I am not sure you would be suited to the joust, Jane," Edward teased, "but we could have you run at the rings if you like, to test your skill?"

I giggled, covering my mouth with my hand. Edward reached over to prise my fingers from my lips, and I smiled. It was our old tradition. "There," he said with satisfaction. "You are pretty when you are merry, Jane. You should let more people see your smile. Wasting it behind your hand is a sin most grievous."

I blushed and looked away. I had never been called pretty before, not by anyone. Pleasant though the compliment was, I did not believe it, but I liked that my brother might think to lie, an innocent lie, to make me feel joy.

"If it is indeed a place at court you wish for, sister, perhaps I can speak to Father on the subject," Edward went on. "You would have to do as I do, as Thomas does now, and work your way up from the household of a rich patron to that of the Queen, but it is not impossible. Queen Katherine admires ladies like you, ones who are modest, humble and sweet. I see no reason why you could not aim to serve in her house."

My eyes darted to his face. His tone was offhand. It was an offer made on the spur of the moment, I knew, but what an offer! Such ambition, spoken so carelessly! How easy it was for men to think of something and then go to do it. How easy the world must look to them, to people who were permitted to do as they wanted.

And what a prospect… To serve the Queen? I had never considered anything of its like before, and yet suddenly I was lost in longing for the dream of which he spoke. "I would love, above all things, to come to court with you, brother," I gasped. "To be gone from… to see the King and to serve the Queen." I cursed my tongue. I had almost expressed a desire to be away from Wulfhall because of Catherine. I could not do that. Edward would ask why I hated my home so.

To be away from this cursed place! Something in me sang like a nightingale.

Edward patted my hand, noting nothing. "I will speak to our father for you, Jane," he assured me. "The court is the best place to find you a husband in any case. You will catch a far grander one if you fish from the halls of court, and Mother would welcome such a fate for you, I am sure. I will keep my eye out for suitable placements, but do not elevate your hopes too much. You know how Mother is; she might decide she wants you all to herself, at home."

"She has Catherine, our sisters and little John now," I said, trying to keep bitterness from my tone. "She has no need of me. And our mother has never liked me, brother. I do not think she would miss me."

Edward frowned, his brow puzzled. "I think you do not see how she leans on you, Jane," he said. He lifted his eyebrows and jangled the reins of his horse. "Perhaps *she* does not see how she leans on you, but I do not think she would have made it through the awful times without you. You are her rock, Jane; quiet and steady."

I thought on his words. Were they true? It was unbelievable to think my mother leant on me, as Edward said. No, I could not believe such a thing. Perhaps by only coming to the house infrequently as he did, he took but the outer show of things as the truth. Certainly, he did not see what his wife was up to under his very nose. We rode on.

"Look!" exclaimed Henry as we rose over the crest of a small hill. "The giants!"

It was unusual to hear Henry excited about anything. He was solid and calm most of the time. My eyes travelled along his arm to where he was pointing and I let out a short gasp. Far away they might be, but I could see how big they were. Standing in the open fields were enormous stones, higher than a man standing on the shoulders of another. Thick and grey, they stood bold on the plains of Salisbury, arranged in a ring, some placed on top of others, making flat arches. Sheep wandered about them. Briars were growing over some, but as we rode closer I could see nothing but them. Some had fallen, but fallen so long ago that the earth about them had risen up to take them back into the body of the world. Something about them made a shiver run down my spine. Spirits of Kings of old had been left here; a hushed majesty, a secret magic.

"What are they?" I asked as we stopped our horses right by them. Up close, they were larger than I had thought. Grey glittered in the light of the sun from their skins of stone.

Edward lifted his shoulders, a careless shrug from one who had seen them before. "There are tales aplenty, Jane," he said. "But none know, really." He shifted his reins into one hand and patted his horse's side. Dust came from the hair, drifting into the light of the sun, glistening as gold. "Some say they are giants made into stone when they dared to emerge from caves into the light of God's world. Some say they were once men, turned to stone by God for breaking the Sabbath. Some claim them as witches, dancing in a circle and cursed to become rock. But none know, Jane. They have stood a long time, and will continue to stand, I believe, when we all are dead and gone."

"Perhaps that was why they were placed here," I said, my eyes dancing over their still forms.

"What do you mean?" asked Henry.

"Perhaps they were placed here to show us immortality," I murmured. "Perhaps God put them here to demonstrate eternity."

Henry and Edward grinned at each other, perhaps thinking me a doe-eyed fool, but I knew what I meant even if I could not express it in words.

"Come," Edward said, drawing me from my contemplation. "We have a way to go before we find the hunting tower."

We rode on, but I did not forget the stones, or the feeling they brought to me. To stand, never moving, immortal, as days, weeks and months of years, of eons rolled over them; to stand through all the ages of man, and never be forgotten.

I could be such a thing, I thought as we neared the hunting lodge that night. Edward had said I was Mother's rock, and even if that was untrue, I could be stone. I could be still and calm. I could watch aeons of time pass over me. A silent watcher ever I had been. In some ways, I felt as stone already, for people think they know all at a glance, but know nothing of the inside of stone.

Did hearts beat in those giants on the plains of Salisbury? Beat, as mine did in me, wishing for a chance at life, for the ambition my brother had placed in me that day, with but a careless promise to speak to our father on my behalf?

Chapter Nineteen

Wulfhall
Wiltshire

Spring 1522- Summer 1523

White flowers on black branches marked the end of winter. Blackthorn burst into life, radiant against a sky of dazzling blue in the morn. Father said it meant a cold spell was coming late; there would be snow again before spring came in, in truth. Snow there was, but not deep. The blackthorn threatened much, but was all tongue and no words that year. Oxlips arrived to welcome spring, but not before the celandine which erupted along banks in the fields and through the forest floor, glimmering as tears of the sun fallen upon brown-black earth.

That year in the spring, as the King rode into the lists wearing the motto *elle mon Coeur a navera, she has wounded my heart* and all said Mary Boleyn, my part-Howard cousin had become his mistress, my mother brought another two babes, Margery and Anthony, into the world at the same time. They almost killed her. The birth was long and she lost a great deal of blood. Mistress Grey was almost beside herself, working so fast her hands became as blurs as she pounded leaves in her pot and made compresses of cold arnica and other herbs to stem the bleeding. My mother recovered, the children were well, if both slight, but she was determined to not bring another into the world. Twins were unusual, and what was more unusual was both survived. But the birth was arduous, and my mother feared Death would come for her if she tried again.

"My days of childbirth are done," she croaked to Edith as the cunning woman spooned chicken broth with rice and almonds, food for invalids, into her mouth. "I need you to help me to make sure I do not bear another."

Edith inclined her head. "Nine children born to any woman is enough, my lady," she agreed. "I will go over the plants you have been eating to ensure regular courses, and think on what else I may bring to you. There are charms we might use. You should not take on another birth, you are right."

Edith went over the ingredients of Mother's *sallats* with me, *tsking* and clipping her tongue. "These are not the best herbs," she noted. "Rue and savin will be more effective. I will prepare a new list for your mother, prescribe a diet rich in herbs and plants that will aid her. We can dry the herbs so she can make infusions in the winter when they do not grow."

Edith did so, and Mother ate each meal thereon accompanied by a small *sallat* of herbs which would keep a child from setting within her belly. Mother approached each of these platters of food as a martyred man would the post on which he is to burn. Father ignored her expression of noble self-sacrifice. I do not think he was concerned that another child would not be born to him of his own wife. He had plenty of sons, three pretty daughters, and he had his mistress to provide children.

Watching my father gloat over his *grandson* was almost more than I could bear. Seeing his face light up when the bastard was brought into the room, watching as he took the boy out and around with him in our house, made me sick to my stomach. I could not love little John, try as I might to not blame him for the manner of his birth. Each time I looked at the child I saw my Father and Catherine. I did nothing to harm the child, but I could barely bring myself to care for him. I felt fiendish, for little John was innocent, but love him I could not.

I found relief in tales from court, as always. I was fourteen, and tales of romance bewitched me perhaps only more than when I was younger. There had been an entertainment put on called *The Chateau Vert*, where a group of ladies, including two of my cousins and the King's sister, had played virtues held captive by vices. *Kindness* was played by Mary Boleyn, which secured the notion in most minds that she was, by that time, mistress to the King. "The King *wants* her kind," laughed Marge, earning a clip about the ear from Mother Cooper.

Mary's younger sister Anne, newly arrived back from France as there was talk of war, was *Perseverance*, and the Duchess of Suffolk played *Beauty*. There were to be more celebrations come May, for the Emperor was sailing to England to meet the King and form alliance against France. They were to war with France, and the King was to stake claim to the lands of his ancestors.

"Was not peace universal and everlasting made at the *Field of the Cloth of Gold*, lady mother?" I asked, quite forgetting we had heard not long after that all that play in France was a huge farce. All I got was a withering glance in reply. I was too innocent, she told me.

But how was I to know something was not, when all had said it was? Perhaps I should have known, for in other ways I saw that which was on the surface was not truth.

*

Church bells were ringing as we went to Mass. They had been for days by order of the King, but not for a child of his being born. His sister had given her husband another boy, and this one was blessed as they had lost their first son whilst she was waiting for this child. They had called their new boy Henry, after his uncle the King and after his dead brother.

"What will become of England, though, with the Emperor our future master?" I heard Bess ask as we walked to the church. The Princess Mary, daughter of the King, had become betrothed to Emperor Charles V, her cousin. When he had come to England it had been with two thousand people and a thousand horse, it was said, and had promised to wed the Princess when she became of an age to be married.

"Mayhap her son will rule England," said Marge.

"Will the Emperor not want his son to rule Spain and the Empire?"

"A second son, then."

"It will be a while before any such son is born, or a second for England," said Bess.

"Then perhaps the nephew of the King will become King after him," said Kat.

"Hush!" Marge said, glancing about. "It is treason to speak of the death of the King."

"Who amongst you will betray me?" Kat asked, and turned, seeing me. "You will not tell your mother, Mistress Seymour?" she asked.

"Nothing did I hear," I said. "I was contemplating the day. All I heard was you speaking well of the King and his sister." I said such things with such innocence that at times they thought I was entirely serious, I am sure. Some of them who knew me better, like Kat, knew I was jesting. We walked on to church to pray for the health of this new babe, whatever would come of his future and ours.

*

"God be praised the King was not killed!" exclaimed my mother, almost falling over as she sank onto a stool. I handed her some wine and she gulped it down. She was not one for strong drinks, and looked more unsteady after the Malmsey.

"God be praised indeed," said my father, his voice ringing with disapproval.

He was not likely to approve of jousting in any case, and certainly not a competition in which the King was almost killed.

It was March, and a rider had come to the house, mud-spattered and wet, carrying a note from Edward at court. The King had been jousting in a competition, winning every match as always. He had ordered new armour to be made, his own design, and had commanded a joust so he could test it. In one of the last matches, pitted against Brandon the King had charged the field, but his visor was not down. The Duke, seeing nothing for it was hard to see in a helmet, charged too, and they clashed. The Duke's lance broke on the head of the King and splinters of wood flew up into the King's face. Our King was knocked from his horse and for a moment lay still on the ground as all the court and commoners invited to watch the joust stared, horrified and amazed.

"All thought he was dead," my father explained, reading Edward's note. "Many ran to him, our kin included. The Duke dismounted and raced to the King, thinking he had killed his brother, but in no time the King was up, laughing and jesting. He insisted on running another six matches to prove he was well."

"If the King had…" my mother said, not wanting to say the words "… Brandon would have lost his head."

"And we would have lost our country," muttered my father.

"What mean you?"

"Without an heir male, there will be war," he said quietly. War was not something my father took lightly. He had fought in enough to have shed the youthful bravado young knights had, had lost enough friends to know that honour and glory come at a high price, one claimed in blood. And civil war, war within his own country, was not something to consider happily. His lands, his family, his kin and friends would all be at risk.

Making war on strangers, for the benefit of England and her King, was one thing. Going to war against friends who happened to support another claimant to the throne, quite another.

War came, but not upon England. That July the King was making plans to invade France and my father was called to court, for experienced soldiers were required and knighted men who had served in other wars were to command troops. "The King will promote him, you will see," said my mother.

She looked as concerned as proud, however. My father had just entered his forty-fifth year and although his was to be a command position that did not mean he would escape fighting altogether. Experience was a good thing for a soldier, anticipation of a foe's movements and greater skill in the sword or lance was beneficial, but youth often grants more stamina than age. Father might find himself outmatched by someone quicker, who could last longer.

One of the youths to go was one I had no wish to see walk to war. My brother, Edward, was to go with Father, we were told. It would be his first experience of war.

In September they marched into France. Brandon, not withstanding the fact he had not so many months ago almost killed the King, was granted command and had ten thousand men under him, my father and Edward amongst them. Proud as I was, I was also consumed by terror that Edward would die. I told people I feared for Father, but he was a seasoned soldier, and besides, I think I had forsaken him in my mind. I loved him for duty, thought him bewitched by Catherine, but I also despised him for his lack of a spine. Why could he not leave her alone, see her for what she was? Why could he not see the humiliation he was inflicting upon his trusting son?

Questions about the conscience of another can never by your mind be answered, I knew that even then, as I knew that humans were a puzzle that never would be solved.

But for Edward I feared, yet should not have. We had reports back swiftly that he was distinguishing himself. Mother burst into tears when we received a letter from Father one wet, raining morning in summer, informing us Edward had been knighted in the field by the Duke himself. "Knighted in the field!" Mother exclaimed. "Then he must have fought well, with honour!"

My brother, *Sir* Edward Seymour. I could have burst for pride.

We went to the chapel to give thanks. Under torn skies ragged with grey flesh and black blood we walked, reaching the door before rain started to fall. As we went in I looked up. White cloud, like linen bandages, was wrapped about the skies, like dressings upon a wound. "Keep my brother safe, Lord of Heaven," I said to the skies. "Bring Edward home to me." Rooks cawed in the treetops. I felt they too were praying for my brother.

When we reached Wulfhall that afternoon, there was another missive, hard on the heels of the first. Father said there was talk the Duke might make Edward his Master of Horse in a few years time. But if Edward did well, the war on France did not.

Ordered to head for Paris, Brandon was to steal away the French seat of power as troops of the Emperor came to reinforce them. But the Emperor's troops never arrived. As winter set in, men were dropping dead of frostbite and cold, the troops were waning and we all feared greatly for Father and Edward. The King sent more men, six thousand, but the Duke turned back. The King was enraged, we were told, but there was nothing the Duke could do.

I did not care for the anger of the King. I just wanted Edward safe, at home, where we could keep him warm and away from the arms of Death. The King raged about the Duke bringing Englishmen home. I blessed him.

Chapter Twenty

Wulfhall
Wiltshire

Spring 1524- Winter 1525

As spring bustled in and little John started wandering about the house in his long infant's gown, crowing like a lord, the King declared he wanted his men to head into France again. Few had the stomach for it. Brandon and his captains were still banished from court because the King was so shamed and enraged about their defeat. Perhaps they too were shamed, but perhaps they also had more idea of the campaign, of what it would cost to win.

Father and Edward had returned home stick thin and skeleton-pale. The rings under their eyes were purple, the weariness upon them settled in their very bones. It took time, much good, hearty food and rest for them to look well again. As soon as he was better, and he recovered faster than Father, Edward left for London again. He was not banished from court, as he had not been one of the leaders of the failed war, and the King admired his knighthood, gained in the field. From a campaign of disasters, it helped the King to see a few victories, a few successes and the King named Edward an Esquire of the Body. It was not a great post, but it was another step up. He was to attend court when there were official functions. It did, however, make him more important in the county. This was recognised as not long after he became a justice of the peace in Wiltshire. He was rising high and working hard. When setbacks arose he overcame them.

The King was not one to accept defeat either. Father said Good Harry did not know how to approach failure, so little had it happened to him. If there was a problem, it was a temporary setback, not failure.

"Sometimes it is as though he is telling a story of his own life, like a man looking back to a legend of the past," Father said. "In such stories there are problems and vexations to try and test a knight, but *always* there is success in the end." He sighed, eyes staring out of the open door where spring sunlight was radiant and sweet. A swallow swept across the doorway, then back, looking for sites to nest. "I think sometimes the King does not see everything the way it truly is. Perhaps it is good, for men in high positions should be capable of high dreams that they might elevate their people into them, into states of wealth and happiness we might not imagine on our own. But I wonder at times... Even upon kings there are limitations."

Father would not condemn the King for being a fantasist, it would be dangerous to do so, but it was clear he thought him one.

"Will you go, John?" I heard my mother ask my father. She feared he would be killed but did not want to say. It was an odd question; even I knew he had no choice in the matter. If my father ruled our house, owned my mother and me and my siblings, the King was ruler of England and owned its men.

"If the King calls, I will answer," he said. "It is my duty as his man, his knight." He reached down and pulled little John to his knee, laughing as the lad wrapped his hands about my father's large fingers and gabbled. John was speaking well, although always a little broken. He loved his grandfather, and his grandfather, or father, whichever he was, loved him. It broke my heart in so many ways to witness. That this child, a pure soul as I wanted to believe little John was, could love my father and my father him was a good thing, yet from evil it had been born. Was it possible goodness could come from evil, that light could be of darkness born? These notions confused my mind, for it was not the way priests spoke of the world, and they were our guides to the will and wants of God. Yet I could see love, pure love, between child and man. I could, at times, too, see that Catherine loved her child with the same purity of emotion. That part of her, at least, was not bound to vice and sin. Placing her heart in the hands of her child, she had surrendered to him. Though I thought her evil, I had to admit she was not devoid of all goodness. *Perhaps the Devil was not either,* said a mean and bitter voice in my head. *He once flew, an angel, with the other servants of God.*

Little John spent time with Dorothy, who cared for him as if he were her doll. She shared her old rattles, balls of pewter with wolf's teeth in them which had been passed down through all of us children, and were said to protect against danger and death. Dorothy had her dolls, real ones made of wood and lead, but John was a good toy too. Sometimes the two of them screaming could be heard for miles when they played, and inevitably, fought.

Elisabeth was gone from the nursery and in the schoolroom. Always my studious little sister could be found, doubled over her hornbook, learning a lesson of the Lord's Prayer, or a Psalm.

At times she joined Mother and me for lessons in the distillery where we preserved the essence of herbs so we could use them all year around. Picking them at certain times of the day, either early in the morning or at dusk, under a full moon or sometimes a new moon, preserved the strengths of the properties we needed them for. Edith Grey had offered much advice in this matter, for she relied on the forest and its plants. Mother adhered to the cunning woman's wisdom and followed it as she would the word of God. Some plants we gathered were used for perfumes, washing waters and soaps, some for medicine. I was good with herbs and by that time, I could remember them and their uses with ease. When I recited them to my mother, Elisabeth watched with shining, admiring eyes. It was not often someone looked at me in such a way. I came to desire it from my little sister, to yearn for it. Curious it was to depend on a younger sibling for support and happiness, yet I did, with Elisabeth. My nine-year-old sister became a balm to my spirits. I was sixteen, and I think I was the one she looked up to in the house, a strange event considering my lowly status within it. Yet as Mother showered Elisabeth with expectations, which she felt heavy upon her young shoulders, I asked for nothing but her company. Perhaps it was a relief.

Elisabeth seemed to drift to me, seek me out, and I believed she loved me. I adored her. She had a gentle nature and a quick mind, a beguiling combination which allowed her to be generous and compassionate. Kindness is a much underrated virtue. I already knew she was cleverer than I would ever be, for reports from her tutors were glowing. "She might almost have a *boy's* mind," one said to Mother. "It happens at times, my lady, that the mind of a woman is blessed with strength almost akin to that of a male."

"Such as in the case of Katherine, the Queen," Mother said. "Or her daughter, Mary, who I hear is blessed with a mind of strength and depth."

"Indeed, my lady," he said. "One must be careful there is not too much lenience permitted, or she will become overbold, but it may mean your noble daughter can be trusted to study deeper, where such things would be considered dangerous for other girls."

His eyes strayed to me, and I put my eyes down. *Hail and well met, floor,* I said to the rushes. His eyes left me. Submission, I had learned, deflected all that threatened me. I could vanish the moment I was noticed. It was as when mice freeze so a cat cannot see them. *Is that why they call me mouse?* I wondered.

"Woman is the creature of God as is man," Mother said later to Father. "If Elisabeth is to go to court, or be a worthy wife to a lord, our daughter should learn all she can."

I could well have seethed in bitterness. When the same discussion had arisen in my past, about my education, the outcome had been so very different. Dull I was thought, and dull I remained because my parents decided I could do no better. For Elisabeth they did more, for her beauty made them believe she had greatness in her. Beauty was rewarded with success and ugliness must be content with failure. But mine became a divided heart, as I had found it often could be. So often we think we feel but one way about something, but rare is the time we are truly in agreement entire with ourselves. More often our emotions are mingled as colours of the dusk skies; blazing blue and sultry red as one, a puddle of colours in the heavens.

Bitter though I was for what my parents thought of me, I was delighted for my sister. I wanted Elisabeth to have a better future than I was thought capable of. She would have to hide a great deal of her accomplishments, as too much book learning was not valued in a woman, but her mind would be sharper than mine. I hoped it would make her happier, take her to court and a fine husband who loved her as she deserved to be loved. I hoped she would be rewarded, not for her beauty, but for the good soul inside that beauty. My little sister was an angel in human form. I had seen what danger could come from a devil placed inside the face and body of an angel.

*

Edward rode to Wulfhall often that year, bringing presents of castile soap for Mother, material for me for gowns, a doll for Elisabeth and often sweetmeats for the babies. He came to visit his son, of whom he was more proud than I think even he understood, and Catherine, hoping to plant another child in her belly. He did not know that Catherine was taking the same herbs as Mother when he came to her. Catherine did not want to bear a child from her husband. She wanted only the child of her lover to grow in her belly.

I had seen her gather herbs by the light of the dawn and at night when she thought no one was watching. But I was always watching her. She revolted me, yet I could not take my eyes from her. *Another power of the witch,* I told myself, not considering that particular accusation made no sense if she wanted to keep her secrets. But I could blame her for all ills. I could not blame myself. Years pressed their hands to my lips, my tongue, as guilt roared as fire in my belly.

Sometimes I started as I walked along a hallway. A figure seemed to loom from shadow, part of the gloom, eyes bright with pain. It never touched me, but I knew it was him. Edmund. A ghost at my back, telling me I should have said something in the past to save his family. And now, to save my own.

*

Sitting at the table one night, as Mother ate her bitter herbs with that now-familiar expression of martyred self-sacrifice and as Catherine charmed all with her conversation, Edward spoke again of the King and the succession.

"The King is restless in his marriage," he noted as he tore a chunk of bread from a slice by his pewter plate. "He knows now the Queen cannot give him another child, and his lords know it too." He mopped the bread in the sweet-sour sauce on his plate, awash with flecks of rabbit flesh and parsley.

"Why can the Queen not produce a son?" Mother asked, picking up rue leaves and chewing daintily with an expression of disgust. When finished, she continued. "She is a pious woman, all know it. The Queen gives alms, prays each day and night and rises three times in the night to hear Mass. Why would God not grant her the happiness many others, including us, have known? Children will come, in time. There is the Princess and a son will follow."

So often had we all heard that, *"a son will follow."* It might have become Katherine's motto, emblazed on her banners and her palaces. It had a hollow ring. When something is said too many times, words lose meaning.

"Some say the King's marriage is no true marriage," Edward said in a low voice. "Since the Queen was married to the King's brother, Prince Arthur, before he died, there are some who say this has cursed her marriage to the King. The Bible says that should a man take his brother's wife in marriage, it is a doomed match and will bear no children."

"But they *have* a child!" Mother's voice was distressed, growing high and shrill. "The Princess Mary, is she not a child?"

"But can she be an heir, my lady mother?" Edward reached again for the bowl of rabbit in sweet and sour syrup, and placed a fresh portion on his plate, dipping his bread in it. "Can a woman be the heir the King, and our country, requires? Can she command men, rule a kingdom, lead men in war and oversee justice?" My brother sighed, lifting the bread although not placing it in his mouth. "And she is but a child still. What would we do if the King were to die this day? There would be war."

"It is forbidden to speak of the death of the King, son," said my father, glancing about as though Edward might have brought the King's guard marching upon us with those words. "Do not forget yourself."

"The King thinks the same thoughts, Father," Edward responded. "I but ape His Majesty's own words. Our good Henry is concerned. He believes something is desperately wrong in his marriage. He speaks often of it and he fears it. Respect and love for the Queen have held him back, but now the years that have passed with no son and the deaths of his children who came so briefly into the world weigh upon him. He cannot believe that he or Katherine have committed a sin so grievous as to deserve such a punishment from God, so thinks they must have offended the Almighty in a way they saw not, or did not want to see. He loves the Queen, he says so often, but he wonders if their marriage is legal in the eyes of God."

"What does the King intend to do, husband?" Catherine asked, her attention for once fixed on my brother.

"I hear he will soon elevate his bastard son, Henry FitzRoy. The lad is young, but is to be granted titles, one of them the Duke of Richmond, a hereditary title of the Tudor line. There is a rumour the King may seek a way to make FitzRoy his heir. But that is not the only rumour."

Edward breathed in and let it out through his nose. "He is seeking to investigate the match between him and Queen Katherine. It was said that since she did not lie with Prince Arthur as a wife, her marriage to the King was legal and she was not his sister in the eyes of the Lord, but the King wonders. He has of late questioned whether the dispensation which allowed them to wed was valid, for if it was not in any way it may be that God sees Katherine as the King's own sister, and will not allow there to be a son born to them for England because in the eyes of God, their union is incestuous."

A flicker in my father's eyes caught my attention. I felt a pain in my heart and I wondered at this law of God of which my brother spoke. Catherine and my Father were related in the eyes of God, yet they had a son. Why would God punish the Queen, yet reward others who sinned in the same way?

"And," Edward went on, "there is another circumstance that has encouraged the King to think more on the subject. Of late, the bonds of love he once held with the Queen have loosened. Perhaps that has allowed him fresh eyes to look upon his marriage and question it, rather than simply accepting it because of his adoration of the Queen."

"You mean he has a mistress, husband?" Catherine asked, her hand playing with her leather goblet. "But that means little, surely? The King is not as François of France who takes a new mistress every day as he takes repast. The King is careful, never upsetting the dignity of the Queen when he takes mistresses, and it is to be expected men will stray, from time to time." She smiled at Edward and then turned that beaming radiance upon the table. "Not amongst *this* company, of course," she added, and I wondered that God did not strike her down for her pretty lies. "But for kings, a mistress is not unusual."

"The King is discreet in his affairs," Edward agreed. "But there is a woman he seems more interested in than I have ever seen before. The younger daughter of the Boleyns of Kent, relatives of the Howards, for this Boleyn's mother was Elizabeth Howard before she married Thomas Boleyn. Her name is Anne, and she has amassed a gathering at court who worship her. She flirts with the King at each event, her tongue sharp and wits excelled by no other. She has become a star of court and serves the Queen. You should see the King's eyes when he looks upon her; it is as though there is no other person in all the world, but she."

"What of it?" asked Mother, her voice curt and wounded. "The King has already had the elder Boleyn girl in his bed, has he not?" She shook her head. "Thomas Boleyn always was a petty climber. He seeks to elevate himself, and has no qualms about using his daughters as whores to do so. I know the family and their father well enough. I served in the household of my aunt, with Elizabeth Howard, before she became Elizabeth Boleyn."

Mother sat back and took up her wine. "Elizabeth adored Thomas, right from the moment they first met, poor sweet fool that she was, but I could see the coldness in him even then. Mark my words, that man will use anything to advance himself, even the virtue of his daughters, but whatever attractions this chit has it does not mean the King would so lightly put aside his wife, who he has lived with for… what is it? Sixteen years now at least! The Queen is regal, royal, of ancient and sacred blood, she is wise, graceful and good. The King is astute and his heart is faithful, even if he is led astray by temptation from time to time. He knows what an asset such a wife is to him, and he loves her. He may cast eyes on other women, but his heart is in the Queen's possession."

"But even if he loves her, lady mother, she cannot give him a son." Edward sighed and sat back, abandoning his rabbit. "I know this pains you, Mother, it pains many of us for there is not a soul who meets Queen Katherine who fails to fall in love with her, but it is true. She has passed the age of childbearing. There will be no male heir of her body for England. If she would enter a convent, the King might wed again, for he is young and vigorous still. And it would be better for England. Any husband of the Princess Mary, any other claimant, would come with troubles for England, and with war on their tail, for unless all men unite under the King's son, there will be a *chosen* heir. Men will argue about who has the most right to rule."

Mother fell silent, and Edward went on. "The King seeks to discover if there is anything ill in his marriage, and he is considering annulling his union with Katherine. It is all over court, although no one has said it openly. It is said Cardinal Wolsey is working on the problem already, that the Queen will be convinced to retire and take the veil. And such a situation is not so unusual. There have been many kings who abandoned a wife in favour of one who could breed sons. Our King but seeks to do what is best for England, and for his people."

"Marriage is a holy estate, sanctified by God Himself," Mother said, disgust crawling in her voice. "The King would not set aside his wife with such callous ease! I do not believe him capable of such… hardness. Just because a new, younger woman comes along that does not mean men should set aside all virtue and loyalty in marriage! What of love? What of loyalty? What of the children she has borne him, the child they have together? What of all her years of good service, and wise ruling of England at his side? Is all of that to be set aside, just for the pretty eyes of a young woman?"

I expected to see my father's cheeks ignite with shame, but he merely coughed and motioned to a servant for more wine.

"Queen Katherine is a pious soul, known for her devotion to the Church," Mother carried on, blithely unaware of her husband's growing discomfort. "If there was anything sinful in her marriage she would not have entered into it in the first place. Katherine would *never* have remained married if she thought for one moment that the King was her brother in the eyes of God!"

Mother was afire now. It was Edward's turn to be silent. "And this is unworthy talk of the King and talk I will believe not!" she went on, "For the King to stray from the Queen's bed is bad enough, but to seek to put another in her rightful place? That would be an insult not only to Katherine, but to her royal house, to Spain! Such an insult could bring about trouble with Spain and the Holy Ro man Empire, even war if the insult was great enough!" Mother shook her head. "I do not believe it, my son. This is malicious gossip spread about court by a cruel heart and a slanderous tongue. You are young, perhaps you do not know that such ill things as this are often spread by those who take delight in working the will of the Devil, in harming those who are good and true of heart, but often it is so. This is naught and will come to naught."

She breathed in. "The King and his Queen will one day be blessed with a son and heir for England. God will bless them at the right time as He blessed Sarah, wife of Abraham. And we must all pray for them, pray that the King will not heed the trappings of temptation and lust, and will remain true to his Queen as she is to him. *That* is the measure of a true man; to stand by the promises he has made, and not to allow sin to enter his life through the wiles of some upstart child thrust into his face by her wily father!"

Mother finished her speech by almost slamming her goblet upon the table. Her cheeks were bright red. I had never seen or heard her speak in such passionate defence of anyone, and with the noise of her goblet striking wood she had declared hers the final word on the subject. Edward did not seek to raise it again but looked utterly unconvinced, and not a little annoyed. It was amusing, in a way, that our mother thought she knew more than Edward, who was, after all, one of the companions of the King and was always at court. But then, Mother always did think she knew everything about everything, on the basis of small evidence. Clearly being told the situation was opposite to how he had interpreted it annoyed Edward, but he said nothing. Yet in those pale eyes I saw anger. He knew he was right and Mother wrong.

I glanced at my father who seemed to be attempting to drown his wife's words in his cup of wine. I wondered if Mother suspected something, and that was the purpose of that long speech about right and wrong in marriage and men. I glanced at Catherine. But she was not looking at me. Her hand stretched along the table and took hold of Edward's. Smiling like a saint in heaven, she regarded him with gentle eyes. Edward smiled back, clasping her hand in his. Anger left his eyes as at her he gazed. Her beauty and, as he supposed, the love he saw in her made all things well. But her efforts were not for him.

At the end of the table, I saw a dark strike of jealousy crest over my father's brow. The affection Catherine showed to Edward was only performed to rile my father. No matter how much evidence she had that her lover wanted her, she wanted him to want her more. Jealousy can be a way to gauge the emotions of another. She wanted Father angry with Edward, perhaps with her. It was a way he would prove his love for her.

I could eat little that night, and went to bed hungry. Catherine was playing games with my family and I seemed to be the only one who could see what she was doing. Like little pawns in her nimble fingertips, she moved the men and women in this household, toying with them, laughing at us all.

*

I sat near the window, the shutters down and watched snow scatter over snow, white on white.

It was March, 1525, and snow was thick upon us. Elisabeth had lost one of her expensive mittens, pretty white wool banded with black, had been scolded hard and long for it, and gone to her room shared with Dorothy in tears. Sorry though I was for her, I wished I could explain she had been gently treated, for at her age had I lost such a thing of such expense, I would have been beaten.

But violence of another kind was on the air at that time.

The King was plotting for war again as a great battle had occurred, the Battle of Pavia. England had played no part, but we were told this battle might open up a chance at the conquest of France for us anew. The Emperor had fought the French King and captured him. It was time for England to march into France and take back those lands that Thomas had told me long ago were ours. Louise of Savoy, the French King's mother, was regent, and whilst France was woman-held it was weak, all said. The King was keen, but Edward wrote from court, saying that Wolsey wanted peace and was getting much money promised, including the return of the dowry of the Dowager of France, in return for a peace treaty with the French. This pleased the King, but still he wanted war.

"Men always do," Mother said that afternoon when I had left my window and joined her in the long gallery. She looked sad a moment, then glanced at Catherine. Her belly had swollen not long after Edward and Father left again for court and possibly for war. Another child, another bastard, or perhaps not? Who could say who was this one's father, if the last was unknown?

I wished her stomach could bring me comfort, wished I could know that if Edward died in France there would be some part of him left in the world. But I did not know, neither did Mother, though she knew it not.

That night I saw a woman in my dreams in the snow. She was looking for something. Into the storm I ran, white-whipped flakes of snow biting my eyes, tearing at my hair.

"Where is my child?" the woman wailed as I reached her.

She turned. It was Mary. In her arms was a bundle of cloth that should have held a babe. As I stared into the bundle a darkness at its centre opened, a mouth. I had time to breathe in once before the maw opened wide, and I was eaten.

Chapter Twenty-One

Wulfhall
Wiltshire

Early Summer- Autumn 1526

The little house was tucked away neatly just out of the village. Close to the edge of the forest it stood, a dwelling which looked as if it might tumble down at any moment, yet in other ways carried an air as if it had stood undaunted since the dawn of time.

Its roof covered in fleshy house-leek, a garden of billowing herbs and vegetables at its front, the house was at once separate from and a part of the land. The open front door gave way to darkness spilling from its inner chambers, like a mouth and throat beyond. It looked inviting, but I shivered in the cool sunlight. I wondered again why I had come, was what I was about to do even sanctioned by the Church? I had come to see Mistress Grey. I had come to find a cunning woman to help me against a witch.

"Stay here," I said to my father's servant. "I need to collect herbs for my mother, but I will not be long."

He dipped his head, took the reins of my horse and led both my mount and his to the open pasture before the house. It was common land, there for horses to be tied up to graze, for travellers and for those of the local area. I looked at the doorway and swallowed the lump of guilt and fear rising in my throat. What I had said was true enough. Mother had sent me to see whether there were other herbs which tasted better than those Edith had prescribed that she could eat to stop a child taking root in her belly. But I was also here to talk to this cunning woman, see if there was a way out of the vow I had made so many years ago. If there was no way out for me, I wanted Catherine stopped.

I wanted justice. I wanted revenge. I wanted that whore meddling with my family to pay for the deaths she had caused, for all the humiliations of Edward, my mother and my father. For all the love she stole from those who saw not her thieving fingers plucking at their hearts. I wanted Catherine punished for her gloating face, for the smug amusement she took in shifting us all about like cards in her hand, controlling all, always in charge. Even my father, who she claimed to love, was just her toy. All this was a game of power and she relished each moment.

Most of all, I wanted to wipe that smile from her pretty face. I wanted Catherine disgraced. To reveal the mask that she showed to the world, reveal how parchment-thin it truly was. I wanted all to see what she was, wanted them to see the demon within.

And yet I knew I could do nothing of the kind. Reveal her and it would hurt my family, disgrace our name. Edward would be hurt. I could not allow that. My brother could not know and disgrace could not touch him, not now. There was too far for him to fall.

The previous year, in the summer, all Edward had said of Henry FitzRoy had come to pass. The tiny boy had been made Earl of Nottingham and Duke of Richmond and Somerset, and a month later was created Lord Admiral of England. FitzRoy had been sent to govern the north. It was, of course, a nominal position since the boy was only six and FitzRoy had a council with him who truly were to rule, but he was being brought up, honoured, like a legitimate son of the King. There were rumours that he might, indeed, be made the heir to the throne. The titles he was given were not the traditional ones granted to the heir, but they were high and all were deeply associated with the house of Tudor.

My brother had been honoured at the same time. He had been placed in the little Duke's household as Master of Horse. Few men were so trusted and Edward had many responsibilities as he had to maintain the stables, organise all travel between houses and castles for his master, and was teaching the lad to ride. It was an important, senior position and if the rumours were correct, it might mean that my brother was Master of Horse to the future King of England.

At the same time, to appease his wife, the King had dispatched his daughter Princess Mary, who was then nine, to Ludlow on the Welsh Marches. She too had a council and was learning to rule.

"The King is hedging his bets," Catherine had said, making my mother look faint with distress.

Catherine thought she was so clever. She was expecting a note any day calling her to the north, or to court would be even better, to join Edward. Edward was dividing his time between Sheriff Hutton in Yorkshire with his master the Duke and the court in London, for he was sometimes called upon to return, being also an Esquire of the Body to the King in times of ceremony. A busy man, my brother had become. Too busy to call his wife to London or to Yorkshire, which made me happy. But he came to see her when he could, get sons in her, and always he looked merry when he was at her side. Catherine had lost the child she carried the year before, but she seemed not to sorrow. A few months gone she had been when the pains came early. The chaplain had blessed the lost child, we had buried what we could. Mother had been concerned, but Catherine appeared untouched by her loss. I had to wonder if she had known it was indeed Edward's child, and for that reason she had not wanted it as she might have wanted one of our Father's.

I resented her. Catherine was loved and did not deserve it, and I was not, and what had I ever done but give myself to them, to my family, in all ways they wanted? Everything was not enough for them. I was taken for granted. What had Catherine done but take and destroy, take and take and take more than even they knew… yet because of a pretty face all they saw were pretty deeds.

I resented my family for not seeing, for being the fools she thought them to be. I hated them for being blind to her ways, enraptured by her body and her face. In a way I hated my family more than Catherine, because they valued her more than me.

I needed help. Soon I would by hatred be consumed. It would rise from within my soul, a mouth and it would eat me. I needed to do something, find a way to stop her and my father without the others knowing, without them finding out I had known, known all this time and said nothing. I wanted a way to stop the sin without inflicting pain. Truth be told, I was there to ask if there was a way to curse Catherine, send her into death.

Many times since the sweat had come, I had thought back to that moment standing over her, the cloth in my hands. Sometimes I knew I had done right and at other times, times when I was safe in darkness and could be honest before the darkness in my soul, I thought I should have done it. Catherine would be gone. There would be no son from her body to confuse the realms of light and dark in our house, to make a mockery of Edward. When Catherine had lost her child, I had found myself wishing she would die too. She would be gone, a simple ending to this tale of horror. Her son could believe her to be the perfect mother, Edward could mourn her, and then he could marry again, heal his heart. My father would have lost his mistress and the sin they wallowed in. My mother need never have known. If Catherine had just died, all would be well. Yes, there was darkness in me, strong and true. It wished for death.

It was not only my father enticed, apparently willingly, into sin. We had heard that in the February that just had passed the King had ridden into the lists wearing a new motto, *declare I dare not*. All said he had a new mistress. Many claimed it was Anne Boleyn, the lady Edward had spoken of. Many more were saying the Queen's heart was broken for the King loving another woman. It seemed to me that those who did wrong profited as those who did good, as surely Katherine of Spain only did, suffered. Why was the world so unfair? In the case of Catherine, I was determined there would be justice.

Quietening my quaking blood, I walked through the small wooden gate and into the garden. There was no sound from the cottage. I walked up the little path to the open door and knocked upon it.

"Just a moment," came the cry of Edith within. "God speed, good and welcome visitor! I will be just a moment."

I waited at the door, watching the delicate stems and flowers of Edith's herbs billowing and bowing in a light summer breeze. There was something so peaceful about the way they danced. For a while I was lost, staring at them. There had been little time for my soul to feel at rest during these years at home. When was the last time I felt peace? Had I ever? Certainly not after Catherine had come, which was more than half my life ago! Had I known peace before then? Perhaps, at times, riding or sewing, my mind settling in its own thoughts, needing no one else.

"Mistress Seymour?" a voice made me start. I turned and looked into Edith's eyes. I had thought them dark, but I realised now, close up, that they were grey. They had orange flecks in the centre, and reflected the colours which she looked upon. When she gazed at plants, they seemed to be green. When she looked back at me, I could see the blue of clear skies in them. Edith Grey had grey eyes. Was it a family trait that somehow had become their name, or had her eyes altered to suit her name? And how had I never noticed? Perhaps I had thought them dark because whenever I had seen Edith she had been in our house, usually in a birthing chamber or a sick room where the windows were covered by shutters, or cloth. She smiled and bobbed a curtsey. I inclined my head.

"I am sorry to trouble you, Mistress Grey," I said. "I have come on an errand for my mother. She wishes to know if there are any herbs she may take to prevent her from bearing a child again, which are more palatable than the ones she presently suffers to eat."

Edith chuckled. "Lady Seymour does not like the taste of my herbs?" She shook her head. "There is little I can do about that, Mistress Seymour. The herbs I have recommended are the best I can offer and the safest I know. Tell her to ask your kitchen women to soak them in honey, but do not allow them to be cooked. If Lady Seymour wishes to stop eating them she risks another child and another bleed. Such horrors only happen more once they have happened once. I would tell her no matter how harsh the herbs she eats are, the taste is better than the bitter tang of death, is it not?"

"I suspected that would be your answer," I admitted. "My mother likes to think all she wishes for will simply come true. I know this is not the way of the world."

"Then you are a wise maiden, Mistress Seymour, for there are not many who understand that the world owes them nothing for having been born into it."

I hesitated a moment. "Was there something else?" she asked.

I glanced about. "There is... but I would not wish to speak of it here, where we might be overheard."

A shadow crossed Edith's face, but she curtseyed, inclined her head and held out her arm, indicating I was to enter her house. I hesitated again, and perhaps she took this as reluctance to enter. "It is not much, compared to your house,

Mistress Seymour," she said, a slight note of annoyance in her tone. "But I assure you, my house is well kept and clean."

"Oh!" I said, surprised. "I did not mean to offend, Mistress Grey, and I am not unwilling to enter your house, it is just…"

"That what you have come to ask of me you are unsure about," she finished for me, gazing at me with solemn eyes.

A raven called in the forest, making my heart jump, and a sick chill swept down my spine, through my blood. She had seen the evil in me. "How did you know that?" I muttered.

Edith breathed in steadily. "Do you know why my sisters and I live on the edge of the village, Mistress Seymour?" I shook my head and she continued. "My family, the women in my family, have long been wise in the ways of herbs, cures, remedies and potions," she said, eyes trailing over a Mary-Bud plant, a common colorant for food and one more affordable than saffron. "We have always used our knowledge for the purposes of good, but there are some in this world who would use such knowledge as we have for ill. When I first came to this house upon the death of my mother, my grandmother told me of this, and warned me that no matter what we did, if we chose to serve our village, as generations of Grey women had before us, we would be suspected of both good and of evil. That is the way of things. People fear what they do not understand, and most people do not understand a lot, so they fear a great deal.

"That is why our cottage and small patch of land lies outside of the village, for here, we are a part of the village and we are apart from it too. It makes people less fearful if we are not too close. As we are outside of their understanding, so we must live outside of their ring of houses. Here we make sense to them, and to ourselves. Within the village we do not. Do you see?"

I nodded.

"And here people come, and they ask us for help. Sometimes it is help we can give and sometimes it is help we do not offer. Sometimes a request comes from the light, and sometimes the dark. There are things people suppose we do because of what we do, where we live, that we do not. And because of past experience, I know you have come to me to ask for something you know is not right, Mistress Seymour. I have seen that look in many eyes before. Uncertainly hovers in your eyes; you know what you are about to ask is not godly."

I flushed, hot and shamed, but she ushered me into her house. I walked past her and smelt a scent of rose and nettle flowers on her clean hair. Even covered by a hood of white wool it was strong. I knew the scent because it was a wash I made with my mother, in our distillery.

Safe inside, I looked around. It was a small dwelling. There were two rooms separated by a curtain which had been carefully mended in several places and embroidered with heartsease flowers in shades of purple and blue that were surprisingly bright. Usually I would think this thread expensive, but I reasoned the Grey sisters would understand how to coax the best dye from forest plants, and most likely dyed their own wool for clothes and thread for embroidery. With the eye I had for detail, I saw this as the careful work of a skilled youngster. Oddly I could almost see age when I gazed at thread and patterns. I could see a heart, intention, in the stitches made by women. An odd talent, but embroidery spoke to me, perhaps because I spent such time in its quiet company.

One room held one large bed, which stood against a wall. It was made carefully, the sides of the bed polished well. Beds were the most expensive piece of furniture any person owned, low or high. They were left in wills, passed down families and given to loyal servants as wedding presents. People took care of them.

In that room too, on the other side of the chamber, there was a fire upon which a blackened pot hung, a pottage of herbs and wild bird flesh bubbling in it. I could smell the gamey scent as I could the tang of the herbs simmering. In there were three stools, of crude but solid craftsmanship, arranged about the fire, as well as several baskets containing needlework and others brimming with onions and small turnips, clearly waiting to be cleaned and stored. *That is their evening work, already set out and prepared,* I thought. I admired their industry. It was clear most items in the house had been made by them. I could almost see them, sisters sitting about a fire in the gathering dark, continuing to toil as they told each other of all the work they had already done that day.

The second room was smaller, and although it contained a trundle bed, was clearly used more for storing produce than for sleeping in. Bundles and bundles of dried herbs hung suspended from the beams, rustling, whispering in the breeze which passed through the front door and out of the open back door. Through that door I could see a plot of vegetables, graceful herbs and delicate salad leaves alongside stocky worts and cabbages, defended by a fence and roof of basket-work bound reeds to keep creatures of the woodland and birds off the produce. Beyond the garden was a small, winding path which led into the shadows of the forest at the back of the cottage. Sweetbriar, the wild rose, was growing about the back doorframe, its sweet scent delicious, apple-like and fresh. I could smell, too, the scent of the linden tree. There must be one or some nearby, or Edith had gathered its flowers, which were good for stuffing into pillows and nosegays, for they kept the scent of the summer in a house all year around.

It was not a large house, but the earthen floor was swept clean, and fresh rushes lay upon it laced with lavender buds, which gave off a sweet smell as I walked over them. Before placing rushes, Edith or her sisters must have dampened the floor, as I could see an earthenware pot used for this task by the door. If the earth on a floor was dampened, dust did not escape through the rushes, filling the house. Such an event was a particular problem in summer when it was dry. The windows were just rectangular holes in the thick outer wall; a woman like Edith certainly could not afford glass and it was a warm day, so cloths that might have covered them were not needed. Her windows would be closed at night, covered by wooden shutters that would be secured to stop thieves getting in. Often thieves tunnelled through walls, finding that easier than breaking through window shutters, but here the walls were thick. No one was getting in, even if they dared invade the home of women rumoured to be wise in cunning and magic.

I knew she had sisters, three at least, though I had not met them, and clearly they shared beds, two in each, for there were not enough for all of them. This was not unusual; even in wealthy houses, like ours, servants shared beds and my sisters did too. Sometimes people shared for warmth, or security and comfort. Even the Queen shared her bed with trusted companions.

The walls were clean, aside from corners where there were large collections of spider webs. It was incongruous to see such a tidy, neat house, then catch sight of those webs, but Edith chuckled as my eyes travelled to them.

"I always keep a hearty supply of spider web in my house, Mistress Seymour," she said. "They are the best fabric for staunching a bleed. They crisp over the top of a wound, slow bleeding and protect against illness. The next time you prick a finger, or see someone with a badly bleeding cut, ball up some webbing and press it to the wound. You will find it most effective."

"That is why you keep it here?" I asked.

"Indeed." She smiled. "All creatures of the world have many uses, even if they are not obvious at first. But it is also bad luck, you know, to kill a spider. When Mary and Joseph were running from Herod with Our Lord Jesus, they hid in a cave. Soldiers who hunted Jesus came into the cave, but found nothing but a mass of spider web. Spiders had flocked forth to conceal the babe and his holy family, spinning silver web over them, hiding them from peril." She glanced up at the webs, dangling in the light breeze, flashing silver and white in the dappled light of the sun. "They are creatures of patience, who weave beauty each day, and I have always thought a house with spiders is better than one with flies and pests."

Her words were true enough; I could see few flies in her house, which was rare. She gestured to a stool and I sat down, feeling the warmth from her cooking fire spread up my legs. Edith sat down too and offered me a cup of ale, which I took, and found it fresh tasting, flavoured with herbs. "Will you tell me now what brought you here, Mistress Seymour?" she asked.

My face coloured. "I do not think I should say," I murmured.

"Do you know why people come to me with the same expression you wear today?" she asked, cradling an earthenware cup in her hands.

"No," I admitted.

She smiled. "They come because they have problems they cannot solve, and they require answers."

"I have a problem," I confessed, staring at my ale.

"What is it?" Edith was gazing at me with a calm face. "Sometimes, Mistress Seymour, it can help more than any potion to reveal what troubles you, and have another listen. So often that is the best service I give; to be an ear to listen, a mouth which will not reveal what it is told." I looked up and she nodded. "I will keep anything you say a secret between us," she went on. "That I swear to you."

"There is an evil presence in my house," I said, "something which works evil, has ill-purpose."

"And you know what this evil is?"

I nodded.

"And you came to ask me to remove it?" she asked. I nodded again. Edith sighed. "I understand from the manner of your speech, Mistress Seymour, that you do not wish to reveal the identity of this presence. That leads me to believe it is a *who*, rather than a what. If you did not know what it was, if you suspected there was a spirit within the house, you would not speak so guardedly."

She placed her cup at the hearthside and took up a long wooden spoon, stirring the pottage thoughtfully. "But I do not work ill against people with my knowledge, or my power," she said. "When I was a young girl, I acted badly in such a way once. I swore never to do so again." She regarded me with those grey eyes, made black from the shadows of her house. "However much a person may deserve evil, I will not do evil upon them. It would place me under suspicion, Mistress Seymour, and in peril, not just of body but soul. Remember, *Vengeance is mine, sayeth the Lord*. The right to punish is not for you or me to decide, it is for God and the law makers of the King. There are many willing to accuse women of cunning, such as me, for tricks of Fate which assail them. If you came to me hoping for something of that ilk, I cannot help you."

"I should not have come, or asked," I muttered, feeling helpless, foolish and out of place.

"But you needed to talk to someone, did you not?" she asked, her voice gentle as a ewe. "Do not make yourself uncomfortable, Mistress Seymour, I can see there is something inside you desperate to be released, and something just as strong holding you back." She got up and walked into the next room, returning with a small pouch. She put it into my hands and sat down again.

"What is it?" I asked.

"A charm to protect you against the evil within your house," she said. "I will not do ill, even against those who work evil, but I *can* help to protect you. This will aid you in your desires, but only those that are good and worthy. And it will protect you from the evil within your house." I went to look inside the pouch and she touched my hand. "It works better if not opened," she said.

"What do I owe you for it?" I asked, reaching for the pouch of coins at my belt, but she shook her head.

"I do not charge money for my help, Mistress Seymour. It has ever been agreed by my family that services such as those we offer should come without payment. We ask that people trade with us, offering what they can so my sisters and I can eat, and continue to serve. But you do not need to trade or pay. You owe us nothing. Your mother has ever been generous to us and to the village. When times were hard, she sent my grandmother a basket of food and fuel each week. She paid for my grandmother to be buried with honour. If anything, we owe your family for their support through lean years, and the employment their house has offered to the people of this village in good and bad years."

I blinked. I knew my mother sent alms to some of the villagers. I had not known she sent food each week in hard times, or that she had paid for Edith's grandmother, dead of the sweat these many years, to be buried with honour in the churchyard.

Edith leaned forwards and curled the little bundle into my fingers. "Keep it with you at all times, even when you sleep, for if I suspect rightly the evil you speak of has a hold over you. This may not release you, not in the way you might expect, but it will aid you, keep you strong."

"I do not know how to thank you."

Edith smiled. "I like to help, Mistress Seymour," she said and chuckled. "And it is not every day one gets to help the daughter of a fine house."

She gazed at me, eyes solemn once again. "Concentrate on the good about and within you," she said. "On good things you want in life, on worthy things you want to do. The amulet will help you to succeed. And worry not on the evil which you feel. If there is one thing I have learnt, it is this; evil does not prosper without a price being paid."

"What do you mean?" I felt my blood run cold even as my heart leapt with a joy so dark it might have eclipsed the night.

"That one day, whatever or whoever it is who does you and your family harm will fall to the justice of God," she said. "Trust in God, for He has a plan for all of us if we but wait to see it. He will rid your house of evil, but He will do it at the right time, Mistress Seymour. God is never late. He knows there is a season for justice as there is for suffering, as there is for sun and for rain. Put your trust in Him, and you will not stray from the path of goodness."

"I almost did today," I confessed miserably.

Edith shook her head. "It is not so, Mistress Seymour," she said with a smile hovering on her lips. "God sent you to me. He knew you were unsure on the path ahead, as He knew that I was able to advise and help you. This day is His doing. He is watching over you, even when you least believe He is there. He is beside us in our darkest times, and in our best. Sometimes we do not see Him, but He is there, holding us up when we think we cannot go on. Trust in Him, trust in goodness, and in yourself, and you will not stray from the path, the Fate, He has designed for you."

I left that cottage after some time in the peaceful, good company of Edith Grey, and as I stood at the end of her path and waved another goodbye, I seemed to see shades at her back: women. A blink and they were gone, yet as I saw the shadow of Edmund in the halls of Wulfhall, as I heard Mary's baby crying, so I knew I had seen them, those ghosts of Edith's family, not there to threaten or reproach, but to protect, guide.

A thousand, thousand lives or more had passed here, unmarked and unremarkable except to them, and yet to them, these people they had known and cared for and adored and lost were everything. All people should be marked and remarkable to someone. All should be noticed, cherished by another. Edith was surrounded by love, the ghosts of her past did not haunt.

As I rode back to the house, her charm placed under my clothing and next to my skin, I felt at ease for the first time in a long time.

The charm never left my side again. That autumn I clutched it to my breast, reminding myself not to do evil because there was evil in the world; not to join with the Devil because others about me had.

She was a good woman, Mistress Grey, and she had helped me. It seemed that her charm worked with swift speed too, for a month into the mist-swathed autumn, I was sent a missive from Edward at court.

He had found a place for me in the household of his once-mistress, the Duchess of Suffolk. His friend, William Parr, had aided him and Edward had called upon his own contacts at court and the King's affection for him. My brother had handed me the greatest gift ever I was to receive. I was to leave this hateful place. I was about to be freed of all which assailed me.

I was to go to court.

Chapter Twenty-Two

Wulfhall
Wiltshire

Summer 1527

I was to leave home! I was to leave home!

Finally a chance to escape this awful place! And to go to court! That strange paradise I had been told of and never had thought to see. I was nineteen and someone might as well have told me I was to walk from a life dreary and unchanging and enter a fairy tale. On the day Edward's missive was read out to me by our clerk I was so happy I knew why butterflies had wings and why birds swooped in the skies. I was to go to court. I was to serve in the household of Princess Mary, the Duchess of Suffolk. I would be a lady attending upon a woman who once had been a Queen. On the woman whose husband had elevated my brother to become a knight! I was to be away from this den of sin and lies. I was to become free.

Free of Catherine, I thought. Never again would I witness her dreadful games of shame and humiliation. Never again would I hear the bed rocking against the wall or see the twisted love in my father's eyes as he gazed upon little John and wondered if he was grandson or son. I did not have to feel a dark mouth opening to consume me. Never again, never again!

I could hardly stop myself from sauntering about with a dazed, smug expression upon my face. When I thought I might look like Catherine I stopped, but inside, under my pale skin and ugly face my heart was alight with beauty, the beauty of hope. My mother was afire with preparations on my behalf, going over gowns, sleeves, kirtles and shoes, repairing what she could, ordering fabric for new items to be made. All my clothes were to be made in the fashions of court, but Mother did not hold with French fashions. She said although I was to go to the household of a woman who still went by the title of Queen of France, even though Princess Mary had only been Queen a matter of months, I would go a good Englishwoman.

"Some of your court gowns we will have to adapt from old ones of mine," she said. "Jane, it will cost a great deal to send you to court."

She flushed. Father had been struggling with money. I knew not how much as he said nothing. He had asked the King some years ago to allow him more time to pay his debts to the Crown, which had been permitted, but I thought them not paid. There had been no wars of late, and Father was too old to be more than a field general in any case, so could not serve and win spoils, titles or rewards. His appointments in Wiltshire and beyond were not remarkable. He was paying for a household of adults, the education and advancement of a son at court, Thomas in the household of the Bryans, and now I was to become another expense. It cost a great deal to keep a child at court. Most who served in grand houses were paid a wage, of sorts, and had other needs such as food provided for by their master, but the clothes required for court alone cost more than some ships. It was said a man might easily wear an estate on his back when he went to court. Court was about the show of wealth, and if one did not have wealth there was more to prove, in a way.

I wondered, at times, if the reason no husband had been put forward for me was because I would bring only a slim dowry, and without dazzling physical perfections that was indeed a problem for most men. They did not want a short, ugly wife who brought no money or land with her. It was not unusual that women of my status were unmarried at my age. The upper ranks of nobility and those of royalty married young, often but not always, but for those of lower station it was more usual for couples to join when they had entered the twentieth years of their lives. But no one had been offered to me, or even suggested, which was more unusual.

"I will not let you down, Mother," I said.

"You cannot hide in a corner, if you are to do well at court," she said, looking worried. Clearly hiding in a corner was all I was good for. She had not prepared me for a life at court.

"I will not, but I will not be bold or brazen, either. My lady mother, you and my lord father have raised me to be good and modest and quiet, and this I shall be."

"Yes," she said. "It is as well. Too many girls go off to court and end up in trouble, or disgrace. You will not be like that." She smiled, looking happier. I was too ugly and too poor to be a target for a fortune hunter, or for a man who wanted a comely tumble in bed. I think that was the first time my mother was pleased about my looks. It almost made me laugh. She thought being ugly might keep me safe.

Clothes that Mother had worn as a young woman were brought out of their chests, shaken and inspected to see what I could use. Some had been eaten a little by moths and mice, so we set to hiding tears and holes under embroidery. Nothing was to be wasted. New cloth for sleeves and kirtles was brought to us so we could make older styles of gowns appear newer by mixing sleeves, kirtles and gowns. Mother was to grant most of her furs to me, for capes and to sew onto the edges of sleeves for winter. Stains were coaxed out of velvet using mixtures of raw red arsenic, *Mertum Cudum* and cinquefoil, then put in the sun, then washed, then dried in the sun. Soapwort, thankfully for Kat's hands, was used for most of the cloth.

"It is much gentler, Mistress Seymour," she admitted. "Much as we're all in joy about you heading to court to serve the Princess, I could go a long time before I use that arsenic mix again."

"Thank you, for all you are doing," I said. "I know the work you do has increased for my new post at court."

Her face puckered with affection. "We never minded, and never will mind, doing aught for you, Mistress," she said. "You never were one to miss when something was done for you and to thank us, and that makes you different. Low or high, many people take what's done for them for granted, and it makes a soul sad to feel what they do out of love is rendered unimportant. You never miss a thing, so always make a person feel special, appreciated."

I think that was the sweetest thing anyone ever said to me, and I could not even tell Kat that, for my throat filled with tears, choking me. She saw and smiled. "You go on now, Mistress Jane," she said. "You have dresses to make for court…" she grinned wickedly, "… and no doubt your fine mother has much wisdom to impart."

She laughed. My face did not change for I was good at hiding emotions, but she saw the flicker of weary annoyance in my eyes. In those days of gown making, before court life began, Mother's tongue had come to life. I had thought she talked before? I knew nothing, for she had been almost silent in the past. Her tongue had life now, and was using it.

Mother lectured me, long and hard, on what was expected of a woman of court, and seemed somewhat amazed that my brother had secured the position for me at all.

"Of course, the Princess listens to her husband, and her brother," said my mother as she sewed furiously fast, making a new set of sleeves for me. If one had several set of sleeves and kirtles whole outfits could be made from relatively few sets, giving the appearance of a grand wardrobe when there was only a slim one. "And the King listens often to your good brother now. I suppose Edward will have told them you are good, quiet and humble." Her eyes leapt to mine. "But you will have to avoid speaking French with anyone," she said. "Or just nod and smile and hope for the best, otherwise they will know your ignorance of that language."

The pleasures of going to court became outweighed by my mother's abject terror of everything I would get wrong, everything she could already see me failing at. I began to think I should not have accepted the post, should have told Father I would stay at Wulfhall, for my mother appeared about to dissolve with terror and anxiety. There were more lessons, more insults, more choice remarks about how little prepared I was for such a life. Over time, I ceased to hear her. I had a strange and sudden understanding which made it all make sense, all of the years of hurt and pain and insult. My mother was afraid.

She was afraid that I would not do well, might make a fool of myself or the family, but she was afraid also to lose me. Perhaps Edward had been right all those years ago and I had never understood until the moment I was to leave that my mother needed me. Whether she needed me as a daughter, in truth, or as something to compare herself to, I knew not, but need was there. It was a revelation. I had possessed power all this time, and had known nothing of it.

And as the days crept past and gowns were made, stored in chests with meadowsweet and cloves to keep fleas and moths away, my heart became lighter. The more Mother tried to condemn me the freer I felt. I knew the frequency of her insults spoke of the short time I had left at Wulfhall.

Catherine was seething with envy. Although she did not want to leave her place here, or position *under* my father, she believed herself more worthy of court than me, and Edward had never asked that she join him. In truth he could not. He had no reason to bring his wife to court and was not rich enough to afford a residence of his own to house her. Perhaps he did not want her there, either. There were pleasures a young gallant might find at court that were not so easily achieved with a wife in tow.

"The Princess will expect you to be talented in music and in reading, sister," Catherine said in a seemingly merry tone across the table one night. "So you will need to brush up on those skills, will you not? For you are lacking in both."

"The Dowager *Queen of France* is aware of my accomplishments as my beloved brother and your husband has told her of them, sister," I replied, lifting my goblet of Rhenish and smiling at her over the rim. I knew Catherine sought to insult me to appease her spite. I was not about to weep for her games, not anymore. "And I believe the Princess values the modesty, *virtue*, and usefulness of a woman over trifling fancies of music and verse. She has plenty of women about her for those things. I will offer her all that I am, and will serve her loyally. I am sure such a princess as she, in all her wisdom, will see my true virtues and be happy with them."

"Well said, Jane," noted my father. I almost choked. It was rare he spoke to me. "Modesty and humility are the best of women's virtues."

Catherine's face clouded. Clearly she did not think such things a virtue. I wondered if she and my father had fallen out.

"But still," she went on, plucking a delicate scrap of capon and wiping it in white wine sauce. "There is much expected of a woman at court."

"I understood you had never served at court, sister," I said, my tone sweet and innocent as honey, "yet you speak with such understanding. I will surely write to you often when I am at court, since you are evidently in a position to advise me on the subject."

"Of course *I* served at court for many years," my mother interjected, unaware of the invisible waves of hatred passing between Catherine and me. I wondered if the smothered rabbit on the table would sour for our spite.

"That is true, my lady mother," I said. "And I look forward to learning all you know." *As if I have not heard it a thousand, thousand times before…*

"And I will advise you in all that you need in order to succeed, daughter." Mother looked pleased and proud. "This is a rare opportunity, one not to be missed."

"I value all you say and tell me, my lady mother," I replied, taking a sip of my wine. It tasted like victory. "It will be good to have someone who actually knows the court as my mentor." As I set my goblet down, my eyes slipped to Catherine and I smiled. Bristling behind her rich velvet gown and fine hood, she glowered at me for a moment then returned to talking with my father on the subject of her son… *their* son. I set down my goblet. She had made the wine in it bitter.

But I would not let her jibes nor her continued liaison with my father defeat my happiness. I endured my mother bleating the same instructions and lessons about court over and over in an effort to prepare me. I endured Catherine seeking to steal my happiness at all turns, and I responded with the sweetness inherent in a person who knows they are almost free of the poisonous bindings which hold them.

Soon, I told myself. At night, in the day, as I went about my tasks, as I sewed with my mother working on my new wardrobe, the same refrain sounded in my head. *Soon*.

Chapter Twenty-Three

Suffolk Place
London

Summer 1527

How I was to pass for a sophisticated woman of court, I knew not. I thought I might at any moment start jumping up and down like a child, or a flea.

Servants of my father's house had brought me to London. On the way we had stayed in the guest quarters of an abbey, a place where both monks and nuns lived in a holy, closed order. I saw only women, of course. I was kept from the men for they were not to see outsiders, and certainly not women.

But that night as the bells called members of the order to Mass I listened and with them, in spirit and prayer rather than person, I had prayed. I prayed that I would not disappoint my new mistress, the Duchess of Suffolk, Dowager Queen of France and Princess of England. I prayed that I would please her enough that I would be able to stay at her side always. That was all I prayed for, not to catch a husband or have children, as everyone thought the sole purpose of my heading to court should be. I had small hopes for a husband, and I was not even sure I wanted one. There was a voice inside me telling me that I would be someone a man settled for rather than wanted, and there was something in me that desired such a stark fate not. Better to be left aside, to be in truth unwanted in marriage than to be taken on as a dreary compromise, something *not quite* what a man had wanted, not quite as good as he had hoped, but was willing to endure.

But I hoped if I pleased my mistress, the Princess, I would be wanted by her. That was what I prayed. A small wish, a simple request; to have a place in life that would satisfy me, a place that could be mine, a place I could be noticed enough to be appreciated. I did not ask to be loved, just not taken for granted.

Along the road heading into London we stopped to water our horses at streams and rivers, fed them horse bread thick with peas. We picked our way about men herding cattle and pigs. My servants shouted at them to move, but with so many beasts such a feat might take all day, so with our quicker horses we picked our way about them. At rivers, small and burbling blue, we passed men fishing and others watering horses. Some horses were wandering along the banks, grazing and scratching themselves on low-hanging branches. They looked up as we rode past, liquid black eyes roaming over us and then away, as to more interesting grass they returned. Sheep in fields gazed at us as they chewed, geese honked from inside willow pens, outraged that we dared to trespass upon what clearly was their road.

As we approached London the next day I thought my eyes might burst from my skull. Never had I seen anywhere so large, so busy, so noisy, and never, even when men had cleaned out the pits near our house, had I smelt anything like the stench that flowed from the city. It wafted from London and raced at me, slapping me about the face. It was a warm, hanging, clinging smell that stuck in my nostrils and took roost in my lungs. Piss, shit, fetid water, horse dung, a tang of ale being brewed, the scent of a thousand women stirring pottages of herbs and bones and meat and grain, hot pies being bitten into as their owners walked the streets, the scent of washing and perfume, bread baking, pigs sweating, horses breathing and water, the Thames, stagnant in places and rushing in others. Such a scent I had smelt nowhere else and never would again. In time I learnt the scent of London changed each day yet never wavered in its awesome power.

High walls and the spires of churches were the first things I saw, along with smoke rising from small houses in poorer areas and from great houses and palaces of nobles, and the

King. My eager eyes saw houses of nobles and lords, then the squat dwellings of common people, crowded brick and wood shoulders pushed together like men in a crowd watching a bear being baited. Grey slate and red-tiled roofs winked in the sunlight. I noted the absence of thatch, which was common near Wulfhall, but I knew it was a fire risk in crowded London. Many houses boasted two or three levels, and many overhung the road; people built out if they could not build up any higher. I could see it made the streets gloomy, even in the light of day.

Highest of all buildings was the spire of St Paul's. It was fitting that the first thing a person saw as they approached London was the house of God. My servants touched their caps when it came in sight and I bowed my head. It was right that we give thanks to God for seeing us safe to London. Outside St Paul's was an open-air pulpit where people gathered to hear sermons. I could see it from the road, clear of buildings but suffocated by people. The surrounding streets were narrow and dark, making it stand out, and they were teeming with people, carts and animals. I could hear church bells ringing for the hour. All over the city they rang; a tumult of noise.

The city wall was ancient. It ran about the east of the city, standing more than twenty foot high, and stretching about three sides of London, with four great gates; Cripplegate, Moorgate, Bishopsgate and Aldgate. Two more gates guarded the river at Newgate and Ludgate. Through the gates and into London we went, passing the heads of criminals on spikes. I averted my eyes. I did not like to see such things. I felt sorry for the men, even though they were dead and past pain. It seemed a thing of shame to be left rotting upon a spike for all to see. The humiliation or shame of others always made me feel ashamed. I knew what it was to be brought low, but it was more than that. Somehow the humiliation of another person became my shame too. I could little explain it, and any member of my family would have called it a foolish thought, for the heads were there to teach others not to sin or commit crimes, but all the same that thought was in my head. Perhaps it was because I was a woman, and we all shared the sins of

Eve. I never thought of men all sharing the sin of Adam, although God had punished men with having to work and toil in the earth. Not all men worked the soil, of course, so perhaps those with more money and better houses had escaped the curse of the first man. Women never could escape that of Eve.

To London Bridge we came. I could see the Tower of London, a mass of towers running along a huge wall circling the central White Tower, which glittered, glaring as snow in the sunshine. "There are many beasts housed there, Mistress Seymour," one of my father's men told me. "Bears, lions, wolves and some strange beasts without names that have spines for fur. People pay a few coins and are let in to see them, or poke them to make them roar!"

I laughed, but later felt pity for the beasts. To once have been free and powerful, only to end up in a cage, poked by passers-by, it seemed a sad fate.

The Bridge was packed so dense with people walking, on horse, or contemplating the wares of shops along the bridge, and with animals being herded, I thought we would not get across. As we clopped slowly over the bridge, I gazed down to see its arches, nineteen of them, reflected in the water. The river was a swirling stream of grey-blue-green water covered in flocks of white swans and hundreds of boats, more than ever I had seen. Some were carrying timber or food into the city from ports outside London, like Plymouth, and some were busy ferrying passengers from one side of the river to the other.

"It is quicker and safer to go by water, for thieves and vagabonds lurk in London's alleyways," my father's man told me, making me wonder why we were heading to the house of the Duchess by horse.

He went on to inform me that only boatmen with the greatest courage, or foolishness, would attempt to take their crafts under the arches of the bridge, for there the water transformed into weirs most dangerous. The reason the bridge was so busy was because it was the only one in the city, and was not only a passage from one side of London to another, but, as I had seen, held shops and houses all stacked upon each other like blades of hay in a barn. There was even a chapel, and people went to the bridge to meet, buy goods, and sometimes just to gossip.

And people I could see. In truth I wondered if I had ever known this many people were in the world. There were bright coats and dun, colourful gowns and serviceable ones. There were men urging on carts stacked high and precarious with barrels of fish in salt from the coast, or honey, or fruit. Markets were here and there, set up for people to mill about and surrounded by maids carrying baskets, sent out by their mistresses to buy food for that day. There were inns and taverns from which men staggered, even so early in the day, although I reasoned perhaps they had tarried late, the scent of ale on the air about their heads. Here and there I could see constables, there to protect the city, property and people, but they were few. The men my father had sent with me stayed close to me, knowing that an innocent such as I was prime game for a cutpurse or thief.

I saw freemen, many with swords and all with daggers. It was usual to see; all people carried a knife for many purposes. As we came from the bridge, after an achingly slow trip across, if an interesting one, we came past more heads on spikes; men who had committed treason and died for it. After the bridge came squares which opened as though they were meadows made not of grass and flowers, but cobbles and grit, in the centre of the city. In such spaces pillories and stocks stood, waiting to correct those who had strayed from the path of the law. Women accused of adultery or fornication would be kept there, and people would hiss at them and taunt them. Sometimes they threw things too. Merchants who cheated customers would find themselves imprisoned there, sometimes with their tainted stock burning under their noses as a lesson not to lie about the quality of their goods. Some believed that women caught in the sin of adultery should be burned to death for breaking a covenant with God. Seeing what Catherine had done to our family, I was tempted to agree, although a small voice inside me told me my father had, too, committed the same sin. For all he had done, for all I despised him for, I could not wish death upon my father. *That is why you hate Catherine so,* the voice said. *You cannot hate your father, for he is your master and sire, but on her you release your hatred of them both.*

I turned away from the voice. Truth it spoke, but I did not want to hear it.

Suffolk Place, residence of the Duchess and her Duke, Charles Brandon, was a new building. The Duke's family had owned another house, which had stood on the same site for many years, but with his wealth finally increasing after years of paying fines to the King for daring to marry the Princess without permission coming to an end, the Duke was in a position to build a residence in keeping with his title. Suffolk Place was in Southwark, on the south bank of the Thames. It was a town house of the grandest kind, and was close to Winchester Palace where the Bishop of Winchester lived. A grand house, with grand neighbours. Southwark was where much of the entertainment of the city took place; bear baiting and plays performed in inns, bawdy houses and markets where men sold ale and women pies, or their own bodies. But it was also where some of the richest of court lived. Here, prostitutes and prelates, bawds and barons lived, if not side by side then not more than a stone's throw from one another.

The street that Suffolk Place stood upon was the main road leading from London Bridge and the city to Canterbury and Dover. It was therefore on a pilgrim route, and was the main road to the sea, to France and to Europe. The house was *most* modern. It made Wulfhall look like an ancient cave. Long halls for walking on wet days met high towers and the outside was covered in carvings in the Roman style, as was fashionable. There were domes on the top of the towers, which looked like little hats from afar. One wing of the house opened out and there was a courtyard in its centre. Long, large gracious gardens and a wide pleasure park stood behind it and there were considerable blocks of comfortable accommodation for guests and for the servants of the Brandons.

"The Duchess and Duke also, of course, have suites of rooms at court," said Lady Guildford, known in the house by the affectionate name of *Mother Guildford*, a title granted by the Princess herself, since this lady had been her governess. Lady Guildford did not serve the Princess all the time, being in her grey hairs and also because she was called on to attend the Queen from time to time, but Mary liked her and retained her often. Mother Guildford had met me at the gate and was showing me about the magnificent house.

"Of course," I said.

I began to feel quite dizzy as she led me about the house. Room after room, all wide and long and high, all painted in bright colours opened out before my eyes. I had not known any house could be so big. There were wide chambers where dark oak panels on the walls were hidden by dazzling tapestry in stupendous colours, and in the lesser chambers there was painted cloth. Emblems of the house of Tudor, of France and of the Brandons were everywhere, a testament to the noble bloodlines that ran in the family. Long corridors were not dark, but were lit by candles and oil lamps, bronze and golden light spilling into the darkest corners, making everything glow like precious metal. There were clocks on many walls, gifts from the King, who loved their intricate workings, as I was told. Portraits of ancestors of the house stared down with unseeing eyes, and grand galleries held glimmering plate of pewter, gold and silver all housed in bold, huge cupboards with open fronts. And glass… never had I seen so much! Thin and stunning it glittered, with goblets etched with roses and vines or the initials of the person it had been bestowed upon. Glass was so expensive it was hardly used. Only the Duke and Duchess, and the King or Queen, were to employ such things to drink from. I was afraid to even go near the cupboard in case I trod too heavily on a floorboard and the cupboard shifted, sending a glass to crash against the side, or worse, fall out to shatter upon the floor.

There was spare furniture, of course, like most houses, but in the Duchess's rooms were masses of brightly coloured cushions made from velvet, linen and silk, the borders embroidered with forget-me-nots and heartsease in thread of azure and purple, gold and silver. The cushions were set about ornate hearths, ready for the women of the household to gossip upon. *You, Jane, are one of her women now,* a voice told me. My heart almost tripped over itself in giddy excitement.

We came to the bedchambers where beds of almost ridiculous size stood hung with thick, embroidered cloth bearing the Tudor rose and lilies of France, with the same symbols carved into the dark wood with intricate grace and craftsmanship. Staring at the roses, I could almost smell them. They smelt sweet, like power.

Stools and trestle tables flanked the edges of the great hall, as though they were maids waiting to be taken out to dance, and in the rooms of my new mistress and master were writing desks inlaid with mother-of-pearl. Like water they shone as the light of the windows, all of them glass, cascaded upon them. Diamond panes made fractured diamond patterns on the desks, on the floors, and glittering from ceilings where the beams were painted in gilt. The effect was such that it made the eyes stream, shocked by the wealth and power the house contained. Perhaps I wept, too, for joy.

"The gardens, where we may take exercise, with her Highness or sometimes with another lady of her house," said my guide, her hand waving at open spaces of green and enclosed sections of trees and flowers.

I glanced from the window, fragrant air rolling from flowers hitting my face along with a faint whiff of the Thames. The gardens were a mass of orchards, flower beds, romantic meads and hidden glens. Rambling lawns of verdant, close-clipped grass demonstrated the wealth of the Duke and his royal Duchess, for who but the rich could afford to grant such space to grass? One could not eat grass or make much from it when it was kept so short. Its appearance, especially in such expanses as at Suffolk Place, demonstrated the carelessness that money may bring, the lack of need to plant only to survive. My eyes crept over the lawns, noting they must be trimmed every day to stay so short, another expense. A job created, perhaps more than one given all the grass, to care for something unneeded, useless.

There were archery butts in open spaces for the men of the Duke, and I was told the Duchess was a fine shot too with her yew bow. It was usual for men and boys to practise with the bow on Sunday, in preparation for war. At the edge of my vision I could see stables that seemed to go on for miles. They were full, I was told, of fine horses and I imagined them snorting with delight as they rooted through sacks of feed. The Duke would feed his mounts horse bread, made of the finest peas, no doubt, and nettles to keep their coats brilliant and glossy. The kitchens stood just outside the main house, and from there wafted the scent of game pies baking, custard simmering, and beef turning on a spit, fat hissing as into flame it fell.

My guide turned, a smile on her face. "The King is *most* fond of the Duke. Our master is, in many ways, closest to the King and all who meet the Princess and Dowager love her. It is impossible to resist her charms!"

I smiled. Evidently Mary's charms were certainly not lost on Lady Guildford.

I had heard that Brandon's were lost on some, however. Charles Brandon was a man who had risen high because he was the friend and companion of the King. Many people did not like it when someone of obscure, albeit noble even if not noblest, origins did well, particularly if they themselves came from more ancient stock than the upstart on the rise. There was a verse that Brandon himself had created when Mary and he had wed.

Cloth of gold, do not despise,
Though thou be matched with cloth of frieze.
Cloth of frieze, be not too bold,
Though thou be matched with cloth of gold.

It was painted under their marriage portrait, copies of which hung all over the house. Mary, naturally, was the cloth of gold and Brandon the frieze. It was the Duke's way of demonstrating his humility, and his deference to her. She was the higher titled soul, the better blood. Many not only agreed with Brandon but thought he had engineered his marriage so he could climb higher. Without an heir of the King in the nursery, Brandon's sons might have a claim to the throne through Mary. I wondered about this myself, but after serving for a time I thought it not so. Brandon was a man of impressive physical power and noble bearing, but he was not the brain in the body of this marriage. That, undoubtedly, belonged to the cloth of gold.

"I did think the closest to the King was his Groom of the Stool?" I asked. "Am I mistaken, Lady Guildford? I am sorry if I am. I am so new to court and to London." I flushed at my ignorance and for having the daring to have asked a question which appeared to contradict something someone told me. At home I rarely ventured opinions. London was having an effect on me.

She smiled again, a touch of pity playing upon her lips, but I could tell she liked my humble manner. All people enjoy feeling wiser than others. Passing on knowledge is a pleasure to all, but some people remember they too do not know all and share knowledge with the humility that comes with that understanding. Others, who think they know everything, tend to impart knowledge which becomes tainted with their own arrogance. Lady Guildford was not an arrogant woman at heart, but neither was she a wise one. The reason I could tell this was because my ignorance pleased her.

"It is easy to suppose such," she said in a kind tone. "The ways of court *are* complex, Mistress Seymour, to the new and uninitiated, but they will become easier with familiarity."

"Thank you, I do so hope so," I said.

"It can be said there are many close to the King, in many ways. The Groom, as you said, Mistress Seymour, is close to the King and must be a trusted man for he attends to His Majesty in the closed stool, and any man in so intimate a position must be trusted since it is perhaps the only time the King may be thought vulnerable. His Majesty also has men who advise and guide him, such as members of his intimate band, and the Council, and he knows them to be loyal. But for true fellowship and honest company the King always has turned, and always will, to his friend the Duke. And the Duke loves the King as his friend and brother."

"Indeed he is both," I said.

"Indeed he is."

Neither of us mentioned that the blood relationship that now existed between the King and Brandon had come about because of scandal. There had been a time Brandon had not honoured his King as a friend and a brother, since he had married the King's sister without permission. Many a man had died for less.

After viewing so many chambers and corridors that I felt light-headed with dazzled wonder, I was brought to the chamber of my new mistress. Outside the door I stood, my throat so dry I thought I might choke. Had I swallowed a desert? A dune was sliding in my throat, sand and grit and wind flaying soft flesh. We entered when we were called and I walked into a glorious room of warmth and bright tapestry. By the fire was the Princess, flanked by her ladies. This was the woman I was to serve who held my fate in her hands. Fail to please her and I would be sent from this heaven, back down into hell.

All eyes were on me as I curtseyed at the door and walked forwards. I could feel the interest of her ladies, sharp as fingernails, poking me all over. They were trying to make out my character, my home, my family. I hoped they would see I was wearing a new gown, and would not see that the sleeves were older, part of a set my mother had given me, adapted to look new.

I came before the Duchess and dropped to another curtsey. It was good, not as poised as many I had seen exacted about the house, but good enough. At least I did not fall over. I kept my eyes on the floor, spotting pretty purple lavender and meadowsweet amongst the rush mats. The smell flew up my nose, suddenly reminding me of another Mary, of dead eyes staring up, of a pale hand on a dead child. I closed my eyes a moment, trying to rid myself of the vision.

"Lift your eyes, Mistress Seymour," said a sweet, authoritative voice.

I looked up and there before me saw such beauty I thought I might lose my breath. Princess Mary Tudor of England was one of the most enchanting women I had ever seen. Erasmus himself, that exalted sage my mother spoke of with reverence, had described her as *"a nymph from heaven"* adding that *"nature never formed anything more beautiful"* than her. I could not disagree.

Her skin was clear and pale and shimmering. It seemed to glitter, like alabaster, and I found later this effect was created by a light powder she wore. Her hair was auburn, partially visible from under a black French hood rimmed with glimmering pearls. Her lips were pretty, full and dusky pink. Her figure was perfect; just the right amount of breast and flesh without ever looking too ample or too spare. Her eyes were deep blue, large and doe-like, with long, black lashes and her expression was gentle, mildly amused. Yet despite this benevolent expression, I could see a flame in her. There was dragon-fire in the Welsh blood of the Tudors and it shone through in their hair and in their spirit.

"Your mistress, the Dowager of France, Duchess of Suffolk and Princess of England," said a man at her elbow, directing his announcement of Mary's titles towards me, as if I could be in doubt of whom I stood before.

The exquisite dragon, the rose formed of flame gazed at me. "Welcome to court, and to the house of my husband, the Duke of Suffolk," said Mary Tudor. "You may call me, my lady."

"I am honoured to be here, my lady," I said. I bowed my head, for the first time in my life not sad to see the floor.

Chapter Twenty-Four

Suffolk Place and Westhorpe Hall
London and East Anglia

Summer 1527

As meadowsweet, my keeper of dark memories, came rambling from shadowy hiding places in hedgerows, as its fluffy blossom started to be found in fields and waysides and women gathered it for strewing on floors, I entered the household of the Duchess, the Dowager, the Princess.

It mattered not what Mary was called. She was easily one of the most titled women in the world, and as had been promised, I fell for her. In her I found beauty matched with courage and a kind nature. To enemies she was fierce and could be ruthless, no doubt, but to friends and to her servants she was the heart of goodness. There was still a touch of the flighty young princess who had gone to France, danced an old husband into his grave then boldly wed the man she loved in defiance of her brother and King in her, but whilst I could see that wild soul, it was matched now, tempered, with a woman of grace and years who had learned who she was and was confident in all she did. I was in awe of her. Many of us were.

My day began with the church bells ringing for dawn. In the maidens' chamber of the Duchess of Suffolk, in the faded blue light before the sun clambered into the heavens, I was woken by the bells and my bedfellow. We washed our hands and faces in cold water in which rose petals had been immersed whilst it was hot. Our maids allowed it to cool before presenting it to us. The Duchess commanded it. Hot water opened pores, making them vulnerable to wandering imps and fevers, but cold water was safe as long as the washer was healthy. We made sure our faces and hands, especially our nails, were clean as each day, before we handled any of her

Grace's food, clothing or combs or jewels, our hands were inspected by the Mother of the Maids, our mistress. If found wanting we might be sent further away than to merely wash our hands again; we might be sent home.

We dressed in gown and kirtle, and our hair was combed, flowing down our backs, as maidens were supposed to wear it. About court we would wear the gable hood, as was proper, or the French hood, as our mistress had made fashionable, but in her house Mary liked to see her maids look like maids. Our cleanliness, too, reflected upon her. If her maids and attendants looked ill-kempt or dirty it might be thought our souls were too, and by association, hers. Our clean hands and well-kept gowns, therefore, were in honour of our mistress. No one in that house was about to shame Mary Tudor, for love if not for fear.

Before leaving the chamber where our many beds stood side by side, by our beds we knelt, thanking God for blessings He had granted, asking for His grace to fall upon all our works. Each morning as thrushes in the trees started their warbling dawn chorus, I thanked God for stealing me away from Wulfhall. I thanked Him for extracting me from the torture of Catherine. I thought there was not much more I dared ask for, but I did. I asked that she be removed from our house, in a way that hurt no one for she had caused enough pain. I asked that as I was free of her, my family be too. I asked God most of all to protect Edward.

"Save my brother, my good brother, from the truth, Lord of Heaven," I mumbled. "The truth can only pain him now. Save him the truth."

Edward was to go to France in a matter of days, with Cardinal Wolsey. I would not see him a great deal, as he had told me when first I arrived. He was a most busy man. Thomas, too, I would not see even though he was frequently at court. He served Sir Frances Bryan, our kinsman, as his personal attendant and so he too was busy. Although I had no wish to see Thomas, and was glad for Edward, I wondered at their missives. It seemed they thought I would have ample spare time, yet I too was an attendant, *and to one of a higher title than their masters,* the voice inside me said. With a pang of guilt, I told it to be silent.

Edward was to go to France for a specific, delicate reason. Odd things had been happening at court. Wolsey had called the King to answer a charge: that the King was living in sin with the wife of his dead brother. Until that moment it had seemed as though little was happening on the matter of the King's fears about his marriage. Until that moment, Queen Katherine had not known the King had ordered an investigation into his marriage, and he *must* have ordered it for Wolsey would not have acted so bold on the matter otherwise. It was said the King had kept his fears quiet, hoping to investigate with subtlety, and that when evidence was presented, Katherine would accept their marriage was unlawful and enter a nunnery, allowing him to marry where he wanted. Some said France would be the birthplace of our next Queen. Others whispered England.

"The Queen will appeal to the Pope," I heard it murmured as I moved through the halls of Suffolk Place. "The Pope alone can decide such a matter as the legality of the King's marriage."

If that was so, I thought the Pope would find for Katherine. It had been the papacy, if not this particular Pope, who had granted a dispensation for the couple to wed in the first place. If the King was right and his marriage was illegal in the eyes of God, that meant the Pope who granted the dispensation had been wrong to do so, calling into question the authority of the Vatican itself. It seemed unlikely the present Pope would undermine his predecessor and his own power by finding in favour of the King.

There was another reason I thought the Pope would support Katherine. Not long before I came to Suffolk Place, Rome had been sacked. In an event which stunned England and all of Christendom, soldiers and mercenaries of the Emperor Charles of Spain, on campaign in Italy, facing France, had entered Rome and attacked. The Pope had fled and was safe, but tales of horrors came to us. Nuns raped upon altars and priests and monks murdered in the streets. It was said our King would aid the French and we would unite against the Emperor and his ungodly troops. I never could keep up with which country was our ally and which was foe.

The Pope was not exactly the prisoner of the Emperor, but he was hardly free either. The Emperor, Katherine's nephew, was in command of Rome. A verdict that the dispensation allowing his aunt's marriage had been faulty, that a princess of Spain had been living in sin with a man, who in the eyes of God was her brother, and whose daughter, the Emperor's cousin, was a bastard born of sin, was not likely to emerge from Rome.

The Cardinal was to go to France, my brother one of his helpers, so Wolsey might talk to the French cardinals about setting up a court comprised of English and French men of God, who, since the Pope was held captive by the Emperor, could decide upon the legality of the marriage of the King and Queen of England. Much as I hated the task Edward was being sent on, it was another sign of trust from the King, and from the Cardinal, who all but ruled England.

My life was more staid than that of my adventurous brother, but that did not mean it was not busy. Once dressed, emerging from our chambers, sometimes we would hear cows in pastures nearby, being herded back to hay fields from outside of the city. There were a few nearby that served Suffolk Place, and after the hay had been cut by scythe and muscle of man, beasts were brought back to nibble the stalks left behind. There were other noises of the city; bells calling people to Mass, maids singing as they wandered in from villages outside of London with milk to sell, men cursing as they slipped on rubbish or shit in the streets.

With our leather boots clipping on flagstones and cobbles, we walked to Mass in the chapel. We stood watching candles burning before images of the Saints, and asked God to forgive our trespasses. We bowed our heads as the priest spoke in Latin over us, sometimes giving a sermon, often about the ills of women. Women were wicked, easily corruptible and corrupting of others, he droned. Women were doomed since Eve to tempt men, and had to be controlled, he said. *Who was controlling Catherine?* I asked myself. My father? My brother? Catherine's own father? None of them appeared capable of controlling her. As far as I could see all of the men who knew her had failed in this duty. I shook my head and prayed for my mistress, trying to set the witch from my mind. I did not want to escape Catherine only for her ghost to haunt me now.

At times, if the priest went on too long, the Duchess would tap her feet, a signal for him to desist. I wondered at times if he spoke so often on the virtues of controlling women because he himself was mastered by one. Perhaps it was a way to vent frustration. He obeyed though, every time.

When God was done with us, we broke our fast on bread and sometimes meat, or fish if it was a saint's day, Advent or Lent, and always said a prayer and made the sign of the cross upon our lips before eating. Then, I went to my duties. No more making medicines in the distillery or listening to Mother for hours on end. There was much to be learned.

My duties were a joy to me. Sworn into her service on the day I arrived, I had made a vow to the Duchess before God that I would be meek, humble, chaste and good. Nothing would I do that would bring scandal or dishonour upon her. We ladies made sure that the Princess had all she could need at her elbow. If our mistress did not have to look for an item, we had done our jobs well. We were to serve her food when it came from her kitchens, refill her wine, and please her guests. At night, if she called for something, we would fetch what treat she desired from one of the hutches, small food cupboards, in her side rooms, and bring it to her. Often, during her second sleep of the night, Mary would call for sweetened ginger to refresh her mouth, or aleberry pudding, which was also a favourite dish of her brother, the King's. Between her first and second sleep we would sit in the bed with her, if she was not with her husband, and talk to her. Sometimes we played cards. It was a time of closeness and confidence, where we shared much. Often she fed us some of the rich treats she was eating, too.

We tidied her rooms a little, but Mary had chamberers who did the more menial tasks, like lighting fires, and scurrying about taking away dirty plates or cups. But we ladies had higher tasks such as taking care of the glorious clothes of the Princess and adornments of her chambers. We kept Mary company, told her what we learned from gossip in the halls and from those who came to the house. Some women read to her or sang, but my reading never was accomplished and I had no voice for singing. I had never learnt an instrument, so I was wanting there, too. I knew how to care for furs, however, and that was a good skill to have in a house where there were so many, and so many of them fine. The Princess was keen with her needle, and admired my skill in that art, so we could talk on that as we sat at the fireside. She had me show her some of the stitches I knew which seemed more elegant to her than ones she was familiar with. I was quiet and humble, which she liked. I did my tasks and I was good at them. I did all I could to please. Of course I did. Suffolk Place and the Princess were my salvation. Always I excelled at things I truly loved, and I loved Mary and her house. Without Mother there, her voice telling me always I would fail, I failed less. My mistress was pleased with me, and under her gentle and encouraging hand, I was turning into, if not one of the most accomplished women of court, a worthy woman of court.

The Duke and Duchess also had a country seat, Westhorpe Hall in East Anglia, where we went from time to time, in summer in particular as plague was rife in the city, but also when the Duke wished to hunt. As I had been told upon arrival, they had chambers at court, in the palaces of the King too, but Westhorpe was where the family of the Duke and Duchess resided, for they had their own children and those Brandon had sired on other women, before his marriage. Some of these children were grown and had flown the rich nest, but others remained. Those who had left, like Mary's stepdaughter Anne, who had wed Edward Grey, Baron of Powys a few years before I came to court, came to see her. Another stepdaughter, Mary, was preparing to wed Thomas Stanley, Baron Monteagle, and was too often with her stepmother. Mary was good to Brandon's children, and to her own. All of them loved her.

In truth, there were some problems, not exactly with their children, but with the status of their legitimate ones. Brandon had had a complicated past when it came to marriage. He had been promised to several ladies at different times, some at the same time, and had been granted a dispensation to marry one woman, which had not been dissolved when he married Mary. This left a question upon their marriage as a promise to wed, backed by papal dispensation, could be seen as as binding as a marriage service. My mistress and master were soon to send a man to the Pope to ensure that their children, Henry, Frances and Eleanor, had the correct status. If their son was ever to be considered for the throne, this was doubly important.

Westhorpe Hall was a pretty house. "It once belonged to the de la Poles," one of the other women told me as we rode towards it on my first visit. "But when the Duke and the Dowager of France took it on they much improved it."

It was grand, a glittering moat running all around it, more for the sake of beauty than defence. There was a large square courtyard in the middle of the buildings, with a fine, tall gatehouse and a bridge leading across the moat on the western side of the blocks of apartments. The chambers of the Duke, Duchess, and the King if he was visiting, and I was told he often did, were on the eastern side. There was a generous great hall, fine for dancing and feasting, as well as a great chamber, a dining chamber, a tower, chapel and ample rooms for guests and servants. Away from the main buildings were the kitchens, the buttery, where sauces were made, and the pantry. The house was the favoured residence of the Duchess. It was where and how she escaped the politics of court.

"What our poor Princess most wishes to escape is that Boleyn witch," said Margaret, one of my new companions, as she took me up to see the view from the tower.

I nodded as I kept my eyes on the spiral staircase, long and dark and twisting. It would be perilous to slip. I knew of what she spoke. I had not been out and about at court since I had come to the service of the Princess. Mary took her more experienced ladies with her to the halls of her brother and often the most beautiful ones. I was a lesser lady of her house, and therefore not as important as others of higher blood or longer standing. I had been assured the Princess would not neglect her duties to me, however. There was a bond between servant and master. As we served them, they cared for us. Taking me out into court would aid my reputation, help me to be seen and known, but at the same time I would be protected by the gentle hand and guiding presence of my mistress. There were few men at court foolish enough to try to impose on the women of the Duchess of Suffolk. But to be seen and known as one of her ladies would improve me in the eyes of prospective husbands. Eventually, no matter how limited the capacity, Mary would take me out with her. But she had not yet.

That did not mean I knew nothing of court. Maids gossiped, as did the Princess, although she was always careful to listen more than talk. She did not want a reputation as a gossip. I had heard talk, ill-boding whispers. The King was making a fool of himself over my cousin, Anne Boleyn, who was at court as one of the ladies of the Queen. All said he was smitten, but although some claimed she was his mistress, others said not. Some whispered she had refused him, yet despite this still he chased her. I thought it was perhaps *because* of her refusal he chased her. I was a good huntress. I knew the thrill of the chase was superior to that of the kill. When death was done and blood was shed, there was sadness, for the excitement was over. Whilst racing into the wind, a horse under you beating the ground with raw power, the screaming of the hunter's horn in your ears, there is anticipation, and there is no pleasure as great as anticipation. It has the capacity to be anything, and anything may come from it. It is an emotion as much fantasy as it is reality. It is a story bound in the arms of emotion; a wish of what may come.

My cousin had thrown such a story upon the King, that what might come would be better than anything ever he had experienced, and the King was lost in the forest of her fable. This was what all said. He was in love. Anne had taken his heart. Some whispered he might think to replace Queen Katherine with Anne Boleyn.

Impossible though it seemed, since Anne, high blooded in some ways as she was, being part Howard, was not royal, it had been done before. Only once, but once a King had married beneath him and for love; the King's grandfather, Edward IV had married Elizabeth Woodville. Lady Woodville, noble though she was, had been thought far beneath him and they had married in secret. There was, therefore, a precedent, and a recent one, for a King to marry a woman lower in station than him, for love.

The difference between our King and his grandfather, however, was that our King already had a Queen. I thought this talk of Anne becoming Queen a fantasy dreamed up by those who liked to gossip. Those who like to listen to scandal and rumour must make each tale they hear wilder than the last, and there is much exaggeration. Scandal is a drug, there must always be more and increasingly large doses of it to satisfy the one addicted to it. Eventually small stories suffice not, so people embellish little tales to make them large. The King had spoken to his men in the past about asking

Katherine to go to a nunnery and taking a new wife, but nothing had come of this for years, until recently. Until coming to court, I had thought my mother was correct and he had remembered his love for the Queen. Less sure as I was by that time that he still adored Katherine as once he did, I still thought the tales of Anne's power too wild. The King might be chasing Anne Boleyn, but it would likely end as it always did, with her as his mistress. If he did set Katherine aside, he would marry a royal woman, I was sure.

We reached the top of the tower and Margaret opened the small, black door and took me out. I could see for miles. Down in the yard at the back of the kitchens a maid was throwing food to hens, green specks of vegetable peels, with some nettle leaves too, no doubt. We fed chickens nettle at home, for it made eggs tastier.

"The Princess is made sad to see the King so open in an affair with another woman," said Margaret. "For it pains the Queen, her sister and friend." She shook her head. "It is too much that a girl may come to court, be graced by the Queen and elevated, and then return that grace with spite, by prancing and simpering at the King so he turns his head from his wife!"

I nodded. I never considered, then, that perhaps the King might too be at fault. He could, after all, have turned his head from Anne and kept his eyes on his wife, the mother of his child. That he chose not to was, indeed, a choice. Willpower was something all people possessed, as was free will. My father, too, could have chosen not to shame my brother.

Yet it was natural to think women to blame. We were held to account for most things, starting with the fall of man from grace. It was natural to think of Anne as being the one to blame in this situation. After all, I more often blamed Catherine for her affair with my father, yet two people were in that bed of sin.

I did not think it perhaps an insult to think that the King had no will power or mind, or conscience, of his own.

Chapter Twenty-Five

**Greenwich Palace
London**

Late Summer 1527

One fine day in the late summer, we were paying a visit to court before heading to the country for a time. The King wished to see Brandon and the Princess before he embarked on progress. He wanted support from his best friend and his sister for his case to separate from the Queen.

The fact that Mary had already made herself quite plain about her support for her royal sister and disdain for Anne Boleyn seemed to pass by the King's nose without notice. As far as he was concerned he was head of England and of his family, and Mary was honour-bound to obey him. That his sister had made herself even more famous than she had been by birth, by marrying for love against his wishes, the King appeared to have forgotten. And my mistress was hardly subtle about her dislike for Anne Boleyn. Mary made pointed, barbed comments, many very witty, about the girl.

Yet the King seemed to hear this not, if any dared to tell him. He was to send men to Rome, to the captive exiled Pope, and those men were to ask the Pope to allow Wolsey to try the case in England. Otherwise legates were to be dispatched from Rome, it was said. Most people thought any man sent from Rome would find in favour of Katherine. Most people thought it impossible she could have been living in sin, in any case. She was too godly, too good a Queen and woman to allow such a thing to occur if against her conscience it went.

And in the midst of this strife, this strange and bitter turmoil, I had come to the court of the King. Perhaps it was selfish of me to find beauty and wonder in a place where so many other darker things seemed to be lurking, yet it was one of the times of purest awe ever I experienced in my life. The household of the Dowager of France had been wondrous enough, but court was another animal, one born of myth and legend.

Sometimes in life, we are disappointed by reality when we have dreamed of something so long, yet sometimes it surpasses all we could have imagined. That was how court was for me. Long had it been my comfort and consolation. Like a tale of Arthur and his knights, or Alfred and his men, court had been a story to me. I had grown up on tales of gowns and dances, of the boyish antics of the King and his men, but nothing prepared me. All the stories my mother told did not come close, could not even touch the hem of the plainest gown, of the wondrous, beautiful, lunatic court.

On my first day, I had to remind my mouth to stay closed and my eyes not to stare at every person and sight I saw. A tight, hard rein I kept upon myself that day.

Ladies' gowns, dazzling in scarlet, azure, glittering white and flashing emerald whispered on fresh rush matting and fragrant posies of fresh herbs as they walked by. Petticoats, always of red, since it was said to bring health to the wearer, poked out from skirts slashed to display the fabric underneath. Noblemen in silks, velvets, cambric and damask, with swords and daggers at their hips were like a host of proud peacocks strutting the halls, their tapered waists held in and padded chests puffed up, and jewelled codpieces jutting out before them, glittering. It was a touch embarrassing if a maid's eye was caught by such a sight, and it was their intention to catch the eye. The nobler the man, the larger his codpiece. The King's were said to be outrageous.

There was, some whispered, another, less honourable reason to wear a large codpiece. If a man had the pox it was treated sometimes with unguents and creams of herbs, grease and mercury slathered upon his diseased manhood. Wear a large codpiece and these treatments and the cloth which covered a man's shaft, holding medicines to the skin, could be concealed. More than a little horrified had I been to think that *so* many men could be wandering about with the pox. I was also told codpieces were often large as men carried things in them, using them as pockets to contain money, missives and other small objects. Some men were said to keep love letters from their mistresses in their codpieces. It seemed an unromantic place to put such things to me, but I could see the logical link.

Perfume rode the air along with the scent of rushes and herbs crushed underfoot, and there were fuming pots in many rooms, emitting scent from burning scented wood, or incense, yet under sweet smells crept a rank stench of sweat, piss and dog shit. About the palaces, the King had instructed signs of the cross to be painted on the floor in red, to stop gallants pissing where they pleased. Some did it anyway, something which shocked me greatly, and others pissed down staircases or into hearths. Few used the houses of easement, or *jakes* as they were known. Women took more care than men, and Mary would not have had any of her women relieving themselves wherever the fancy claimed us.

But a pungent scent, or pretty one, was not the only assault on the eyes. Court was so bright in some chambers it was like staring into the sun. Walls blazed, plate glittered, gilt shone and vivid colours burst out from every part of the palace and her people like an army of cutpurses in a darkened street. It was a constant attack on the eyes. I found mine darting all the time from one object to another, flabbergasted by each in turn until my mind became dim under the onslaught of sensation. It was as though court tried to tame each person who came into its halls, subdue them with this onslaught of wealth and colour, smell and sensory excitement, teasing and tickling the mind so that eventually it shut down, exhausted, and then they could do nothing but obey, follow their master in stupefied wonder. Perhaps it was a trick of the King.

Court was a wonder. There was more wealth here than ever I had seen, and more people willing to do anything they could to gain more. There was a rampant, predatory sense to the halls of the King, only kept in check by the rules of chivalry and the grace of the Queen. Katherine, truly, was the steady hand upon the youthful arm of court. She reminded us all to be the best we could be, by being the best she could. Even before I met her, even though she spent a lot of time in her quarters, it was felt; a presence like a spirit flowing from the chambers of the Queen, keeping peace, keeping order.

And yet, it seemed she was in danger. Lose the love of the King and the world could become a dangerous place. I learnt that truth fast, and never was I allowed to forget it.

But for me, at that time, court was more about pleasure than fear. I had seen Edward, albeit sparingly, a few times since I had come to court, and since he had returned from France, his mission largely uneventful. The Cardinal had not managed to convince his French brothers of God to form a council to hear the King's plea about his marriage. Thomas, too, I had seen along with Sir Frances Bryan, our kinsman. Thomas I cared nothing for, and he was only a visitor to court. Edward I loved seeing, missed each moment I did not, but he was busy often, making a name for himself and serving the King. When I heard good reports of him, my heart glowed. I wished I could feel as happy for the Queen.

Perhaps it was the adoration my mother had for her, or the way she was spoken of so well by all in Mary's household, but I felt connected to Katherine before I met her. It was the way of good Queens. As the King is the justice and law of a country, so the Queen is mercy and charity. She was love, as the King was fear. Both are needed if a country is to obey its leaders. There must be fear enough to prevent rebellion and love enough that commands are followed with hope and belief. Katherine was the heart of England, and to me it felt as if that heart was wounded, perhaps broken.

But on the day I met her, little prepared as I was, I found that what is broken is not weak; that which is wounded is not devoid of courage. I found the opposite of what I had long thought true, to be true. I met a Queen one day, and encountered a warrior too.

We ladies were walking with our mistress the Princess in the gardens at Greenwich, along paths of swept sand made smooth each day by those who toiled to make the gardens a wonder. In places that sand was crafted into large patches, coloured, and arranged to make Tudor roses bloom in sand and grit upon the floor. Striped poles stood in beds of dancing blooms, beasts of heraldry upon the tops, growing lions and wide-grinning dragons. There was the scent of roses, abundant and soft, on the air, the whiff of the river, an ever-present smell of London, and the far off smell of creatures roasting and pies baking in the kitchens. Gently we conversed as we walked the paths, our boots of good leather crunching the slippery sand underfoot as over our heads light, white clouds bustled swift and busy in a sky of brilliant blue.

The Queen and her attendants came in sight. Although she had not known her sister was in the royal gardens that day Mary was pleased, for she loved Katherine.

As we two groups sighted each other, Queen Katherine came close, an expression on her face of beatific happiness. "Sister," she said in a voice warm as gentle sunlight as Mary curtseyed to her. "It is good to see you this day."

"You look radiant, Majesty," Mary replied.

Radiant was a strange word to use for the Queen, for a beauty she was no more. She looked weary, truth be told. I had been told that, as a young princess come to marry Prince Arthur and even when she had wed the King, Katherine had been a beauty with her long auburn hair and clear skin. But when I first met her I thought she looked worn. Not old exactly, but like a path walked too long and hard so the stones that line it become scattered, leaving impacted earth. There was pain in her, something she had carried a long time and dealt with each day. Since I too had borne the burden of pain, I could see it in the Queen, and I could see the strength it took to bear that weight and to smile with the love she offered her sister, Mary. When we know suffering, sometimes our hearts retreat, unwilling to encounter love or compassion, or offer whatever of good we have left because of the agony we bear. Katherine had not chosen to do such a thing. Here was a woman who had lost much in life; family, her country when she came to England and her children, all but the Princess Mary, but the Queen had not allowed it to make her bitter. I understood there are some who endure the pains life offers and become wise and gentle, as some become brittle and brutal. Katherine had taken on understanding in place of self-pity, endured pain, but the suffering she carried was her own and she did not pass it on. What she passed on was love.

Her eyes were captivating; bright and intelligent, like coal glittering underwater they seemed both deepest black and blue in the same moment. Under those eyes were great rings of purple and grey darkness. Sorrow had painted shade there, but so too had her habit of rising through the night, each hour, to pray to God. She heard Mass in the night, I was told, and made constant offerings to the Church. Katherine believed in doing good, and did it. Many people just think of doing good and never do. Katherine was a woman of immense piety, and her devotion and love for God was writ upon her face and form.

Her gown was glorious, black, the most expensive dye, with bright white lace at the cuffs and hem of her chemise. Her jewels were many, but she did not look overdone as some at court did. But her figure was thick from bearing child after dead child, and the weary pain of that loss was a cowl upon her. She carried her children with her, all of them, just as she carried the love she bore for the one who had lived, her daughter, who had been named for the woman she greeted with such warmth that day.

The Queen held out a hand to the Princess, who rose from her elegant curtsey. Katherine's hands were lovely; pale skin, clear of any blemish, and her fingers were elegant, only more so for the plain rings of gold upon them. And no beauty could match the wisdom and calmness of her expression. The Queen had a soul more beautiful than any beauty could have ever been. I, who had seen what evil may lie behind a pretty face, did not hold physical beauty in high esteem. If I was to love a person it was for the inside, even if I was impressed with the outside. But from the first moment I worshipped Katherine, seeing in her the wonder of an exquisite soul.

Katherine held out her arm and Mary took it. We ladies, two groups of attendants, fell into pace behind them, the highest of Mary's ladies talking to the noblest of Katherine's, and the lowliest, like me, grateful to have the lowest of Katherine's talking to me. As the two Queens, one of present and one of past fell into conversation together, we maids did the same.

"You are new to court, Mistress Seymour?" asked Anne, one of Katherine's maids of honour.

"I am indeed, Mistress Stanhope."

"You are enjoying life in London?"

"It is a wonder to me, daily." I smiled shyly at her, resisting the urge to cover my lips with a hand. "I was only and ever in my father's house in Wiltshire before now, so all I see is enough to make me quite dumb with wonder."

She laughed a little, and we both ceased to talk as we rounded a corner and entered a small clearing surrounded by high hedges, leaves clipped and manicured. Here, we wandered in small groups, some ladies sitting on meads of flowers and some standing. And from here, I could hear the two Queens.

"How are you, sister, truly?" I heard Mary's soft voice press Katherine as she held her arm. Even above the buzz of conversation about me, I could hear urgent concern in her tone. There was respect in Mary's voice, the respect due from a younger sister to an elder. Sisters they were because of marriage, but I knew then that Mary saw Katherine as her older sister in truth.

Katherine sighed. "These days are hard for me, dear sister, as I am sure you understand."

"Of course," Mary replied, pressing her hand into Katherine's arm. "But my brother will come to his senses, Majesty. This raven-haired chit is a passing fancy, all know it. When he has opened his eyes to see the tricks and whore's wiles of that girl, he will return to you. He has loved you, and still loves you, since he was a young man. Long have I known both of you, and never was there a happier marriage that I have ever seen."

"Besides your own, but I thank you, sister." Katherine's voice was low with sorrow. "But this girl… I think she is different to others he dallied with in the past. He always kept them secret, and always I knew of them, but there was no need to say anything. Much as once it wounded me so sore, I came to understand and have now long understood men struggle to be constant when there is such temptation presented. It is not his fault; girls were thrown at him by ambitious men. Were it not for his friends, I think he would always have been faithful, for once he loved me as no other. Once I was the only one in his heart, the only one his eyes searched for. It is not so now."

"But always he has returned to you, for you are his true love."

"I love the King with all my heart, and I always will, but I think his love for me wanes. Always I will be his one, true love, for there is no woman, no person, in the world, who loves him as I do. But that is my heart I speak of, not his.

"I am older than him and when we were young together it mattered not, but now he notes it. Still he comes to ask my counsel, still we talk of our daughter, and we are friends, but the fire that once ignited in his eyes when he looked upon me has faded." Katherine set her shoulders back. "I see it kindle in his eyes, when on her he looks."

"She is nothing, what is she?"

"Oh," said Katherine, shaking her head. "One should never underestimate a person just because we do not like them. My mother taught me that when to war she took us children to teach us the ways of the world." She smiled sadly at Mary. "I know you say such to cheer me, but this girl is not nothing. It is true she has no great looks to boast of, but Anne has wit and cleverness. It did not take her long to shine at court, where there are many more beautiful women and with better blood than her. Men started to see her before they saw beauty, and that is a rare talent. There is a quick, keen mind behind all her prancing and prattling, and she is using it to bind my husband in a web of deceit. If only he could see her true nature. She is a wasp, soon she will sting."

Anne Boleyn again. I wondered at times if anyone at court, or in our country, was speaking of anything else. It reminded me of when Catherine had first come to Wulfhall and she was the only thing people could see, the only topic of conversation. Anne Boleyn was the same.

There were rumours building. Since Wolsey had called on the King to answer a charge of living in sin, it was all anyone could talk of. I felt so sorry for Katherine. To have a charge of living in sin, in *incest*, with the man you had lived with for twenty years as a beloved husband was an ill enough slander on anyone's name, but that her husband had *brought about* the charge? It was hideous. To be shamed in public by the person you loved, had thought loved you? And all for this girl. All for Anne Boleyn.

It was common knowledge now that the King supposed his first marriage illegal. The Bible agreed, he said, for it said in one passage that if a man married his brother's wife they would have no sons, for the match was cursed. But Katherine's supporters noted that another passage of the Holy Book said a man *should* marry his dead brother's wife, for he was duty-bound to protect her and continue the family line with her. The King countered by claiming his lack of sons demonstrated God did not gaze on his marriage with favour. If he had no son the future of England was in doubt, said the King, and this was why he was investigating his marriage, but other people whispered he had been thinking of ridding himself of Katherine for years, and, gossips said, Anne Boleyn had seen that if she held the King at bay she might win more than passing favours and a bastard babe… she might become Queen. Listening to rumour leap back and forth at court reminded me of tennis matches we watched the King's men compete in.

"She is a little fool, Majesty, soon she will fall."

"If only that were true, Mary, but I do not believe she is foolish. She has found a way to play my husband. He is a hoop racing down a hillside. She is the stick which beats him on, whips him to go faster, and who makes him fall if so she wishes. If only I could take him back into my bed, remind him of how it once was between us, remind him of the years of gentle love, all we have faced together and overcome… then, I am sure I could win him back from this girl. But to me he will not come."

"He will see her ways himself, soon enough." Mary spoke with stout resolve, but her hand pressing on Katherine's arm, on her sleeve of purple velvet, seemed to convey quite another meaning. It was trembling with anger and perhaps fear. My mistress was not sure at all of the words of comfort she spoke. "He will come back to you, Majesty. You are his true love. You have his heart in your keeping, I see it."

"To me he comes these days as a friend and mother, more than wife," said Katherine. "When there is trouble, he comes. When he needs his ambassador, as always I was, he comes. There is still the love we knew between us, but also between us is the girl." Katherine smiled. "God will find a way to open the King's heart to me again," she said. "I must be patient, and patience is something I have been taught before. I learned my lessons well. But God must have more to show me in this hard classroom. I will do as the Almighty desires, and I will learn what He wishes to teach me."

"Jane?" A voice at my elbow broke my concentration. I looked around, dazed, and saw ladies staring at me, giggles ready to burst from their throats. Evidently I had been lost, listening to a conversation not my own.

"I am sorry…" I muttered and flushed bright scarlet. My pallid cheeks turned hot as flame as I curtseyed. "I was thinking of something else. I am sorry, my Lady Exeter, what did you say to me?"

I was more shamed by the fact I had failed to note a woman of consequence was talking to me. Gertrude Courtenay was one of Katherine's ladies, one of her favourites. Her husband was Henry, the first Marquis of Exeter and a close companion of the King's, having known him since he was a boy. Gertrude's father was William Blount, Baron Mountjoy and her stepmother was Inez de Venegas, one of the women who had come with Katherine from Spain so many years ago when she was to wed Arthur. Gertrude was said to be like an older sister to Mary, Katherine's daughter, and was a daughter of England's old blood both by marriage and through her own family.

"You looked as though fairies had stolen you away for a moment," she said, chuckling. "I was asking how you liked court."

"Oh, well, very well indeed, my lady," I answered, feeling more foolish than usual. She did not look displeased, which calmed my heart a little. "I had never seen anything as grand as London when first I came here. My eyes were ready to fall from my skull in wonder at it all!"

"You resided in Wiltshire, did you not?" she asked and I inclined my head. "Is it a wild place, where you live?"

I smiled. "Perhaps, compared to London, my lady, but it boasts beauties and graces. The forests are thick and fine near my father's house, Wulfhall, and the hunting is good. There are places in the forests where the oppressive sun of the summer cannot touch a rider; places where snows of winter never fall, so deep are the cover of branches and trees."

"You make me almost jealous, Jane," she went on. "Perhaps one day you will show me your home, if we get the chance. On progress, perhaps, if your father is honoured by the King? Your brother does well at court, and many warm to him, so perhaps one day we will all see your family home and ride in those forests."

"I would like that, my lady," I replied warmly, trying to stave off thoughts of Catherine and my father even as I spoke.

Gertrude opened a twist of fabric in her hand, revealing comfits of caraway, which she offered to me. I took one and sucked its sweetness as we walked along. Our mistresses had started to stroll again, so we followed. It was the way of things.

We walked on, and came to a fountain in the gardens. In the centre of the pool was a statue of Venus and Cupid, he playing at her feet, she gazing down on him with pleasing eyes of gentle marble. Were there thoughts inside that marble-formed mind of hers? Were there passions? What secrets did such a motionless face hide? What truths that no man or woman would ever know were there, lying just under that impassive staring face?

Am I of marble made? I asked myself. A wit would say I was pale enough. Sometimes I felt I was crafted of rock, for few would ever know me. I trusted not many, so few ever saw past my pale and plain face.

Our deepest thoughts and feelings are impossible to describe, all people fail, even poets. That is why they write so often and so much, seeking to attain the impossible. Within us such emotions and thoughts fall as light upon ash, shifting, changing, flickering; a thousand colours trapped in grey. And so was I, this face of stone, a myriad of colour and emotion beneath.

As the other ladies sat at the poolside, talked and chattered to each other, I wandered to one side and stood looking at the view of the palace. I noted a late aquilegia bloom, its petals almost fallen, green seed pods forming. Gently I crouched down and put a hand to it. As I did, the last of the beautiful petals fell away. Without meaning to I let out a short sound of sorrow.

"Do not grieve," a voice said. Surprised, I stumbled to my feet and found myself gazing into the dark blue eyes of Queen Katherine. I fell into a most inelegant curtsey before her, and rose with my cheeks flaming. *Ungainly fool!* said the voice of my mother in my mind.

"Grieve not for the flower, Mistress Seymour," Katherine said again. Before I had a moment to wonder that she knew my name, she spoke again. "Its first flush of beauty is gone, but it has a greater purpose now."

Katherine reached out and touched the sticky seed pod. "Soon, she will be a mother to many." Katherine smiled sadly at me. "They rise from the earth every two years, these plants," she continued. "Did you know that? So they do not just flower, seed and die, but return into the world when they are ready, when they are strong. She will show beauty to the world again, Jane. So do not grieve for the loss of her petals. She is about to become a mother. That is the best of all graces in the world. Although people may look on her loss of the first flush of loveliness and mourn it, in truth she is about to become more beautiful than she ever was. Motherhood is the most blessed of all states, the most glorious."

Her voice was deep for a woman's but not gruff. It was musical, singing with notes of Spain lying upon English words. It was lovely.

"Yes, Your Majesty." I bobbed into a better curtsey than the last, and looked up into her eyes. There was sadness there. It had not overtaken her, as one day it would, but it was present. Katherine emitted something. There was sorrow in her air, yes, but grace too. She was dignified without arrogance, graceful of spirit without selfishness. She held her emotions in, unleashing only the worthy as much as was possible. I felt calm with her, sated, as though all would be well as long as she was near. Perhaps it is the feeling that wisdom bestows upon others. Each moment I was with her she became more beautiful.

"Do you like flowers, Mistress Seymour?" she asked, indicating that we were to take a turn about the pool together. As we started to walk, other women gawped in astonishment. They could not understand why the Queen would be so eager for my tedious company. I understood their confusion perfectly.

"Are there any who do not like flowers, Your Majesty?" I asked. "If so, I pity them for they must be empty souls. I love to see gardens and flowers, but those I love best perhaps are wild blooms that gather on the edge of the farmland in my father's lands. I find myself lost in meadows, the glare and glow of the many flowers, all growing without order, within them. I love their beautiful confusion and chaos. They are not as cultured or grand as those which grace the gardens of court, but I find in them a simple beauty which I love."

I blinked, surprised at myself. That was the longest I had spoken since coming to court, perhaps since coming into the world, and it was honest, revealing something I had not said to others. I thought it remarkable that in a moment the Queen had teased such secrets of my soul, my loves, from me, but Katherine had a talent in that respect. She asked, then remained silent, allowing you to spill your heart. She could have stolen secrets of the angels and demons with ease. It was an uncanny talent, and I suddenly realised why the King had relied on her so completely when first he was King and many times since. She was a statesman who just happened to be a woman.

Katherine chuckled. "Indeed, Mistress Seymour, many would be astonished at your love of wild flowers, but I am not. Some cannot see beauty in wild things, but I can. In my homeland of Spain, in the mountains, there were blooms that would bring all to silence when they beheld them. Such a riot of colour, such hardy little buds and petals, thrown haphazardly over fields and hillsides as though God scattered seeds without thought or purpose, and yet, if one thinks on it God always has purpose, always a plan. If we cannot see it, it does not mean it is not there. As a girl I would stand amongst those flowers and I would barely think, for the wilds stole my breath and my thoughts. Perhaps that was God's purpose; to bind man in silence for a moment, so we might appreciate the glory of God."

She smiled at me. "Many of the flowers of which I speak grew in spare soil, with little rain, yet they survived, and were glorious to behold. There is a beauty in that which is wild and free, Jane. There is wonder in confusion, in having a question but no answer. I am glad that you see it, as I do."

She stopped at the edge of the pool and let out a sigh.

"Are you well, Majesty?" I asked with concern. "Would you prefer to sit?"

Katherine reached out and pressed her hand upon mine. "I am well, Mistress Seymour," she said. "It was just… you reminded me of Spain. It has been a long time since I saw the lands of my birth, more than twenty years! There is much in me which still misses it, even though I adore England as my own land as well."

"I am sorry if I made you sad, Majesty." My face flamed again. I was mortified to think I had caused her any pain.

Her eyes were soft as she looked into mine. "There is often not just one emotion which comes to us when we think of home," she said. "You brought sorrow to my heart, yes, but you also brought joy, Mistress Seymour, and all joy, no matter how small or passing, should be something we know gratitude for." She touched my cheek. "Be not sad, for you brought sorrow to me, yes, but also happiness.

"I recollect the times when my sisters and I wandered in the gardens of our mother and father, my gracious parents the King and Queen. I think on the loving eyes of my mother as she sang to us under trees where blossom danced, the sharp eyes of my father when he came riding home and called for us to gather so he could inspect us." She laughed. "He was an exacting man, my lord father," she went on, those dark eyes twinkling. "I am sure you understand what I mean when I say at such times as those my heart raced, thinking he would find fault with me and then burst into joy when he kissed my head, told me I was a good girl."

I nodded, although in honesty it had been so long since I had thought about my father with any emotion other than disgust and shame that what she said was almost unimaginable to me.

Katherine patted my arm. "Do not fear, Mistress Seymour, for you have brought me much this day that is pleasing to my heart. Sorrow and joy are ever entwined in life. Such is the way of things. But you have brought me both this day, and I thank you for it. I believe I will think much of home, of the past, today, but at the end of the day I will take to my knees in gratitude. I will thank God for the blessing of my family, for the love they offered me as a child, and I will ask that those who are in Heaven with Him be taken care of, as they took care of me." She nodded. "And I will pray for you, ask God to be kind to you, in thanks for reminding me of my youth and the flowers of the mountains."

"I will pray for you, Majesty," I said, although in truth I could not think of anything Katherine could possibly do that would upset the Almighty. She was a saint already, I was sure. Yet saints suffered, did they not? And she suffered, for the King was making her sad. Clearly she had borne enough sadness for a lifetime. *And now more, because of my cousin,* I thought.

So perhaps I did have reason to pray for Katherine. Not because her soul was in any danger, not because I believed God did not love her, but because mere mortals were treating her badly, not upholding her, not standing with her, as they should.

Katherine called for her ladies to come to her. They were bound for their evening meal, she said. The Princess, who was to eat her dinner outside, for Mary had set quite the fashion for dining outside that summer and wanted to continue it, said we would walk a little longer.

As she left, the Queen turned to me. "Thank you for our talk, Mistress Seymour," she said. "I find you pleasing company. I will look for you again."

"My thanks, Your Majesty." My tongue fumbled the words, but Katherine smiled, not displeased by my inelegant ways or crude country manners. She reached out and touched my face. "You are pretty when you allow yourself to smile, Mistress Seymour, but you look as though you require more practice. Perhaps you have not had much reason to smile in your life, but I am sure that this will change."

Two days later, my mistress Mary of Suffolk called for me. She had astonishing news to impart. Queen Katherine had personally requested that I enter her service. I was to leave the Princess, to serve the Queen of England.

"I will be sorry to lose you, Jane," Mary said. "But the Queen was impressed with you, and my good sister should have all that she wishes for."

"Yes, my lady," I said. "I am honoured beyond measure."

"The Queen said she remembered your mother fondly, as Lady Seymour has served my royal sister in the past on state occasions, and the Queen believes you will serve as well, if not better. She likes your humble nature, and thinks you quietly intelligent, Jane."

I flushed, my cheeks roaring, flames against marble. "The Queen is gracious to me," I said. "I shall not disgrace you, Your Grace."

Mary smiled; it made her face light up so she looked no more than fifteen. She had that blessing some women are granted, that in joy they lose age as a tree sheds leaves. She could have been any age when she had happiness upon her. "I never thought you would disgrace me, for a moment," she said. "I have been pleased with your service, and I know you will serve the Queen as well as you have me."

Mary hesitated a moment as though she wished to say much and knew she should not. "Take good care of the Queen, Jane," she said. "She is not only a good Queen. She is a good woman. She deserves only happiness."

I knew what my mistress was trying to say. Mary wanted me to uphold Katherine in friendship and love, to pay her more honour and respect than the King was paying her at present. She wanted me to be a woman who held love and gratitude for the Queen in my heart, unlike my cousin.

"I promise to do all I can to reward Her Majesty's trust and yours, my lady."

Chapter Twenty-Six

Greenwich Palace and Richmond Palace
London

January 1528

"You have not said that you have sought the lady out, nor do I hear that you have met. I would have an answer to this riddle, daughter!"

I sighed as the clerk read the missive aloud to me. "Thank you," I said when he came to the end. Offering a sympathetic face, he nodded to me and left. He was to read other letters sent from families to other ladies of court, to all of us who had limited skill. For their sakes, I hoped other letters from other homes were gentler than mine.

Shrill words had seemed to leap from the pages towards me, claws extended to rend flesh. No matter how far I travelled from my mother, her voice could be relied upon to sound in my head at a moment's notice. She was a worm in my mind, one with a voice that whispered, always telling me what I was doing wrong. Had I ever done a thing right?

You now serve the Queen, said a rebel voice in my mind. *That was something done right.* I sighed. Sometimes I believed that, sometimes I wondered how it had come about that I had moved up into the service of the Queen, as though it was a mistake that someone, the Queen most of all, would soon notice and I would be sent away from her chambers, gales of laughter following in my wake for the thought that I, the little Seymour mouse, could have been thought worthy enough to wait upon the Queen of England.

It was just after the New Year. I had been in the Queen's chambers a few weeks and was doing well, so I thought. So I hoped. I had stayed long enough with the Princess to see the wonder of the Southwark Fair the previous September, one of the biggest in London. Huge crowds had gathered, and there were markets and entertainments, bear baiting and bull baiting too. We ladies had wandered, carefully guarded by Brandon's men, to watch rope dancers and tumblers, and hear players perform and singers sing. The Princess was cheered everywhere she went. Although Mary only came out for the afternoon of one day, the people loved her for it, and men were commanded to hand out free ale and wine from her stores on the last day of the fair.

St Luke's and St Crispin's Day had flown past, as well as Allhallowtide where we prayed for the souls of the dead and the saints in Heaven. My duties kept me busy, but time truly seemed to take to the wing that autumn, sending me feeling unprepared, sprawling, into the service of the Queen.

Sad though I was to leave the Princess Mary, especially as new women like Katherine Willoughby, a ward of the Brandons who was to wed their son Henry when he was older, and Margaret Douglas, daughter of the Scottish Queen and English Princess Margaret Tudor, therefore the niece of Princess Mary, had just joined the household. They made the already exciting chambers of the Princess only more so. But something about Katherine and her chambers called to me. There was more peace in the presence of the Queen than I had felt anywhere else, at any other time in life. I had little known how much I craved steadiness, stability, or how much gentle affection meant to me. With Katherine I did not feel haunted or hunted; I did not feel as though I was constantly under siege... aside from when my mother wrote to me. I was calm, drawing peace from my new mistress.

There, with the Queen, my inside matched my outside for the first time. Calm on the outside, seemingly at peace I had always appeared, yet not so was I inside. But with Katherine I *was* peaceful, I could be content. I felt not lacking anything or anyone. I was enough. That was a special feeling and all who have felt lacking, inadequate, will know what peace may come when that feeling dissipates. In truth, I was becoming reliant on Katherine, addicted to her.

The Queen's household was more demanding than the Duchess's had been. We women of her chambers worked in shifts, and each was gruelling. We rose with the Queen often in the night, for she would hear matins at midnight and Mass again at dawn. She prayed for hours in her chapel, and although we were permitted cushions, Katherine laid her knees to the hard floor. Often her knees were cracked and dry. Sometimes they bled, crimson creeping, seeping from deep, deep cuts, for only deep wounds could find the blood inside her body, her knees were so hard. We rubbed olive oil on them but it made no difference. She had been doing such for years, and there was leather on her legs now where skin might once have been. She never complained about the pain, and thanked us for each attention. Her goodness made my heart break.

Katherine went to confession three times a week and heard Mass several times a day. I wondered what she had to confess, for she was the best of women. She was kind, a virtue so often overlooked and yet one that requires infinite patience, understanding and courage. It is so easy to be cruel. During the day we read to her from books of devotions, or rather other maids did as my skills were poor, or we walked in the gardens, sewed and sometimes played cards. Studious and godly though the chambers of the Queen were, Katherine had a sharp sense of humour and a ready wit. She never used either meanly, however, which others at court did not hesitate to do, and perhaps that was why she was not as known for her wit as other women and men were. But it was there.

As Katherine made my soul joyous, I was also bewitched by the glory of her chambers. Ornamented ceilings, with balls and ribs tripping gaily along, flanked by octagons and lozenge shapes shone down on us, gilt paint and shimmering reds, blues and greens reflecting on our faces. There were heraldic beasts and symbols on the walls, such as Katherine's pomegranate and portcullis, shimmering with gold and entwined with lovers' knots, painted in a time when the King had loved her and no other. Many of the Queen's rooms were dressed in verdant green and glaring white, or royal purple and eye-watering crimson. Each day I carried items for my mistress along halls lined with huge cupboards holding plate in gold, pewter, silver and gilt. Katherine's bed was draped in thick, embroidered cloth encrusted with pearls and jewels which glimmered in the morning light as we took down the shutters. Chairs were upholstered in velvet of purple and crimson, and the fireplace was surrounded by large cushions, on which we sat to sew with our Queen.

I was often chosen to sleep on the Queen's floor as a companion, my dreams held safe by a soft pallet bed. Some women, I think, resented the task because Katherine rose often in the night to hear Mass and to pray. It was not unusual for people to take two sets of sleep, especially in winter, but Katherine rose almost on the hour. Some women found it hard to be of good cheer when serving as a bedchamber companion, due to tiredness. I did not. I did not complain or allow myself to seem tired or weary of spirit. The Queen appreciated that, and called for me often to serve.

Some would have called our days dull. The King was retreating from his Queen more and more in the days I first came to court, and that left the Queen's women spare of companions to laugh, dance and flirt with. But I had not encountered much in the way of flirtation at Wulfhall and found it somewhat confusing and very much false. Courtly love, much as I had admired it from afar, had small interest for me. It seemed to make women cruel and men moaners. And I did not find days with Katherine uninteresting. My life at court was more wondrous than anything I could have imagined, especially when I compared it to the strain and stress I had felt in my own home. Removed from Wulfhall, I saw how afraid I had been, what the secret I had carried had done to my mind. I had barely thought of a thing but Catherine and my father all my life. I had barely lived, for the lack of security they had instilled in my soul, and the fear they had implanted in my heart.

It is a thing horrific, to know fear in your own home, in the one place you should be entirely safe. Until I left, never did I know how heavy it had weighed upon me. Until the burden lifted, I had no idea how light everyone else in the world must have felt every single day.

As we worked on altar cloths or clothes for the poor, Katherine told us of things we never had seen in Spain, in England, in books and legends, and whilst some never can keep a tone of condescension from their voices when imparting knowledge, there was not a scrap of that in Katherine. She imparted knowledge with passion and never made the other person feel small. That was her greatness. She stood high not by standing on others, but because she was great in herself. She honoured others, made them feel taller, bigger, more important. Nothing was beneath her notice, and no one. With her I felt noticed, worthy and never taken for granted. In her eyes I was special. Finally I understood why my mother had worshipped her so, loved her so dear and with such devotion. I fell in love with Katherine, my Queen. She made it so easy, for she exuded love as a scent, as a sense, and it flowed from her upon all she met.

I could not understand, therefore, why the King was not infatuated with her as always he had been. Katherine was the perfect woman.

The Queen's greatest joy was when her daughter was at court. It was rare, but Mary came from Ludlow, where she had been sent by her father to learn how to rule by ruling Wales, from time to time. She was studious, kind like her mother and a pretty girl; I loved Mary and she was gracious to me.

If only my mother were so gracious.

The Queen had dispatched her request to my parents that I alter household, but even this, apparently, was not enough for my mother. Stupefied though she had been to try to imagine how I had ended up serving the highest woman of the land, Mother thought she needed to advise me. Clearly I had done well on my own, but this was not the way Mother thought. If anxious she had been rendered by the notion of me serving the sister of the King, she was twice if not thrice more worried I was to serve his wife, the woman she worshipped.

My mother thought I needed help and had written again, telling me to seek out Mistress Anne Boleyn. Not only was she my kinswoman and one of the Queen's ladies, she was obviously successful at court. Mother, removed from court as she was, believed nothing of the rumours that Anne might replace Katherine. Mother thought her a good connection for me to gain, one that might lead me to the Howards, and a higher husband.

I did not like the idea. The more I heard of Anne Boleyn the less I warmed to her. All said she was bold and outspoken. She seemed to have the whole court and all its men wrapped around her finger, and was drawing the love of the King from my new mistress. I had seen Anne in the chambers of the Queen, of course, but we did not always work at the same time and Anne, although she did her duties without fault, often seemed distracted. She also was not there a great deal. Katherine, in fact, seemed to call for Anne as rarely as she could, and certainly did not invite her to be a night-time companion, as I so often was. I had not sought Anne out. I had no wish to.

I loved my mistress, gentle and wise Katherine. Anne Boleyn was not a friend to her, as well I knew and all who were enemy to Katherine were, too, to me. Had I been brave enough I would have shouted Anne Boleyn down in the hallways of court for trying to steal the love of the King from Katherine.

I do not think it had occurred to me that love is something that cannot be stolen. It is given, it is taken back, but it cannot be snatched away. If someone chooses to no more love where once they did, that is their choice, and it is down to them. If the King loved Katherine no more, it was not because another had taken his heart. He had given his heart to another.

But, little as I liked the thought of meeting my kinswoman who was causing so much trouble, my mother's orders were my mother's orders. I was bound to obey her as my parent. I sought out Anne, my second cousin. Poor relations though we were to the likes of the Howards and even Boleyns, kin we still were.

I found her, as directed by the note she sent in reply to mine, in her father's chambers at Richmond Palace. From the first moment she turned her face to me, looked me up and down, and allowed an expression of mocking despair to flow over her face, I disliked Anne Boleyn.

She turned to me and smiled, her hands on her waist. Anne's waist was slim and taut. Gowns seemed to hang on her as though they were but a part of her own skin, as though they were water and she a smooth rock that waves crashed over, slid from. Her sleeves were long and hanging, in an almost ancient style. I had seen others wearing the same about court, but none wore them like she did. She was fluid, smooth as a snake. The scent of her skin was jasmine and honeysuckle. When she laughed or smiled, it made me want to know the same joy she demonstrated. There was much that was merry in her, and it was mesmerising. Sadness pushes people away, but to find a heart lit with joy draws people in.

Anne was middling tall for a woman, taller than me, elegant and lithe. Her face was not beautiful but it was symmetrical. When she smiled it lit up with a natural grace, a joy in life. Her hair was dark, which was not desirable in a woman, but it was long and shone like the mane of a well-brushed horse. There were flashes of blue and red in the black, silken tresses. And there was a sensuous confidence about her which struck me immediately. She was enchanting because she was confident, not confident because she was enchanting. Her eyes were almost black, and they were large. They were captivating, those eyes, I will allow her that. They seemed to draw you in as you gazed on her face, as though you might become lost. It was like staring into the endless skies of night. Anne had a musical, pretty voice when she was singing and when she was not, and she was the most stylish woman I had ever seen at court, even above the Duchess of Suffolk. When Anne moved it was as though she was dancing. Her feet trod light upon the ground. Her laugh was throaty, like Catherine's. It made you want to make her laugh.

Perhaps that was the secret of her charms, in truth. There seemed hidden delights in Anne, not things of the bedchamber necessarily, but hidden things, like that laugh. Her lips often twitched when she found something amusing, and when your eyes saw that, it made you want to jest, just to hear her laugh. When she looked at another, you wanted her to look at you, just to see those bright, black eyes. That is the best way I can describe the secret of her allure. She was the sunlight on the horizon, the pretty glade just out of sight. It seemed she was full of secrets, secrets that any who met her wanted to know. She was a box of delights, but you had to be worthy of the key. Anne was anticipation, the treat always in sight and out of reach.

I could see why so many men flocked to her. She had a teasing, confident, playful manner which seemed to suggest that she was ever open to conversation of dalliance, and yet was always just apart from it. Those black eyes snapped, brilliant and bright, and her tongue was always ready with a quip, often cruel but also often amusing, about a situation or person. She was intelligent, her wit was sharp, and yes, she was captivating, I could see that. She was all I was not and never would be. Confidence sang from her as though it ran in her veins instead of blood.

And yet, for all her graces, my heart ran cold as I looked on her.

I had met a creature like her before. Right from the very first, Anne reminded me of Catherine. Was it just that they both had chased a husband not their own? That they were humiliating others, Catherine my mother and brother, and for Anne the Queen, who was a better woman than any in this world? Perhaps it was that. Perhaps it was that from both I thought I felt a gritty, worldly selfishness. They wanted their pleasures and cared nothing for what it would cost others. I felt the joy Anne exuded was stolen goods. She had no right to it.

For one like me who had been told her entire life to surrender what I wanted to the whims of others, Anne was alien and at the same time intoxicating. I wanted what she and Catherine had, this ability to surrender consideration for others, to not care what others thought. I knew I would never have it. I would not have withstood the guilt. I had been trained too well and too long to abandon myself and give to others. I had been taught that what Anne and Catherine were, was wicked.

But how I wanted it, that ability to care for oneself first. And how I hated that others had it! I thought not of that then, of course. Easy it is to look back and see why we did something and often the answer is so simple we wonder how we did not see it plain at the time, but we do not. We do not because emotions whirl, a mill pool of water churning in the soul, confusing you, making you believe you feel something for one reason when in fact you feel it for another. So much of life may be put down to so few feelings, and most are born of either love or fear. I wanted what Catherine and Anne had, and I feared what they had. I was jealous. I did not like what they did to others, to people I loved, yet I wished I could care so little for the good opinion of others. I possessed wonder, admiration, love… and hatred for them.

In a moment, for that was all it took, in a glance of her eyes sweeping over me it was done. Anne and Catherine and all the feelings each roused in me at different times, became one and the same. One fair and one dark, perhaps that only made more sense in the twist of my mind where they became looped. Anne was the dark shadow cast by Catherine, Anne was the echo of all the hurt Catherine had caused, but Anne had become amplified, not faded as an echo becomes. Catherine had wielded pain in a small sphere, Anne brought it into the world, cast it upon our leaders, our people, the Queen.

Suddenly I realised she was speaking. Perhaps she had been lecturing me for some time as we stood in her father's gracious rooms, I knew not. In truth I had trained my face so well that people barely noted when I was or was not paying attention. I nodded, and that was enough, so it seemed, to fool them.

"You must do your duties quietly and carefully to gain the affection of the Queen," Anne advised. Her hand was on the marble mantelpiece. Her father had good chambers at Richmond, perhaps paid for by the whoring of his eldest daughter, or this one. "You seem intelligent enough, and you are humble and meek, she will like that. Do you read? The Queen enjoys hearing works of devotion read to her in her chambers."

I shook my head. "I do not know how to read or write a great deal, cousin," I murmured, feeling my cheeks flush. Books; the old shame, the old humiliation. "I can sign my name, but my father did not believe reading and writing were honourable or necessary pursuits for women."

I tried to straighten up. Next to Anne, my figure felt dumpy, fat and graceless. I smoothed the front of my gown and tried to stand taller to make myself comparable to her. It did not work.

She arched her eyebrows at me in disbelief. "But you know your prayers and Scripture, I am sure?"

I dipped my pale face. There it was, another floor. "I learned by heart all that was thought appropriate for me to know." I looked up.

She was gazing at me in a pitying manner, and it angered me. So I did not know all the things this lady did... what of it? There were plenty of women at court who knew not how to read, and could only sign their names on parchment! Just because I had not been drowned in education as she had, and sent to France and Burgundy to learn arts and allurements, that did not mean I was worthless.

I kept my face calm and steady, no matter the anger within me. Anne was gazing at me thoughtfully, and appeared to be already dismissing me as a rival in the games of courtly love. *She is thinking I am nothing,* I thought, *that I am no one, nothing to trouble her as she cavorts about court making eyes at all men and boys!*

"The Queen will like your quiet character and your virtue," she reassured me, in an apparently kindly tone, but I bristled. I hated being pitied as much as I hated being bullied.

"Does she like *your* virtues, cousin?" I asked carefully. Anne started, suddenly unnerved.

"What do you mean?" She grabbed my arm and drew me close. Looking about, as though all that she said was being noted by some unseen spy, she pulled me to the fire. Perfumed logs burnt hot and bright in the hearth. They sent richly scented smoke up the chimney, leaving a little to linger in the chamber. Ember and ash which smelt of culture and court remained, specks floating up. One landed on Anne's sleeve, but she noted nothing. A tiny grey stain clung to the rich fabric; a tiny imperfection, on a creature of glorious grace.

I hesitated, feeling a fool. "There are rumours..."

"Of what?" She grabbed my arm hard. It hurt. I could feel her sharp fingers digging into me and I liked not the insistent way she leaned in right to my face. I could smell her breath, perfumed with mint and sage, on my cheek. Anne's proximity reminded me of the day Catherine had attacked me. I had been a fool that day too. I would not be again. I would be careful. I had to stop my face twisting into an expression of dislike. I did not take my arm from her grasp, but I did wince as I felt Anne's fingernails dig deeper into my flesh through the velvet plush of my russet gown, another of Mother's old court cast-offs.

"There are rumours that perhaps you do not love the Queen as you love the King, cousin," I said, diplomatically. "They say the Queen is sad because you have taken the King's heart from her."

"*They,*" she snapped, black eyes flashing, "can say what they wish. The more time you spend at court, Cousin Jane, the more you will realise that listening to gossip does not help a lady; she is better off making her own judgements rather than bending to the will and rumour of others."

I removed my arm gently but insistently from her claws. "I shall endeavour to take your advice, Cousin Anne." I folded my arms, tucking my hands into the folds of my over-hanging sleeves lined with furs. "I shall make my own judgements and not bend to the will of others." *And I judge you, strumpet!* something in me crowed.

She nodded, still frowning. Her eyes roamed my face, searching for more than I wished to share. Then she breathed in and started anew, in a louder voice than before. "Now," she went on. "Let me show you the Queen's chambers and introduce you to your duties there. Although you are new to court, I have been here some time and before now was in service to Claude of France and Margaret, Archduchess of Austria. I can show you how to be a good servant to the Queen."

I smiled with mirthless humour. "I long to benefit from your... *experience*, cousin."

There it was again! Another sentence just slipped out. Some rebel was rising up within my soul. I was going to have to be more careful. This was not Wulfhall, and Anne was not Catherine, no matter how similar the two seemed in spirit. This was another woman, one in high favour with the King and admired throughout court. No matter my feelings of disgust I could not allow it to show so openly in my face or my speech.

Anne glanced at me with sharp eyes, but I kept my face blank, innocent. I had learnt to manage my expressions when I had a need to, and I believed I needed to then. Anne *must* dismiss me from her thoughts as unimportant, as so many others had. To gain an enemy at court, especially one so high in favour, would be most dangerous. I felt my heart freeze. *"Little mouse,"* whispered Thomas's voice in my mind. I felt hunted, by her, as I had as a child by him.

Her eyes travelled over me for a moment, searching my blue eyes with her black ones for any deceit, then she lifted her chin as though pushing me from her thoughts and waved an arrogant hand for me to follow her. I scampered at her heel. Anne strode off, walking fast as though to demonstrate she had more energy and spirit than I possessed. As we walked the halls of court, me ruddy-faced at her elbow, heads of all courtiers we passed turned to watch her. If they looked at me it was only to give me a passing glance, or have a titter at my red face. I must have looked like a donkey chasing a stallion.

I know not if Anne was aware of her effect on people, it seemed to come so naturally. As she strode past those people, not giving them a second glance, heads turned like sunflowers to the sun. Anne stood out. She was the flame eyes are drawn to in the dark of night. She was not beautiful, no, but she had no need to be. She had everyone in her thrall, everyone perhaps but me, Queen Katherine and a few spare others.

Anne talked as we walked, seeming to never grow out of breath as she marched and spoke at the same time. She told me of meals I was entitled to, of dogs I was allowed to keep, and of my duties. All of this was said in such a straightforward manner, as if I might have been a kitchen maid learning her duties for the first time. I resented the manner in which she spoke. She was high-handed and overbearing.

I also knew all that she told me already.

It was a stunning realisation. Apparently I was so unremarkable that Anne thought I was fresh to court that day. *So unremarkable that she has not seen you in the chambers of the Queen!* I thought. Of course I had always known I did not stand out, often I took pains not to, but despite this I resented that she had not seen me. Perhaps she was distracted by her dalliance with the King, and we were not in the same dormitory of the Queen's women by night, but even so we had served in the Queen's chambers together three times at least. There were other women there, of course, but she had not noticed me at all. I was a stranger to her.

I hated her for it.

Anne made me feel more invisible than I already was. I could have been a rush mat upon the floor for all the notice she took of me. It stung, an old wound ripping asunder, an old voice mocking me, laughing at me.

She left me with the Mother of the Maids, and I was glad to be free of her. All that there was about Anne reminded me too painfully of Catherine to be borne. *I shall take one piece of her advice,* I thought as I excused myself from the Mother of the Maids, who was entirely baffled as to why I had been brought to her as if I was new to court. *I shall indeed form my own judgements.*

*

As winter went on I heard foxes in the grounds screaming and shrieking. Something in the sound reminded me of the wind in the days before my mother gave birth to Elisabeth, that wailing and crying. Something in those screams brought on the same feeling I had then. I became restless, although I was happy where I was. In time I came to think it was not restlessness but anxiety. Something was about to happen, I could feel it.

It came from home. The scribe who read my mother's letter to me could hardly keep his countenance as his eyes and lips travelled through the words.

I listened quietly and sent him away quickly. I asked him not to say anything to anyone. He promised, but I knew he was lying.

My brother had discovered his wife's infidelities. He had found Catherine in a compromising situation with another man. Although the letter did not state whom, I knew who he had found her with.

In a week there was more news. My brother was seeking to annul his marriage to Catherine, and also to bastardize the son he had by her, and the child she was carrying. I had not known she was again with child.

He knew. Edward knew everything. Catherine was the whore of our father, and Edward's sons were, in truth, his brothers.

And it would not be long, I knew, before everyone else knew. Unnoticed I had gone at court, for the most part, yet I was about to be seen, in the worst way imaginable.

Suddenly I wished that everyone at court had the black eyes of Anne Boleyn, so I would vanish, unseen and unheard, so I would not be found. I wished I had an attic or a barn in which to hide. I wished I could become stone, my outside hard as rock, so I could not be shamed by everyone knowing our secret, so I would not feel the pain my brother felt. Edward's world had just crumbled. The last of a bonfire lit to celebrate a wedding fading in the wind, glowing sticks once solid, crumbling, falling to ash.

Chapter Twenty-Seven

Greenwich Palace
London

Spring 1528

Although we tried, the news was too scandalous, too inviting to the trip of malicious tongues to be hidden. It leaked out through court, for all knew that Edward was seeking to annul his marriage upon finding he had been played for a cuckold. And played as a cuckold by his own father, no less! Gossips had a rare treat with our pain that season at court. They had a good, long laugh, our agony and shame tickling their throats and chests.

The manner in which people began staring at me weighed on my shoulders. Where before I had largely gone unnoticed at court, now eyes lingered, but not with interest and adoration as they did when they saw my cousin Anne. No, no such graces were for me. Everyone looked on me with disgust. I was a daughter of a house where the father had made a whore of his daughter-in-law. I came from a house where sin reigned, incest ruled and virtues were light and free. I became suspect, stained, because of the actions of my hateful father and his dirty little whore. As Eve's sins had become those of all women, Catherine's became mine. I was painted dark, sullied deep because of her.

I hid even more so than usual. I had learnt to do this well as a child, and now I was grateful for every time I had gone unnoticed, un-remarked upon. How I wished for the dark shadows of the barn at Wulfhall to hide myself in. How I wished that I had remained unnoticed, unremarkable, unseen. Never had I understood what a blessing it was to be unknown. Never had I appreciated that to be anonymous was to be safe.

The Queen was kind. Shocked though she was to hear the gossip, Katherine did not treat me as though I was cast down into a pit of sin, as others did. Katherine sent me to quiet chambers often, but not for shame or spite. She did it to save me. Other maids frequently burst into laughter near me. Anne was one of them.

"What a story!" I heard her crow to a group of men, her handsome brother amongst them, in the gardens. "One has to wonder how true it is."

For a moment I was grateful to her, at least for planting doubt in minds where so many had already decided the truth, but then she said something I did not hear. All the men burst into raucous, admiring laughter. I bristled, my soul burning with anger, for I was sure it had been something cruel, her jests often were, at the expense of my family.

In truth, I had no proof that was the case. But I believed the worst of Anne first, and always. Mine was not a forgiving soul, and I was shamed deeper at that time than ever I had been.

Edward sought me out at court. I had been dreading the day when I had to reveal to him that I had known about this affair, and I knew it had come. He called for me in the Queen's chambers. Katherine received him with tact and warmth, as was ever her way. She did not mention the scandal, but merely held his hand and said she hoped his troubles would find an end soon. My brother's cheeks had turned ruddy for her words, but he accepted them with grace.

We went into the gardens together and sat by a pool where a Tudor dragon stood bold and true in the centre, water pouring from its mouth as though it were fire. I glanced at Edward. He looked old, his pale eyes haunted. Sorrowed and aged had my beloved brother become. My heart broke to see it.

"Jane, I must ask you something," Edward said as we sat on a small wooden bench of good oak.

"She told you that I knew," I said. I had known, of course I had. Catherine would do anything to displace blame, thrust it on another. She would have tried to turn Edward's anger from her, onto me. It was her way.

Edward narrowed his eyes. "I did not think it was true," he said, staring at me with pain in his face. I put my hand to his.

"I was a child when first I found out," I whispered. Where words had failed me and silence had held me captive so long, suddenly something burst inside me. Words poured out. I rambled, words that had been prisoners inside me leaping over one another in their rush to be free.

"I went to Catherine and asked her to stop the affair. When I confronted her she threatened me. She said she would speak to our father, have me branded a whore and sent from the house. She made me swear I would tell no one, Edward, and she made me swear on the Holy Bible itself. I could not break such a vow, for fear of my own soul. I should have, though. It was not to my honour that I was scared into silence. And then after, even when I thought it would be right to break a vow made before God if it would reveal such evil, I could not. I had been silent so long I knew not how to talk. I knew not how to explain that I had known and I thought I would not be believed. I am so sorry, brother." I shook my head. "I should have tried," I said. "I have felt guilt, all these years, not knowing if I should say or not say, not knowing if I would be heard."

Tears which I had long held inside for my forced deceit came to me. I put my hands to my face and tried to bury my shameful eyes. "I am so sorry," I said, weeping, gulping. "And then it had gone on so long and she had such power in the house, over father, over mother, you… I thought I would not be believed. And then there was the child. You thought John your son and you were so happy and the thought of hurting you and the thought I would not be believed was too much." I stopped and sobbed, gasping for air. "It was all too much. I knew not what to do or what was right, and what was right for me was not for you, and Catherine said no one would believe me and she said I would be sent away, and she said…"

"Jane…" Edward's voice was soft even as it was harsh. I could hear emotions battling in his soul. My hysterical tongue stumbled to a halt and I looked up at him, my face red and ugly from my tears.

"I am so sorry," I said again, choking on my words. "I should have spoken out. I should have said something. But I believed that if I did then she would have me punished. No one in Wulfhall ever believed me about anything, and yet Thomas and Catherine, they were always believed! But I tried, Edward! I went to Mistress Grey. I asked her to help me, to help you. But she would not curse Catherine for me. She said she did not do such things… but I tried, Edward, I tried!"

Fresh sobs broke. I was shaking and shivering, my nose running and eyes blinded by tears. Through grief breaking in me like a storm tearing apart summer skies I felt my brother reach out, pull me to him. For a long time we merely sat, thus. My brother holding me, me sobbing upon his shoulder.

I sat back. "It should be me comforting you, Edward, not the other way around," I noted, drawing in a long, wet and sodden sniff.

"It would seem, Jane, you have been carrying a weight I knew nothing of, and you have carried it a long time on my behalf." I looked up, wiping my eyes, and nodded. Edward's face darkened. "It was not you at fault, sister," he said, gazing out over the pool so that the blue of the waters was reflected in his eyes. "That woman has done much harm, and for the other man caught in all her sin to be our own father…" He breathed in deeply, hands twisting into fists upon his knees. "I cannot think of it without fury possessing me. I had to leave when she told me. I thought I might kill Father, or her."

"You have been wronged by two people who should have loved and protected you, brother," I said. "What could make a person angrier?"

He let out a barking laugh without mirth. "That the children I thought were mine are most likely my bastard siblings," he murmured bitterly.

I put my hand over his fist. "It is Catherine who is the evil in our house," I said. "It was she who enticed our father into sin, I saw it, and she held him as her captive. I heard her, brother. I heard what she said to him and what she did. She said that she loved him, and only wanted to bear his children. You were used by her, brother, used so she could gain a place in our house, be near to our father. That was what she wanted from the start."

"And she terrorized you, and charmed Mother into submission." His tone was amazed as he thought on his wife.

"How is our mother?"

He paused and breathed in again. "She has not left her chambers for many days. She will not see Father. She will not see Catherine or little John. She has shut herself away." He gazed at me. "She would like to see you, though, Jane," he went on. "She spoke of how she had ever underestimated your worth, now that she sees Catherine for who she really is."

"She thinks of me as a faded weed left at the edge of the garden," I said. "She only wishes for me now because I am not a conniving whore who has torn apart our family and ruined our standing in the land." As another wave of anger passed over Edward's face, I clenched his hand in mine. "This will pass, brother, in time. Soon enough there will be another scandal for court to talk of, and this matter will be forgot."

"I will never forget," he murmured. "I have petitioned for an annulment of my marriage. Catherine will have nothing from me and I will not have her stay at Wulfhall, neither will Mother. The whore can take her bastard children and return to her father's hall, if her family will have her. I will never see her again."

"And the children?" I asked. "They may still be yours, Edward, and one is unborn. And little John? He is not to blame for this."

"I cannot be sure they are mine," he sighed. "And the anger within me, the pain, it poisons the love and pride I had for John, for Catherine's swelling belly. Ready as I was to kill Father, and Catherine, I remain the same towards them. I cannot look on those children, even one unborn, without seeing their mother's sin. They disgust me. But I will not see them made beggars on the streets, even though I care not where their mother ends her days. In time, I will see they are taken from her, set up in other houses. I will not recognise her offspring as my legitimate children, for I know not if they are, but I will see they are raised in a good house." His face twisted as if he was eating something sour. "After all, Jane, they are either my children, or they are our siblings, so they are kin no matter what I do."

"Edward..." I rested my head against his shoulder. "You are a good man, brother. Many men would not do so much for the children of such a woman."

"Do not suppose I do anything for *her*." He pulled me close. "The witch! How could I have not known her true nature? How could I have been so fooled?"

"She played her part well, Edward," I counselled. "She was a fine liar."

"As were you, sister," he noted grimly.

I struggled up from his arms. "Edward, I failed you, and I am sorry. There are not words enough to express my sorrow. But if there is ever a way I can repay you... if there is anything I can do, I will do it. You have only to ask it of me, and I will make it so. This is my promise, my oath to you."

"More oaths, sister?"

"This one I enter into freely, of my own will. Hold me to it, brother, and I will not let you down. I swear. Think of any service you would have me do for you, and I will see it done. I will not fail you this time. This is my oath to you, and to God. My soul and place in Heaven is upon this vow. I am yours to command."

My eyes must have reflected my earnest heart, for he smiled a small, sad smile. "Very well," he said. "I will find a task someday, and it will be yours. And then that will be an end to this."

A breeze blew, as though God sighed, and I knew somehow that this was the right thing to do. It felt as though the Almighty had approved; that one vow made in silent desperation which had kept evil flowing and alive, wounding those I loved, could be washed away by another made in liberty, from love for a brother.

It is right and it shall be done, I said to God. *This is the vow I make before you, my Lord of Hosts. I am my brother's to command.*

Opening his arms again, Edward took me in his embrace. I rested my tear-stained face on his shoulder. "I loved her, Jane," he said. "She did not love me."

"She did not," I said. "No one who loves someone could do something so cruel as she did to you."

We were silent a while. *It is as well you are now property of your brother,* said my mother in my head. *For what man will want you now?*

I did not care for what she said. I had not thought a man would want me. It was true, however, that one of the few virtues I had possessed had been coming from a good family, albeit one of lesser nobility. And now, thanks to Catherine, a good family we were no more. Stained and sullied was our name, shamed was our reputation.

We sat there for a long time without talking, as our eyes watched water spurt from the mouth of the dragon, as the balmy wind sailed, caressing our cheeks still wet with tears cried for grief, for shame and for secrets. We did not know that was the day the King announced that a legate from Rome was to come to England to investigate his marriage. There would be a trial, in public. I was not the only one to feel shame fall upon me that day. It fell on Katherine, my good mistress.

But we did not know, we children of the house of Seymour, eldest daughter, eldest son. By the time we left the gardens we would hear it everywhere. The scandal which had wrapped itself about us, born from Catherine's spells, would be soon forgotten. The King's scandal, his *Great Matter*, would become more important than we ever could be. Even in disgrace we never were the most important of court, not then.

But we knew that not, Edward and I, as we sat comforting one another by the pond in the gardens. I thought of Wulfhall, the nest I had flown, nest of ashes and broken dreams. I thought of the dreams I had now, at court; small dreams but dreams enough and ones I hoped Catherine could not touch.

We did not know, did not know the future had become uncertain as we mourned what had passed. We simply sat, the breeze washing over us. Outside of the kitchens a maid dropped a pail of ashes and ember from the fires. There was a curse which died on the wind.

Over the wall of the gardens the contents of her pail washed, grey ash sparkling as diamonds on the breeze. Embers burned bright once, then faded. For a moment I thought I could with those ashes cleanse myself, allow them to drift over me, become purified by fire. I watched as into air the ash whipped, softer than snow. Then it was gone, as if never was it there at all. For that is what comes of ashes. They fall to nothing. Into the wind went the past. I hoped never to see it again.

**Here ends *Nest of Ashes*,
Book One of *The Phoenix Trilogy*, Story of Jane Seymour.
In Book Two, *The Worm and the Fledgling*,
Jane will witness the fall of Katherine of Aragon and the rise of Anne Boleyn, and will come to understand the fragility of power
as she herself catches the eye of the King.**

Author's Notes

This is a work of fiction. Although I try to stick to known facts, there are certain elements I created in this book. All conversations are fiction, although where the words of the characters were set down in historical record, those words are used. The characters of the people involved are my invention, although based on study of their lives and actions. I used a great deal of sources for this book, and mean to include those in the bibliography at the end of the series.

I include a few notes on the book here. For those who do not know the story covered in this book and future ones in the series, a warning: I discuss matters that might spoil the tale to come.

Jane Seymour is an elusive character, even for the Tudor age where so many people are mysteries. There is scant detail about her early life, and even her early career at court. I admit, therefore, to using imagination to fill in the gaps. This is the right of an author of historical fiction, but for clarity I will explain in these notes what I created and why. In this book I created more character for Jane than I have done for any character of history, as so little is known about her apart from in the last few years of the story when she became the love of Henry's life, then his wife and Queen.

I wanted to create a character for Jane that would explain the myriad of qualities she seemed to possess. Whilst most people described Jane as "good" and "mild" when she was Queen, I believe she must have possessed some strength and indeed, ruthlessness, of character in order to play the part that she did in the fall of Anne Boleyn. There is an argument to be made that she may not have had a choice, that when the King's eye fell upon her she was thrust into the role of Queen-in-waiting by her ambitious family, but Jane played the part very well, a little too well in my opinion, for her to have been a simple pawn. This does not mean, however, that I believe she was a creature only of ambition, or that she was inherently a bad person. I wanted her to have a back story which explained many of her actions.

Jane, as I saw her, was credulous, quite innocent in many ways, but with a hard core. She loved deeply and fiercely, but as she is often disregarded in this book, as I think she was by many until King Henry happened to see her, she learned to hide her emotions. When *my* Jane is noticed by a person, she loves them with all her heart and would do anything for them. When she is ignored she becomes resentful, as many of us would. There are times in the book where Jane steps close to truly terrible actions, such as when Catherine is ill and Mary dies, but she refrains from her worst impulses. This, although created, was a way for me to introduce how she may have approached her part in the fall and execution of Anne Boleyn.

I painted Jane's mother, Margery, in a poor light in general in this book and I have no evidence to suggest that her character was like this at all. This was done to aid Jane's development as a character, and to explain why she might have learnt to hide as a child, creating a mask which served her well later at the Tudor court. I also painted Thomas Seymour as a bully, which is something I believe has some weight. Thomas Seymour's behaviour as an adult was often wild, always selfish and entitled and his attitude towards women in general was horrific. I see him as fully accountable for his treatment of his later wife, Katherine Parr, and for the abuse of Princess Elizabeth Tudor when she was a young child. It was not hard, therefore, to work backwards and suppose what he might have been like as a child. Jane and Thomas were close in age and would have shared lessons. That they were not close as adults pointed me in the direction that they were not as children. Given Thomas's later behaviour, and their lack of closeness, I believe it not unreasonable to suppose he bullied his sister.

Painting both Thomas and Margery Seymour as bullies was done to explain Jane's extreme submission. Although it was a common trait for women to assume, there were many hints during the fall of Anne Boleyn and during Jane's time as Queen that Jane's submission was more an act, or a defence technique, than natural meekness. I think she learned early on that to submit was not only the only path open to her, but was the safest. It is also true that those who experience bullying often develop a strong, tough core, which I think she had.

Jane's childhood is largely unknown. For her education I worked on what was known of her later abilities, and what was standard for girls of the time to learn. She may have been more literate than I have made her, but certainly she was not well educated by the standards of Katherine of Aragon or Anne Boleyn. We know that she could sign her name, perhaps write a little, although it is possible surviving letters were written by clerks and she copied them out. It was not unusual for women, even of the nobility, to be less educated than their male counterparts, even though literacy was on the rise in the Tudor period. Jane certainly seemed to be unfamiliar with French, as she struggled to speak to ambassadors in that language as Queen. She shines in embroidery and riding, which I have emphasised in the book.

Jane being a lady in the household of the Duchess of Suffolk may or may not be true. It would appear she served in another noble house before heading into that of Katherine of Aragon, but the actual house is unknown. A few historians have put forward the theory that Jane served Princess Mary and since her brother had before, when Mary married into France, this seemed possible. It would also explain how Jane managed to get a post in the household of Queen Katherine. Jane's meeting with Queen Katherine is again my invention, but I think her devotion to Katherine stemmed from a place of love, and the Jane I see is a person who longs to be noticed, often is not, and when she is noticed by a person, they steal her heart. This is *my* interpretation of her character.

Jane discovering her father and Catherine's affair is my invention. Although it would appear the affair happened, as her brother Edward did indeed disown his wife for having an affair with his father, there is nothing in the historical record to suggest Jane knew. I invented her finding this out as I wanted her to have a reason later to instantly dislike Anne Boleyn. Catherine Fillol and Anne Boleyn both became the mistresses of married men, and in Jane's eyes, and arguably many others, both wreaked devastation. (I would point out that the men involved in the affairs also played a part!) I wanted Jane to have a personal reason to dislike Anne, in order to explain her later actions. The oath Jane takes on the Bible, and her later one to Edward, are also my inventions. I would also like to point out that I do not feel the way Jane does in the book about Anne Boleyn. I admire her greatly.

It is true that Edward refused to recognise either of his sons as his legitimate children. Edward may also have married Catherine at as young an age as 14. Most sources think he was married before 1518, so I had him promised in marriage and married at 17.

I found different birthdates for Edward's sons. I chose to accept an early date for John, the first son, and what appears to be the agreed one for Edward, his second, as those suited the story. Catherine Fillol was not recorded as having a miscarriage, that was my invention, but it was not unusual. Catherine's character is also my invention. There is little about her in the historical records. Personally I feel more pity for her than Jane does in the book. There was little freedom in those days for people to fall in love, and to be able to be with the person they loved.

Jane may not have been the eldest daughter of the Seymour line. I have found numerous and varied birth dates for the children, and for some of the Seymour siblings I merely accepted one date over another. John was the eldest and appears to have died young, although there was a date I found for his death suggesting he may have been in his early twenties when he died. I invented the notion that he drowned.

Edward was certainly the second son, and became the eldest, and the one who seems to have been promoted the most. Henry and Thomas come next in line, with Jane probably following them. There may have been another son, also called John, which was a not unusual event in noble houses. Often if a house wanted a traditional name to live on, they named more than one child by that name, particularly if the first child bearing that name was ill or died. Mary Tudor and Charles Brandon, indeed, named their second son Henry after the death of their first son who carried the same name.

Dates for the births of Elisabeth and Dorothy, as well as Anthony and Margery vary. Anthony and Margery were unlikely to have been twins. I included this because I wanted to explain about the rarity of twin births, and as a reason for Lady Seymour to want to cease to have children, which led to Jane going to see Edith Grey.

Edith Grey is an invention, but cunning men and women existed and were employed by noble and common people alike as physicians and midwives. Cousin Edmund and his wife Mary are also invented characters.

Jane Seymour was indeed related to Anne Boleyn, and also to Catherine Howard. If you have read my series on Queen Anne Boleyn, *Above All Others: The Lady Anne*, you may well recognise the first meeting between Anne and Jane in this book. Since writing that scene in the Anne series, I have wanted to show it from Jane's perspective, and did in this book.

One of the reasons I wanted to write about Jane was because of the myriad of qualities which in historical records we only glimpse, which she appeared to possess. Meek and mild and quiet, yet ruthless enough to aid men who engineered the fall of Anne Boleyn, Jane apparently was. Humble and submissive, and yet strong and bold enough to attempt to stand up for the King's daughter, Princess Mary, she was later in life. This is an odd mixture of character traits, which always suggested to me that the meek, quiet Jane was a mask, hiding a much bolder character underneath.

I wanted there to be reasons for Jane's willingness to supplant Anne later in this story. I wanted to understand her motivations. That Jane was dedicated to Queen Katherine and later her daughter Mary seems to be borne out by historical fact; Jane supported Mary, at times to her detriment, when she became Queen. But Jane's willingness to replace Anne, certainly at one stage knowing it would lead to her death, I wanted to understand. I thought a combination of factors had occurred. Jane's dedication to Katherine was one, but I thought her father's affair with Catherine, her sister-in-law, also played a part. Jane had seen how a scandal of that kind, and indeed betrayal, could soil her family name and destroy the trust, perhaps the love, in a family. I believe she saw Anne as another Catherine, as is stated in the book, and took a personal dislike to her because of this. This is just a theory, and one unlikely to ever be proved, but I hope it makes sense to you, reading this, and I hope you, like me, warmed to the Jane created for this novel. Whilst not perfect, as none of us are, the Jane I saw had a fierce ability to love, a devotion to those she cared for, a strength which sadly would be put to both good and bad purposes later, and a simple wish, to be seen, and not to be taken for granted.

Thank You

…to so many people for helping me make this book possible… to my proof reader, Julia Gibbs, who gave me her time, her wonderful guidance and also her encouragement. To my family for their ongoing love and support. To my friend Petra who took a tour of Tudor palaces and medieval places with me back in 2010 which helped me to prepare for this book and others; her enthusiasm for that strange but amazing holiday brought an early ally to the idea I could actually write a book, begin a career as an author. To my friend Nessa for her support and affection, and to another friend, Anne, who has done so much for me. To Sue and Annette, more friends who read my books and cheer me on. To Terry for getting me into writing and indie publishing in the first place. To Katie and Jooles, Macer and Heather, often there in times of trial. To Leeann and Will, old friends, who, along with their lovely children took me on a walk through the countryside in which the book is set, and planted many thoughts in my mind during that walk. And to all my wonderful readers, who took a chance on an unknown author, and have followed my career and books since.

To those who have left reviews or contacted me by email or Twitter, I give great thanks, as you have shown support for my career as an author, and enabled me to continue writing. Thank you for allowing me to live my dream.

And lastly, to the people who wrote all the books I read in order to write this book… all the historical biographers and masters of their craft who brought Jane, and her times, to life in my head. I intend to include a bibliography at the end of the last book in this series.

Thank you to all of you; you'll never know how much you've helped me, but I know what I owe to you.

Gemma Lawrence
Wales
2020

About The Author

I find people talking about themselves in the third person to be entirely unsettling, so, since this section is written by me, I will use my own voice rather than try to make you believe that another person is writing about me to make me sound terribly important.

I am an independent author, publishing my books by myself, with the help of my lovely proof reader. I left my day job in 2016 and am now a fully-fledged, full time author, and proud to be so.

My passion for history began early in life. As a child I lived in Croydon, near London, and my schools were lucky enough to be close to such glorious places as Hampton Court and the Tower of London, allowing field trips to take us to those castles. I think it's hard not to find characters from history infectious when you hear their stories, especially when surrounded by the bricks and mortar they built their reigns and legends within. There is heroism and scandal, betrayal and belief, politics and passion and a seemingly never-ending cast list of truly fascinating people. So when I sat down to start writing, I could think of no better place to start than a subject I loved and was slightly obsessed with.

Expect *many* books from me, but do not necessarily expect them all to be of one era. I write as many of you read, I suspect; in many genres. My own bookshelves are weighted down with historical volumes and biographies, but they also contain dystopias, sci-fi, horror, humour, children's books, fairy tales, romance and adventure. I can't promise I'll manage to write in *all* the areas I've mentioned there, but I'd love to give it a go. If anything I've published isn't your thing, that's fine, I just hope you like the ones I write which *are* your thing!

The majority of my books *are* historical fiction, however, so I hope that if you liked this volume you will give the others in this series (and perhaps not in this series), a look. I want to divert you as readers, to please you with my writing and to have you join me on these adventures.

A book is nothing without a reader.

As to the rest of me; I am in my thirties and live in Wales with a rescued dog, and a rescued cat. I studied Literature at University after I fell in love with books as a small child. When I was little I could often be found nestled halfway up the stairs with a pile of books in my lap and my head lost in another world. There is nothing more satisfying to me than finding a new book I adore, to place next to the multitudes I own and love... and nothing more disappointing to me to find a book I am willing to never open again. I do hope that this book was not a disappointment to you; I loved writing it and I hope that showed through the pages.

This is only one of a large selection of titles coming to you on Amazon. I hope you will try the others.

If you would like to contact me, please do so.

On Twitter, I am @TudorTweep and am more than happy to follow back and reply to any and all messages. I may avoid you if you decide to say anything worrying or anything abusive, but I figure that's acceptable.

Via email, I am tudortweep@gmail.com a dedicated email account for my readers to reach me on. I'll try and reply within a few days.

I publish some first drafts and short stories on Wattpad where I can be found at www.wattpad.com/user/GemmaLawrence31 . Wattpad was the first place I ever showed my stories, *to anyone*, and in many ways its readers and their response to my works were the influence which pushed me into self-publishing. If you have never been on the site I recommend you try it out. It's free, it's fun and it's chock-full of real emerging talent. I love Wattpad because its members and their encouragement gave me the boost I needed as a fearful waif to get some confidence in myself and make a go of a life as a real, published writer.

Thank you for taking a risk with an unknown author and reading my book. I do hope now that you've read one you'll want to read more. If you'd like to leave me a review, that would be very much appreciated also!

Gemma Lawrence
Wales
2020

Printed in Poland
by Amazon Fulfillment
Poland Sp. z o.o., Wrocław